TAP DANCERS

BY

CHRIS SIMOND

ABOUT THE AUTHOR

Chris Simond was like many Covid lockdowners, who when the 2020 pandemic struck found himself in need of a project to wile away hours (ultimately two years) of lengthy incarcerations in Sydney, Australia.

A background in marketing then television news and current affairs (ABC and Network Seven) had fired up his concerns for the vulnerability of the world's water supplies. With 97% of the planet's aqua resource coming from the oceans only 3% is fit for human consumption. Most of that 3% is found underground or from glaciers leaving a miniscule 1% to be drawn from lakes, rivers and dams. Alarm bells should be ringing.

How protected is our planet's liquid gold? How easy is it to seize control of reservoirs and catchments, even poison them?

In recent times we've witnessed terrorist threats, cyber attacks on corporations, website seizures and ransom demands paralysing communities, cities, even countries. What's next?

In Tap Dancers Chris visits real possibilities following the brazen seizure of a water utility that cripples a city. A city afraid to turn on its taps.

While organisations, characters and storylines are all fictitious it explores realistic and 'tongue-in-cheek' scenarios that might just force municipal and government instrumentalities to heed the warnings and take a closer look. Are their protection, surveillance and security procedures adequate? Are their risk assessments water tight?

Most importantly are there fully established disaster plans in the event of an emergency?

What happens if there's a catastrophic shutdown?

That day when there's no water.

What then?

For Molly and Nicola

Dedicated to all those good folk who started a project
during the 2020-22 Covid pandemic.
With a special mention to those who completed it. I applaud you.

To Ramona heartfelt love and thanks for the encouragement
to keep writing.

A general appreciation from family and friends for applying pressure.
"How's the book coming along" guaranteed its completion.

1

The neighbourhood was not amused.

Outrageous misbehaviour from one wayward household had woken an entire street. An evening of alcoholic excess and childish party games had spilled into the road, resulting in numerous complaints and a police presence.

An out-of-control hokey-pokey chain dance was the main culprit. Windows from the reveller's house had been opened, allowing heavy music decibels to flow into the street. Pumped-up sounds along with boisterous foul-mouths reaped immediate on-the-spot fines. One guest, urinating in a neighbour's garden was apprehended and immediately fined for offensive conduct. Another was charged with indecent language and obscene exposure to a female constable.

For good measure, the party's host was nailed for creating a public disturbance.

The police were forced to return a second time when an inebriated foursome started a house-to-house doorknock, singing Christmas carols. Especially odd for the month of June.

A sergeant clearly short on patience and humour laid into the intoxicated host.

"We've received dozens of complaints. Twice now we've had to come out. If you don't…"

The lead carol singer immediately leapt to the defence of his makeshift choir. "Officer, it's the season of good cheer. Santa's not going to visit your house now, is he? Why don't you take that sleigh of yours with the flashing blue light and head back to the North Pole?"

Another warning with the threat of more severe consequences, including an overnight stay at the local police station, finally hammered home the message. The party was officially over. At least the noisy street version.

It was the kind of behaviour that might have been expected from teens and twenties at an out-of-control rave party where hair would be let down, alcohol poured down throats and interesting substances consumed. But this unruly mob, mainly aged in its forties and fifties had clearly decided to re-live adolescence, for one memorable night.

After all, it was a special occasion, and in their minds, totally justified disorderly conduct.

Finally, the street had quietened down, and the police departed to a chorus of cheers, wolf whistles and blown raspberries. Much to the relief of neighbours, taxis were called to remove the trouble-making carousers, all of whom were promised hangovers for the morrow. Inside the party house, celebrations quickly dwindled to just one guest couple, the pair who'd been the most garrulous all evening.

"Let me top up that vino," insisted Mack. Birthday boy and party host.

"I really think I've had enough," said Dino, resting an open hand on top of his glass.

"Oh, go on, I'll call you both a cab later, we see so little of you."

"All right, twisted my arm."

"You're an easy touch," laughed Mack, filling Dino's outstretched glass.

"Let's hope I can tempt your lovely wife too?"

"Yes, I'd love one," shouted Sacha from across the room.

"Me too darling," said Jacki, Mack's wife, kicking off her shoes and rubbing her feet.

It had been a wild evening full of catchups and laughter. Thirty friends who had never stood in the same room at the same time. Mack's 50th birthday had managed to draw them all together. He was popular, the life and soul of any gathering. Tonight, was no exception.

Macdonald Shackleton Grayson, 'Mack' to all who knew him, was born in Scotland to an English father and a Cambodian mother. The name Macdonald had been his father's nod when it came to christening the lad, synonymous with perhaps the most famous of Scottish clans.

Shackleton, Mack's middle name, was chosen following his father's obsession with the exploits of Antarctic explorer, Ernest Shackleton who had led three expeditions to the South Pole in the early 1900's. These name selections said a lot about the man's idiosyncrasies and sense of humour. Mack's father, Stanley Barraclough Grayson was a renowned after-dinner speaker, ladies' man and a more than capable golfer. He lived in the Scottish Highlands working as a psychiatrist for 23 years, until he was struck off in sensational circumstances. A major family disgrace that Mack had never properly come to terms with.

From a young age Mack had buried himself in the art of photography, aiming to become a globetrotting photojournalist, telling news stories through pictures. He quickly became obsessed. As his camera-eye witnessed major events he wrote detailed captions and text to support their images. While the old adage of a 'picture is worth a thousand words' may be true, he believed just a hundred of his words linked to a striking image, could speak volumes.

His star-studded career in photojournalism stretched over 25 years. He had been working for the largest Australian newspaper and television organisation, The TransNational Media Corporation, in their various overseas bureaux. He was now back at the group's Australian HQ, in Sydney, as a staff photographer on The TransNational Times. And he hated it. There were still occasional overseas assignments but with a growing family he decided, or his wife Jacki, decided for him, his international jaunts for months on end, were over. With two failed marriages behind him, he didn't want to risk a third.

The frustration of being one of the photographic elite but no longer working the frontline, was tearing him apart. Tonight's guest list was full of the media profession's highest achievers, top operators, producers, journos, and cameramen. Altogether, a brilliant eclectic mix of artists, technicians and news analysts, many of them Mack's closest friends. This respect for the top performers in his field had led to a problem at home.

The small, cramped house he, Jacki and their three children had lived in for five years had been turned upside down. Their rundown hovel needed a major makeover for the party. For one reason, mainly. Thousands of magazines and newspapers strewn across every available space, every corner, even high-rise piles in the kids' bedrooms.

While these newsprint mounds represented Mack's love affair, some would say unhealthy obsession, with media reportage and glossy pictorials, it had become excessive beyond reason.

The family's combined lounge and dining room had become a repository for his overflowing print and photographic library with individual articles, features and supplements from assorted newspaper and magazine mastheads. A few decades' worth of the planet's magic moments, some in which Mack had been intimately involved. Others had been the handiwork of photojournalists around the world, people whose work and skills he admired. Presidential elections, political skulduggery, celebrity gossip, natural disasters, every imaginable scandal, all now laid meticulously, one above the other. Most would remain undisturbed probably for years, maybe forever. No one was allowed to throw anything away, let alone touch. They were Mack's extended family.

A tidy up for the party meant Mack's collection of print and photo memorabilia had to be shuffled and piled up into columns, many reaching to the ceiling. Stacked one above the other, everything from major international newspapers to National Geographics, New Yorkers and Vogues. Locating one specific front-page photo or article from the Everest of print in each room was always a labour of love. Jacki dreaded those days when Mack went in search of a particular gem with his familiar air of confidence.

"I know it's here, somewhere; I'll find it."

He rarely did. On these occasions Jacki raised the question of a serious cull.

"Isn't it about time we returned the house to some normality and reduced your mountains to mole hills, manageable piles?" Jacki would plead.

It always led to an argument with Mack saying it gave their rundown home real character and took attention away from its drab décor. With little artwork adorning dull unpainted walls he was convinced this homage to photography and journalism made its own artistic statement.

With a chuckle he once said,

"These towering pillars of history's highlights I'm sure would even make Callicrates and Ictinus quite jealous.

"And who are they?" groaned Jacki.

"The great Greek architects of the Acropolis and the Parthenon. They knew all about column inches!"

Jacki didn't find it at all funny. She would be silenced one more time. His stubborn heels had become so submerged, would she ever break through? She prayed one day, she would. Due to the birthday boy's party celebrations, their much-strained relationship was on hold. A where-to-from-here discussion was long overdue.

Despite a dark cloud hanging over their marriage Jacki had been planning his party for weeks and singlehandedly produced a sumptuous sit-down feast, that became peppered with speeches and joke-telling, well into the night. Mack was 'roasted' by most of his guests with exaggerated stories of past times spent, especially about the ladies who had the dubious honour of being his partner, in two instances his wife. Jacki was not amused.

In the main it was his 'war' stories, of times in the field as an award-winning 'snapper' journalist. He'd been stationed in the Middle East, covering numerous war zones. Most of those gathered were media veterans who had worked alongside him in newspapers, TV, radio and wire services around the world.

Everyone was well lubricated thanks to an open bar and an over enthusiastic waiter, hired for the evening, to keep glasses brimmed.

That was what led to the street knees-up, igniting interest from the local constabulary. But peace had now broken out. 2am came and went. And sauced party guest, Dino, still had his newshound nose on duty.

"So, how's the weird and wonderful world of photojournal-ism? Been taking your camera on any exciting assignments?" asked Dino, slurring his words.

"Let's give work chat a rest, me old mate," Mack replied firmly, patting Dino on the back.

"How are your boys?" Mack changing the subject.

"What happened to that story you were working on about the cutting off or poisoning of our water supply?" persisted an inebriated Dino.

"Shoved on to the back-burner for now, a bit of a storm in an old teacup if you ask me," lied Mack.

That wasn't quite true. Mack was well aware a whistle

blower was wanting to spill the beans about the current risk of contaminated drinking water in the main Sydney catchment and he wasn't about to give Dino the inside drum. Mack had been tipped off, if he could gain access to the control room of the city's main water supply, he'd be able to observe how easy it would be to cut off or poison the precious natural resource.

The Whistleblower gave Mack graphic descriptions of the horrific effects toxic drinking water could have on unsuspecting consumers. Over the phone Mack wasn't sure whether the whistle blower was certifiable or if there was genuine substance to his claims. Whatever the scenario he wasn't about to give Dino the heads-up. He loved getting his teeth into a good scandal. It was in his blood.

The highly strung Italian-born loudmouth, tall, slim and permanently tanned, presented a top rating afternoon talk-back radio show in Australia's harbourside city.

Typical ON-AIR flash:

"This is Dino Lombardi on radio A2Z, the station shaping you a better world."

Dino: *"What's on your mind?"*

Caller: *"Dino I'm in serious trouble, I need your help,"*

"That's why I'm here, talk to me.

"It all started about three weeks ago… (FADE)

Dino had a reputation for solving listeners' problems, sniffing out stories from seemingly innocuous beginnings. Any time there was a whiff of an 'exclusive', an 'exposé', a 'skeleton in someone's closet' Dino was all over it. He had won numerous awards for exposing corruption, often within senior government ranks. Recently a federal minister was forced to resign after it was revealed he'd been receiving kickbacks for granting defence contracts to organisations, who'd miraculously avoided the official tendering process.

Another star performance from Dino revealed that one of the nation's most celebrated authors, Malcolm Flashman, was shown to have plagiarised large sections of a well-known Russian novel. Flashman, an ageing writer without a best seller in years, had foolishly assumed he'd get away with translating into English, word for word, stealing from the original text. The obvious conclusion, all the material had been lifted, illegally obtained with Dino the hotshot talkback jock, basking in the glory, once again. Meanwhile, Flashman was disgraced, pilloried publicly, never to write another word.

Dino's contacts were impeccable. Sources from all levels of society and authority meant he was always the 'go-to' individual for anyone peddling controversy.

There was no way Mack was going to even hint he was sitting on something with serious scoop potential.

"But you gave me the impression you had a tiger by the tail," Dino persisted.

Mack zipped his fingers across his lips, declaring an end to the matter.

"Oh, come on Mack. You're hiding something, you told me a few weeks back we should all be worried when we turn on our taps."

"I never did. Mate, I think the grog has got the better of you."

"Bullshit," spluttered Dino, sweat drops descending his

brow. He drew out a handkerchief and mopped the shine from his bronzed, bald crown. Mack decided to shut him down before it got out of hand.

"You're on a fishing expedition now and there's nothing to hook my friend."

"You definitely said…."

"Just drop it mate, maybe it's time for that cab?" joked Mack.

The few seconds of awkward silence that followed were broken by Mack's mobile phone, vibrating in his pocket.

"Bloody hell, 2.30 in the morning, it can only mean one thing. Actually two."

"Who rings at this time?" slurred Dino.

"Well, if it's not my dippy mother wanting to know what I want for Christmas, it'll be… Yes, it is."

Looking at his phone confirmed the call was from the Chief of Staff's desk at Mack's employer, The TransNational Times.

"You've woken me up," lied Mack. "It better be good."

"All hell's broken out, Mack. It's a big one," said Wesley Markowitz, Chief of Staff, at The Times.

The on-duty night crew had been despatched to a beach suburb over a hundred kilometres away to stake out a brothel story about illegals from the Philippines. Mack was the only standby option in the event of a major breaking story. And it was.

"There's a massive fire at the Continental Apartments on Buckingham Parade and police radio's saying dozens of people are trapped. It looks serious Mack; can you get out there?" Mack heard the urgency in Wesley's voice.

"Geez Wes, I've been drinking all night, it's my birthday for fuck's sake, I'm in no fit state, isn't there anyone else you can send?"

Mack's plea was a hollow one. He knew there was always a slim chance he'd be called out. Months had passed and he hadn't been shaken from his sleep to front an overnight story. So, he'd taken the risk when another journo asked him to swap shifts because he wanted to spring a surprise on his girlfriend and propose. This romantic wanted to drop to one knee on the night of Mack's party. Soft-hearted, Mack agreed, thinking nothing will stop him celebrating his birthday. While the odds were against a call out, the Gods tonight had other ideas.

"I'm afraid you're it. The overnight crew is chasing that brothel story up the coast, Zak's on holiday and Cameron's still sick," Wes was about to blow his stack when Mack interrupted him.

"I've had too much to drink, I can't drive, in fact I can't talk at the moment, Wes pleeeease?"

"I've booked you a cab, it'll be with you in ten. Ring me when you get there, the boss wants it in the online edition ASAP." Mack heard the phone go click.

"Shit! Bugger! Crap!" exploded Mack.

"What's up darling?" asked Jacki sidling up with Sacha, the pair having evacuated their couch corner where they'd been exchanging quietly, out of earshot, for quite some time.

Jacki and Sacha were joined at the hip, two peas in a very similar pod, each other's best friend. Both blessed with exceptional looks. Jacki short blonde hair, slim figure, always stylishly dressed. The perfect mother of three who made it regularly known that she was made for much more than just motherhood. Her career as a child psychologist appeared to be permanently on hold.

Sacha was the bright and highly competent GP who specialised in fertility issues at a local medical practice. Always impeccably groomed, her long dark tresses received a weekly tease, at a local salon. A three-inch scar on her jawline from a dog bite, when she was a child, worn with pride.

'The Girls' as they were fondly referred to, had been in deep conversation. Sacha was convinced Dino was screwing around. Ever since his 5am return home from the radio industry's Bugle Awards a couple of weeks before, he'd been acting strange, often taking phone calls in the garden, to not be overheard. Then justifying them, by saying it was a sensitive staff issue. Sacha had always been his confidante over such problems at the radio station in the past, so she was convinced this was something else. An affair maybe and she'd felt the need to unload her concerns on Jacki. Jacki had her own thoughts.

"There's a massive fire at the Continental Apartments in the city and they want me in there pronto."

"You're kidding, you promised this weekend was work free."

Mack went to grab his camera, tablet and notepad.

"Where's... my... wallet?" Mack was now yelling. "Sorry Jacki, I didn't tell you but I swapped shifts with Daniel Lacrosse. He was originally on the call-out roster but he wanted to propose to his girlfriend tonight. I didn't think I'd be..."

Jacki interrupted "You didn't think all right. And you didn't even think to tell me!?"

A car horn sounded; Mack's cab was outside. Waving at everyone but no-one in particular, he made a dash for the door.

"Ring me, let me know," cried Jacki, throwing her hands in the air.

"Happy birthday" chorused Sacha and Dino.

2

Haunting sounds from multiple alarms filled the air as police, fire and rescue vehicles joined the municipal melee. Telescopic ladders rose to attack the blaze.

Hoses zigzagged each other as their jets belched water toward the inferno. Firefighters in full protective gear and breathing apparatus disappeared behind clouds of toxic smoke.Controlled mayhem had broken out.

From Mack's taxi the glow in the sky could be seen from miles away. His head was throbbing, and annoying hiccups were interrupting his breathing. He was certainly feeling the effects of the night's indulgence, proving cocktails and cognacs were not good friends, en masse. He knew he was about to be sorely tested for the task ahead. He'd done it before and was hoping experience would see him through, one more time. Staring through the cab's windscreen at the approaching fire something stirred within him. It didn't feel right. And it seriously disturbed him. Once again.

3

An elderly couple in night clothes was running from the awninged portico of, what until minutes before had been the entrance to their swank apartment block. Shouting at each other, pale-faced, eyes wide with fear, not sure whether to exit left or right. Full of panic, each ran in the opposite direction, immediately losing sight of the other. Her screams made him turn but with the stinging smoke in his eyes he failed to locate her in the blackness.

"Over here," he cried, struggling to catch his breath. The intense heat from the burning building had singed his hair, smoke was now rising from his head.

"Sadie" he croaked. The volume of his cry dulled by the toxic fumes he was now breathing in.

Smut-stained tears rolled down his cheeks as he strained to call out, one more time.

"Sadie, where are you?"

There was no reply.

4

The taxi pulled up with a screech. Mack was thrown forward, the sudden jolt digging the seat belt into his shoulder.

"I'm not going any further," shouted the cabbie

"Just through that gap," urged Mack.

"Not another inch. That fire's crazy Dude, I can feel the heat from here."

"Up behind that fire truck, over there."

"No way. That's 18 bucks, cash only."

"Can't do that," said Mack, exiting the cab, pulling out his wallet.

A figure waving both arms and a torchlight was signalling the cab to reverse.

"Jesus Christ, now this cop wants me to back up," yelled the cabbie.

"I've only got plastic." Matt thrust his card through the window.

"Card machine's on the blink, cash only."

"Move it, you're blocking access." The police officer flashed his torch at the arguing couple. "Out of here now... oh no, not you again."

Mack looked into the same angry eyes he'd seen a couple of hours earlier. It was the cranky sergeant who'd turned up at his house to deal with the unruly mob in the street.

"You seem to be making a habit of getting in my face. What the hell are you doing here? Haven't you had enough for one night?" shouted the policeman.

"I'm covering the fire for The Times and I don't have cash to pay the cab, only a card," explained Mack.

"You two, sort it right now or you'll be facing your second fine of the night."

Striding away the lawman started yelling at rubberneckers to get behind the barrier. The fire had escalated, drawing a crowd of onlookers, perving at the fire scene, with outstretched mobile phones. It was now threatening to engulf apartment blocks on either side.

"I want my money and I want it now," shouted an increasingly agitated cabbie. He was now out of the taxi, standing nose to nose with Mack. Large, muscled arms, a shaved head, wearing a T shirt printed with the legendary Clint Eastwood threat 'Go Ahead, Make My Day'. With the temperature rising and the cabbie clearly spoiling for a fight Mack, felt he had little choice but to hold his ground and make his predicament crystal clear. Flicking back his dark mop he placed hands on hips, accentuating broad shoulders. He hoped his almost 2 metres of height would combine to intimidate.

"Get it into your skull, I don't have any cash, what I can do is..."

At that moment part of the roof of the apartment building fell in with a deafening roar. Mack ducked as flames exploded into the night sky. The updraft from the collapsing roof jettisoned debris across the fire scene, showering embers at his feet.

He felt a shiver down his spine. An immediate flashback to a moment he'd spent years trying to forget.

It reminded him of an incident he'd witnessed in Sao Paulo, twelve years ago, on assignment to cover the Brazilian general election. He'd been monitoring an anti-government rally when protesters firebombed the electorate office of a leading candidate. Flames had quickly spread to neighbouring shops and residential villas. Two large retail stores were consumed in the blaze. One was a shop selling paint supplies, the other a haberdashery, with rolls of highly flammable fabrics.

At the back of the paint shop an explosion had blown out its front window. Cries from within suggested people inside had been injured. At that moment Mack had been faced with the most challenging decision of his life.

5

"My newspaper will send you the money," promised Mack.

"Look, I'm not in the habit of giving free cab rides at three in the morning," said the cabbie.

Mack looked at his wrist, for his watch, thinking it could be his security, a temporary trade, to shut up this ranting cab driver. A Rolex presented to him in London after a five-year stint, producing photographic gems in Iraq and Afghanistan. It was engraved 'To Mack the image maker. Love your work. Universal Media.' But in the rush to leave home he'd forgotten it. In a snap decision, he slipped a ring off his finger.

"This'll guarantee your lousy eighteen bucks, don't you dare lose it."

"I don't want your ring, man."

"I promise you; I'm going to want it back."

"Chrissakes get this cab out of here." exploded the returning cop.

Mack slung the camera over his shoulder and headed toward the Fire Commander for a media update, his heart beating fast. That flashback to Brazil had really unsettled him. This was not the moment to be losing control. And his head still ached from the night's alcoholic onslaught.

"Happy fucking birthday to me," he mumbled under his breath.

"This means nothing to me," yelled the cabbie, waving the ring before slamming his T bar into reverse. Glancing over his shoulder, he gunned the cab twenty metres, before grabbing the hand brake and spinning the car into a 'one eighty', narrowly missing a paramedic crew, running toward the fire scene.

Mack turned quickly, making a mental note of the taxi's number. No argument, he had to get that ring back. Shaky marriage or not, he'd be mincemeat if Jacki found out he'd just pawned his wedding ring to a cabbie, for a lousy eighteen bucks.

6

With the fire out of control the enormity of the task was patently clear. Twelve fire trucks from six brigades were now assisting, backed by a strong police and rescue unit presence. Casualties were receiving on-site attention before being stretchered to ambulance crews and dashed to one of three nearby hospitals. Burns units had been placed on full alert.

Mack's camera was working overtime. His knack for seeking out shots that spelled drama as well as aesthetics was legendary. Faces of suffering, victims of famine, battle weary soldiers, many telling images, winning prestigious awards. Often risking life and limb to capture the moment. He'd hit the fireground running, so many opportunities, so much on offer. He had taken the standard action pics of personnel at full stretch doing what they did best. Then, had moved in close, to catch anguished faces, streaked in soot and sweat, mouths wide open shouting orders, stressed paramedics tending to lifeless figures. Once again, he was in his element. His hangover was gradually retreating.

And then he saw it. A lone face at a window, little fists beating on the glass. A gust of wind had temporarily blown a clear patch in the smoke to reveal the building's upper floors. He could just make out a child on the sixth floor, screaming its lungs out, deaf to those on the ground. Mack released a barrage of shots, feeling guilty he was taking a picture he may never release commercially. A gut-wrenching he had experienced many times before. If it potentially had fatal consequences and the child did not survive it crossed his ethical divide. Never show images of dead children. Or children about to die. No negotiation. This had got him into trouble in the past with various employers wrestling him and his conscience, to no avail.

The trigger for his decision had come in 2013. Mack had been covering the Syrian War when he witnessed a chemical weapons attack, outside Damascus. He photographed helpless civilians, convulsing, foaming at the mouth from the effects of mustard gas and the nerve agent, Sarin. Then he saw something even worse. Terrified children and babies, panicking, struggling to breathe. As his camera devoured the horror images, he experienced his moral and ethical epiphany. Mack's shots of babies with contorted, grotesque faces following their agonising deaths, still haunted him. 1400 people died that day. He was wearing protective gear and felt profound guilt for surviving the attack. But something far deeper had stirred within him.

It was this, that had led him to the decision not to allow his work to ever be released against his will, for what he called public titillation.

He was quite prepared to assist Royal Commissions and Government enquiries regarding images of dead and dying children, if it would assist a good cause, or provide an outcome to a worthwhile inquest or hearing. But a photograph commercially released to boost television ratings or newspaper circulations was against his moral code. End of discussion.

"Look. There's a child at that window." Mack shouted above the roar of the fire.

A fireman training his hose through the blazing lobby of the building looked up. There was no face at the window, just a bright glow engulfing the back of the same room. Clearly the fire was taking hold but the young face was nowhere to be seen.

"A child, boy or girl I don't know, a second ago there was a face at that window," insisted Mack.

The firefighter yelled at the man beside him.

"Sixth floor, third window from the left, this guy reckons

he's seen a young kid."

Three faces looked skywards... and there it was. The face had returned but was now lower, a child on its knees, no doubt in a state of collapse, smoke billowing around it. But now, an adult in the background, had staggered forward and was wrestling with the window, finally managing to prise it open. One of the fire department's telescopic ladders was immediately directed toward the desperate pair, an adult female and a young girl, now waving, shouting from the open window. Mack's camera absorbed each tense moment of the nail-biting rescue operation. He knew how each second was vital. How quickly things could change. The difference between life and death. He knew because he'd been there before, many times. On one occasion in particular.

7

It had been the spine-chilling cries from the back of that paint shop in Sao Paulo that still haunted him. Covering an anti-government rally, he'd photographed protesters firebombing the offices of one of the major political parties. The fire had quickly spread to adjoining buildings, in particular the paint supplies shop. Mack had captured the key shot, just as a massive explosion blew out the shop's front window. It was the screams that followed which had become the nucleus of his sweat-filled nightmares. Jacki had woken him many times after he'd relived the moment, when he entered the burning building, drawn to the sounds of human pain and panic. He'd found bodies, some dismembered, parts scattered across what was obviously a paint storage area. It was macabre. The explosion had blasted hundreds of paint tins, of various colours, across this horror scene resulting in a gut-wrenching, multi-coloured bloodbath. It was as if some demented artist had curated the darkest of artworks possible. Mack had immediately thrown up.

It was the young boy propped up in the corner who had then caught his eye, clearly alive, not uttering a sound. The shock from the bombing had obviously stunned him. As Mack made his way through the acrid smoke, he saw the boy was cradling the remains of his left arm. Covered in paint and bleeding profusely from his gaping wound the boy looked into the eyes of the approaching stranger. It was a look Mack would never forget.

He quickly took off his shirt and wrapped it around the boy's mutilated arm, in an attempt to stem the flow of blood. The young lad uttered something in Portuguese. Mack didn't understand him but immediately responded, knowing his own words would also not be understood. Soothing words in a foreign language, better than no words at all, he thought.

"We're going to get you out of here my young friend, get you some help."

He carefully picked up the boy before stepping over two bodies and making his way toward what was once the front door.

"I am sure there'll be a nice doctor we can find to look after you, at the hospital. You'll have your family around you. I'm sure they'll be here soon."

As he said those words, he realised some of the boy's family may well be lying on the floor behind them, dead to the world.

8

As the ladder swung toward the window Mack reeled off a series of shots. The woman and young girl were now seconds away from being consumed by the raging inferno.

A large crowd of bystanders was having its morbid curiosities massaged. Shocked screams rang out.

"Quick, quick, get them out, get them out," shouted a lone voice in the crowd.

A TV crew trained on the action, spun around to vox pop the crowd.

"They're going to die, somebody do something!" screamed a distraught woman.

"I can't look," said another.

By now a number of crews from TV networks had arrived to record the unfolding drama. Mack nodded at a couple of familiar faces, reporters, cameramen, sound recordists he knew from various gigs at home, in Australia and overseas. All of them, like him, hauled away from their Saturday nights to file what had quickly become a major news story.

Then it happened. Mack's legs gave way as he collapsed in a heap. His heart beating overtime, a wave of nausea consuming him. He struggled to remain conscious. Memories of that explosion in Sao Paulo and the young boy who had battled to stay alive, had revisited him, flattened him. Here we go again he thought. Yet again lives hanging by a thread.

He had visited 11-year-old Pedro Ferreira in a Sao Paulo hospital every day for three weeks. He was the child's only visitor. His mother, father and two sisters had been killed in the explosion. And then the heartbreaking day when he visited the boy to find his empty bed and a tearful nurse. She had explained how the brave little fighter finally succumbed to his injuries and had passed away. Mack openly wept. The nurse and he had clung to each other and sobbed.

9

The intense heat should have forced the fireman to retreat but breathing heavily into his oxygen mask he had reached through the window space. Quickly snatching the woman and young girl, balancing them momentarily on his cramped platform before starting their steady descent. Flames immediately erupted in the space they'd just left. A split second after their evacuation, the room exploded.

Onlookers broke into spontaneous cheers, instant applause

as the ladder lowered the trio to the ground, to safety.

With his head still spinning Mack recovered briefly to capture the moment. Three people, the rescuer and the rescued, silhouetted against the flaming eruption behind them. No doubt a photo destined for tomorrow's front page. He then closed his eyes shutting out the madness for a few moments. He didn't know for how long but a passing paramedic checked to see if he was okay. At the same moment his mobile burst into life.

It was Wes wanting to know what Mack had scored. "I need your best shots pronto. And a few paragraphs of support copy. Number of dead and injured, any detail on what caused the fire etc etc, ok?".

"I still have a bit to cover. I think you'll need comments from two lucky survivors I'm about to photograph."

"Your birthday party's over now Mack," said Wes. The phone went dead.

"Bastard," thought Mack. He and Wes had never got on well but tonight had taken their strained relationship to a new low. Mack's reluctance to turn out for this fire story had definitely raised the temperature. He knew he was the designated overnight photo journo but had attempted to wriggle out using birthday celebrations and drunkenness as feeble excuses. Not a good look, he had to admit. He'd have to deal with Wes later. For now, there was a story to cover and two very lucky ladies to interview.

As he made his way toward the back of an ambulance where the rescued couple from the sixth floor were being treated, a familiar TV face emerged through the smoke. It was Phil Lok, a veteran news cameraman who worked for TransNational TV News. Like Mack's newspaper, The Times, he was also part of the TransNational Media Group. They often shared resources at incidents like this. They had first met in the organisation's Beijing office, ten years earlier. His name had been immediately Australianised.

"Bit late aren't you Lockie? Some of us have been here for hours," quipped Mack.

"I know, don't rub it in," a clearly distraught Lockie.

"What happened?"

"My sound recordist needed to be picked up, his car wouldn't start, he lives miles away."

"Your competition has shot the shit out of the fire's early horrors, some great footage I reckon. I'm afraid I can only offer you stills," said Mack, holding up his camera.

"I guessed that. You won't believe it."

"What?" said Mack.

"It gets worse," admitted Lockie.

"Why?"

"Bob Bradley, the reporter who was meant to be here with me, his wife has gone into labour, he's raced her to hospital. So, I've got no 'talking-head' to front the story, conduct interviews, put it all together, for the early morning news."

"Can't your Chief of Staff send someone else? Surely, he can drag another body from its bed?" offered Mack.

"Too late now. It'll be daylight in an hour," whined Lockie.

"Your best bet is to see whether the other networks might share some of their footage. Cobble that together with wire service info on the fire and edit it, into a quick one-minute package, Bingo," said Mack, making it sound easy.

"I've got a better idea, Mack."

"Got to fly Lockie, I need to get comments from two of the luckiest people on earth, captions for my photos," said Mack, walking away.

Mack and Lockie had worked on the same stories in the past. There had always been good camaraderie and banter. In Beijing they regularly turned up at the same event. While they both worked for the same corporation, their roles were quite different and neither was formally obliged to assist the other. But here was a work colleague in need and Lockie was quite insistent.

"Mack, could you do me a real favour?"

Mack turning around. "What kind of favour?"

"Can I shoot your interview with these two ladies for TV News?"

"You know we can't do that," said Mack. "We're two different animals, serving different masters. I can't be seen to be acting as a reporter for your network".

"Why not?"

It would be a moment before Mack replied.

Why not indeed? Technically they did serve the same master, albeit through separate media, newspapers and television. Ever since Mack had taken up his position at The Times he'd been frustrated, he was no longer in the frontline. Few foreign assignments to far flung hotspots. Twenty-five years in the sweat and grind, chasing the ultimate image in one overseas conflict after another, had taken its toll. He admitted he was burnt out and was no longer coping with war zones and the threat of terrorist attacks. Constantly working around the clock, accommodating different time zones. It often meant sending material during the night to fit in with newspaper deadlines back home in Australia. A lack of sleep was a major contributing factor to extreme fatigue.

He definitely needed a change but the wrench from being an award-winning international photojournalist to a home-based snapper was a bitter pill to swallow. His family had suffered too. Jacki had borne the brunt of his absences, raising their three children, practically on her own. The boys, Dylan and Jake, grew up virtually fatherless and the youngest, Amy, reached the age of eight, before he'd even noticed. As a result, she'd now established a strong bond with Jacki.

He'd lost intimacy with all of them, realising there was a yawning chasm of lost ground to make up if he was to restore relationships.

He was also aware of the strain he'd placed Jacki under. She'd known when she married him that she would be doing a lot of solo parenting but when it came to the reality of day-to-day routines, she found she was doing all the heavy lifting. With the kids at three different schools, she spent half her life behind the wheel, orchestrating drop-offs and pick-ups. Throw in a mix of netball, soccer, violin and trumpet and you got the picture of a woman who was just hanging on, hanging in. And that was before she accommodated the domestic scene, the cleaning, laundry and kitchen duties. And the ever-present mountain of ironing.

While her career as a child psychologist was placed on hold, her knowledge and expertise on the subject helped her cope with the rigours of raising three completely different children as she juggled their needs, demands and idiosyncrasies.

Mack was well aware he had an uphill struggle on his hands to save his marriage and regain his family.

And so, he had pulled the pin on his Boy's Own travels, turned his back on globetrotting and taken the job at The Times back in Sydney. But its humdrum predictabilities were suffocating him. He was struggling to adapt. Most stories he worked on, to him, were parochial yawns about faceless men and women of State politics or petty squabbles in Canberra, the nation's capital. From a photo opportunity point of view, all offering bland imagery.

His photographic genius was not allowed to roam, at will.

Boredom was helping him crawl up the wall. And it didn't help that his Chief of Staff and nemesis, was hellbent on making his life a misery.

Now, here was cameraman, Phil 'Lockie' Lok, pleading for assistance and unwittingly offering Mack the opportunity to adjust his sights, perhaps his life. Thoughts of combining his career experiences to date and blending them to create TV stories of substance, perhaps exclusives, had always been of interest and carried great appeal.

Years of sticking to what he knew best, and was clearly good at, had impeded any move.

Until now.

While he knew he just might be getting ahead of himself, prematurely, he felt a shiver of excitement. He thought of the water contamination story. It could provide such an opportunity. An exclusive exposé that would serve the community, save lives. It could be the fresh direction he craved. It might also provide the happiness key to rekindling efforts on the home front.

Maybe, with a bit of luck and ingenuity he just might be able to manoeuvre this moment into a life changing opportunity. Here. Now.

Mack turned to face the veteran camera jockey.

"Lockie are you seriously suggesting, I become a TV reporter for the day?"

"I think you'd be good at it. And you'd be getting me out of a massive hole."

"I'm a stills photographer, not a full-on TV journo, surely that's unethical, risky at best!?"

"I'm desperate Mack. I'm sure I can explain to my News boss we had no choice but to hook you in. Without you, we have no story. We arrived too late, missed all the action. My reporter had to rush off and cry 'push' at his pregnant wife's side! You've got the field-experience, you know the drill better than anyone. I've been around the traps, a few times too. Together, I reckon we could pull this off, don't you?" Lockie's eyes pleaded.

"It could be the end of both our careers," laughed Mack. "We'll be pushing the proverbial uphill, to get this filed and on-air in the next couple of hours.

"Look, to do this properly we'd need to interview the on-site fire and ambulance commanders, those two survivors over there and Lockie, you'll need to lean on the bosses in your Network newsroom. Get them to somehow beg fire footage shot here by one of your competitors.

They'll have to negotiate an 'I owe you' because without that, you're right, we don't have a story."

Lockie had already pulled out his mobile and was punching in the office number.

"Don't ask them, just tell them what has to happen, if they want this story. And Lockie, best not mention I'm working with you," said Mack smiling.

Lockie walked toward a quieter space between two ambulances as Mack bailed up the fire chief and a Salvation Army officer for an incident update and interview request. He then introduced himself to the two survivors rescued from their blazing apartment. Mother and daughter had a lucky escape with only minor burns thanks to the extraordinary bravery of their heroic rescuer. They were among a dozen casualties being treated by paramedics, most for smoke inhalation, all of them for shock. They had not only lost their homes but their lives within them had been reduced to smouldering ash.

An old man who earlier had become separated from his wife during the chaos had been reunited with her, much to their joint relief. They clung to each other in silence, truly thankful for their survival but grieving their shared loss. Smoke still rising from his singed hair.

While the fire was now well under control, the apartment block was no longer recognisable.

Lockie had finished the call to his Network's newsroom and

joined Mack.

"What did they say?"

Lockie didn't sound confident. "The on-duty news producer said he'd do a ring-around with the other networks but wasn't sure he could pull it off."

"Let's just pray he'll be able to weave some magic. Let's get cracking. You prepared to let me take the lead from here?" said Mack.

"What's first?" said Lockie, lifting the camera onto his shoulder.

"Follow me, I've got a vague plan, I just hope it works," said Mack.

10

The four-wheel drive crunched over gravel, pulling up in a layby. The moon, almost half full, cast a moody glow over the lake. The night still, almost windless, an occasional puff creating gentle ripples on the water's surface. The driver opened the door, stepped toward the railing and lit up a cigarette. The passenger was finishing a phone call.

"Anyway, see you tomorrow. Your husband's still away? Good."

The view from the lookout was spectacular in daylight but at night the inky darkness betrayed its beauty. As the moon disappeared behind a cloud it switched off the only light source. In the pitch blackness it was impossible to distinguish where the water met the backdrop of night. You just knew it was there. Its catchment spread over eight thousand square kilometres, its foreshore stretching four hundred and twenty kilometres. Massive, largely unprotected, a real bonus. Most of its geography out of sight from closed circuit tv coverage. But not all of it.

The passenger joined the driver at the railing.

"Clear drinking water. Without it, a community's health, its economy, its security, just collapses."

"Contaminating this precious drop would bring a city to its knees, create mass hysteria, until it paid up?"

"By contaminating, you mean poisoning?"

"Yes."

"With what?"

"From one of hundreds of germ banks worldwide I am assured we can get exactly what we want. My preferred option would present a serious threat, an iron fist in a velvet glove. To actually use it would have dire, possibly fatal consequences. I'm hoping it won't come to that."

"And what might that be?"

"All in good time."

The moon emerged from its cloud cover, shining on three thousand gigalitres.

The city's largest water supply.

Jacaranda Dam.

Exposed and vulnerable.

11

It was the usual tabloid fare from various desks at The TransNational Times, Australia's leading daily newspaper, hard copy and online. Stories under their familiar banners: General News, Courts and Legal, Business and Finance, Foreign Affairs, Education, Environment, Arts and Entertainment, Rumour Mill/Social Page and Sport. They were all there.

But it was the day's headline that had blown everyone's morning cobwebs into the ether. A real blinder guaranteed to divide the nation. It screamed **Government to Recruit Teen Warriors** with subheadings **Two Years in the Frontline and It's Compulsory.**

The Federal Government had launched its grand plan to re-introduce conscription, sending young men and women, over the age of eighteen, into the armed forces, for a minimum of two years. It had been mooted for months but today, emphatically front and centre, it was government policy.

A controversial move to re-introduce a National Service Scheme for the first time since Prime Minister Robert Menzies' Federal Government legislated one in 1964, as a forerunner to involvement in the Vietnam War. Five hundred and twenty one Australians would ultimately die, three thousand would be wounded. They had been selected by a random lottery system. Dates drawn from a barrel signified those born on that day, aged between 18 and 26, would be forced to serve their country. Today's article predicted if a similar selection method was employed now, it would guarantee a massive backlash with protesters taking to the streets.

Follow-up commentaries from assorted experts and columnists had dissected the subject in minutiae. How would commerce and industry survive, if a large percentage of the nation's youth was serving the country rather than its economy? The lead article suggested there was a lingering threat. Dissenters and conscientious objectors could be jailed if they refused to comply.

The TransNational Times had covered all the extreme opinions. Pro-groups insisting the commitment of ill-disciplined youths to front-line duties is exactly what society craved. You could hear selective cheers from the sidelines. Others proposed a reworking of the judicial system. Instead of prison, why couldn't young, low-key offenders, serve out their sentence militarily? Existing inmates could also be considered for active duty, as an alternative to serving time in jail.

Extremes? Maybe not, according to some scribes.

The rest of the Times' offerings for the day's edition had been somewhat swamped. An article on global warming and the planet's increasing temperatures entitled **Cooking the Continents** had been downplayed into a couple of paragraphs while a scandal involving a government minister and a 14-year-old altar boy had been buried on page twelve.

A devastating fire in a block of apartments in the city hadn't even made it into the morning's edition. The newspaper's print deadline had passed as flames licked the building's façade, even before anyone was despatched to cover the story.

A photographer had been cabbed to the scene and was due to file images for the paper's online edition. As yet, nothing had arrived and the Chief of Staff was checking his watch. He knew other media were already broadcasting details and pictures of the tragedy. Three people had died and five were being treated for burns and smoke related respiratory conditions. It was a big story and so far The Times had nothing.

Wes Markowitz had rung the snapper, Mack Grayson, a dozen times. With no answer, he'd sworn at the ceiling.

He needed Mack's photos and a couple of lines of copy to upload onto the Times' web version. He was half expecting a call from his boss, Mason Green who would want to know why there was nothing online.

As publisher Green never missed a thing. He was permanently glued to radio and TV news outlets. A bank of monitors tuned to networks, locally and overseas. His desk would be piled high with the morning's early editions and he'd be plugged into websites and news wires for any updates or breaking items. His office was often referred to as Mission Control, the nerve centre of the media group.

By now, Green would be well across the city fire, wondering why there was nothing online. Other mastheads had their sites posting updates. Where was The Times?

Markowitz rang Mack Grayson's phone, one more time.

12

From the first day they'd worked together things had careered off the rails. The superstar photographer and the ageing Chief of Staff had clashed on Mack's first morning. Wes had introduced him to other staff as Matt not Mack Grayson. Despite being corrected, it happened several times. Mack was sure Wes was getting it wrong, on purpose. Then after a corridor collision with a production secretary, Wes tipped the contents of his coffee cup down the front of the white shirt Mack had ironed a couple of hours earlier. Wes overdid a profuse apology.

Everything comes in threes, so they say. And it did.

The car parking space allocated to Mack was withdrawn as there had been an apparent clerical mistake in Human Resources. It had been promised, to another staff member as directed by Wes Markowitz.

Pure coincidence? Yes, probably. Lousy luck? undoubtedly. The end of a relationship before it started. Most definitely.

From that day forward they never really got on. There was always the undertow of bad blood. Mack put it down to the fact he was popular and had achieved far more than Wes ever would. Pure jealousy.

Wes thought Mack an ego-maniacal, stuck-up prick, with tickets on himself. Locked-in opinions unlikely to change.

Ever. Never.

But bad things apparently can also happen in fours, not just threes. Because on Mack's first day, after borrowing a clean shirt to replace the coffee-stained version, Wes gave him his first assignment.

In an upcoming issue of The Times, the much-revered chairman of the entire TransNational Media Corporation, Sir Phillip Daniels, was to be featured in a thirty-year retrospective of the paper he founded. Casual and formal photos were requested for this special tribute. Mack was to take portrait shots of the media baron along with images of the great man at his desk, eye-balling the newspaper's historic editions from decades before. A reflection on how much had been achieved under his stewardship, over the years.

Mack couldn't believe this was what his life had been reduced to. From the battlefronts of Iraq and Afghanistan, ducking gunfire, photographing the horrors of war, what's next, he wondered, weddings?

Mack had travelled to an address Wes had given him. He was told it was where Sir Phillip had requested the photo session should take place. It was at a luxury apartment, in a beachside suburb, an hour out of town. On arrival he'd rung the bell and knocked on the door several times but received no reply. He tried the handle and the unlocked door opened. Standing in the foyer he called out.

"Hallo, Anyone at home, Sir Phillip?"

He walked into the living area and was immediately struck by the stunning beach and seascape view. The 180-degree uninterrupted vista was spectacular. While the outlook took his breath away it was the massive lounge space dripping with style and good taste that really impressed him. Pure luxury. Plush furnishings, Persian rugs, ornate mirrors and prized artworks appeared to be the finest money could buy. Mack's artistic knowledge was limited but he couldn't fail to see paintings bearing the signatures of Warhol, Hockney and Picasso, just some of the priceless gems, in Sir Phillip's private collection. Strange, he thought, that the front door had been unlocked, with treasures like this left unprotected.

"Anyone at home?" Mack called out again.

From upstairs there was what sounded like a panicked exchange between a man and a woman. Mack couldn't make out much of what was being said but clearly heard.

"Quick, in the bathroom. Go."

Seconds later a woman tying up her dressing gown leant over the upstairs balustrade. Her well blessed figure making an immediate impression on the silky fabric. As she pulled the material closer to her upper body her sizeable bosom almost escaped. Both nipples seeking immediate attention.

Mack tried not to notice.

Her face displayed a pained expression, suggesting everything from outrage to embarrassment. Mack thought, this is the kind of woman who's not used to being caught in a state of undress, with her hair in total disarray. It wasn't just the hair, this attractive woman's smudged make-up, also spoke volumes.

"Who are you, what are you doing here?" she shouted, tightening her dressing gown cord.

"Mack Grayson from The Times, I'm here for a photo shoot with Sir Phillip."

"How on earth did you get in?"

"I rang the bell and knocked a number of times. The door was unlocked so I came in and called out," said Mack.

"Sir Phillip isn't here, I'm Lady Daniels, I'm here on my own. I don't know anything about a photo shoot."

"I was given this address for a midday appointment," explained Mack.

"He conducts all TransNational's business from his office at our other home in the city. I suggest you've been given the wrong address. Now, please leave."

"Apologies Lady Daniels, I didn't mean to disturb you."

"Well, you have. Now go!" she screamed.

With hands in the air, Mack retreated to the front door, closing it behind him. Florence 'Flo' Daniels, Sir Phillip's much younger wife, watched him depart, before returning to the bedroom. She prayed her secret remained intact.

As soon as he was outside Mack called the office. How could Wes have given him the wrong address? More importantly was Sir Phillip waiting at his other home, right now, for the photographer, who never arrived? What an impression to make on your first day in a new job. And with the Chairman.

"Wes you dickhead, I'm an hour out of town, at the wrong address," exploded Mack.

"Don't talk to me like that, what are you blathering on about?"

"Sir Phillip was not at the beach address you gave me.

According to his wife he always handles business from his city office, never at their holiday home. She was bloody ropeable, being disturbed," said Mack.

"I'll ring his office and explain there's been a mix up and check whether he's free later on for you to take your happy snaps," said Wes, with a touch of sarcasm.

Mack drove back into town, banging his hands on the wheel, shouting through the windscreen, at everything and everyone. And so, it was confirmed, things don't always happen in 'threes' they can sometimes jackpot to 'fours'. While he believed each of these adverse experiences had brought immense joy to one person in particular there was a silver lining. It was the knowledge of an apparent double life of a media baron's trophy wife.

13

Morning radio was conducting live crosses to the city's fire scene for talk-back updates. TV news packages were revealing the magnitude of the tragedy. Websites were bleating blame and culpability along with graphic photos of the smouldering remains of the apartment building.

Wes Markowitz was beyond angry. He'd failed to raise Mack's mobile for an update on the likely arrival time for photos. Two hours had been and gone and there had been no phone pick-up, no call. Meanwhile, all the Times' competitors, local and national, had their websites streaming visual and editorial gems from the fire scene. Many mastheads were planning mid-morning editions as the overnight fire had missed earlier print deadlines. Still nothing from Mack and Wes was fuming.

After another half hour Mack finally submitted highlights from his night's shoot. All stunning examples of the true professional he was. While the blaze in its ferocity was the main focus, he'd also captured numerous human touches. Close-ups of courageous fire fighters carrying residents from the burning building and frantic paramedics tending to dozens of injured and frightened survivors. All typical images bearing Mack's heart-warming signature.

Together with Mack's emotive captions Wes uploaded the photographs to TransNational Now (TN-Now), the online website for the Times. Web staff immediately posting the images on its front page.

It was the very last site to carry pictorials of the fire. What had been the delay? Wes knew he and Mack were heading for a showdown.

It wasn't long before Wes would see Mack but it wasn't face to face. In the newsroom TV wall monitors bleated bulletins all day, every day. The Times' television partner TransNational News (TNN) was just commencing a half hour of updates from across the globe and was now flagging a 'breaking' local story. The newsreader made it clear the lead item was just in from the scene of this morning's fatal city fire.

"Good morning and in breaking news, the death toll from the fire at the Continental Apartments in the City has now risen to four. Just minutes ago a seventy-three-year-old grandmother passed away in hospital. Six people are in intensive care, treated for serious burns. Dozens of residents are now homeless. The question being asked is how did this catastrophic fire start? As Mack Grayson reveals, in this exclusive report, expert opinion suggests this is a tragedy, that could so easily have been avoided."

Wes screamed at the TV monitor.

"You're fucking kidding. That's why he hasn't been answering his phone, he's been moonlighting as a bloody TV reporter."

Cheers from newsroom staff as they rushed to watch Mack's debut as a prime-time news reporter.

Mack's voiceover opened the story with horror visuals of the burning building. Lockie's efforts in begging some amazing pictures from other news networks had clearly worked a treat. The images were shocking. Mack's story immediately came alive.

Mack's Voiceover:

"For three hours the city's fire brigades battled the CBD's worst blaze in over twenty years. Around one-thirty this morning flames spread from the first floor of the Continental Apartments in Buckingham Parade, quickly engulfing the 14-storey residential block. Flammable panels on the building's facade giving the inferno extra ignition, blasting it toward upper floors. Brigades from four council areas fought to bring it under control.

Fire Chief, Rick Charles' first priority, rescuing trapped residents."

"We're throwing everything at it, evacuations where possible, ladders up, pumps at full tilt, just praying we'll be in time to rescue as many as possible.

Mack's voiceover continued:

"Some residents escaped with minor injuries or suffering smoke inhalation, others were trapped behind a wall of flames. This rescue by one fireman risking life and limb was nothing short of miraculous. Seconds after a mother and daughter were plucked from their apartment, it exploded behind them. The ladder bringing them to the ground and safety greeted with instant applause from the crowd of bystanders."

"We so lucky, to be alive," said the mother, in an eastern European accent.

Mack's Voiceover continued:

"Immediately treated by paramedics the stunned pair, spoke of their relief and gratitude following their amazing escape, despite losing everything they owned".

"It was you, my daughter say who notice her at window and tell the fire people to bring their ladder to us, thank you, thank you. You saved our lives."

The little girl leapt forward and put her arms around Mack and wept.

Back at the Times, Wes swore at the TV monitor.

"I don't fucking believe it, the happy snapper's now the hero of the fatal fire."

Mack then emerged full frame to deliver his piece-to-camera. He looked confident as he strode across the fire scene, not distracted by the comings and goings of firemen, paramedics and rescue personnel cutting across him as he walked toward the camera.

"Four people dead, six in intensive care, many residents now unaccounted for, grim statistics. And as fire investigators sift through the smouldering rubble to determine the cause of the fire, I have just been informed the building's management had ignored numerous requests to replace its failed sprinkler system. TransNational News can now reveal it has been out of action for 18 months with the finger being pointed at the building's body corporate. Jack Rankin, the City's Safety Inspector for residential property, explains how his department did everything possible."

"We've visited, we've met with the committee, we've advised on the need for a total overhaul, placed demands in writing, several times. We could not have done more. No action was ever taken. It's now a case for the Coroner."

Mack's voiceover continued:

"This tragic story is only just beginning to reveal the facts, the true cause of this devastating fire. As friends and relatives of the dead and injured come to terms with this heart-wrenching disaster many will no doubt be demanding answers about a fire which, it's alleged, could well have been avoided. This is Mack Grayson for TransNational News"

Phones immediately sprang into life. At the Times, at the desk of publisher Mason Green, at Sir Phillip Daniels' city office, even at Mack's home where dozens of calls, to confused wife Jacki, applauded her husband's bold entry into the world of TV news presenters. She hadn't even seen the story and immediately rang Mack several times, only to hear constant engaged tones or his message bank.

Wes was livid, his temperature at boiling point. Mack had been a reluctant, inebriated participant at the outset of this photographic assignment. Then he'd gone rogue, uncontactable and tardy, in despatching photos back to The Times. Now, the bastard was becoming bigger news than the fire itself. Wes seethed as he answered call after call about how Mack had acquitted himself, wasn't he brilliant, he'd definitely found his true calling, could you give me his mobile number, I'd like to congratulate him. Wes had no choice but to comply.

But it was the call from TransNational's lord and master, Sir Phillip Daniels, that had Wes standing to attention.

"Certainly Sir, as soon as he comes in," Wes scribbling down Sir Phillip's private phone details.

Sir Phillip hadn't said why he wanted Mack to call him but judging by the deluge of hero-worshipping backslaps flooding in, it was clear the media group's main man was mightily impressed.

Within the hour Mack's story was repeated in a news update. Wes nearly lost his lunch as he struggled to swallow a schnitzel sandwich, whilst reaching to turn down the volume. Just then, Mack walked in, Wes was forced to leave the story with the sound-up, to complete its second run.

The newsroom spontaneously erupted into cheers and high-fives as journos mobbed the man of the moment, eager to know how he'd switched from stills photographer to star TV reporter. As his story played out on the monitor behind him Mack started to explain how he and News cameraman Phil Lok had joined forces because his reporter had raced off to hospital with a pregnant wife.

"It was a split-second decision, we just raced around the fire scene recording everyone and everything we could and…"

Wes bellowed from the other side of the room, "That's quite enough, back to your desks, there's work to be done, a paper to print."

Groans from the floor and a shuffling of feet as bodies dragged themselves back to hot desks.

"Beers and all the bullshit tonight at The Back Page" said Mack, a suggestion greeted with a chorus of "you bet", "right-on" and "we'll be there."

Across from the Times was the newspaper's watering hole. The back bar at the Page and Inkwell had been nicknamed the Back Page and was full every night with the comings and goings of the newspaper's various shift personnel. Whenever you went to the Back Page there was always someone you knew. A dangerous place to go for one quick drink, on the way home.

"Mack, my office now," yelled a clearly pissed-off Chief of Staff. His string bean body was visibly vibrating. Long greasy hair flailing, both hands gathering it behind his neck.

Mack made his way to Wes's corner office to newsroom taunts "Who's been a naughty boy?" and "Maybe the principal wants you to stay in after school?"

He entered Wes's office and shut the door. Wes closed the blinds blocking access to prying eyes. While journos and admin staff couldn't see what was going on, they certainly heard it.

"What the hell were you playing at? You work for this newspaper not the Group's TV news department. You disappear for hours on end, you don't answer your phone, you send back photos, long after everyone else has filed theirs!"

Mack had a well-prepared reply. "TransNational's TV news crew was in a real bind, their cameraman begged for my help, when his reporter was forced into a mercy dash to hospital. We're all part of the same organisation, I thought I'd help out the Group."

"Don't give me that bullshit" Wes kept up the attack "You're in serious trouble, you've really crossed the line, this time."

Wes's tirade was interrupted by his desk phone. He picked up. It was Mason Green, the Times' publisher, asking if he was alone.

"I have someone with me." said Wes. Green wanted a private, confidential chat and said he would ring back in a couple of minutes.

Wes put down the phone and pointed a finger at Mack.

"It's got to be about you. That was Mason Green he needs to talk to me urgently. It looks like opportunities for you here could be evaporating before your very eyes. You may want to consider a new career. How about happy snaps for kids' birthday parties? Now get out of my office."

Back in the newsroom Mack received a standing ovation. Wes appeared in the doorway, red-faced, hands on hips. His phone began to ring.

"I want to talk to you about Mack Grayson and his piece on the fire this morning." said Mason Green.

"I've just spoken to him and given him a spray about how he's let down the newspaper, the staff...."

"What are you talking about" Green immediately interrupting Wes. "His report was sensational, my phone's ringing off the hook. Sir Philip Daniels reckons TransNational has found exceptional new on-air talent".

"But surely, he failed in his duty to The Times?"

"How wrong you are. Forget he was working solely as a photographer for The Times. He not only fulfilled his responsibilities to you and this paper, he went on to champion the story for our TV news. And in a major way. We were the only media outfit to expose the failure of the fire building's sprinkler system. It's already sparked a major enquiry, brilliant stuff. All because Mack Grayson took the initiative. That moment when the mother and little girl thanked him for saving their lives and the little girl hugging him, was pure gold."

Wes had just thrown Mack out of his office and was now hearing his boss anointing Mack as the fire's superhero.

He attempted to wriggle his way out. "I grant you he was able to help out on this occasion, but I think his track record as a photo-journalist proves where his true talents lie."

"Absolute Bull!" argued Green. "He's clearly capable of so much more. Sir Phillip plans on talking to him about television. Mack Grayson's career is about to take a new direction and I doubt it will involve you or our newspaper division."

14

"I think I've got about ten messages from you," said Mack.

"I've been trying to phone you all morning. People have

been ringing me left, right and centre. Looks like you've created quite a stir. I haven't even seen what it is they're talking about," Jacki clearly frustrated at being the last to know.

"I think I became a TV reporter for the day," quipped Mack. "The fire's tragic loss of life appears to have certainly shaken up a few folk and sparked an enquiry. TransNational News is running it every hour. You could catch its next bulletin."

"How are you bearing up Mack? Last time I saw you was around two this morning, pissed and angry, as you jumped in a cab leaving me with a drunken Dino and Sacha," laughed Jacki, sarcastically. There was an edge to her voice.

"Did they help you clear up?" asked Mack.

"Did they heck? I've had my tits in the sink almost since they left, about an hour after you went off to be a super star. What a mess everyone made, Mack. With all the bottles and glasses littering the street, it looked like the detritus from an Armageddon farewell party! How could so few people make so much mess?"

"Great party, the way you organised the whole show was just magic. I hope none of my piles of newspapers and magazines suffered in any way?"

"Well, since you ask. There was one little accident. Dino was..."

"I knew it. I knew it. Had to be Dino!"

"As Sacha and Dino were leaving, he saw an issue of Time magazine poking out from one of your columns, some revelation about John F Kennedy's assassination. Anyway, as he tried to slip it free, he lost his balance and lent against your pillar of print. Down it came" explained Jacki.

"He was as pissed as a parrot, the bugger, I bet he did it on purpose."

"Don't worry, I've put it all back together."

"But it won't be in the same order."

"I shouldn't have told you. You won't notice any change. Anyway, why should you worry about a pile of old mags, when you're the flavour of the moment?"

"No one cares about my print library. It's my past life, my current life and it's the future. A history of the world's greatest moments, something to pass on to the kids."

"I'm sure they can't wait. Will you be home for dinner?"

15

The next morning's edition of The Times was all about the devastating city fire. Two people had died overnight, bringing the total to six. Three others were clinging to life, including a two-year-old boy with burns to seventy per cent of his body.

There was an impassioned editorial marvelling at the rescue efforts of the city's fire brigades but impressing how many firemen had risked their lives unnecessarily because safety regulations at the apartment building had allegedly been ignored. The newspaper's editorial called for a full enquiry into how the fire started and why the sprinkler system had been inoperable for eighteen months, despite numerous demands from the City's safety inspectors.

But it was the images that took up most of the front page that were the talk of The Times newsroom, TransNational's boardroom and many of the paper's loyal readers.

It was the split-second moment when a mother and daughter were plucked from the sixth floor of their blazing apartment building. A courageous fireman had managed to snatch both instantaneously, tucking one under each arm, just as the fire before him erupted. Facing outwards two terrified faces captured in close-up at their life-saving moment. It was a study of agony, foreshadowing a miraculous outcome.

A second photo showed the couple now safely to earth, staring back at the flaming shell that was once their apartment. Faces etched in pain.

Overall, two classic images focussing on human survival, the bravery of rescue personnel and the acuity of a photographer.

In the bottom right-hand corner of each photograph, the name of the person credited with creating this 'stills' magic. It may have been in small print but the genius responsible for the overnight fire's stunning pictorials was quite clear. It was Mack Grayson.

16

A sweat-making shared climax left both of them breathless. He lay there for a moment before rolling off her ample body, on to his back.

"You're getting quite good at that," she said with a laugh. "Timing's perfect too. Seems we've found magic synchronicity."

"I still think we need to get together more often to practise."

"Twice a week for six months now, let's hope we can keep it up."

"I hope *you* can," she giggled.

She reached between his legs as he reached for the TV remote.

TV news channels were running updates on the city fire and its mounting death toll. TransNational TV was showing highlights from an earlier story including extended interviews with two survivors who were thanking a journalist for saving their lives. Material not featured in the original story had been edited into a longer piece following conversations with the Fire Chief and City Safety Inspector. Sharp, incisive questioning, from the reporter.

"So, you believe the fire that started in a first-floor kitchen could easily have been extinguished if the sprinkler system had been operating?" asked the journalist.

"I do, no doubt about it" replied the Fire Commander.

"I think that was the man who interrupted us that day," she said.

"What man?"

On screen, Mack Grayson was then seen asking a city council employee about his visits to the doomed apartment block and how he'd been thrown out of a Body Corporate meeting.

She turned the volume down.

"A month ago, when some photographer guy was looking

for Phillip. He was supposed to turn up at his office in the CBD, not here. It was a mix up, but I sent him packing. He was only here a minute or two."

"You don't think he suspected anything do you?"

"No, not a chance, you were tucked away, out of sight, nothing to worry about."

17

"We nearly met about a month ago when you were scheduled to take portrait shots of me," said Sir Phillip Daniels.

"Yes, I'm sorry about that, a mix up with the choice of location," Mack explained.

Finally, Mack had been granted an audience with the media titan to photograph him for the TransNational Times' 30th anniversary supplement. A firm handshake as his boss returned a fob watch to a waistcoat pocket with the other hand. The 77 year old's ruddy complexion betrayed a well-lived life. Portly of average height he was wearing a pinstriped Saville Row suit, cleverly tailored to hide obvious girth, as a well-crafted hairpiece did its best to shave years off its wearer's age, with questionable success. While four disastrous marriages had taken their toll the multi-million dollar man clearly remained in charge of his empire.

"I understand your Chief of Staff gave you the wrong

address. It gave my wife a bit of a shock as well. I gather she was taking a nap when you called."

A nap indeed, thought Mack. There was no sleep going on when he was there. Quite the opposite. Flo Daniels had been caught in flagrante delicto and she had no idea she'd been sprung.

"I apologise for that too," said Mack.

"No need, no need. I left later that day for meetings with our Network partners in New York, it wouldn't have given you much time for your photo shoot. Today we have all the time you need."

"Do you mind if I take shots while we talk? I find the results will be more natural than posed set-ups." Mack started to erect studio lights and a tripod for his reflector umbrella.

"Good idea," agreed Sir Phillip.

"Can you take a book from your library shelf, walk towards me and settle at your desk? I'll snap away, then move the lights to get some close-ups."

Sir Phillip's splendacious office was typical for a man proud of his achievements and wishing to display the ornaments of his success. Oak panelling, leather upholstered lounges, a library littered with first editions and paintings like those Mack had seen at his beachside apartment. He noted a Jackson Pollock and a Picasso. Then, there were the photographs with the rich and famous. Sir Phillip with Bill Clinton, Tiger Woods, Oprah Winfrey, the Dalai Lama. And on his desk a picture of the main man with his young bride on their wedding day. He looked ecstatic. She with a forced smile.

"Florence is my fifth wife. We met at a New Year's Eve party two years ago. It was love at first sight. At least it was for me. She's been a special friend, an amazing companion."

It was obvious Sir Phillip had said more than he intended, as he quickly changed the subject.

"Anyway, your Chief of Staff Wesley, um…"

"Markowitz."

"Markowitz yes, unreliable fellow. I spoke to him after your news story on the fire to ask you to call. I gather you never received that message?"

"No, I didn't," said Mack leaning over the knight's desk, reeling off a barrage of shots.

"I'm hearing there's a great deal of unrest amongst newsroom staff. How do you see it?"

The magnate was grazing archive copies of The Times from thirty years ago. He was just plain Phillip Daniels in those days, the founder of a radical tabloid that became the flagship of a global empire. The enterprise had mushroomed into today's media conglomerate of international press, radio and television properties, and with it, came a knighthood for its creator. Now, here was Mack sitting on the media baron's leather-bound desk, snapping close-ups, about to discuss his future. Talk about Mohammed and the Mountain. A few weeks ago, he thought his career might have been on the ropes. Constant clashes with Wes Markowitz were getting to the point where one of them had to go or there'd be blood on the floor. Was this an opportunity to bury Wes?

"Sir Phillip I shouldn't be telling tales out of school but I get the impression you already know he could be a major liability."

"Yes, I have heard rumblings. But you're on the inside, how bad is it?"

"He's a serious thorn in numerous sides. Rubs people up the wrong way and as Chief of Staff has made some unforgiveable mistakes. Personally, I can't stand the man and would do anything to see him on his way. Right now, morale at the Times is at its lowest ebb."

"I'll have a word with Mason Green. As publisher he's in charge there. Perhaps he can shake some sense into the man or perhaps we should be looking for a replacement?"

As Mack continued to point his lens, capturing dozens more close-ups, and posed shots, he wondered whether he may have gone a little too far in condemning Wes. Telling the Chairman his publishing sensation was suffering because of the man was probably not a bright move. His priority should be this photo shoot. He needed to ensure the portraits were perfect and the subject ecstatic with the results.

Mack's mind was in overdrive. Still reflecting on how his fortunes had changed, in such a short time, since his birthday. The night of the fire he and Phil Lok had pulled off a major coup compiling the now much talked about five-minute story that Mack dreamed could lead to new career opportunities. The story, shot in record time, had been edited at the fire scene by Lockie and uploaded to his producer at TransNational TV News. There, the fire footage begged from other tv stations was added and the exclusive report was delivered to air, with just seconds to spare. The success of that lead news item had now brought Mack to the seat of power. To the office of the man who could re-shape his life. Add to that, two front-page photos in The Times. Mack's images of the rescued mother and daughter had award potential written all over them. He had pulled off the magic double in one day and, as the flavour of the moment, was now poised for greater things. It just needed the Chairman to start the conversation. Mack had now been in the mogul's office for over an hour and was beginning to wonder when serious chat might break out, or whether he was just there to take pretty pictures of the boss.

When Sir Phillip's personal assistant rang to make the appointment for the photo session, she indicated there were a number of other things he may wish to discuss. Despite Mack pressing her for further detail she politely shut him down. Leaving him in the dark. And intrigued.

Patience will ultimately be rewarded, he thought. If it wasn't, he'd weigh in with a vision of his preferred career move and wax lyrical to hopefully impress. At the same time, cautioning himself not to be too cocky. He may well have caused quite a stir with his emergence onto the news reporting scene but should not get ahead of himself. He was new With his fiftieth birthday just passing he knew time was not on his side. This might be the last chance to change career horses. So, he had come up with some ideas in case he needed to kickstart the conversation. Without doubt the fire story demanded follow-ups to further explore breaches in safety regulations, the coroner's report was due and the Continental Apartment's management committee and body corporate was in the firing line for negligent culpability. Six people had now died and three others were clinging to life with third degree burns. If they survived their futures looked bleak at best. There would also be interviews with hero rescuers and the rescued. And with the winter ahead he would propose a special investigation with guidelines into how the dangers and risks of accidental fires in the home could so easily be avoided. In essence a public education special on the dos and don'ts designed to save lives and property. And once those yarns had been put to bed he could hopefully be trusted to pursue, research, report on tastier morsels. One example could be the water contamination claims that could threaten the entire city.

"Have you got enough now?" asked Sir Phillip.

"I would like just one more beside your trophy shelves over there. That silverware is really quite impressive," replied Mack.

"I can't take the credit for any of these awards. We have a fantastic team of seriously capable pros that are the true engine room of TransNational. They're the ones that deserve the accolades. Richard Ogilvy head of TV for News and Current Affairs is the genius behind a lot of these statuettes. Top rating programmes, best story categories, gongs for exceptional presenters, reporters, producers, cameramen, editors, they're all there."

Finally, the conversation swung toward the elephant in the room.

"Talking of awards Mack, I quite understand photo-journalism has been your life for years and your reputation, your track record, your awards, obviously speak for themselves. If you still see it as your future that's fine but I have to say your recent story on that tragic fire in the city was an excellent piece, under difficult circumstances. It created a lot of positive comment here with many in NEWSCAF thinking you could be a valuable asset to their division."

"Thank you, Sir Phillip. I must say how much I appreciate the opportunity to discuss this with you. The fire story has given me an extraordinary insight to the world of reporting. I enjoyed the immediacy of it. The responsibility of telling a story fairly and accurately, while exposing weaknesses and righting wrongs. It's a powerful tool. The visual combination of pictures and words to communicate, to educate, to entertain, certainly is a powerful art form".

"I can see you're quite passionate about this, which is good because I've asked Richard Ogilvy to have a chat with you. He's got a number of ideas that could ring bells for you both. Under him are programme producers who no doubt will also have opportunities worth discussing. Richard has a handle on all of that. He's expecting your call."

As Mack packed up his gear and made his way to the door, Sir Phillip called out. "The photographs had better be good Mack. Your future here may depend on it," he laughed. "My wife is banking on you making me look ten years younger, don't you disappoint her now."

"I'll do my very best," said Mack with a smile and a goodbye wave.

Closing the door behind him Mack felt sorry for the famed media man, clearly unaware his wife, more than likely, would be the one to disappoint him.

18

"The Chairman is spitting chips over the way you've been running things lately. The morale at The Times is at an all-time low, you've really dropped the ball, Wes. What's the problem?"

"Our circulation is the highest it's ever been, we're up for more awards than any previous year, advertising revenue is through the roof," argued Wesley Markowitz.

It was a showdown that had been looming, for weeks. Mason Green, media legend, publisher and guiding light for Australia's leading daily newspaper, The Times, versus his Chief of Staff. The location, Mission Control, Green's nerve centre. A bank of TV monitors tuned to local and international news channels filled one wall. Newspapers and magazines in racks against another wall. A contraption on his desk allowed him to dial up any radio station in the world. Around the globe whatever was going on, he had it covered. He never missed a breaking story, worldwide contacts tipping him off or updating him on the progress of a political coup, a Royal scandal, or a stock market crash.

A confirmed bachelor, overweight with a shaved head, he was an outwardly proud homosexual supporting a number of 'rainbow' causes. His reputation in the media was impeccable. He lived and breathed his passion for news dissemination in the printed word. He'd held numerous positions at the Times over the last twenty-five years and won prestigious awards for exposing everything from corrupt corporate captains to a paedophile ring in the top echelons of the Roman Catholic Church.

"Yes, we're selling more copies than ever before and advertising revenue is blitzing the bottom line but you're missing the point. All those achievements are a result of many people's sweat and tears. People who you are meant to be directing, motivating, inspiring. And the feedback from the newsroom is none of that is happening. In fact, the opposite," shouted Green.

Mason Green's door had been revolving. Editors and feature writers coming in to complain about an atmospheric stench in the newsroom. How the air could be cut with a knife. Wes ruling his domain with an iron rod, barking at everyone, everything. Many staff members were at their wits' end, wanting to leave. They named Wes as their prime reason, citing his atrocious attitude, lack of support, and regular administrative stuff-ups.

"And the way you handled Mack Grayson over that fire story. His stills photography plus fronting for TransNational TV News was nothing short of spectacular. You should have been helping him, not hounding him."

"He was meant to be working for The Times not TV News," countered Wes.

"He works for the TransNational Group and obviously saw how he could fulfill two roles. News had lost their reporter, I gather rushing his pregnant wife to hospital, so Mack seized the opportunity and saved the day."

"Well, he was drunk on duty. He was the scheduled standby

in the event of a call-out during the night."

"What? I don't believe…"

"When I rang him around 2am to assign him the fire he tried to wriggle out of the job telling me he was too pissed," argued Wes.

"I'll hear his version before I pass any judgment on that. He must have recovered fast, to have delivered that TV news story."

"Fucking show pony…swollen head, tickets on himself."

"You're already in hot water, don't make it worse. It's as if you've got a vendetta against Mack."

"Bullshit. He waltzes in from our Asian HQ, Mr Hotshot. Carries on like he owns the joint but I still treat him just like everyone else."

"That's not what I've heard."

"Which is what?"

"That you've got it in for him, that you criticise his work, you give him poor briefs, inaccurate assignment details. It's as if you want him to fail, so you can jump on his back."

"Who's saying that?"

"No names. Suffice to say my office door has been run off its hinges, with constant traffic from senior staff, complaining about you."

"Looks like the vendetta's against me."

"Brought this on yourself. You've been here fifteen years Wes and until recently a key and valued member of the management team. Unless there's a massive change in you, your attitude, your performance, your time here may be coming to an end. Sir Phillip is already calling for your head."

19

"Hello Stranger, nice to have you drop by," Jacki, dripping with her usual sarcasm.

"Hi darling, hi kids. Sorry, I haven't been around, it has been a mad few days," explained Mack.

"Usual story, nothing new there, Dad," said Dylan, without looking up from the television.

"You missed my school concert, you promised you'd be there," whined Jake.

"I painted a picture for you Daddy," said Amy, handing over her still-wet artwork.

"Ever since that story on the fire you've been out early, back late. Is this the new timetable we must get used to? Never home for dinner, no help with school activities, the kids' sports and you missed Jake's concert. The whole idea of returning from overseas was for you to take a job with regular hours and for us to have a normal family life," moaned Jacki.

"I thought you'd all be pleased. This could lead to me breaking into television. More money, maybe a move to a bigger house, the kids getting their own bedrooms."

While Jake's eyes lit up at the thought of getting his own room away from his untidy brother, Jacki and Dylan appeared unimpressed. Mack knew he faced an up-hill struggle. He hadn't even had his interview with the head of TransNational

TV, Richard Ogilvy, but all the buzz was suggesting his days in the print media were about to be traded for television.

Programme producers in the current affairs division had stopped him in the corridor and in the lift to congratulate him and suggested it was a lay down misère that Ogilvy would swing the door wide open, at their planned meeting, tomorrow.

Mack knew if he was offered a job in television, he would want to bury himself in the new opportunity. That would mean trips away, late nights, impossible deadlines, and lost weekends. More importantly from a family standpoint he'd be missing out on even more school concerts, soccer matches and family celebrations. He'd missed so many birthdays and Christmases, even Amy's birth. There was always a war, a peace treaty, an air raid, or a bombed city to cover, all seemingly far more important than home affairs. He could never quite understand why no-one saw his passion, his commitment to the cause as vital to the world. Perhaps it was just his world. A world nonetheless that paid all the bills, at home.

He had never been able to properly find the perfect work/life balance and here he was hurtling toward another black hole, likely to consume him. He had made promises to Jacki about spending more time at home, more involvement with the kids. She also had hopes she might be able to return to her job as a child psychologist.

But first things first. Another problem had raised its head. "Mack, you're not wearing your wedding ring. Why? Where is it!?" Jacki screamed.

"I can explain."

"You'd better. And now."

In all of the chaos and excitement of the past week Mack had not given one thought to chasing down the taxi driver who had accepted his wedding ring as temporary payment on the night of the fire. Mack had made a mental note of the cab's registration number with the intention of tracking the cabbie down, paying the $18 fare and getting the ring back. Now, his memory of that number was hazy, at best. He'd meant to write it down but had raced off to cover the fire. He would have to find out which cab company had accepted the job. Tracing it from there to a 2am booking that Sunday morning shouldn't be too difficult but it would mean talking to the person who ordered it. Someone he'd managed to avoid since being on the receiving end of a serious dressing down. That was when he was threatened with losing his job and would end up snapping photos at children's birthday parties. It meant he would have to talk to Wes Markowitz.

"It's a long story," sighed Mack.

"It had better be a good one," said Jacki, hands on hips.

Mack began his explanation, making it more dramatic than the true version. He finished up telling Jacki he had tracked down the driver and just had to pick up the ring and pay the fare. There was nothing to worry about. The ring would be back on his finger very soon.

But something else was really worrying him. A closer look at the wet painting Amy had given him revealed an adult with long golden hair with the word 'Mum'. Around her were three children, she'd named in blue, 'Dylan', 'Jake' and 'Amy'. And the heading at the top said, 'My Family'.

A family that appeared to have no father.

20

The first thing you noticed walking into Richard Ogilvy's office was his raised desk, giving the impression he presided above the room, like a judge in a courtroom. While visitors' chairs were scattered around his elevated space, the main meeting area appeared to be on the lower deck. There, you had two choices. Couches and armchairs arranged in different groups for casual encounters, as in a gentlemen's club. Then the formal conference option. A massive boardroom table seating up to sixteen people with plush ergonomic leather chairs. Each seat with its own power points for laptops, tablets, and phones. A large screen built into one wall with cameras set into the ceiling opposite. Electronic blinds provided a total blackout for viewings. At the head of the table, a large high back chair, that resembled a throne. Alongside it a keyboard from which all of the room's gadgets could be operated. A touch of a button and sliding out of the wall appeared a full bar with every imaginable beverage. Mack found it hard not to be impressed.

"Welcome Mack," said Ogilvy, TransNational TV's El Supremo and part-time barman, extending an outstretched hand.

"You've had a big week, what can I get you?"

"Thank you, a Scotch would be great."

"Ice, water, soda?"

"Just straight, thanks."

"Good man, something we already have in common," Ogilvy poured two generous slugs of Scotch, before pointing to a pair of leather armchairs.

His was a striking presence. Two metres tall, broad shoulders atop an athletic build. Mack's eye was immediately drawn to a shock of grey hair pulled back into a ponytail. He'd been involved in university and club basketball for many years but had retired from active competition and was now known as a keen rock climber. It was his reputation as a TV executive, gifted with exceptional talent, where he had truly made his mark. Apart from his success in revamping the Network's news and current affairs (NEWSCAF) programmes he was one of the pioneers behind early breakthroughs in reality TV. He had created the first talent competition (Showtime), a cooking competition (Plate Up) and a dating show (Match Me). All of them ratings winners. Mack knew he was in the presence of TV royalty.

"You've certainly stirred up the joint this week, Mack. I've been receiving emails and texts, raving about our new reporter. I had to admit I hadn't met him yet," chuckled Ogilvy.

"I have to say the last few days have been something of a whirlwind. Meeting Sir Phillip, now you," said Mack.

"So how does a stills photographer with impeccable pedigree jump the great divide into TV reporting and become an instant hit? What's your secret?" quizzed Ogilvy.

"Probably because I've been around the traps a few decades, hung out with TV crews, reporters and presenters, all around the world. Seen them in action, been in the same environments, sensed the same story opportunities, it's become second nature."

"Yes, but to turn a story around from a standing start into the gem you put to air last Sunday morning takes a certain skill, years of hard yards."

"I had great support from my cameraman, Phil Lok and sound recordist Dave Saddler. Lockie did most of the editing on location, so it was a team effort."

"You're very generous in dishing out the credit but your role is what I'm talking about. So, you've written and presented this one story for television. Was it a fluke or do you reckon you could produce more engaging stories of that calibre?"

Mack felt he was in the box seat, confident of producing more stories of similar quality, perhaps even better.

He was finding it hard to believe that just a short while ago Lockie had approached him at that city fire, begging him to hook up as reporter for TransNational News. Now, he sat before the one man who might be able to steer him toward new horizons. He immediately gave Richard Ogilvy a full rundown on his ideas for follow-up stories on the fatal city fire and how he intended to nail the inadequacies of the body corporate at the Continental Apartments. The key being to highlight the importance of malfunctioning sprinkler systems. This would lead to an in-depth fire safety 'special investigation', educating the community about the risks and remedies, how to avoid a fire in your home.

"Excellent idea, you'll need to be quick while the fire's culpability issue remains topical, controversial. I'd like you to talk to Clyde Jameson, he's the Executive Producer, over at TransNational Tonight, our nightly current affairs show.

I've already told Clyde you could be coming on board so he's expecting you to drop in at the earliest. He'll give you all the support possible, researchers, camera crews, editors."

"Great, thanks for the opportunity. Um, regarding my current position with The Times, do I take leave, do I resign?"

"I've spoken to Mason Green and he's arranged for your temporary absence. I gather you'd be happy about that, something about bad blood between you and your Chief of Staff there."

"Yes, a difference of opinion, I think."

"Sounds more than that. I gather he's even complained to Mason about you being drunk at the fire story."

The bastard. Mack tried to contain his anger. Wes was trying to derail his new career before it even started.

"It was my 50th birthday, I confess to a couple of glasses."

"I'm not going to buy into the argument now.

Suffice to say we don't tolerate drinking on the job.

Best of luck with Clyde."

21

When Wes Markowitz ripped into Mack for moonlighting with the Group's TV news subsidiary on the fire story, he made a fatal mistake. Mason Green had read the riot act, now Sir Phillip Daniels insisted on more drastic action. With The Times 30th anniversary celebrations Sir Phillip wanted to protect the masthead from negative publicity or gossip. A special colour supplement featuring the legend behind the newspaper's success was about to hit the streets. A supplement that would hopefully carry flattering photographs of the media mogul. Every precaution had to be taken to ensure The Times' thirtieth birthday was a roaring success.

Wes had therefore been relieved of his position and sidelined to a menial production job on the paper. His future looking rocky, at best.

In Wes's defence he and his family had experienced seriously tough times in the past. In the early 1980's they were subjected to widespread poverty and starvation, in their native Romania, under the communist regime of Nicolae Ceausescu. Wes's mother and father, anti-government activists, had been shot and killed during one of the many demonstrations that finally toppled the dictator. Wes's life had been miserable and deprived. Raised in one of the country's notorious orphanages he was subjected to constant hunger, sexual abuse and regular beatings. After the fall of communism, Wes's uncle applied for them to come to Australia. Here, he learned English, completed his school education and with impressive writing skills scored a job on a local suburban newspaper. He worked hard and was rewarded with regular promotions, finally rising through the ranks at The Times.

He had been married but was now divorced, with a ten-year-old son, who lived with his mother.

While his miserable and tragic past would no doubt have a great deal to do with his personality, his demeanour today, there was little sympathy from the newspaper's management. Their firm opinion? There was no excuse for his recent behaviour. The fuse, signifying Wes's imminent departure, had been lit.

Not knowing Wes had been demoted, Mack expected to find him at the Chief of Staff's desk in The Times newsroom. Instead, he was directed to a far-flung corner office, where he found the man hunched over his desk, eating a schnitzel sandwich, with both hands.

Wes glared at Mack through thick rimmed glasses, that needed their smeared lenses cleaned. Brushing crumbs from his thick black beard he stood up.

"Come to gloat at the fallen eh Mack?"

"Not at all. Just want to know which cab company you called on the night, or should I say morning, of the fire story. I need to track down the cabbie."

"The fire story, that fucking fire story, the bane of my life, that's what's led to me sitting here in the dock, awaiting sentence," said Wes.

"I think it's a bit more than just that one occasion. You've had complaints from all over."

Wes quickly moved to Mack's side of the desk, prodding him in the chest.

"Yes, people like you, stabbing me in the back, you bastard," said Wes.

"Looks like you've been doing your own share of telling tales, snitch."

"What do you mean by that, asshole?" Wes shoved Mack against a filing cabinet.

"Telling Mason Green I was drunk on the job."

"You were!" screamed Wes.

"I was not drunk, I'd had a few but I got the job done, quite well it seems, according to everyone. Everyone but you."

Wes raised his fists and dropped to a boxer's stance, readying himself to land a punch.

"Not a wise move Wes, you could find yourself out of here in a flash."

The next thing Mack knew, he was on the floor, blood pouring from his nose. The southpaw's direct hit had landed him on his back. As he staggered to his feet, Wes launched a quick-fire volley, sending him flying across the room. Newsroom staff, who'd been watching the argument unfold, leapt forward to overpower Wes, placing him in an arm lock. Two guards alerted from security arrived bringing the one-sided fight to a close. Mack hadn't even raised his fists or attempted a response.

"You're going to so regret that Wes," said Mack dabbing a blooded, swollen nose. The front of his shirt soaked in red. "You've done everything possible to make my life hell, in an attempt to destroy my career. I think you failed there. Looks like it's your career that may have hit a brick wall, whereas mine could be about to take off," Mack offering a sardonic grin.

"Ever since you arrived back from overseas with your superior, 'I'm better than everyone else attitude' you've rubbed so many people, up the wrong way," sneered Wes.

"On the contrary, it's you who has lost the respect of your colleagues. Why do you think you're here in the naughty corner? You're a complete waste of space, I won't be forgetting this.

You'll pay, you'll suffer, I can guarantee that."

Wes attempted to wrestle forward and break free from the muscled security. He failed but did manage to land a spit ball on Mack's blooded shirt. Jacki had given it to him for his birthday. She'd no doubt be highly delighted that it was now, not only soaked in his blood but in the struggle one of the sleeves had almost separated itself from the body of the shirt.

And there was still the question of the cab company, the cabbie and the missing wedding ring.

22

Clyde Jameson had put Mack to work immediately. The interview set up by Richard Ogilvy led to a backslapping chat about the original fire story. Like many others Clyde was an instant fan but alluded to the fact that one story does not a prime-time reporter make. There was still much to prove and Mack would be given every assistance to pull more rabbits from assorted hats. There was then a quick round of introductions to staff at TransNational Tonight, colloquially referred to as TNT, the nightly current affairs programme that had become well known for stories that packed an explosive punch.

(Trinitrotoluene more commonly known as TNT, an alternative to dynamite, and a convenient acronym for a television programme that flew the flag, patrolled the nation's waterfront, responding to its needs, its challenges.)

As its Executive Producer, Clyde was regaled as the brains behind its success, forging a mix of 'need to know' information, 'know your rights' support, backed by an all-out effort to expose corruption and represent the defenceless. All in the name of entertainment. Bearded Clyde, father to six girls, had been a university lecturer in mass media communications before Sir Phillip poached him to spearhead the programme. Mack realised he was surrounded by people who really knew their business. With eyes and ears wide open he was under no illusion. There was a steep learning curve before him. Desk space was cleared, a pass key made available, and a list of story priorities agreed. Mack hit the phones setting up interviews and booking a camera crew, for the following day.

He was on the treadmill, his new career off to a flying start.

23

Returning home last night had resulted in a mixed reception from Jacki and a startled scream from little Amy when she saw his blood-soaked shirt.

"Poor Daddy, what happened?" shrieked the 8-year-old.

Then from Jacki "That was the shirt I gave you for your birthday."

"Wes Markowitz decided he didn't like me or the shirt. He

tried to punch my lights out and break my nose."

"He's really got it in for you, what happened?" Jacki feigning concern.

"He's blaming me for ending his career, I think he did that, all on his own."

"Did you put him down Dad?" said Jake.

"Knock him out cold?" asked Dylan.

"I didn't even get to throw a punch."

"What!" from Jake.

"Pussy," from Dylan.

"Thanks for the sympathy, everyone. I wasn't about to give him the satisfaction of responding to his anger with even more violence. I'm thinking of pressing charges against him for assault."

"I'm not sure who I feel sorry for," said Jacki.

"I don't believe it, you've got to be kidding, thanks a lot."

"By the way, where's your wedding ring? Still not collected it. Too busy being the new hotshot?"

"I haven't had a moment to pick it up but don't worry I will."

"By the way we've received an invitation to celebrate thirty years of The Times," said Jacki waving a heavily embossed invite.

"Who from?"

"Sir Phillip and Lady Florence Daniels," Jacki in a la-di-da voice.

So, a get-together at Sir Phillip's with his trophy wife, Flo. That could be interesting. Mack wondered if she'd remember him and whether she was aware he knew her bedroom secret.

While The Times birthday celebrations and catching up with Sir Phillip's unfaithful wife was an occasion to look forward to, there were more pressing issues right now, requiring urgent attention.

Mack was quickly realising, as his star rose on the job scene, it was plummeting on the home front. Jacki was permanently hostile. His constant absence was becoming a major issue. But a total lack of concern for his punched nose and veiled support for the man who caused it, was quite disturbing. Hurtful. The kids were equally negative, no doubt driven by their mother who made little attempt to mask her anger or disdain.

Mack's promise to himself and to Jacki that he would count domestic issues at the top of his priority list, was already stretched and strained. He needed to talk to someone, he needed some sound advice. If his new work life was to proceed, he was going to be busier than ever. How could he take a step back to address this gaping hole with the family? How could he stop this runaway train from derailing itself?

Later that day his prayers were answered with an out-of-the-blue phone call from Sacha. He hadn't seen her since his birthday party, when she and her husband Dino had been the last to leave. He'd dashed off to the fire leaving a drunken Dino to tip over one of his towering columns of magazines.

Mack had always had a soft spot for Sacha. He admired how she had created her own medical practice, how as a GP she wanted to be part of a bigger entity. She had gathered around her a group of practitioners with separate specialities. It was a full house. Apart from the general practice the clinic offered psychology, dietary and nutrition advice, naturopathy, chiropractic, as well as her own credentials as a fertility expert.

Recently she had taken the space next door to her surgery, hired a licenced chemist and opened a pharmacy. It had become a one-stop health clinic.

Apart from her medical and business acumen Mack thought she was one of God's special creations. Clever, funny and beautiful, with a fuller figure, just short of voluptuous. Her long brown hair against her dark skin gave her an exotic look. Mack could never understand how her marriage to Dino had survived the years. He was loud and crude. Sacha the opposite. Mack had always felt she was a kindred spirit but because of her almost incestuous friendship with Jacki, he never really got the opportunity to exchange meaningfully.

"How's the gorgeous Sacha?" purred Mack.

"Bloody awful."

"What's up?"

"Lots, can we meet for a drink?"

"Of course."

"Don't tell Jacki," said Sacha firmly.

"Oh, ok, no problem."

Sacha and Jacki were supposedly best friends. Any issues of concern would normally be thrashed out between them. A quiet word away from Jacki's ears immediately intrigued Mack. At the same time a catchup with Sacha would provide him with a sounding board for his own problems at home, especially some reason for Jacki's constant antagonism toward him. And this discussion over drinks would be off the record. Perfect. He respected Sacha's rational thinking; she'd hopefully have an insight to his dilemma. And he to hers. Whatever it might be.

24

There had been four cab companies operating on the morning of the city fire and phone calls to each finally tracked down two cabbies who were operating in the area around 2.30 am. The first driver Mack spoke to was a young student who clearly was not the cranky soul who had taken off with his wedding ring, as security for the eighteen dollar fare. On the second call he found his man, recognising the voice. Problem was, the cabbie claimed he was nowhere near the fire that night, he would have remembered.

"I've checked. All my rides were out of town that night." he explained.

"I'm sorry my friend but I took down your number," Mack lied. "And I distinctly remember your voice. You dropped me at the fire."

"No, it wasn't me, you've got the wrong guy." In a wavering voice, the cabbie was beginning to sound less convincing. Mack went for the jugular.

"You're lying and I will report you to the cab company and the transport ombudsman. You'll probably lose your licence."

The cabbie immediately caved in. "Look, I've had a rough few weeks, my wife's in hospital having our fourth child. I needed cash that night, not a ring, it was a nightmare, the credit card machine wasn't working."

"Yes, Yes, I'm sure it was very stressful for you, forget all that. I'll give you the $18, you give me the ring, we call it quits?"

"Well, that's the problem, I don't have it anymore!"

"What do you mean?"

"I was desperate, I needed the money so I, um, pawned the ring."

"You what?" Mack yelled down the phone.

"Yes, the next day I pawned it."

"I bet you got a lot more than $18."

"A bit more."

"A lot more. How much did you get for it?"

"$50."

"What! That gold band is worth over five hundred bucks, it's my wedding ring."

"$50 was all I got," grovelled the apologetic cabbie.

"Well, you're going back to that pawn shop with $50 and buy it back."

"I've been back, I felt bad, I went in with $50 to get it back"

"And?"

"They'd sold it."

25

Clyde Jameson had made it clear what he wanted in the way of follow-up stories on the fire.

"The first should be about the notorious sprinkler system

that failed to function at the Continental Apartments. What have the fire investigators unearthed? Is there a Coroner's report? Can the Body Corporate be nailed? Will anyone be charged?

"Then there's the mother and daughter who were miraculously rescued. We should visit them, where are they living? Has the mum got work? Is the child back at school etc?

"Both of these stories will give us the opportunity, the excuse, to show the magic pics of the fire again. Sexy stuff, good promo material too." Clyde was almost salivating.

Mack wasn't sure about milking vision of the fire for the sake of a hike in the TV ratings. It was his first glimpse of the raison d'être behind commercial current affairs TV. He was quickly realising that bums on seats, cranking up audience numbers, was what it was all about. The more people watching a programme, paved the way to increased rates paid by advertisers, which in turn generated more revenue for the TV network.

Mack thought as long as the business realities didn't cut across his grand plans for good, honest reporting, everything would be fine. He realised it might turn out to be wishful thinking.

He decided his first story would be with the rescued mother and daughter. Selecting a suitable location to conduct the interview was important. It was probably poor taste but he started by asking Olga, the mother, whether she and her 11-year-old daughter Nina would be prepared to meet him at the fire scene's charred remains. They had not been back to what was left of their former home. Despite initial doubts, they agreed to meet Mack and his camera crew at the site. They decided it was the only way they could begin to rid themselves of the demons from that terrifying night and start to rebuild their lives.

The ash blackened shell, still cordoned off with police tape presented a depressing but poignant backdrop to the interview. With criminal charges against the building's management likely to be laid, Mack easily justified the choice to himself. He was convinced the grim reality of this setting was key to his story's presentation. The imagery something his photojournalist's eye was well trained to identify. The part of the building containing what was left of the couple's apartment was hardly recognisable. A section of ceiling, in the room they were rescued from, remained intact. A shattered chandelier candle swung eerily from a loose wire. Somewhere in the mound of burnt rubble at ground level were the remains of everything Olga and Nina used to own. Everything.

Apart from personal possessions, especially their photographs, there had been a living joy in their lives, a dog. Boris, a much-loved Labrador pup had perished in the fire, his little body now cremated within the crime scene. Nina had not only lost her new best friend but also treasured trophies and medals from her gymnastics competitions. Olga had a reputation as a portrait painter. At the time of the fire, she had been working on two part-completed commissions. They were now buried in black ash.

It was a grim scene. Shattered lives, dashed dreams. All that was on offer now, an uncertain future. Mack had his work cut out.

As the camera rolled the devastated mother and daughter walked toward Mack joining him, just metres from where they used to live. Olga looked sad and gaunt. Her unwashed hair hung loosely around her shoulders. The cotton smock she wore was many sizes too small, accentuating her emaciated frame. It was no doubt a charity hand-out, as all her clothes would have been destroyed in the fire. Nina clung to her mother with one arm, the other clutched a small stuffed rabbit, probably provided by the hostel where they were now temporarily housed. She trembled visibly. A frightened child, clearly not comfortable, she was about to be confronted by the projected lens of a television camera. They stared at the space that was once their home. After a minute of stunned silence, observing all that had been before, but was no longer, Olga turned to Mack.

"If only my husband here, he know what to do."

"Tell me about him Olga?" Mack knew there was so much more to this unfolding tragedy. To have survived the devastating fire and be left with nothing was one thing but to have emerged with a young daughter and no supporting partner was another. While Olga's English was limited, her husband had spoken it perfectly.

"My Sergei. We come here from Russia, 12 years ago, when I pregnant with Nina. He work hard but get sick with the cancer."

Olga gave Mack the full story of their family life in Australia. About a loving husband and father who was totally dedicated to his wife and daughter. How he had worked two jobs to provide for them. On the production line of an auto-parts company by day and as an industrial cleaner by night. Six days a week.

Not only was he the major breadwinner but also the chief decision maker, on every aspect of their lives. So much so, when he died of prostate cancer two years ago, Olga and Nina's lives fell apart. Olga had a breakdown and was hospitalised for months. Nina had been placed in foster care. Only six months ago they had been reunited and moved into this apartment. Now, they were homeless. It was a story to break any heart and Mack knew that careful editing of these tearful moments would have a major impact on viewers. He was already getting the handle on how he might be able to milk key moments for maximum effect. Mercenary, perhaps, but in the end, the story had to pluck heart strings, reach out and touch a sympathetic audience, whilst still qualifying as entertainment. Perhaps, most importantly, Olga and Nina's plight would hopefully provide vital ammunition to the negligence case against Continental Apartments and its body corporate. Theirs would be just one testimony. Others from families of the dead and injured would add further weight to a justifiable class action.

Mack and his crew, a cameraman, sound recordist and production assistant spent the next hour reliving the horrors of that night. Through the eyes and words of Olga and Nina they learned how the fire roared down the corridor outside their one-bedroom apartment, flames licking at their front door, finally burning it down. How the thick smoke choked them to the edge of asphyxiation. Finally, after prising open the window, the moment they were plucked to safety, just as the room behind them, exploded.

On a cue from Mack's production assistant, a lone figure started to make its way toward them. The camera swung around to capture the moment. Olga looked at Mack as if to ask, what was happening. The figure came closer. The smile on its face spoke volumes. The khaki uniform with yellow reflector strips gave away, what the individual did for a living. It was a fireman, not just any fireman.

"Olga and Nina, I would like you to meet Duc Tran. You've met before. At the top of a ladder. The ladder that came to rescue you. This is the fireman who saved your lives."

Immediately there were shrieks and tears in between multiple hugs as Duc re-lived the moment with them. While the intense heat had been deflected by his flame-retardant uniform, he could not believe how they had survived in their flimsy nightclothes. While they were treated for minor burns and smoke inhalation, a few seconds longer in the burning building and two more names would have most certainly been added to the list of fatalities.

Mack had stood back allowing the camera to absorb their tearful reunion. Everything was going to plan. In a moment he would involve himself in this emotional exchange, gleaning from Olga the next steps in rebuilding their lives. He also wanted Duc to share reactions from his workmates and family.

He didn't get the chance.

Olga suddenly let out a high-pitched scream and flew into an instant rage.

"You should have let us die, we lose everything, now homeless, living in church hostel, we better off dead," wailed Olga.

Nina burst in to tears and threw her arms around her mother. Duc was dumbstruck, as if his lifesaving efforts had been for nothing. Had the rescuer failed the rescued? Back at brigade headquarters the young firefighter had been hailed a hero and been nominated for a bravery medal. Was his heroism about to be questioned?

Mack knew he had to intervene and save the pre-planned centrepiece for his story from becoming a total disaster. Especially since all eyes would be on his first TV outing for TransNational Tonight (TNT). Clyde Jameson would be expecting a stellar performance. As Mack stepped into the space with the weeping mother and daughter, he knew whatever happened now, one thing was certain, he could not fail. He had to regain control of the situation.

"I know it may seem hopeless right now Olga but I can assure you help for you and Nina is on its way."

"How can you say that, we have no home, no clothes, no job, nothing," sobbed Olga.

"I believe many people watching this story now will want to reach out and help. People at home, thinking, if the tables were turned and they were suddenly left with nothing, how would they cope?"

"But they don't know us, why would they help," asked Olga as she dabbed her eyes with Mack's offered handkerchief.

"Why would they help Olga? That's a very good question."

Mack's calming words soothed the moment as he turned toward the camera to deliver an impassioned appeal to the viewers of TNT. He hadn't advised the crew he was about to deliver this piece-to-camera, he hadn't even rehearsed in his head, what he wanted to say. He just knew that the spontaneity of the moment, fresh from Olga's painful outburst was key to the impact, he was hoping to make. Anyway, this wasn't live-to-air, just a series of taped interviews and moments to be added to the existing drama-packed file vision from the night the apartment building burnt down. Those pictures were what Clyde Jameson insisted should be liberally sprinkled throughout the story for maximum effect. Mack was beginning to understand how flexible one can be, how parts of a story can be re-worked, re-shot or re-edited and how music can be added later to play a large part in plucking heartstrings for a story like this.

Mack turned toward the weeping Olga.

"Why would they help you and Nina? You're right, they don't know you but many will feel your agony. As you say Olga, you may have no home, no clothes, no job. No one would want that. They see what you're going through and pray they never have to experience something similar themselves. I am quite sure there are people watching right now who may be able to help."

Mack walked away from Olga and Nina. Their tears had stopped and they were listening. Possibilities dawning on them. The camera followed Mack to the charred landscape. No words were required, the magnitude of the disaster spoke for itself. The stark backdrop, the building's skeletal remains made their own depressing statement, in total silence. The only movement, a loose section of police tape waving in slow motion, thanks to a light breeze. Overall, a sober reminder of how bleak a survivor's outlook must be, how impossible the notion of starting over must appear.

"Your whole life reduced to this" Mack pointed to the blackened shell that was once the Continental Apartments.

Mack began his delivery to camera:

"We now know the Coroner's investigation into the cause of the fire has levelled serious allegations of culpability. So, who is responsible, was there negligence regarding inadequate safety procedures? It appears so, but it could be quite some time before a decision is reached and a satisfactory outcome compensates victims like Olga and Nina. What's really important is the here and now. The true objective must be to help those struggling to piece together their lives and start anew. To help those who, right now, cannot help themselves."

Not missing a beat, Mack then launched into his key communication. Without a second thought as to what Clyde may think or whether prior permission, should have been sought. The only saving grace, this pre-recorded material could be edited in order to add, subtract, or clarify.

Mack continued his piece to camera:

TNT has decided to create a Trust Fund to assist Olga, Nina and all those families seriously affected by this tragic fire. Donations can be made via the website, on your screen now"

Mack presumed an on-screen caption for the website's details would easily be inserted when he reached the story's editing phase. Just another assumption he was making, something to sort later. Meanwhile there was the plight of a desperate mother and daughter to consider.

"Olga and Nina clearly have tough times ahead. Their needs are obviously immediate. Perhaps you can help? Their first aim would be to find

accommodation. Then Olga needs to find work.

"I am very good cook" said Olga sidling up to Mack, linking her arm in his. Nina at her side.

"Olga taught art at a school in Russia. In Australia she has been successful with portrait commissions. Sadly, all her recent artworks were destroyed in the fire. Maybe someone can help her with some artistic endeavour?"

"And sometime after they've found a new home, I'm sure Nina would love to replace the pet dog she lost in the fire."

"Yes pleeeease!" shrieked a clearly much happier Nina.

Mack wrapped up his lengthy piece-to-camera with a final impassioned plea for generous donations, encouraging visits to TNT's website for further information.

He realised his decision to hijack the story and commit TNT to a fundraising role may have exceeded his brief and management's expectations. He could be in trouble with Clyde but remained confident his approach would ring the right bells with viewers. Possibly generate high ratings too, particularly if the story was pre-promoted properly. Anyway, there was always the fallback position. Nothing had gone to air yet so the shape and content of the story could still be re-worked to suit other opinions. If push came to shove.

Mack hoped it wouldn't come to that.

26

So much had happened to Mack in such a short space of time. Predominantly good but each advance had a stressful consequence. Hurtling towards a series of new challenges was a real turn-on but, in its wake, a crumbling home environment, that was only likely to worsen.

A lack of understanding from Jacki had led to her poisoning the children. Particularly concerning was Dylan's negative attitude toward everything. Leaving school this year and joining the workforce, any workforce, was going to be a shock to his system. His enthusiasm, or lack of, a major stumbling block. No visible drive or enthusiasm for a possible career direction. Not a healthy state of mind for a 17-year-old. And his father was worried the distance between him and his son had a lot do with it. And the gap widened even more, by the day.

Mack had been sitting at the cocktail bar on the 45th floor of the Majestic Hotel talking to the barman about the recently announced conscription programme. The 22-year-old was concerned he could be called-up to serve in His Majesty's armed forces if the date of his birthday was one of those selected from the Government's lottery system.

"My father was in the air force," said the young man as he shook a Margarita into life. "He's trying to get me excited about the opportunities it could present, particularly with career prospects in the future. I can't think of anything I'd rather do less, but I may not have a choice." The young man's dream of pursuing his first love of playing the pipe organ at the City Cathedral would have to be placed on hold. Mack reminded himself that Dylan would be 18 in five months. Maybe the future will be decided for him. A stint representing 'King and Country' may not be such a bad idea.

"Sorry I'm late, surgery ran overtime," said Sacha kissing Mack on both cheeks.

"Not to worry. We've been discussing the future protection of the nation and how some of our young men and women will be called up to join the ranks."

At home Sacha had two worried sons "Both my boys are shaking in their boots right now, neither are keen to serve but what can you do, other than cross fingers and toes. We're all waiting for the announcement, whether its odds or evens for birth date selections."

"If I'm called up, I'm going to declare myself a conscientious objector on the grounds of my religious beliefs," said the barman.

"I've certainly walked in on something really deep," said Sacha signalling she'd go the Margarita route as well. Immediately offering her philosophic opinion.

"It does seem unfair that a few hours difference between one birth date and another sets you up to fight for your country, no argument. And those few hours of difference could send you to foreign parts, fighting for your life, even risk losing it."

Mack's mind went into overdrive. It could be dangerous but it could be the shake-up and discipline Dylan desperately needed. Especially if it could be linked, in some way, to his IT and online passions. Serving his country could be a great idea if it involved computers. Dylan had spent half his life at the keyboard, staring at a screen, playing games, hacking into secure sites, communicating on the 'dark web' with unsavoury individuals. No doubt cruising porn sites too. There wasn't much the teenager couldn't create, unravel or repair. He had a certain affinity with the IT world. He found traversing its offerings easy navigation, frequently guiding family members into or out of frozen screens and crashed hard drives. Would the armed forces be able to straighten out a petulant youth by acknowledging his computer skills, at the same time injecting purpose into an otherwise rudderless life? Dylan's birth date might dictate no choice but to serve Australia but if he could see out much of his national service staring at a small screen, he might just learn something he could use career-wise, upon its conclusion.

"Let's take that booth over there," said Mack pointing Sacha to the quietest corner of the cocktail lounge.

"No rush, but can you bring us two more of those Margaritas?" "Certainly," said the barman, deep in thought.

"So, how's the world according to Mack?" asked Sacha with a cute smile that made Mack return something similar. "You've certainly stirred up the airwaves, bit of a rising star?" she said, sliding into the cushioned corner. "Haven't seen you since Dino and I drank the bar dry at your birthday bash. Hasn't a lot happened in a short space?"

"Yes, and mixed blessings there," said Mack, throwing a

long face. "While this sudden rise in the employment stakes really excites me there's almost too much going on."

Mack launched into a potted appraisal of the past few weeks. His meetings with Sir Phillip Daniels, Richard Ogilvy and his TV debut. How praise was being heaped upon him, how the fire story catapulted him into the front line and how various doors had slammed wide open. Then, there was his run-in with Wes Markowitz and the potential for legal action. Finally, his unpopularity at home, Jacki's constant whingeing and the growing distance between him and the children.

"And I thought my life was complicated," said Sacha with raised eyebrows. "For a start, you'd be mad to take Wes Markowitz to court, just as all the talk about you is so positive. You could undo all that good work. As much as you may want to nail the bugger, I seriously suggest you back off. Also, a case like that could go on for weeks, cost a fortune and have no guarantee of a satisfactory result. Anyway, Wes is mounting his own case."

"What! against me?" blurted Mack, as the barman arrived, placing drip mats, settling two more Margaritas. Sacha drained her first cocktail, handing the barman her empty glass, waiting till he departed before replying.

"No, not you, TransNational." Sacha drew the afternoon edition of the Chronicle from her briefcase. The lowly competitor to The Times had taken great pride in its prominent front page article, crowing how the newspaper's Chief-of-Staff was suing his employer, over claims of wrongful dismissal.

The article stated, 'Mr Markowitz was relieved from

his position yesterday following a series of incidents and indiscretions, including an assault against a member of staff.'

"Nobody told me he was being fired. It'll look like his attack on me was the decider, that showed him the door, that I sealed his fate. I could be called to give my version."

"All the more reason, to shelve any plan to sue him. He's lost his job. That may have to be sufficient reward for your bleeding nose," said Sacha trying to lighten the mood.

The article went on to say, 'Mr Markowitz claimed racism was rife within the TransNational Group and that he had never been treated fairly when it came to promotions.' His back story had cited a deprived upbringing under the Romanian dictator Nicolae Ceausescu when booth his parents had died in an anti-communist demonstration. As a result he'd spent his early years in one of the regime's notorious orphanages.

"He's certainly playing the sympathy card, milking it for everything he can get," said Mack downing the remaining half of his Margarita in one slug. "Fucking Wes, he's trying to bring me down. I need a scotch, no, a double." Mack was waving at the barman.

"Mack, there are bigger fish to fry right now, worth much more than this stoush with a disgruntled ex-employee. TransNational's legal advisors will probably head it off somehow, or settle before it becomes an embarrassment, you may never even be called to defend or respond."

Sacha was trying to reduce the temperature and change the subject. There were other issues on each of their agendas, their reason for a quiet get-together. So far, the evening had been hi-jacked by Wes Markowitz.

"Double scotch for sir. And for madam?" asked the barman clearing away demolished Margaritas.

"A bottle of your Chenin Blanc please, I think we're going to be here a while" Sacha placed her credit card on the barman's tray. As he departed, Sacha lent forward. "Mack, I've never seen you so agitated."

Mack hardly needed to be told, his stress levels were through the roof, plenty of bottled thoughts in a knotted stomach.

Before replying to Sacha, Mack knew he would have to separate his Margarita-ed mind from switching the conversation on to a more intimate level. He felt each time he'd seen Sacha recently his heart thumped as an unspoken frisson fizzed between them. Lingering eye contact, moments that, he thought, spoke volumes. Maybe it was his imagination and he'd completely misread signals but he believed he wasn't alone with these impressions and feelings. Anyway, tonight was definitely not the moment to enquire about the possibility of a shared crush. Lives were complicated enough right now and with Mack married to Sacha's supposed best friend it probably wasn't a bright move to broach the subject. And all the more confusing when Sacha asked Mack not to mention this drinks' meeting to Jacki.

What was all that about?

"Sure, my plate overflows right now but let's just turn the tables a moment. When we spoke last week, you seemed in a bad way."

Sacha needed no prompts, immediately delivering both

barrels on her frantic life, at work and at home. Her newly expanded medical practice was operating at full tilt but there was a major drama. An internal rift over profit sharing, with the partners, had reared its head. And the licensee of the new pharmacy she'd opened next door was being taken to court after negligently dispensing a prescriptive overdose, resulting in a patient being hospitalised in a coma.

"And that's just the start of it," said Sacha reaching for the bottle of white wine, topping up her glass, downing it in one gulp. "What's really got to me, is the fact I think Dino is having an affair."

"No, that can't be true, what gave you that idea?"

"He's been acting strange for weeks, always home late, takes phone calls in the garden, in the car, anywhere out of earshot."

"He has a very demanding job Sacha, hosting a talk back radio show is full-on 24/7." Mack offered a reasonable explanation.

"It's more than that, he just seems so distant, so pre-occupied. Even the kids have noticed he's not tuned into their world, like he normally is. And to make things worse I was taking him a drink in the garden last week when he was on the phone yet again. He was arguing with someone and I distinctly heard the voice of a woman. When he came back inside, I asked him who he'd been talking to, and he told me it was David one of the panel operators on his show. I said nothing but suddenly felt the wheels coming off my marriage. He's having an affair Mack," Sacha burst into tears.

"You don't know that Sacha, surely there's got to be a perfectly reasonable explanation," Mack wrapped Sacha in his arms.

"What excuse could there be?" sniffed Sacha.

"To put your mind at rest you're just going to have to confront him, ask him straight out, what's going on?" said Mack.

"I can't."

"Why not?"

"Because I recognised the woman's voice"

"Who was it?"

"It was Jacki."

27

It was a miserable night. The rain had been descending like stair rods, all day. Pissing down. A vertical unrelenting downpour, almost tropical in its ferocity. Once again, La Nina had chosen to make her grand entrance, with flooding rains and cooler daytime temperatures. In recent months she had rescued Australia from the wildest of weather patterns. From a catastrophic drought that parched landscapes and emptied dams, leading to record rainfalls, flood warnings and overflowing catchments.

Tonight, was definitely not the night to be out for a casual stroll. The streets near his rental accommodation were poorly lit, the pavements uneven. It would have been easy to lose one's footing, even in favourable weather. But this evening's inclemency, with no umbrella, suggested getting soaked was an acceptable outcome. A stumble or two in the dim light, a likely consequence.

With head down, jacket collar turned up he leaned into the weather with a purpose that lacked concern for the conditions.

At first, swearing silently to himself. Then, as if struck by lightning an outburst, full of venom, as he yelled at the heavens in a foreign tongue. Whatever his plight, whoever his target, the words fell on deaf ears. No satisfaction of a reply. While his diatribe was unintelligible, he appeared to be appealing to a loved one. Reaching out with both arms, embracing an imaginary soul, perhaps a mother, a child, a kindred spirit. As his wailing increased, he clasped his hands together, praying, seemingly pleading for guidance.

His agony was to be prolonged as he started to relive a recurring nightmare, a fixation on a children's dormitory, from a faraway time. He could see the anguished faces of his fellow sufferers and the leering joy of their tormenters, their evil masters. Orphans at their peril. Having lost parents in tragic and horrific times to then be cast into hellish conditions only to be used and abused, starved and beaten, most importantly unloved, for years. In many instances, for ever. In those dormitories terrified to fall asleep, in case something, someone, would wake you, torture you. Threaten you, unless you performed a despicable act, forced to be the plaything of one of these monsters of the night. Resign yourself to its inevitability or suffer the consequences of a sadistic response. He would later escape outdoors, relishing a downpour, to cleanse the horror of his latest encounter. Rain was his friend, rain his saviour. He was known to seek the joy of a deluge whenever life threw him the darkest of curve balls. Tonight, a new excruciating heartache, needed to be drowned.

He fell silent as he approached a streetlamp that finally illuminated his pathway. Standing beneath its floodlit glare he stared up at the source, hypnotised by its glow. Resuming his vitriol, he howled into the light's shaft as if seeking some divine intervention. A one-way conversation loaded with questions, providing no answers, as the rain continued to pound the night.

The cascading rain formed rivulets, pouring down his creased face, a picture of total desolation. A broken man reaching the end of his tether. Raindrops from above, teardrops from within.

On this same night, at this very moment, in this filthy weather, windscreen wipers were working overtime. Each corner taken at reckless speed and then corrected by wrestled over-steers. Tailspins accompanied screeching tyres, a driver on a mission with a clear disregard for other road users. Or pedestrians. With few vehicles on these soaked suburban back streets, an apparent freedom to apply a lead foot and a thumbed nose at safety.

As the man shuffled away from the overhead streetlamp the headlights picked him out on the sidewalk. His shadowy silhouette immediately filling the wall beside and behind him, several times his size. A giant image for a diminished soul. Talking to himself he ignored the approaching vehicle assuming, it would turn away, taking off down the street. Instead, it headed straight for him. The impact tossing him into the air and against the wall, metres off the ground.

His body dropped to the footpath with a sodden thud, still and lifeless.

The car reversing back, sat idling for a moment, the driver

no doubt absorbing the magnitude, the gravity of its creation.

As groans began to emanate from the crushed body on the ground, the car backed away a little further. Then with engine revving, sped toward the injured man, who by now, was attempting to sit up. It hooked him onto the bumper bar finally slamming him, once again, against the wall.

With reversed wheels screaming, the vehicle backed off the pavement instantly grinding into a noisy first gear, hightailing a speedy exit.

The relentless rain pooled a pinkish red around the body as a life ebbed away and flowed into the gutter.

28

Of course, he'd been there before, albeit briefly, but walking through the front door to be greeted by the 180-degree ocean vista, once again, took his breath away. The view, the artworks, the four-piece band on the vast balcony, the well-heeled guests, many a familiar face. It was like a scene from a Hollywood movie classic. Jacki wide-eyed, her open mouth full of wonderment. Mack had to ask her to close it. A tray of champagne cocktails pressed by a tuxedoed waitress was their starting point, as a familiar face weaved his way toward them, with a wave.

"Mack, so glad you could make it."

"Congratulations, Happy 30th Anniversary to you and TransNational," said Mack. "May I introduce my wife, Jacki. Jacki, Sir Phillip Daniels."

"I think we can drop the 'Sir' for tonight. Phillip Daniels, delighted to meet you," said the media baron lifting Jacki's offered right hand, kissing its back, exchanging meaningful eye contact.

"A pleasure to meet you Sir Phillip, sorry Phillip!" all three chorused a laugh.

"I have to say Jacki your husband has certainly impressed many of us at TransNational. I think he could be destined for great things. You must be very proud."

"Um, yes of course. It's all been a bit sudden really. Just a few months ago he was snapping photographs for the Times, now he's presenting stories on primetime TV. I hardly see him, the kids don't…"

As Mack threw a wide-eyed glare at Jacki, Sir Phillip continued to wax lyrical.

"Some of his stories on the fire scored the highest viewer ratings this year for TNT. Amazing stuff. By the way Mack, Richard Ogilvy and Clyde Jameson want to talk to you about maximising public donations."

Mack was sure Jacki wasn't interested with how successful he'd been with the fundraising but pressed it home anyway. "Yes, over a million dollars already raised for the victims which is great news, I've got a few ideas and…"

"Is that a real Picasso," said Jacki interrupting.

"Yes, my dear," Sir Phillip rested a hand on her shoulder,

guiding her toward the famous artwork.

"It was among his early work, when he was hardly known, I picked it up for a song, many years ago now. Mack why don't you mingle, while I show Jacki some of my collection."

With a nod and a breezy wave Sir Phillip whisked Jacki into his gallery corridor where individually lit artworks and sculptures led to an atrium with a gushing fountain. Mack could just make out a chubby cherub with water spurting from its penis.

"Now, this one he painted in the 1920's," said Sir Phillip commencing his guided tour.

Mack turned away from the illuminated aqua delight, dripping in rain forest greenery. For the first time he was able to take in the enormity of the occasion. It was certainly a star-studded guest list. Apart from the obvious TransNational throng there was everyone from Government ministers and corporate captains to actors, supermodels and socialites.

And then, there she was.

As Mack made his way through the well connected, well dressed and wealthy he came face to face with Florence 'Flo' Daniels, Sir Phillip's trophy wife. With the look on her face showing she had no idea who he was.

"Lady Florence, Mack Grayson," said Mack introducing himself with out-stretched hand.

Tentatively offering hers, she gave him a confused look.

"Have we met before; the name rings a bell, but I can't quite place the face?"

Florence or 'Flo' as her intimates called her, was wearing a shimmering gold-mesh floor sweeper. A classic gown designed to show off her hourglass figure and accentuated bosom. She had succeeded in drawing attention to herself as the night's hostess. Her prominent cleavage stealing the show, introducing itself ahead of its owner's arrival. Upon this immense hooter-shelf, a corsage offering token decoration, to her fleshy outcrop, a hint of respectability.

Her hair was piled high with twirled ringlets dangling around her shoulders, like serpents in search of someone to bite. The highest of heels ensured she teetered precariously. It was hard to discern whether inebriation or stilettoed altitude was the cause.

If her intention was to look exotic and sophisticated, she had sadly fallen short. Instead, something tragically brassy had taken its place. One could see how an ageing media tycoon with four failed marriages might woo and snare her, as wife number five. Forty plus years younger than Sir Phillip, Florence knew it was no love match but the obvious advantage of money, a title and the lifestyle was hard to ignore. Completely foreign to her previous existence. As an all-singing, all-dancing cruise ship entertainer she had been thoroughly swept off her feet by a passenger, a shining knight, from a first-class cabin. After a six-week whirlwind romance they were married in Monte Carlo aboard a luxury yacht. Now, two years later, their relationship remained intact. Just.

"We met once before, it was here, a couple of months ago," explained Mack.

"Really, what occasion was that?" said Florence furrowing her brow.

"I came to photograph Sir Phillip, for the anniversary supplement for The Times."

Florence's jogged memory immediately unsettled her.

"Oh, that was you. Yes, in the wrong place. I remember you woke me up. Those photos were quite good of Phillip. You definitely got his good side. Anyway, do excuse me, I must keep circulating. Lovely meeting you."

A slight farewell bow from Mack and Florence tottered off on her high-rise heels. Guests separated, like the parting of the Red Sea, heads turning to take in the view.

Mack was quite sure Florence had remembered him. She obviously had no idea he still held her secret.

"The old man would have fun with that, when the lights go out."

Mack turned to see who was observing their departing hostess with such caustic appreciation.

The boss of TransNational TV, Richard Ogilvy, with an ear-to-ear grin and a glazed look, was obviously having a good time.

"We're having our best year, Mack. I have to say I'm in celebration mood tonight. As the Group clocks up thirty years, it's fitting the most profitable division is TV. Ratings are up, advertising revenue is at record levels, programme planning for the New Year has some genuinely exciting prospects, couldn't be happier. Cheers." Mack and his excited, well refreshed boss, clinked glasses.

"Cheers and congratulations," Mack replied.

"Obviously a good time for me to be knocking on your front door. I'd like to think I can bring something to your grand vision for the New Year."

"Mack, if you continue to impress. Look, your follow up

stories on the fire have blown people away and with viewers throwing their cheque books at us in support of that Russian mother and daughter, the sky's the limit."

Mack's punt with Olga and Nina had paid off. His bold assumption during filming at the burnt-out building that he could commit TNT to a fundraising campaign for victims, turned out to be a stroke of genius. More than a million dollars were raised in the first 24 hours.

Then, the heartfelt appeal designed to help the Russian mother and daughter start new lives together had an extraordinary response. They were offered a fully converted boatshed at the bottom of a waterfront garden as a temporary home until they found something more permanent.

Olga was deluged with job offers for portrait painting assignments. Two schools wanted to discuss teaching positions in their art departments. Having alluded to the fact that her culinary capabilities were more than passable Olga was approached by a hotel and a number of catering companies, interested in talking to her.

The biggest response had come from Nina's plight, after losing her Labrador pup, Boris, in the fire. Dog lovers, breeders and the RSPCA gave the young Russian girl plenty of choices and a difficult decision. Dozens of pups were offered up but it was finally whittled down to one, a newborn black Labrador from a family who had recently rejoiced in a litter. The dog was instantly christened 'Vlad'.

More and more stories went to air as a semblance of normality returned to their lives. Olga took up two jobs as a cook and an assistant art teacher in a local primary school. She also received a marriage proposal, which she politely declined.

One story had turned into multiple yarns. By now Mack's morals and sensitivities about not showing horror visuals from the night of the fire within each story, had softened. He had already grown used to his boss, Clyde Jameson, insisting the 'sexy fire pics' must be woven into every one of these follow-ups. Mack could now see how dramatic pictures drove a story, ignited emotions. He had to admit the impact of TV footage versus a stunning stills photograph was a debate about to wage within him. Capturing a single telling image and for it to be compared to audio and moving picture stimulation is unfair. Each has its own strengths and merits. But in a short space of time Mack felt compelled to place photojournalism and TV current affairs on trial. So far, stills photography was leading the way with the recent announcement that the photograph of Olga and Nina being rescued from their flaming apartment had been short-listed for several national and international awards.

And there was still the most important story of all. The ongoing court case against the negligent body corporate at the Continental Apartments, continued to dominate the headlines. There was growing confidence that significant compensation would be due to the families of those who had perished and the survivors whose lives, properties and possessions had been destroyed. Mack was proud his efforts had delivered such positive outcomes.

While each story had been a touching tribute to the mother and daughter bravely piecing their lives back together, there was so much more. Mack had been front and centre as the driving force, full of empathy and sensitivity. His pieces-to-camera always natural and genuine as he delivered updates or appealed for support. Judging by viewer reactions to the programme's website and phone-ins to its production office, TransNational Tonight had unearthed new talent with exceptional flair. TNT had discovered an emerging star.

"Don't get ahead of yourself Mack, there's still a lot for you to learn but your contribution to date has not gone unnoticed," said Ogilvy.

Mack was listening, at the same time casting his head over the crowd, hoping to catch sight of Jacki. She didn't know anyone at the party and would no doubt whine that he had abandoned her. She had last been seen on the far side of the atrium entering Sir Phillip's library, where further artistic treasures were known to be on display.

"I know Clyde over at TNT has high hopes for accelerating your profile," continued Ogilvy. "Talk of the devil."

"I hope you're not trying to steal Mack away for one of your New Year projects," said Clyde Jameson, raising his glass.

"Yes, I've booked him to host a new dating show for the over 60's. And he's just accepted," joked Ogilvy.

"Mack, I've been trying to marry off my mother, I can offer her as a contestant on your first show," said Clyde.

"Sorry, first season's fully booked. If there's a second series, might fit her in then," said Mack, smugly tossing his head.

"Yeah, yeah, very funny. Seriously for a moment. We've just been talking about what could be up ahead for Mack," said Ogilvy.

"I'd rather save that discussion for the office, I'm not talking shop tonight, other than to say Mack let's move on from all those fire stories. I want to raise your profile and get you into some new, meaty topics. Let's talk next week."

Clyde departed through the noisy throng to catch up with TNT's host presenter, Quentin Street. Street had been the front man for the programme for the past eight years and while he had been a solid contributor to the show's success his tenure was now under question by many, including Sir Phillip Daniels, who thought it could be time for a change. Clyde was a staunch supporter of Street and was resisting attempts to unseat him. Meanwhile Street, aware the writing was on the wall, needed reassurance.

Mack had had little to do with Street, who had welcomed him on day one. Apart from a few compliments regarding his stories he'd kept himself to himself in a corner office, separated from the programme's nerve centre. He rarely emerged to mingle or enquire of one's workload. Mack assumed that was a presenter's prerogative, coming alive, fully informed, at showtime. On air, he was slick, a sharp interviewer with a ready wit. A slim build with a baby face, he looked much younger than his forty-three years. Permanently tanned and always sharply dressed he gave one the impression that his wardrobe at home would be fastidiously well maintained. His bathroom products might be many and varied. The sort of person who you could imagine would iron his own underpants. Mack had ignored the office gossip about him. Being the new boy, he opted to remain neutral.

As the familiar strains of Van Morrison's 'Moondance' filled the air, Mack wandered out onto the sizeable balcony that stretched toward a stunning Pacific horizon. The very capable jazz funk foursome had encouraged dozens of increasingly lubricated couples to take to the dance floor. The number of younger women dancing with much older male partners was quite noticeable.

Couturiers had obviously been raided. The finest evening gowns were on display, supported by a glittering array of 'look at me' baubles. Mack was convinced the Tower of London had been raided and the Crown Jewels shipped to Australia. The crème de la crème of society was here tonight, money dripping from every pore. This two-hundred-person spectacle of extreme wealth made Mack uncomfortable. He wondered how many used their bank accounts to assist worthy causes rather than topping up well-lined pockets. On his global travels as a photojournalist he had seen so much suffering, so many needy charities. Third world problems that could so easily be supported by these first world wallets. And yet, a self-centred greed, ignorance and 'turning-a-blind-eye' had resulted in numerous cold hearts.

Mack had suddenly realised the growing contradiction in his life. What a hypocrite he'd become. Hobnobbing with the rich and famous, drinking vintage champagne and on the launchpad of a new career, financed by such people. Two hours of having his glass constantly topped up by an army of wait staff had somehow relaxed any outrage. Had he reached the crossroads? Were his growing career prospects with their seductive fame and financial benefits, proving too irresistible? Maybe he had no choice but to park his moral and ethical imperatives for a moment and indulge himself.

At least for a while, perhaps.

Just as he was sidelining the guilt pangs he noticed two familiar faces, late arrivals, being handed bubbling champagne flutes, as they mounted the two steps to join the party.

He hadn't expected to see them.

The Odd Couple, the Lombardis, Dino and Sacha. No surprise. After all he was the celebrity top jock at a radio station owned by TransNational and no doubt closer to Sir Phillip than Mack. He would have interviewed his lord and master many times. He was still the last person Mack wanted to see. Dino's interrogation at his birthday party over a whistle blower's claims of threats to the city's water supply had left him with a bad taste in his mouth. Add to that Sacha's belief Dino might be having an affair with Jacki and the hackles were rising.

Dino was weaving through revellers, dragging Sacha behind him. A sight for sore eyes, she looked sensational. In a short black cocktail dress, her hair up, tied with a shimmering gold scarf. Stunning. While it was only a few days since their 'deep and meaningful' cocktail moment he realised, she had been on his mind. His heart willingly leapt a beat. Her smile appeared to respond.

"It's been a while sport, haven't you scored a goal?" said Dino overdoing his lyrical waxing, with a slap on the back.

Sacha stepped in for a two-cheek kiss.

"Good to see you, Mack, this looks like quite a show, so

many famous faces." Sacha nervously downed the remains of her glass, attempting the matter-of-fact look.

There was an awkwardness, felt by two out of the three of them. The third, blissfully unaware, immediately piped up.

"Where's Jacki?" said Dino. Mack and Sacha exchanged quick glances.

"Having her art appreciation massaged. She's on a grand tour of Sir Phillip's private collection."

"Right, I'll catch her later. A few people here I need to connect with, you two all right for a moment?"

Without waiting for a reply, Dino exchanged his empty glass for a passing refill and bounded over to a nearby throng, shaking hands and kissing air as he went.

"Good to see you," Mack started.

"You too," Sacha gave him a knowing look.

"Bit strange this."

"An understatement."

"I've thought a lot about our chat, we certainly covered the waterfront."

"I don't remember the last time I felt so at ease, so safe."

"So comforting to know there's someone who understands."

"I'm not quite sure where one is supposed to go from here."

"We need to keep talking and more often."

"Not quite sure how, but I agree."

"How's everything at home?"

"Indescribable."

"You?"

"Same."

Dino returned almost as fast as he left, whisking Sacha away to join a group of familiar actor faces. She gave a wave, a frown and a shrug.

Neither Jacki nor Sir Phillip were anywhere to be seen.

As the night wore on and the music continued to encourage dancing feet, a warm breeze wafted in, tinkling decorative windchimes made of seashells and glass. Part of Florence Daniels' well-known obsession with Feng Shui.

Recognising many familiar faces from film and television Mack was tempted to dive in and introduce himself. Instead, he was waved over by some TransNational types for what turned out to be boring office small talk. He decided he was ready to call it a day, for the night.

"Dear boy, I've been looking for you everywhere."

Mack swung around to face his host.

"Jacki has been taken poorly and I tried to find you but in a crowd like this, I gave up and called her a cab," explained Sir Phillip.

"What's wrong with her, she was fine?"

"She complained of a blinding headache, then fainted and was out cold for a few minutes. She's better now but under the circumstances, thought it best to head home, when we couldn't locate you."

"I've been out here on the balcony for ages, I'm surprised no one could find me. I better get home and see if she's ok. Thank you Sir Ph... Phillip... for an enlightening evening. What a party, I think it might be going on for a while yet."

He looked toward the crowd hoping to see Sacha, so he could say goodbye. All he saw was Dino locked in animated discussion with Lady Florence.

"I'm sure our paths will cross again soon," affirmed Sir Phillip. "Do send my best to your lovely wife, I do hope she's feeling much better."

Mack made his way to the front door, nodding farewells as he went. A bunch of cabs waited at the curb. He slid into the back seat of the first one with immediate thoughts as to the reason for Jacki's strange turn.

Was she really ill?

Had she drunk too much?

Or was it something else?

29

"Horrific injuries, nearly every bone in his body was shattered. By the time the paramedics got to him, he was long gone. The coroner says this was no average hit and run. No accident. The wounds were so severe he reckons this man was run down more than once," said Detective Inspector Brian 'Deeks' Deacon.

The Incident Room was full.

Briefings on various ongoing investigations and their updates were quickly dispensed with. It was this suspicious death that had all the hallmarks of an intriguing homicide. The case had already created some media gossip because of the deceased's profile and recent history.

Brian Deacon was a career cop of 27 years and chief of the homicide squad for the past 8 years. Recently married for the second time bringing his two children and his new wife's three, from a previous relationship, under one roof. Fingers were crossed the new Brady bunch household dynamic would survive. Top that off with his poor diet, ever-expanding waistline and an addiction to nicotine and many considered him a ticking timebomb. But a timebomb with an eye for detail and a nose for sniffing out the unusual. Overall, a revered and feared reputation, with a temper to match.

"The storm that night was the worst in months, deluging rain and blowing a gale. Why would anyone step out in it unless they really had to? Was he planning on meeting someone? And the fact there were no skid marks, suggests no attempt to brake. A deliberate attempt to knock down and kill. Ladies and gents this to me, smells of murder," shouted Deacon, hitting the whiteboard with his knuckles, drawing attention to the gruesome crime scene photos. Various angles of a pulped body showed not just impact injuries from the vehicle itself but the results of it being crushed against a brick wall. Twice. This blunt force rendered the man almost unrecognisable. It took a week before he could be formally identified, thanks to partial dental records.

The media had been unusually vigilant in its pursuit of the story. One of their own had been run down and killed. Allegedly on purpose. This reeked of a planned execution, they howled. Column inches of newsprint and minutes of radio and TV airtime were devoted to seeking answers, encouraging anyone with information to come forward.

The deceased was, until recently, Chief of Staff at the TransNational Times.

30

When Mack slipped his key in the door, he assumed he would find Jacki in bed, recovering or sleeping off the earlier headache and fainting episode, Sir Phillip had explained. Instead, music was playing loudly. Jacki was propped up on the couch, scotch in hand, singing along to the Best of the Bee Gees. Mack picked up the remote and turned it off.

"You've made a quick recovery," he said.

"I feel much better, thanks for asking."

"What happened? You were fine when you went off for a tour of Sir Phillip's art gallery."

"I've been feeling off for a while, I reckon I've got some viral flu or something. I feel permanently run down."

"That's the first time you've mentioned it."

"Well, I would have but you're never here."

"Why didn't you find me before leaving?"

"Sir Phillip thought it best to go home and rest. Trying to find you in that crowd could have taken for ever. Anyway, I'm off to bed now."

Mack was becoming increasingly aware that viral flu or no viral flu his relationship with Jacki was deteriorating by the day. And as his new career trajectory took flight her resentment was becoming more and more obvious. He was convinced her performance at the party was no coincidence. It spoke volumes. He was trying to make an impression. She was doing her best to derail it.

He was almost tempted to ask her if she'd seen anything of Dino recently. With Sacha convinced she'd overheard an intimate phone conversation between Jacki and her husband, Mack wanted to see the look on his wife's face, when he asked the question.

Now, was not the time.

"Good night," he said.

"Don't forget the boys have got soccer in the morning," said Jacki, closing the bedroom door behind her.

Mack was curious. Could Sir Phillip's guided tour have provided more than an artistic appreciation?

31

Lake Jacaranda was, once again, bathed in moonlight. Their meetings in the secluded layby on the western edge were becoming more frequent as plans for **Strike One** took final shape. They both felt increasingly confident they were about to shatter the city and shock the nation, while pulling off the cyber-crime of the century.

There was something else on which they were both in silent agreement. Bringing the city to its knees and making their fortune, in the process.

"I've been doing some research. There's some serious history behind threats to poison water supplies while holding cities to ransom."

"How successful have they been?"

"All of them created widespread panic, paralysing state and national authorities. In 1984 the Rajneeshee religious cult in the U.S. contaminated an Oregon water supply with Salmonella, making 750 people critically ill. In 1992 The Kurdish Workers

Party successfully poisoned the main water supply, for the Turkish Airforce, with deadly potassium cyanide. In 2000, workers at a French chemical plant, protesting against workplace conditions, poured thousands of litres of sulphuric acid into a local river. In the end, they all got what they wanted, attention to their plight with all ransom demands met in full.

"Despite decades of examples from around the globe, little had since been done to address glaring weaknesses. Amazingly it's in our favour. No country had actively introduced sufficient defence measures to protect their most vulnerable of natural resources. One might think the very threat of an entire city being held to ransom would put municipal authorities and law enforcements on high alert.

"Even as far back as the 1960's published reports in the United States revealed how a large dose of LSD (Lysergic Acid Diethyl-amide) a psychedelic hallucinatory drug, colloquially referred to as 'Acid', introduced into the water supply could disable an entire city. Someone with an axe to grind, could easily take control, until de-mands were met. To date it appears no one has been bold enough to carry out such a daring attack. At least, not yet.

"There are also lethal viruses to consider. And not just for the poisoning of water supplies. The American Anthrax scare of 2001 paralysed an entire nation, one week after the September 11 Twin Towers tragedy. Five people were killed but millions feared for their lives. An important lesson was learned. When you bring a nation to its knees everyone's life hangs in the balance until demands are met

"Terror is a powerful weapon and Anthrax just one of the

many choices we have to wreak havoc. While its catastrophic effects on a town's water supply are yet to be fully tested, trials to date, suggest its lethal potential. Scientific studies have confirmed weaponised Anthrax can easily be manufactured as a liquid slurry, already known to be fatal in animals. "It is almost certain to be similarly life-threatening to humans.

So far, no one has been bold enough, or mad enough, to put it to the test.

Just a question of time perhaps before someone decides to poison a city's water supply. Why shouldn't it be us with Anthrax just one of the key weapons in our deadly arsenal."

Confidence was peaking for the trio. Especially for one of them. A personal secret lay just below the reservoir's surface. In ten metres of water, an ugly 'hit and run' accomplice, still smeared with its victim's blood.

A wrecked blue Ford Falcon with enough DNA evidence to close the books on a certain murder enquiry.

32

"Picasso was obviously one of the greatest artists of all time but he had a very complicated private life. During two marriages he had numerous affairs, multiple mistresses, often all at the same time. It's believed it was his intense sexual drive that inspired many of his masterpieces," said Sir Phillip, launching a guided tour of his personal collection.

"He must have been permanently exhausted," Jacki offered with a chuckle.

"Half his luck!" Sir Phillip, with a dirty laugh.

"Picasso's treatment of women is legendary, he equally adored and despised them. He's famously quoted as saying 'there are only two kinds of women, goddesses and doormats' and that 'women are machines for suffering'. That certainly rings true when you realise one of his wives fatally shot herself and a spurned lover hanged herself," grimaced Sir Phillip.

"That's tragic, how could a genius like that be such a monster?" questioned Jacki.

"My dear many of the world's greatest talents have dark secrets and warped desires. Very often it's that which fuels their creativity. Now, this one is perhaps his most famous, The Weeping Woman, painted in 1937. Its analytical cubism features his lover and favourite muse of the time, Dora Maar. Her known depression is used here to depict universal suffering...

...My dear what is it?"

"I just find it so sad, women being used, abused and exploited," said Jacki chasing a tear from her cheek. Her obliging host quickly whipping a silk handkerchief, from his top pocket.

"Here, I'm sorry I didn't mean to turn this into a depressing lecture on Picasso's proclivities and obsessions. A bit of a preoccupation of mine, I'm afraid. Why don't we sit in the library a moment, perhaps I can get you a drink?"

Sir Phillip, smiling inwardly, unable to dismiss the irony of being sandwiched between two weeping women, swung open the solid oak door to reveal the most sumptuous of settings. The scent of leather and polished timbers greeted nostrils as the eye took in something far more than a room, with a few books. The walls were lined with a multitude of tomes, illuminated by dozens of small spotlights. From a control panel, Sir Phillip dimmed a massive ornate crystal chandelier. A press of a button and curtains buzzed along rails, closing out the night. Another button and suspended tv monitors retreated into a ceiling recess. A third button and the main bookshelf split itself in two, revealing a fully stocked bar.

"Now, what will you be having, my dear?"

In no rush to return to festivities and engage with his VIP guests the forever flirtatious knight appeared unperturbed, far happier chatting to the stunning blonde, he'd just met.

"That painting and Picasso's lifestyle clearly disturbed you?" said Sir Phillip, handing Jacki a strong gin and tonic.

"I think it was a trigger. There's a lot wrong in my life, right now. I don't want to bore you with it. This is your night, your celebration. We hardly know each other, not to mention you're my husband's employer!" said Jacki, gulping down the contents of the glass, handing it back to Sir Phillip, with a look that suggested a refill would be appreciated.

"My dear, feel free, let loose. If I go back in there, I'll only be talking shop. I'd much rather chat to you. I'm not a bad listener, give me a try."

"Why on earth would you want to listen to a whingeing housewife with three demanding children and a husband who's never home?"

"Because you strike me as a woman of substance, who's not afraid to speak her mind. I admire that. And might I say, very beautiful."

"I must admit I feel very comfortable here with you. It's the first time in ages anyone has shown an interest. And you do mix a mighty fine gin."

"Can I top that up for you?"

"Just a little one, thank you."

"My dream was to be a full-time child psychologist. I qualified and was in practice when I met Mack. I fell pregnant and was soon a stay-at-home Mum while Mack trawled the world's trouble spots, snapping their horrors. My career was temporarily, then permanently on hold. Two more children and my child psychology focus became very domestic. I now have three clients aged 17, 12 and 8."

"Now, that he's off the world circuit couldn't Mack lighten your load, perhaps give you the space, to resume your career?"

"He's busier than ever and now that TransNational's TV heavies think he should be primed for even greater things, I can only see it getting worse…"

Jacki burst into tears.

"I just can't see a way out."

Sir Phillip moved in to embrace the inconsolable Jacki, whispering a quiet word into her ear.

"My dear there has to be a solution, you must talk it through. You both have needs and demands but right now it does seem as though only one of you is being fulfilled."

As the tears flowed, Jacki pulled Sir Phillip a little closer, well aware how her bosom would flatten against his chest. Innocent, yet easily construed as something else. She then pulled back.

"You are so sweet, thank you for listening." She kissed him on both cheeks.

"My dear anytime you need to share a moment, let me know."

"I can't go back out there now, my eyes are red and puffy, what would Mack think?"

"I could say you felt sick and had to leave."

"A migraine perhaps? I do suffer from them."

"I couldn't find Mack in the crowd, called you a cab and you went home."

"That'll work, is there another door out to those taxis waiting in your driveway?"

"Follow me" said Sir Phillip.

On her way home, Jacki felt pleased with herself. She'd just made a special new friend who could come in rather handy. For good measure he was also a billionaire and an obvious flirt.

She wasn't quite sure what would be her next move. In the end, it was made for her.

The following week Sir Phillip rang and asked her out to lunch.

33

"Right now, it's 32 degrees across the harbour city. Weekend outlook, thunderstorms. Saturday, keep those umbrellas on standby. Sunday, blue

skies, mid-thirties, sun-cream for you beachgoers. "This is Dino Lombardi on Radio A2Z, Sydney's number one talk-back, the station that shapes you a better world.

"This is Dino"

"Dino?"

"Yes, it's me, who else would it be?"

"Am I on?"

"Yes, go ahead."

"I'm very nervous."

"No need to be, it's just you, me and half a million of my friends listening in, what's on your mind?"

"I believe our water supply is under threat."

"In what way under threat?"

"I know there are people planning to poison our water."

"Who are these people?"

"I can't say"

"Why not?"

"I'm afraid."

"Afraid of who?"

"Them."

"Who's them?"

"I can't say."

"Do you have knowledge of a particular plan?" pressed Dino.

(Silence)

"Are you involved and you're having second thoughts now?"

"Certainly not. I just know that's all."

"What do you know?"

The line went dead.

Silence

"Well, that's a strange one. Why did he call if he wasn't going to tell us anything? We'll keep an open mind on that one. I'll do a little digging with people I know, see if it rings any bells.

This is Dino Lombardi at Talk Back A2Z. Shaping you a better world"

As he came off-air Dino had a flash-back to a conversation on the night of Mack's 50th birthday party. Mack had denied receiving information about a possible threat to the city's water supply. Their conversation had abruptly ended when Mack was called away to cover the city fire, that ended up launching his career as a TV reporter.

Dino thought it was about time they had another chat.

34

As he switched off the car radio, he knew Dino would soon call and grill him about their unfinished conversation. Mack was convinced the mystery caller he'd just heard on Dino's radio programme was the same man who had made similar wild claims with no proof to back-up his suspicions. With Mack's plate overflowing with work commitments, it had not been a priority. Perhaps now he should chase it up, before super sleuth Dino landed another of his scoops.

Mack already had a distinct advantage. He hadn't spoken to the man, but his email had given a phone number.

35

Two weeks had passed and despite a public appeal for information no leads had been received on the 'hit and run' that had now become a murder investigation. The late Chief of Staff of The Times, Wesley Markowitz had been deliberately targeted in a brutal attack. An unidentified vehicle had mowed him down, more than once, leaving the controversial journalist with horrific injuries, crushed and dying. The driver's objective had clearly been achieved.

The foul weather that night meant few people had ventured out. There were no witnesses, no clues to follow up. But there was an interesting development with a recorded phone message that had immediately prompted homicide detectives to pay a visit to a local hospital.

From Markowitz's mangled mobile phone, retrieved from his dead body, access to his message bank revealed a call from a nurse at St Margaret's University Hospital. The muffled voice had delivered devastating news.

"Mr Markowitz, Nurse Janet Strange, from St Margaret's Hospital. So sorry to be the bearer of such sad news but your son Thomas was brought in to Emergency a short while ago, with head injuries from a skateboard accident. We have been unable to contact your wife, so I'm calling you. To inform you that Thomas was placed in an induced coma but the brain damage was so severe we have had to turn off his life support...."

"This Janet Strange clearly does not exist. St Margaret's say no one of that name has ever worked there," Det. Insp. Deacon was addressing his troops in the Incident Room.

"What's more, no hospital would ever leave an insensitive recorded message that a family member had just died. It's a total fabrication. Young Thomas is fit and well, we've checked with his confused mother. Markowitz apparently gave the boy a skateboard last Christmas but had not given him the all-important safety helmet. Hence the suggestion the boy had succumbed to his brain injuries, thanks to Dad failing to purchase any head protection. .

"That phone call was clearly designed to send him off his trolley, unhinging an already troubled mind. While most sound-thinking folk would reject such a crank call, this was not a happy man. Separated from his son, he'd lost his job and was suing for wrongful dismissal. He got sucked in. The coroner says his blood alcohol level confirmed he was totally sauced. Pissed and on the edge of insanity, it's not surprising he should wander out into the downpour and be struck down by his murderer. We're going to find who did this," Deacon thumped his fist on the desk. Detectives had trawled through Markowitz's sad life trying to find a link to someone who may wish to see him come to harm. And while very few of those interviewed, especially workplace colleagues, had much to say of a positive nature, about the man, one name continued to crop up. Someone who was constantly at loggerheads with the newsroom boss and regularly traded verbal blows.

On one occasion it had even become physical.

36

Following Dino Lombardi's exchange with the mystery caller to his radio programme Mack decided it was time to show renewed interest. He rang the number he'd been given weeks ago. Could this be the genuine whistle-blower?

"I wondered if you'd get back to me."

"I've been a little busy." replied Mack.

"Saw your stories on the city fire. TV more your game these days?"

"Might be. Thought it was time we had a chat. Like to hear more about your time with Metro Water."

Within minutes Mack knew he was talking to the real deal. A former employee with extensive knowledge of Metro's inner workings. He obviously knew what he was talking about, describing the control room at Lake Jacaranda, in minute detail. He had worked in the facility's nerve centre, playing a key role in the administration of the city's main water supply.

Over the years he'd become increasingly concerned about protocols for security procedures being totally inadequate. In particular, outdated guidelines on how to respond to criminal or terrorist organisations who might be tempted to hold the city to ransom, threatening to poison its drinking water. There wasn't even a contingency plan to deter fringe or environmental groups who might use the catchment's surface to wage on-water protests and demonstrations. The Board's management had ignored all his criticisms and recommendations, declaring a report he authored a gross exaggeration of the potential danger, a total over-reaction. They had shredded all copies, declaring current systems more than adequate.

As a result, he had resigned. Unable to remain silent, he considered his next move carefully. Where could he go, where his claims would be seen and heard as legitimate? He wanted to highlight the deficiencies within Lake Jacaranda's network, expose its weaknesses and failings. Most importantly how the supposed fail-safe devices could be overridden by someone in the know. When it came to the facility's computer systems it was more a question of cyber 'insecurity' rather than 'security'. His scathing report had revealed, in graphic detail, how easy it would be to seize control of the information hub and shut down the central pumping system. Or add deadly chemicals to the outflow and risk the lives of an entire community, millions of Sydneysiders. His damning report, in the wrong hands, would be dynamite. He had texted Mack, whose work he'd admired for years. His unique ability to expose issues photographically, often gaining covert access to forbidden sites, risking life and limb, to deliver the truth, was legendary.

The former Metro employee was hoping Mack might be encouraged to take a closer look at potential threats to the city's water. They had exchanged emails, Mack promising to follow up.

"You reckon the defences at Metro Water's HQ could easily be penetrated?"

"My report to the Board spelled it out, exactly how anyone

with criminal intent could seize control, easy as.'"

"I'd like to see that report, get an idea how vulnerable our tap water might be."

"I'll flick you a copy online. Take good care of it. In the wrong hands, it could…"

"Don't worry, it'll be safe. What are the chances of me getting into the control room of Metro Water on the pretext of a general interest story for television?"

"Almost impossible. They're not keen on the media getting up close but I can give you the name of someone you could approach, he'd be your best bet."

"After hearing you on Dino Lombardi's show I got the impression there was an imminent threat."

"That wasn't me!"

"What do you mean, it wasn't you?"

"That's why I thought you called, because of that talkback call. I heard it too."

"I assumed it was you. So, who was it, someone from Metro Water?"

"I know the people there, it wasn't one of them."

"Whoever it is, he seems to know something we don't."

"If he's to be believed, he knows about some current threat to poison the city's water. It's exactly what my report to the Board red flagged. Chapter and verse, all the tricks on how an attacker could bypass the system and petrify the community.

"You should also read an article, from a few years back, lamenting our main natural resource as an ignored commodity when it comes to its protection. It was in TransNational

Geographic. Nothing seems to have changed."

"Look, if this mystery caller is no crackpot and his claim is genuine, the risk could be very real."

37

It was obvious Mack was going to have to call Dino and see if he'd made any progress following his caller's claims of an imminent attack. What Dino didn't know was, there now appeared to be two whistle-blowers. For now, it was important he was under the impression there was just the one.

Mack needed to get his hands on a back edition of the TransNational Geographic article, his whistle-blower insisted he read. A computer check gave him the magazine date from two years ago. He instantly knew where he could lay his hands on a copy.

As he slipped his key in the front door, he prayed no one was home. With no car in the driveway, Jacki was obviously out. It was early afternoon. Fingers-crossed, all the kids would be at school.

He crept upstairs thinking he would start in the boys' room. "I know it's here somewhere, I'll find it," he said to himself.

TransNational Geographic was one of the many mastheads Mack had worked on. Two years ago, he'd contributed to a series of glossy features on Tribes of the World. He'd travelled extensively, spending time in jungle communities, living with the inhabitants, photographing them, their cultures, their traditions. He had his photographic thumb print on every quarterly issue for ages. He knew the edition he was looking for was here somewhere.

In the boys' room alone, there were over two thousand magazines, piled one above the other. Four columns from floor to ceiling. Mack's love affair with photography and printed reproductions in black and white and colour, a blinkered fascination since a young lad.

It was his first camera, a Kodak Instamatic, that started his obsession with photography. The Instamatic came with its film in a unique plastic cartridge, no threading and winding for the youngster, who was keen to 'point' and 'press' at anything, quickly earning the nickname, 'Snappy Mack'.

Now, decades later after a decorated shutterbug career he'd surrounded himself with a plethora of the camera's printed gems. Some were his creations, but most were examples he admired. The work of fellow practitioners. Whether it was from war zones, in jungles, being at one with nature, or just capturing a split-second image of jaw-dropping beauty. They were all there.

While he was in love with his photo library, Jacki hated the chaos and clutter it created. Their already stretched relationship was compounded by an on-going stoush over the columns of news and feature material that dominated most rooms in the house. A constant request for the piles to be dismantled and disposed of were greeted with deaf ears, ignored demands.

Mack just needed to find the specific periodical from two years ago and he'd be out of there, hopefully before anyone turned up. The spines of magazines protruded from the stack, with some titles and dates, just visible. Most needed to be tugged from the heap for a closer look. When it turned out to be the wrong issue, sliding it back into place was almost impossible. Hundreds of journals, weeklies, monthlies, and quarterlies weighed down on the withdrawn periodical, making it impossible to return it to its original place. It would need a forklift truck to raise and replace. Consequently, with numerous magazines half-in, half-out, the swaying columns were beginning to lose their centre of gravity.

"I know it's here somewhere, I'll find it," he repeated to himself.

Eventually Mack abandoned the pillars of press coverage in the boys' bedroom in favour of a floor-to-ceiling tower in a corner of the kitchen. Working his way through the mountain he immediately came across a copy of the magazine's title from two years past, but it was not the edition featuring the 'Water' article he wanted.

Half an hour later, with a shriek of "eureka", he pulled his prize from the stack. The piece he was searching for just happened to be from the same issue in which Mack had covered a story on Land Diving, the extraordinary precursor to bungee jumping. He'd spent time in the South Pacific on Pentecost Island, Vanuatu, where men launch themselves from wooden towers, 30 metres above the ground, with tree vines strapped to their ankles, to break the fall. Death defying dives to prove virility and masculinity of the island's tribesmen.

Sitting on the floor, he flicked through pages of photos he had taken, reminiscing on the memorable assignment. He'd earned the trust of the villagers, living with them for days, as he learned their culture and the history behind the land diving rituals. As he re-lived the flashback, a recollection of his over-dosing on Malok, a Kava type local brew, that had rendered him unconscious for hours. He'd been keen to follow the example of the locals but found his constitution was not as strong as theirs. Times well spent. Stories begging to be told. Photos that spoke volumes. Great memories.

The sound of a key in the door.

As Jacki entered the kitchen with bags of shopping, she was shocked to see Mack sitting on the floor, reading a magazine.

"Mack, you nearly gave me a heart attack, what are you doing here?"

"I needed to get my hands on a magazine article from a while back. I knew exactly where it was. I found it straight away."

"That would be a first," scoffed Jacki.

"Must get back to the office," said Mack jumping to his feet.

He was keen to make a hasty exit before Jacki had a chance to raise the old chestnut of a household cull of all print media.

As he reached the front door and released a quick "See you later" the sound of a mini earthquake from upstairs.

He closed the door behind him.

"Mack, Mack!" shrieked Jacki

38

Mack drove his car around the corner to avoid Jacki's hot pursuit. After inspecting the demolition of the boys' bedroom, she would no doubt want to nail his genitalia to the wall. He applied the hand brake, turned off the engine and absorbed the article's content.

While two years had passed since it was published the concerns then seemed no different to those of today. No action from government or municipal authorities to address overdue security reviews. With no warnings heeded and no action taken, the ever-present threat remained.

Water Wars
Is enough being done to protect our precious drop?

Liquid gold.
Pure, unadulterated drinking water. Without it, mankind would perish.
If it's that important to society, why does it remain so vulnerable to outside forces?
Why isn't the protection of the planet's most precious natural resources? watertight?

It's not surprising that throughout history, battles, feuds and hostilities have attempted to seize, take control of, or destroy such a vital commodity. The ultimate aim, to create chaos, gain strategic advantage and panic populations.

Throughout recorded time there have been over 900 serious water related conflicts. Across the globe, poisoning public water supplies has a dark past as warring factions attempted to gain upper hands, politically, socially, or economically with everything from bombings to chemical contamination.

Early simplistic attempts were to cast dead animal carcasses into local water supplies. Now, the current and more pressing threats of bio-terrorism result in ransom demands and widespread public mayhem. So far, everything from deadly potassium cyanide and sulphuric acid to salmonella and ethylene dichloride have targeted reservoirs. Many of these attempts have been thwarted by last minute tip-offs but not before paralysing governments and terrifying communities.

In these uncertain times of changing international politics and arguments over borders, nuclear weapons, trade wars and divisive pandemics, the future is far from clear.

And we're not just talking much discussed protagonists like Russia, China and North Korea. Who knows who may bear a grudge? A deranged citizen with an axe to grind, a wronged corporate entity, a left-wing anti-government movement, anyone wishing to inflict terror and disruption to fulfill objectives military, political or financial. The bottom line? Water, the most precious of natural resources, right now, is probably at its most vulnerable. So, why are authorities who oversee and maintain security measures for their catchments, blissfully unaware how easily their defences could be breached?

At Sydney's Lake Jacaranda reservoir, we're reliably informed the most advanced technology, an over-arching security system, protects its daily operations. Hailed as world's best practice, we're advised it successfully monitors and controls every aspect of the water's treatment and distribution.

Could its real weakness be the ambivalence of those who choose to bury their heads in the sand? Recent threats around the world, notably in France and Canada, have resulted in computer hackers infiltrating operating systems, making ransom demands. In both cases sizeable amounts were paid to re-start equipment, shut down by a hacker's computer.

A temporarily stalled system is bad enough, inconveniencing consumers for a few days. Imagine an entire water catchment forced to close down because hackers had seized control. Ignoring concerns to penetrate water's nerve centre, most importantly its filtration system, could be disastrous. These concerns have been continually shrugged off by each administration who stress total confidence in their existing surveillance with its in-built failsafe systems.

How foolproof is any system when powers hellbent on taking control, armed with the most sophisticated IT weaponry, will do anything to seize such a vital resource?

Especially if they know we can't exist without it.

It could happen tomorrow.

Are water's gatekeepers are about to be challenged?

Mack felt a shiver. The realisation that the city's drinking water was an easy target.

39

Firmly planting tongue in cheek, hoping to get information without giving any in exchange, Mack called Dino.

"I wondered when you'd get around to it," Dino's usual sarcasm, alive and well.

"Get around to what?" said Mack, in offhand fashion.

"Stop it, Mack. My whistle blower got your interest, right?"

"Do you think he's the real deal?"

"I've spoken to him a couple of times 'off-air,' he seems to have knowledge of something going down. Looks like he'd rather talk to me, than you."

"Not much point, if he's not telling you anything," dismissed Mack.

"He will, eventually. I've had stacks of other media trying to muscle in, wanting a piece of the action. Newspapers and TV. I'm convinced this guy has something. For now, I'm keeping it to myself. If you're thinking, Mr TV, you're going to partner me on this one, think again.   At your birthday bash I knew you were hiding something.

Got to go. Bye."

The thought that Dino might want to join forces, his radio programme and Mack's tv current affairs show was clearly not going to happen. Combining the two media to deliver a more substantial outcome, was now a popular modus operandi. As media outlets became increasingly stretched following downsizing, retrenchments, and budget cutbacks, it was becoming common practice. An investigation in which a newspaper or magazine joined forces with radio and TV programmes to share information, resources and costs had many advantages.

But it wasn't going to happen this time. Well, not yet.

While Mack reckoned Dino exaggerated the validity of his whistle blower's claims, he was aware the shock jock would quickly gain the upper hand if his man provided strong evidence of an impending strike against Metro Water.

Mack remained confident, trusting his earlier conversation with the former Metro Water employee.

Within the hour he'd received the promised damning report. Downloading it, he printed off a copy and headed for Clyde Jameson, at TNT.

"This is the road map on how to hold your city to ransom," an incredulous Clyde, flicking through the report.

"In the wrong hands it's 'friggin' dynamite and Metro Water's ignored every word of it." Mack was shaking his head.

"Do you believe this guy's claims are genuine? He's not a disgruntled ex-employee attempting to blow the sour grapes whistle?" Clyde needed convincing.

"I've yet to meet him but everything he has told me so far carries the authority of someone who knows. I reckon this document speaks for itself."

Mack knew his short time with TNT had been eventful, his rise meteoric. In a few months he'd fronted numerous stories, apart from the city fire series, and already gathered a healthy fan base. Tall, handsome, broad shouldered with his mop of unkempt dark hair provided a physical presence that had not gone unnoticed. A hint of Asia, thanks to his Cambodian mother, added to striking good looks. Already, groupies requesting selfies and autographs, hung around the entrance to the TV studios, hoping to catch the new face of current affairs television. With proven journalistic talent and obvious on-camera appeal the future was looking bright. His tenure as a photojournalist with The Times had ended and a lucrative contract signed as a reporter with TNT.

If he could now uncover a major threat to the city's water catchment he'd be in clover.

"Book a camera crew and record his story ASAP. I want you to prioritise this, Mack. And stitch him up with an exclusivity arrangement. It may be a while before something breaks but when the balloon goes up, we need to make sure he's ours, contractually," stressed Clyde.

Mack decided to pitch the second string to his story.

"I'd also like to get a crew inside Metro Water's main control room on the pretext of a general interest piece, nothing that will raise suspicions, just to get an idea of the set up."

"Tread lightly there. You don't want to alert anyone that you have ulterior motives."

"Don't worry. While I'm finding this cloak and dagger stuff quite addictive, I wouldn't risk blowing our cover."

"Good work, keep me posted. And monitor your shock jock A2Z mate, looks like we may have two whistle-blowers!"

After the meeting Mack set up an interview with his whistle-blower who revealed himself as Professor Victor Denton, former Operations Manager at Metro Water. Victor was chomping at the bit. He couldn't wait to spill the beans and was quick to provide the name and phone number of the man who could possibly grant access to Metro's nerve centre for a supposed 'colour piece', general interest story. Mack rang the man, who politely turned down the request for a television interview and tour of facilities. But when Mack offered himself as interviewer, just with his own 'stills' camera, he broke through.

The photojournalist was back in business.

40

It had been a productive day with two planned 'shoots' now in motion. Confirmation that his whistle-blower's report exposed chronic weaknesses was, however, more than disturbing. How the entire city could be held to ransom, panicked, and poisoned, spelled it out in frightening detail. Alarming facts with damning predictions, if ignored.

Conversely, how vital resources could easily be brought to bear to avert the threat of water contamination. But as those proposed resources and measures had been rejected and dismissed by those administering the liquid resource, the ever-present risk remained.

There were shocking examples of how a public health disaster could paralyse a municipal water system threatening the lives of millions of consumers. The 1993 Milwaukee Cryptosporidiosis disaster was the largest waterborne disease outbreak ever recorded in the United States. It was caused by a deadly parasite in cattle run-off, drained from pastures flowing into water treatment plants. Cryptosporidium, a chlorine-resistant pathogen causes gastrointestinal diseases, in particular chronic diarrhoea. Within days more than 400,000 Americans fell ill, 4000 were hospitalised, 54 died. It cost the City of Milwaukee half a billion dollars in infrastructure upgrades and repairs to restore water purity.

While it was not a criminal act, it highlighted how quickly a community can be struck down. More importantly how easily the responsible authority can lose control.

If Dino's informer snitched and a genuine danger was revealed, one would pray that the limited counter defences currently available within Metro Water could be employed in time. With so many reported deficiencies and glaring inadequacies, this seemed unlikely. There were no guarantees. The complete shutdown of the entire water supply to five million homes and businesses was a real possibility. Failing to act could have colossal consequences. Not to mention, tragic loss of life.

There was much to digest and plan for the coming weeks.

Meanwhile Mack had others to consider. A wife who despised him and was probably having an affair. Three kids he loved but from whom he was becoming increasingly estranged.

Regardless of this picture of gloom, he had a family to support.

Having not seen his children for any quality time in recent weeks he decided to take an early mark, ringing home to say he was on his way. On hearing his father's voice, Dylan sounded his usual disinterested self. That was until Mack offered to pick up pizzas. As Dylan advised his brother and sister, there were shrieks of approval and immediate requests for specific toppings. Did Mum have any preferences? Jacki wasn't home. No one knew where she was. Mack rang her phone, letting her know he was on the pizza run, leaving a message.

Driving home Mack contemplated his soaring career and his crumbling marriage. Wondering about Sacha's fears that husband Dino might be having an affair. An affair quite possibly, with Jacki. Could that be who she was with?

He parked the car, crossed the road and entered the pizza parlour. Still wondering about Sacha. Their last get-together had been over a handful of Margaritas in a booth on the 45th floor of the Majestic cocktail bar. Both experiencing deteriorating marriages, both aware of the ever-present, unspoken electricity that surfaced each time they shared a rare moment alone. How is it, he thought, other people, other women, especially attractive women, married to someone else, understand you, your quandaries, and struggles, far better than the one person you chose to be tied to, legally, supposedly for life? Mack wondered, why are joyous, intimate, thought-provoking discussions limited to people you're not married to? Strange that.

Full of warm thoughts and armed with hot boxes of

mixed pizza delights Mack stood kerbside, preparing to cross back to his parked car. He pressed the remote key lock and heard the familiar beep. On the other side of the road his central locking system released all four doors. At that moment a speeding car accelerated past, blocking his path, preventing him from crossing over. In those four seconds Mack's world turned cartwheels. When he finally could cross the road, he could see one of the car's back doors was now open. A hooded figure was reaching inside. Dodging traffic, he raced across, dropping pizzas, finally launching himself at the figure.

At that moment the thief who Mack could now see was wearing a full-face mask, beneath the hoodie, struck him with a heavy object, knocking him to the ground. By the time he'd staggered to his feet, a motorcycle had pulled up. His assailant had climbed aboard, the pair disappearing at speed.

Tucked under the arm of the pillion rider, a black briefcase. A briefcase that had been used to strike Mack. A brief case that contained one explosive document.

After phoning Clyde Jameson and Professor Denton to advise he'd been mugged and robbed, it was agreed he should not report the theft to police. In fact, no one should know about the stolen document. Not yet. A meeting was hastily convened for the following morning.

It was clear now. There was so much more on the veiled threat to the city's water supply. A document spelling out the methodology for an attack was now in the hands of someone who could wreak havoc. Was this in any way related to Dino's talk-back caller? Mack wouldn't be ringing the radio shock-jock to find out.

Arriving home with cold pizzas, whose boxes had bounced off bitumen, did nothing to improve relationships with Dylan, Jake, and Amy. While leftover cold pizza from the fridge was normally a hit, the promise of the hot version, two hours earlier, was what was promised. And not delivered. By the time Mack had returned to the pizza outlet and rustled up a fresh order, his angry brood had hoovered up available morsels from their pantry and were no longer hungry. His popularity rating plunged even further.

And Jacki was still not home.

41

She had splashed out on a new dress, one she hoped would be appreciated. Low cut but tasteful, revealing a subtle swell of bosom that quietly said, hello.

Their last meeting had been fraught with emotion, a bout of tears and an extraordinary frank exchange that belied the fact they'd only just met. The sizeable age difference suggested a platonic relationship, a friendship, could be the only realistic outcome. But at their first meeting each had waved subtle indicators, hinting a more intimate conversation, may have potential.

When she kissed him on both cheeks in the library, at the same time pressing her breasts against him, she lingered extra seconds, sending an unspoken message. He had complimented her beauty and played amateur psych, unravelling her woes, offering a willing ear and shoulder. They were clearly poised for an interesting second meeting. After all, both had unmet needs. Each was trapped in an unhappy marriage, unaware of a shared burden. Neither had enjoyed bedroom calisthenics for months. Both were looking forward to lunch.

"My dear, may I say you look absolutely stunning."

Sir Phillip Daniels planted a welcoming kiss on a well-turned cheek. Jacki acting with early reserve.

"Thank you, Phillip, what a lovely restaurant. The man outside whisked my car away and another brought me to you here, in this private room. What beautiful flowers."

"I'm glad you like them."

"Like them, Birds of Paradise, Orchids and Dahlias, I love them, they're my favourites."

"I know," said her host with a knowing wink.

"How do you know?"

"Your Facebook page is actually quite revealing."

"You have done your homework. How did you get the restaurant to display them?"

"It helps, if you own the restaurant."

Only a couple of minutes in and Jacki was trying not to drop her jaw or declare she might be a tad impressed.

"Phillip, I'm touched, thank you."

The popping cork behind her signalled the arrival of a vintage Dom Perignon and the beginning of a lunch that clearly was in no rush.

42

The early morning meeting to discuss the robbery of the whistle-blower's document was to be brief. Clyde Jameson flagged there was another more pressing issue he urgently needed to discuss with Mack.

Mack wondered what could be more important than a city facing the potential threat of a terrorist attack, as his boss launched a salvo of criticism.

"Who knew you had this document? How did they know it contained such explosive information? Why did you not have it, under lock and key? It was sitting on the back seat of your car, for Chrissakes! How did they know you were going to that pizza shop? Somebody is one step ahead of you Mack, what is going on?"

Clyde was apoplectic. The atmosphere could be cut with a knife. There were no answers to any of Clyde's questions. Someone had scored a home run, snatching an explosive document that gave chapter and verse, on how to exploit Metro Water for ransom, for profit, for political gain. Whatever evil hearts desired.

With little ammunition, the TV programme's production team wrangled the disastrous predicament, thrashing out best options for an effective, strategic response.

The whistle-blower, Professor Victor Denton would be

interviewed as arranged and grilled on the glaring inadequacies of Metro Water's security system. He would need to reveal the weakest links from his document. The most likely targets.

Mack would immediately action his inside story on the water utility. He'd need to be more direct in his questioning than originally planned. Hopefully unearth any threats or cover-ups that may have arisen since the document was stolen.

Dino Lombardi at Radio A2Z should be chased up, a subtle enquiry, could his whistle-blower informer have links to the robbery.

Contacts in security and armed forces were to be sounded out on the City's ability to respond in the event of a full-scale assault. While much of their information would be classified, knowledge of training exercises and access to available video footage would be crucial. These enquiries would need to be based on potential stories on the protection of State assets. The real reason for the sudden interest should remain under wraps. With an agreed plan of attack, the team scattered to implement priorities. A progress meeting was scheduled for that afternoon.

It was quite clear that if an exposé of this magnitude broke it would be of national and international significance with kudos and notoriety for the media outlet breaking the story.

There would be bonus follow-ups and updates providing the latest information. A gift that would keep on giving with accolades, of course, for the creators. But with it came expectations and responsibilities. Dark, possibly tragic consequences, almost impossible to contemplate. It was as if the reality of such a catastrophe occurring, would be the equivalent of placing the city on a war footing.

If it wasn't so serious, one might be laughing one's head off at such a B Grade movie script. But in this case fiction could quite quickly become fact.

Clyde's instruction to his team was to treat this as their toughest assignment ever. Dedicate with haste and focus, remembering the three P's. Patience, Persistence, Perspiration. While they were at it, add two more, Pragmatism and Perseverance with no room for Pandemonium, Procrastination or Panic. Far too much alliteration from Clyde but it showed the ringleader was fired up, in his element, cracking the whip, revving the troops, motivating them into action.

It was the first time Mack had seen his new boss in full battle cry. While most of the meeting's bombast was aimed at him, he was impressed at the speed and certainty of the proposed action plan. Quickly realising with nightly current affairs television how prompt, accurate knee-jerks must always be of the essence, with speedy, accurate turnarounds. Exclusive stories, focussing on issues of major public interest. Always with the intention of gaining the highest possible viewer ratings, the yardstick that separated the best from the also-rans. All with the aim of gaining a sizeable audience, knocking off competing programmes from the other television networks.

With his recent fire stories, he had been assisted by various production staff, working at his own pace. While he was learning on the run, he knew he had to now lift his game if he was to survive in the fast lane.

He needed to become more involved in the mechanics

of a story. Researching, producing, shooting, and editing a piece involved several individuals within a tight knit team. Each played their part, to meet strict deadlines, while still guaranteeing speed and accuracy. He had to learn from them, understand their roles, their individual contributions. And there was even more on this steep learning curve. Fact checking, the legal parameters, industry regulations, supporting graphics, captions, special effects, and music selections were all additional components of this well-oiled machine that pumped out stories, night after night. As the supposed new gun reporter, he needed to be across all these elements. From now on, to drive each story, he knew he had to lead, not follow.

"Mack, my office now," barked Clyde.

43

With the Dom Perignon long gone and a French Sauvignon Blanc in fast pursuit, lunch for two in the private dining room had taken on an air of levity.

Between us we've had six marriages, quite busy people aren't we?" chuckled Sir Phillip.

"I suppose one just keeps on doing it, until you get it right," Jacki raised her glass, clinking it against her host's.

"Do you think you've got it right?" said Sir Phillip, fishing.

"Well, I've only wed the once, my husband has had two

previous attempts, I gather you're now on your fifth. I must be slipping!"

"It's not a contest, I didn't set out to give four previous candidates a house and a pile of pocket money. But life's too short, definitely not a rehearsal. This is it. And if you or your partner are unhappy, cut your losses, move on." Sir Phillip waving a knife to make his point.

"That's easily said but when there are children involved and massive financial implications, not everyone is as blessed as you Phillip."

"I grant you, I'm not short of settlement funds. It's cost me a fortune. Several. But let me tell you, I have three children from my first marriage. I'm close to two of them. The third has never forgiven me for leaving home and taking up with her mother's best friend. Two out of three's not bad though!"

"Naughty boy, in the past you'd be labelled a typical cad, a bounder, even a rogue."

"A loveable rogue, I hope?"

"Well, you have some endearing qualities, a man of good taste with an impressive art collection, who's very generous, very attentive and doesn't hide the fact, he's an outrageous flirt!"

"How am I doing?"

"Does your wife know you're lunching alone, with a married woman today?"

"Oh, don't spoil it."

"Well, does she?"

"Of course, not. Does your husband know you're lunching with me?

"No!"

"Well, then. "

"Touché!" Sir Phillip raising his glass, triumphantly

44

Silence as Clyde poured two black coffees, without asking Mack whether he wanted one, or how he liked his brew. He passed him a cup.

"I was probably a bit heavy in there, in front of everyone else, but Mack, what a disaster. We've lost the advantage. Until that document was stolen it was only speculation of a major threat to the city's water supply. Now, it's a cert and someone has got a head start on us. We must use all our resources to seize back control. From a story point of view, this is a potential blockbuster."

Mack wasn't going to whinge about the public dressing down he'd just received in the conference room. He knew he deserved it but as the new boy in front of colleagues, who were still making up their minds about him, he'd winced with embarrassment.

Instead, Mack offered a glimmer of hope with possible redemption. "I've still got the online version of the document, I want to go through that with Vic Denton and identify the riskiest, the most vulnerable areas and see if that throws up any pointers, any clues, as to who might be behind this.

"Plucking at straws, aren't we?" Clyde screwed up his face. "Maybe it's our only hope of finding the key to unlocking this one. Give that Dino Lombardi a shake-up too. If he's got something, he may want to share it. He'd get good exposure, working with us."

That was one directive Mack planned to ignore. Trying to work with Dino only spelled trouble.

"Mack, I want you to helm this. You started it, you got us into this latest mess, I want you to see it all the way through. I can allocate resources, people, whatever you need, whenever you need them.

"There's a lot riding on this one, not just from TNT's perspective. The protection of this city's most precious resource and its potential impact on millions of residents is at stake. Remember, they're our viewers too.

"Mack don't let me down.

"Now, the real reason, why I called you in here…"

45

The entrée of tapas selections was cleared. A Beaujolais then poured by the sommelier in honour of the arriving blue-eyed cod, poached in an onion and saffron broth, with asparagus and sweet potato. Normally white wine would be chosen with fish but Sir Phillip's investment in a certain French winery insisted they break with tradition.

With a silent bow the waiter retired, closing the door behind him.

"What a treat, thank you Phillip, it's not every day I get to experience being fussed over so."

"I thought you deserved some serious time out. When we met the night of the party you were clearly unhappy. I trust things have improved."

"Oh Phillip, I don't want to spoil this lovely lunch, delving into my gloom and doom. Suffice to say, my marriage is heading for the cliff."

"My dear, I am sorry. Looks like we have a lot in common, mine too, hovering on the edge of that precipice, just a matter of time."

They both burst out laughing, raising their glasses to each other, before diving into the cod. Apart from the occasional clink of cutlery, there was a minute's silence, before Sir Phillip chilled the air.

"I think your husband may be in a spot of bother."

"What do you mean, I thought he was your shining star, right now?"

"Well, he is, I'm not sure how long that's going to last."

Jacki's eyes widened. "What do you mean?"

"It seems a number of TransNational's staff have been interviewed by police over the suspicious death of The Times' Chief of Staff, Wes Markowitz.

Apparently, they now want to interview me."

46

"This is really quite serious" Clyde leaned forward in his chair.

Mack Immediately thought the growing disquiet over the death of Wes Markowitz must have finally reached senior management's ears. His fight with the late Chief of Staff, followed by wrongful dismissal claims may be hard to explain. With his star in its current ascendancy, was he about to be smeared by the controversy?

Wes had been a right royal pain in the neck, there was no denying, but the suggestion he could be responsible for despatching him to the Almighty was unthinkable. Information on the hit and run was sketchy. Police releasing few details of the incident, other than it was now a confirmed murder investigation.

The funeral had been a grim affair. With a small group of Romanian friends and an even smaller group of TransNational staff, headed by Mason Green, as Wes's immediate boss. He was feeling uncomfortable as only weeks earlier Mason had dressed down the former Chief of Staff before forcing his resignation. Wes's young son clung to his mother with one arm. Under the other, the last present he'd received from his father, its four wheels a stark reminder of the link to this tragedy. But now there was an eerie addition.

Ten-year-old Thomas had chosen to wear a safety helmet to

his father's funeral.

Markowitz's body had been withheld by the coroner for three weeks until the police had completed a thorough investigation of all the physical evidence. Flakes of a blue/grey paint and tiny fragments of glass had been extracted from the battered corpse with hopes they could be matched with the type and make of vehicle involved in the crime. Possibly even with its year of manufacture.

The dust-up in the office when Mack was floored by Wes had been witnessed by a handful of staff, including security guards. Mack had not thrown a punch, retaining a passive stance throughout the ordeal, much to his son Dylan's disgust. To anyone observing the fight it was quite clear who started it, who was the aggressor, who was landing the punches and who chose not to respond. At least physically. Verbally, Mack was well aware he had given Wes a monumental spray. A vicious tirade that could have implications at a later date.

"We've lost Quentin," blurted Clyde.

"What are you talking about?" Mack was instantly relieved he wasn't on the end of a 'please explain' about Wes Markowitz.

The presenter of TNT, Quentin Street, was an unusual cove for the host of a TV current affairs programme. Instead of the anticipated, outgoing, gregarious soul he bordered on the anti-social. He may have seemed the friendly 'hail-fellow-well-met' type but away from the studio lights and on-screen presence, a different persona emerged. Never getting involved in any staff parties or seasonal celebrations. When viewer ratings screamed another success story it always meant an open assault on the bar fridge in the boss's office. He always had a prior commitment or pressing engagement.

"He hasn't answered his mobile or landline, last night or this morning. No reply to texts or emails. I sent a production assistant around to his home, no answer."

"Is he away, out of phone range maybe?"

"We have a show to put to air, where would he be going? He's not on any assignment. He knows he's hosting tonight's programme. Right now, we need him to voice the promos for the lead story. Apart from TNT's on-air spots, radio stations are bleating for our ads, scheduled for live-reads by their programme jocks, within the hour." Clyde was clearly stressed, sweat patches under his arms were growing.

While there had been rumours Street's eight-year tenure as the show's front man was under review, his no-show was totally out of character. All TV presenters feel the relentless pressure, their positions are constantly under threat. It's the nature of the beast, known as television. Street was a competent host and interviewer but recently both his in-office and on-air demeanour had changed markedly. Everyone on the programme suspected it was because he had recently ended a relationship with his live-in male lover. He had no idea that everyone on TNT knew about his private life, assuming he'd also been successful in keeping his 'behind doors' secrets away from the prying eyes of the gossip media and paparazzi. Was the stress of it all a factor, was he lying low somewhere? If so, why not call, why not ring in sick? As Clyde ran a hand through thinning whisps of grey hair, he took off his glasses, throwing them down on the desk.

"If Quentin doesn't come in, in the next five minutes, I want you to voice the promos for tonight's show."

"Me? Right. No problem, surely Quentin will turn up though?"

"And if he's not here in the next half hour?"

"Yes?" Mack looked uncertain.

"I want you to host tonight's show."

"What! I've never, I'm not ready!"

"Mack, with what you have achieved in the past few weeks, it's a logical next step. Maybe a little sooner than expected, I grant you,"

"I'd say so," said Mack, nodding madly.

"You've become a fan favourite judging by the mail we receive and the selfie-hunters outside. The viewers are definitely ready for you."

"But I've never worked a studio before."

"I've booked the studio for a practice run. Our Director and production staff, including an autocue operator are going to turn you into a TV presenter, before show time. I have every confidence in you. Take the advice you're given, keep practising until you feel comfortable talking to camera. Act natural, you can do it, Mack. Piece of cake," chuckled Clyde.

"If it's that easy, why don't you do it?"

"I don't have the flair or the ability. You have both. If you can make this work Mack, the opportunities are endless."

"But I'm no show-pony presenter, I'm 50 for God's sake."

"Get ready to break the mould. Here are the scripts for today's promos, they're your first priority. Then down to Studio

One for the schooling. After that you'll need a shave before going to make-up. Then, it's on to wardrobe for a suit and tie. I don't think our viewers are ready for your ripped T shirt and shorts look, just yet!"

Clyde hurried Mack to the door.

47

As he walked the corridor toward the audio booth to record his dulcet tones, Mack rehearsed out loud.

"Caught living the high life. The property developer selling non-existent apartments, gouging millions from buyers. We track him down in the Caribbean.

The Government Minister, the City Councillor and the TV Chef. The Love triangle that has the whole world talking.

And the two-legged dog, looking for a new home.

That's next on TransNational Tonight"

Mack entered the sound-proofed booth, putting on the headphones. After the audio engineer gave him the thumbs-up he delivered half a dozen versions before being told the last one had nailed it. He was enjoying himself. He was beginning to get the taste of being in the hot seat. At the same time he had to admit there was something he found rather unsettling. This supposed hard hitting current affairs show, about to reveal the potential exposure of the City's water supply to terrorism, was also spruiking a love triangle and a two-legged dog!

Welcome to nightly TV, he thought. Give the viewers what they want. The content mix must have broad appeal, something Mack was becoming increasingly aware of. Get used to it. In the end, it came down to viewer ratings generating advertising revenue. The more people watching, the more dollars could be charged for a 30 second commercial slot. He felt a growing uneasiness. Not so much about how his moral compass was under attack but an uneasiness about how comfortable the whole tv merry-go-round was becoming. This latest door opener of hosting tonight's show packed an addictive punch that already had his adrenal glands standing on hind legs.

The problem was he was loving it.

And the runaway train had only just left the station.

Next stop, camera, lights, action in TransNational's main TV studio. The on-camera run-through for that evening's show.

He slipped into the host's chair as floor crew rushed around him positioning lights, attaching a lapel microphone, checking sound levels. An autocue was activated. Words rotated at speed until they found their start point. Staring at Mack was his introduction.

Hallo, Good Evening and Welcome, I'm Mack Grayson, This is TransNational Tonight.

The floor manager told Mack to read through the first few story intros to familiarise himself. A production assistant had given him a hard copy of the same material. If the autocue failed, or some untoward moment meant you had to fly by the seat of your pants, you had the printed version, as back up.

A booming voice from the darkness introduced itself. The Director was in a control room, high above the studio, heard but not seen. His friendly, relaxed tone, prepared Mack for a trial run. Everyone was fully aware that within a few hours he would be on-air presenting the programme, live to Australia. This would be his only rehearsal. No point accentuating the bleeding obvious. Getting it right, was paramount.

While there appeared to be no rush, all the time in the world, nothing could have been further from the truth. Purposely, no one had told Mack that Studio One was only available for half an hour. Regular bookings for news bulletins and pre-recordings for reality shows would soon take priority.

This precious thirty-minute window was all the preparation time he was going to get, before addressing the nation.

48

"I really should be getting home" said Jacki slipping off her shoes, dangling them over her shoulder, by their straps. Stepping into the lift with a hint of a stagger, she issued a loud hiccup.

"It's definitely the longest lunch, I have ever been to."

"Where shall we go for dinner?" giggled Sir Phillip, glazed and eager.

"Dinner! I won't need to eat for a fortnight".

"How about a drink then?"

"Where are we going?" Jacki saw floor numbers 24, 25, 26, flash by.

"To the moon," Sir Phillip pointing to the lift's ceiling.

"What?"

"Not quite that far, 45th floor to be precise."

"What's there?"

"A teeny, weeny glass of champagne."

"Phillip, you're not trying to get me drunk, are you?"

"Am I succeeding?"

"I think a black coffee would be a far better idea," Jacki wagged a judgmental finger.

"Maybe a little lie down?"

"Certainly not, Phillip I'm not that type of girl."

"A lie down, on your own, I mean. I wasn't suggesting a twosome nap. Unless you insist?"

Sir Phillip gave her a naughty boy look.

"Nice try!" laughed Jacki.

Jacki was pleased her plan was running like clockwork. She had Sir Phillip under her spell. He'd hopefully be putty when the moment came to reel him in. There was only one drunk person following their five-hour lunch and right now his numerous inebriated attempts to insert a key into the front door were proving to be quite an ordeal.

Jacki on the other hand, throughout lunch, had been carefully donating the contents of her wine glass to pot plants around the private dining room. Some of the fine whites could now be described as quite floral. Literally. An expensive vintage or two finding themselves tipped into vases of dahlias and birds of paradise, thoughtfully provided by her generous host. She had been able to strategically spill most of her wine while Sir Phillip was absent on one of his frequent visits to the boys' room.

All she had to do now was play act at being tipsy and go to work.

"Where exactly are we, Phillip?"

"Just a little pied-a-terre, I have for special occasions, discreet private meetings."

"Does your wife know about it?"

"Of course not" Sir Phillip let out a snorting laugh "But you do, now."

"Yes, and I'm sure your intentions are not honourable."

"I will be a complete gentleman, but who's going to know if we decide to have a little fun."

"We have one lunch, and you think I'm going to jump into bed with you?"

"Look, we've both admitted our marriages are on the rocks, don't we deserve a little joy."

Sir Phillip topped up Jacki's Pol Roget, as both pondered the moment. He appeared ready to pounce. She wasn't about to succumb to his obvious intentions. Not yet.

"I reckon my marriage is hanging by a thread," began Jacki.

Sir Phillip was quick to match up. "Mine's heading for the lawyers. But this time I think I'll be able to negotiate a more realistic severance. Dear Florence, has been a very naughty girl. Do you think your husband has been sharing favours elsewhere?"

"I would have no idea, he's never home, he could be having multiple affairs, for all I know. I'm more concerned at the gossip surrounding the death of Wes Markowitz. The police haven't interviewed Mack yet but there are rumours already, volunteered statements, declaring he had the motive. Am I supposed to think Mack had something to do with Wes's murder?"

"I think it was well known they hated each other. Then, of course they had that dreadful fight which led to Wes's sacking," Sir Phillip sat down beside Jacki, resting a hand on her knee.

"My marriage would be well and truly over if he was found to have killed Wes Markowitz. What would happen to me and the kids?" Jacki's eyes welled up. Sir Phillip moved a little closer, his hand advancing fractionally from knee to thigh. Jacki responded firmly, quickly returning his hand to her knee.

The new dress she'd bought, especially for the occasion, discretely displayed her cleavage and had certainly caught her lunch partner's attention. Now, that she was sitting next to the knight rather than across the restaurant table, she was aware the garment's risen hemline displayed more leg than she realised. It was as if it now signalled an invitation to explore.

She decided not to pull down the dress or adjust her position.

"You mentioned earlier that the police wanted to interview you. What do they think you can tell them?" said Jacki accepting a champagne top-up. She had already committed most of the last two glasses to a potted palm, when Sir Phillip had obliged the ensuite.

Sir Phillip knew several TransNational staff had already been interviewed by police.

"They've spoken to the Times publisher Mason Green who made it clear Wes had blown the whistle on Mack, ratting him out for being drunk on the night of the fires. That could give Mack motive, perhaps."

"Richard Ogilvy, head of TV, confirmed there was obvious bad blood between the two but not to the extent of killing someone.

"Then, there were the journalists in The Times office and the security officers who witnessed the fight. Apparently, the fiery exchange between the two of them suggests Mack said something about, *'I'll make sure you suffer, you can guarantee that.'*

"I think they want to talk to me about Markowitz, how I'd received various complaints about his performance, how he'd been accused of constantly abusing and harassing staff. I'd suggested to Green maybe it was time to find a replacement. I seem to remember Mack and I also talked about it, when he took photos of me for The Times, thirty-year anniversary."

"Do you remember what he said?" asked Jacki placing her hand on top of the one on her knee.

"From memory, he was really quite angry. It all started when I rang The Times to congratulate Mack on his debut fire story. Markowitz failed to pass on my message and phone number. That's right, he then gave him the wrong address for the photo shoot. Mack turned up at my beachside address instead of the city office. My wife was quite taken by surprise. We had to postpone the session and set another date, weeks later. It was as if Markowitz was constantly going out of his way to muddy the water between himself and Mack."

"Did Mack give any indication that he could possibly take matters into his own hands?"

"I do remember him almost apologising for his outburst. What did he say about Markowitz now? Something like *'I hate the man, I'd do anything to see him on his way'*."

"So, what will you say if the police ask you whether you think Mack is capable of murder. Markowitz's murder?"

"I'll have to give that some serious thought," said Sir Phillip. A pair of knees parted, ever so slightly.

49

Mack's premier performance in TNT's host chair went smoothly. He introduced the programme, saying he was 'filling-in' for an unwell Quentin Street. The half hour show was relatively straight forward, no live interviews, no changes to the promoted rundown. Three stories back-to-back, plus a trailer for the overnight promotion, a teaser for the following day's program.

He read the autocued story introductions and back announcements, seemingly unaware around two million people were sitting at home watching him. Particularly one home which he'd forgotten to advise that he'd be addressing the nation that evening. His gobsmacked family just happened to be watching and jumped out of their seats. And their skins. Mainly taken aback, because for the first time in his life, they saw him wearing a suit and tie.

At the end of the show programme staff were rushed off

their feet as viewers rang in to say how much they liked Mack 'in the chair'. Although many complained, a suit was not his look. Dress him without a tie, maybe even without a jacket, they urged. His stories on the programme to date had been largely a jeans and t-shirt affair. Loose and natural, apparently that's what they wanted. Clyde Jameson, amazed at the torrent of calls, noted the comments, conscious that this was just a one-night phenomenon. Tomorrow, Quentin would be back on deck.

One of the calls was directly to Mack, from Sacha Lombardi. After showering him with praise, she made it quite clear she needed a catch-up drink, for an update on each other's travails. Their last conversation, she'd shared the extraordinary fear that her husband might be having an affair with Mack's wife. If for no other reason the need to review that bombshell, was long overdue. They made plans to share a bottle.

Mack then returned home to a hug from little Amy, a grunt from Jake and a surprising high-five from Dylan. The normally non-communicative seventeen-year-old son had momentarily suspended his 24/7 anti-Dad campaign. Not a word from the kitchen, where Jacki was preparing dinner.

"That was cool Dad, but you on 'Teev' wearing a suit, so not you. And what about that mangy two-legged dog, appealing for a new home, what the...?"

Dylan had just delivered two sentences. Two sentences more than he'd uttered to his father in the past month. Mack tried to hide his surprise with a quick reply.

"You won't believe it but we had around 30 or 40 calls and emails from people willing to take on that crippled Corgi. I gather it's stories like that people remember and react to. More than say, that story tonight about the dodgy property developer we caught up with."

"Yeh, I wasn't really watching that."

"See what I mean," laughed Mack.

"Dad?"

"Dylan?"

"What would be the chances of me getting work experience, a trainee position at TransNational?"

Mack was shocked rigid. He made sure it didn't show. It seemed his teenage son had just woken up from a coma of complacency. Before this moment, there had been total disinterest in anything other than video games, violent movies, and an obsession with social media and its dubious connections.

There had been no regard or application to the fast-approaching Year 12 Higher School Certificate, with career prospects beyond that a complete unknown. Yet now, a blinding flash, a bold enquiry that blew the dust off his usual indifference to almost everything. It suggested a genuine interest, in life after the classroom.

Mack felt he was dreaming, almost leaping forward to check Dylan's pulse, in case his oldest offspring had been struck down by some life-threatening affliction. The devil's advocate was ready with a reply.

"It's pretty tough. I gather TransNational receives requests from dozens of keen students every week, looking for apprentice-ships," lied Mack. He had no idea how many students applied, or even if there was a trainee programme. He just wanted to see if

Dylan had given any thought as to how he might sell himself if there was competition for work experience opportunities.

"I'd like to see how a newspaper works or a TV programme is put together, get some idea about who does what," said Dylan.

"Any idea what you might want to do, what skill you'd like to learn?"

"Definitely don't want to do what you do, Dad. Don't want to wear a suit either," Dylan laughed. "Something to do with computers, I reckon."

And then a surprising announcement that even had Jacki emerging from the kitchen.

"There's been a fair bit of chat from the teachers at school about this compulsory conscription and the chance you could get called-up to serve in the armed forces when you turn 18. Most of my mates hate the idea. Others see it as a way to learn a craft and setting yourself up, for a career, down the track. I know it all depends on the Government lottery that draws birth dates and decides, who gets called up. But I thought..." Dylan was interrupted by his younger brother.

"Would you have to go overseas and kill people?" shouted Jake from his glued position, in front of the television. "Or be killed?"

"Jake that's enough," Mack closing down the unhelpful aside, just as Dylan was getting into his stride.

"Well, would you?" persisted Jake.

"Jake, please!"

"I just thought," said Dylan picking up the threads of his extraordinary revelation "quite a few of the guys at school have got plans after the HSC. I don't and have to accept I probably won't pass. Without any qualifications it'll be difficult to find a job. Maybe work experience will get me a foot in the door, somewhere. If not, maybe the army?"

Dylan looked as though he was about to burst into tears but just managed to exercise self-control in time. Jacki moved towards him, arms wide, suggesting a hug was on offer. Dylan pushed her away and ran upstairs to his room. Jacki gestured to Mack, as if he should follow.

"Leave him be for the moment. That was amazing. Brave stuff, expressing himself like that."

Mack was proud Dylan had honestly confessed to his own shortcomings. In front of the rest of the family too. The fact that his historically poor application to schoolwork would give him limited employment prospects, had finally dawned on him.

If there were any work experience opportunities at TransNational, Mack was going to find out.

That's if the military didn't intervene first.

50

Typed and un-signed, the note read:

The consequences of harbouring lifelong secrets have been inexplicit agony. Years of play-acting, spinning yarns, avoiding the truth, just to keep family and friends in the dark. The pain of telling constant lies has tortured me to the very core of my being. I am now terrified and conflicted by my choices. If I reveal my true self I will hurt my nearest and dearest. With my secret shared will I gain the peace I crave or suffer the wrath from those I have deceived. Their judgement could be unbearable. Alternately, I could seize the moment and end the pain. Suffocated by indecision, I have made my choice. To all I have disappointed, my heartfelt regrets and sorrows. To those I have loved and have loved me, my deepest, sincerest, thanks.

True love to all.

A strange unpoetic farewell. Flowery eloquence from a gay man, afraid to leave the closet? Threatened with exposure, faced with shame, given no alternative? Or a well-crafted exit, designed to deceive?

Because of the Wes Markowitz murder enquiry Inspector 'Deeks' Deacon had been called in following another suspicious death linked to the TransNational Group.

The morning after Mack's debut performance, as temporary host of TNT, calls to mobile and landline phones of the programme's resident presenter, Quentin Street remained unanswered. With no reply from his knocked front door and fearing he may be sick or injured, a locksmith was called, and the police alerted. After gaining entry to Street's luxury apartment, grim findings.

"It was probably typed up on his laptop and run off on this printer here. Strange that he didn't sign it though. Nothing handwritten to prove they're his final words," said Deacon, stubbing out yet another cigarette.

It was well known at TNT, Street had been grieving the

breakdown of his relationship. His live-in lover of 12 years had decided to move on, leaving him devastated. It had been a 'behind doors' partnership he insisted was kept totally private. They never appeared in public together. He wanted his family, his friends and most importantly his television audience, his fans, to see him as 'straight'. On his rare appearances, where a 'handbag' partner was required, he'd escort gorgeous women, friends, glad to spend the evening with a celebrity. He would then race home to be with his lover.

Today, Quentin Street's face, his expression, looked a long way from being at peace. He'd been there for more than 36 hours, Already, a grey tinge to his usual tanned visage had given him a touch of the hideous. Bulging eyes wide open, almost pleading. Etched in pain. All the more macabre, because the usual snappily dressed, perfectly groomed TV star, had decided to make a final impression, a parting fashion statement. He chose to make his grand exit, wearing full evening attire. Dressed in tuxedo, wing collar, bowtie, silk handkerchief in the top pocket, carnation in the lapel and glistening patent leather shoes. Grotesque imagery. Sartorial elegance wrapped around a corpse. A weird, artistic statement. One could imagine it, at some dark avant-garde exhibition entitled, 'Hanging Out in Black Tie'.

One small contradiction failed his pitch for tailored perfection. A now wilting carnation.

A breeze from the open patio door and Street spun slowly.

Deacon wasn't sure yet whether it was a crime scene or a tragic suicide. He was renowned for switching mindsets from an innocent death into a case of murder. Often successfully. No one dared challenge him.

"Belts and braces," uttered Deacon under his cigarette breath. He believed in being proactive now, rather than regretful later.

A laptop, personal files and an answer machine together with footage from outside surveillance cameras, were taken away for analysis. A fingerprint sweep on door handles and windows was added to the gathered evidence.

After dozens of photographs were taken Street was lowered from the lounge room's central beam and laid on the floor, before being placed in a body bag.

A chair, on its side, four metres from where he'd been hanging suggested it was the suicidal mount, which after being climbed upon, had been kicked away.

Deacon wasn't convinced. Could the chair have been propelled that far from a dangling body, even if it was lashing out frantically?

51

Mack spent two hours conducting an on-camera interview with former Operations Manager for Metro Water, Professor Vic Denton. The more questions he asked, the more disturbed he became. Critical vulnerabilities at Lake Jacaranda, the City's main reservoir, were confirmed to be at the will of anyone with dark intentions.

Denton had resigned from Metro after the report he'd written, exposing dozens of weaknesses, was rejected by its Board. Whistleblowing to Mack had led to him forwarding a copy of his damning allegations, only for it to be snatched by thieves on a motorcycle. Some organisation or terrorist group was now armed with numerous opportunities to wreak havoc.

Denton had briefed Mack on what to look out for, what to photograph, when he toured Metro's facilities. He had arrived for what was agreed to be a light-hearted colour story. Its management had disallowed film crew access to the inner sanctum but granted permission for a 'stills' camera within selected stations, at their discretion. Mack was immediately subjected to a formal clearance procedure, form filling and a photo taken for a security pass. So far, quite impressive.

It was the first time he'd played photojournalist in many months. A lifetime of 'snapping' had given way to viewing life through a different lens. The adrenalin rush associated with covert photography had been his drug of choice. And he could feel the familiar on-coming buzz, the challenge of confrontation, coursing through his veins. So many flashbacks, so many moments. Not all of them joyous but most achieving outcomes that helped settle scores or expose injustices. Bottom line, his image offerings to the world had given him rock star status.

Fighting for a cause or righting a wrong was something he'd

wrestled with for years. Ever since his father's public disgrace forced the family to flee the Scottish Highlands. He had been peddling fast ever since, to erase the shame.

Mack's father, Stanley Barraclough Grayson had been a psychiatrist for 23 years, when he fell in love with one of his patients, a Cambodian woman, many years younger than himself. When she became pregnant with Mack there was much consternation over his professional ethics, as a relationship between doctor and patient were grounds for being struck off the medical register. Despite vigorous protestation, he was unable to convince authorities their professional relationship had finished long before their personal one began. It signalled the end of his father's career. It was seen as a cardinal sin, a male psychiatrist, suspected of taking advantage of a vulnerable woman, who had been seeking professional therapy. The medical fraternity, friends and neighbours had turned their backs, making it impossible for the family to remain in the area. They were forced to move from the country to the city, to Edinburgh.

Mack attended local schools and ultimately Edinburgh University where he majored in journalism. But it was his passionate love affair with the camera that occupied all his spare time. From a Kodak Instamatic to a parade of Nikons and Canons. It wasn't long before 'Snappy Mack' gained his nickname and a graduation to serious professional photography, working freelance, for a while, on the Edinburgh Evening News. It helped the young man grow into his adult skin, while his father's world sadly declined. Stanley Grayson never practised psychiatry again, his mental health deteriorating to the point of hospitalisation. Family life was at its nadir. Without notice, Mack's mother, suddenly, inexplicably, left home one afternoon, never to return. His shattered father, died, broken-hearted, six months later.

Parentless, Mack was forced to re-shape his now solo world. Photography saved his life as he struck out to forge a career that might pay the bills. Confidence grew, as his work became noticed, gaining professional recognition and impressive local awards. At that stage the main focus was his infatuation with moments frozen in time. Weather shots, a baby's cry, a geriatric's smile, a cat's yawn. But they didn't pay the rent, so he sought projects that showed ingenuity, a point of difference. Initially he chose to roam the freelance world but infrequent assignments and slow paying clients, made it difficult to survive.

Still in his early twenties, he financed a trip to Beirut toward the end of the Lebanese War in early 1991. He managed to embed himself with US troops and score telling shots of what remained of a devastated nation. It had lost 150,000 of its citizens and displaced a further 900,000. It was here his photo sensibilities were truly born. The trashed landscape. Bombed buildings, blown apart, revealing former lives, in former homes. Family photos on mortar-blasted walls, furniture clinging to collapsed floors, curtains waving from shattered, glassless windows. The shells of one-time domestic normality, now post-apocalyptic skeletons. All amid the stench of death.

The standouts were his images of survivors. Broken souls with creased faces, picking through the rubble, that was once their homes. Mack's graphic interpretation, the depiction of the human toll from war was being noticed back in Australia. The young photographer had caught the eye of one of the nation's leading newspaper publishers, Mason Green at the TransNational Times, (The Times).

In November the same year Mack pulled off a world exclusive that sealed his future and an offer to roam the globe as a contracted staff photographer for the Times. It was his exclusive photos of Aung San Suu Kyi that launched Mack into big time's fast lane. The Burmese Opposition Leader had been awarded the 1991 Nobel Peace Prize medal and diploma as "an outstanding example of the power of the powerless". While Suu Kyi had convincingly won the previous year's national election, Burma's military junta refused to hand over control, placing her under house arrest. With the Laureate unable to travel to Oslo, Norway to receive her Nobel award, Mack decided to attempt the near impossible.

Flying to the Burmese capital Yangon he bribed officials to reveal the location of Ms Suu Kyi's confinement. For three days he camped outside the compound where she was being held under house arrest, hoping for a glimpse of the woman who had made world news as a beacon for democracy and human rights. Late on the third afternoon the political prisoner was seen to stroll in the garden at the rear of the property. He was able to engage her, seeking comments on her Peace Prize award and gaining her approval for photographs to be taken and released to the world's media. When asked for her reaction on hearing the news of her Nobel anointment her thoughts from a place of detention were full of humility.

"It did not seem quite real because in a sense I did not feel myself to be quite real at that time." - Aung San Suu Kyi, November 1991.

Photos of the Nobel Peace Prize winner in her backyard prison circulated around the globe. Exclusive pictures appearing on front pages of most international dailies. One in particular, the TransNational Times in Australia. Mason Green was quick to congratulate Mack, inviting him to visit Sydney next time he was in the country, to discuss full-time employment.

Once contracted as a Times staffer he roamed the world for more than two decades. Wars in the Gulf, Afghanistan, Iraq, and Rwanda fuelled his appetite for photographic statements, endorsing political or social objectives, at home and abroad. His stark and revealing images struck a chord with the newspaper's readership. His lengthy captions and editorials, a vital part of the overall communication, with much of his work submitted for local and international awards.

He received frequent World Press Photo of the Year nominations and on two occasions scored the coveted first prize.

Invariably these winning images were casualties of war. His most famous picture a family of a dozen Afghanis gathered at a cemetery for the burial of a baby, killed in an air strike. All twelve faces looking toward the camera, all showing the pain of their loss. It was entitled 'Slaughter of an Innocent'.

He spent months working alongside Médecins Sans Frontières to highlight the tragic consequences of war. Many of his photos were used in poster campaigns to raise funds for medical facilities or infrastructure rebuilds in bomb-flattened communities.

TAP DANCERS

During this time, he was married and divorced twice. His obsession with war zones showed where his priorities lay, partnerships always playing second fiddle. Rare visits back to Australia strained his private life, while his star soared on his professional one. Two wives abandoned him, as a lost cause. A very expensive lost cause. His meagre savings just managing to reach satisfactory settlements. When he met Jacki in early 2003, he decided he would slow down, spend more time at home, with the new love of his life. Third time lucky, he hoped. They married and within months Jacki was pregnant with their first child, a son, Dylan.

Mack thought if he spent time away from battle grounds, it might cure his shutterbug lust for theatres of war. Best intentions often have poor outcomes. It didn't help that the TransNational Group's editors were always keen to parachute their best photographer into the action, invariably overseas. At a moment's notice, Mack would be boarding a plane.

Jacki's dream of opening her own practice specialising in child psychology seemed permanently on hold, especially when she became pregnant with their second son.

His third marriage became severely challenged towards the end of 2004. A quick overseas gig was planned to have him in and out of the country, home before Christmas. TransNational Geographic, the Group's environmental masthead was granted exclusive access to the threatened Sunda Tigers, on the Indonesian island of Sumatra. Due to de-forestation and poaching these magnificent animals, with their strikingly distinctive black and orange stripes, were listed as critically endangered. The objective of the photo-shoot was for Mack to draw the world's attention to the plight of the few remaining tigers, facing extinction in their fast-disappearing habitat. He satisfied the brief, capturing stunning pictures of the wild cats, writing an emotionally charged piece appealing to the world to take action. In essence, save them before they disappear altogether.

He finished the assignment just before Christmas, expecting to fly home in time for festive celebrations with the family. Alas, his flight was cancelled due to a last-minute industrial dispute. With seat availability during the holiday period as rare as hen's teeth, his only chance was a 'standby' option in two days' time. A shared turkey on December 25th with Jacki and his two sons was now impossible. To say Mack was unpopular at home was an understatement.

As it turned out his delayed departure meant he was the only internationally recognised photographer on the spot, when one of the world's worst natural disasters devastated Sumatra. It would mean his proximity to its mayhem, its horrors, its tragic aftermath, would be his alone as the rest of the globe's media struggled to gain access.

A tragedy of immense proportions was about to make Mack Grayson known the world over. It was just two days later, after he had spent a quiet Christmas alone. Boxing Day 2004 at Banda Aceh, on the northernmost tip of Sumatra, the mother of all tsunamis struck. Giant waves up to 30 metres high. Widely regarded as the deadliest in recorded history. The force of a gigantic, under-sea earthquake, was measured to have 1500 times more energy than the atomic bomb dropped on Hiroshima, Ja-

pan in 1945. A three thousand tonne ship was flung 8 kilometres inland. Trains were swept from their rails. Homes, cars,
human beings, swallowed up, consumed by the out-of-control
maelstrom. For anyone to survive such a cataclysmic nightmare
was a miracle. So much so, 227,000 people died that day.

Staying at a hotel close to Banda Aceh's Kedatangan
International Airport in case a ticket home suddenly became
available, Mack had no idea he was about to witness the most
horrific scenes of his life. Tsunami warning sirens in Indonesia
were not uncommon, 150 earthquakes being recorded over
the past century. When the alert sounded no one knew of the
threatened ferocity. Maybe another false alarm, perhaps a small
wave about to splash ashore? Grabbing his camera, jumping
into his hire car, he headed to higher ground above the city,
just in case there was anything visual worth capturing. Over
the next few gut-wrenching hours, hundreds of pictures would
become indelibly ingrained into his very being, not just his
camera. Never to be forgotten.

In the distance he picked up mildly steeped waves generating
a gradual inland creep. Nothing that suggested it was the calm
before the worst storm ever. As if propelled by some evil, an
unprecedented force, a secondary wall of water then bowled
over its predecessor and charged inland.

Within minutes the streets were flooded with torrenting
water, its endless power sweeping all before it. A traffic jam of
exiting cars in its sights. Fleeing individuals on foot, begging lifts
from vehicles, only to be carried away in the surging inundation,
just seconds later.

Mack's camera devoured the extraordinary scenes before him. The gigantic wave began to mow down individuals, cars, homes, businesses, everything forced to join the swirling non-stop river of debris. Among the floating flotsam, men, women, children, facing their final seconds, waving at someone, anyone, to rescue them from what was to be an inevitable death.

Hours later Mack descended to the tsunami's graveyard. The sights that greeted him gave him further photo fodder but by now his stomach was churning. The wholesale annihilation of a community, the pungent odour of death was indescribable. With all his experiences on war-torn battle grounds nothing came close to what he was witnessing now.

It dawned on him how unlikely it was that anyone else had secured pictures of the unfolding drama, its peak horrors, its aftermath. The world needed to be informed, aid agencies alerted, thousands had been injured and displaced.

With the airport decimated and all communications down, he needed to let the world know of this horrendous human disaster. Since his hotel had been washed away, he drove south into Sumatra to find a post office where he could send out pictures with details of the tsunami's destructive path.

Apart from helicopter TV coverage, no one else from the media was on the ground for the next two days. Mack's photos were seen across the world. Selected shots, revealing nature's horrific attack on humanity. Survivors searching for lost loved ones, amid the rubble, that was once their home. He remained in Banda Aceh for a week before flying home, a physical and mental wreck. Being the main witness to the tsunami he had been interviewed by numerous media outlets. He and his photographs, receiving widespread coverage.

He was almost forgiven at home. His star rising briefly with his kids. It didn't last long. Jacki continued to grumble over his yuletide absence.

Within a month he was back in war-torn Afghanistan, doing what he loved best.

His extraordinary photos of the tsunami were featured in an exhibition displayed at Canberra's National Gallery.

Yet again, he received photographic award nominations and won another World Press Photo of the Year.

All that was quite some time ago, now.

A recent move into television had given his 'stills' camera a rest. Until today. At Metro Water.

He had been well briefed by TNT's research team. In addition, his own digging for background information had unearthed disturbing details on the inadequacies of the State's catchment security. What he found was not at all reassuring. In its latest report, an organisation called The Reservoir Security Council of Australia had made startling claims, almost relinquishing its regulatory responsibility to act as its organisation's name might suggest. To protect reservoir security. Instead, it appeared to wash its hands declaring:

"Incidents of security breaches were so negligible there was no threat to the community."

The report also confirmed it was not responsible for regulating security against vandalism, damage to equipment, poisoning of water supplies or preventing security breaches.

Mack was dumbstruck. If the Security Council wasn't responsible for key security measures, then who was? And what, if anything, was the Council administering? More importantly, wasn't every major water catchment now a sitting target?

Today's Metro tour was ostensibly a public relations exercise, a magazine colour piece for TNT. Mack knew he couldn't ask questions about potential security risks. He needed to keep eyes and ears open for anything that might throw light on yawning gaps or ineffectual procedures he could exploit.

As Mack was led through a series of corridors, he received an innocuous brief on how water is mankind's key natural resource.

"Only 3% of water comes from the earth's surface. 97% comes from the oceans," drawled Magnus Flume, Metro Water's new Operations Manager, Professor Vic Denton's replacement.

It was his ill-fitting suit, with pants far too short, revealing electric blue socks, that Mack noticed first. And it was as if Flume had no neck. His chin was almost inside the top of his open neck shirt. Physically he was no work of art. The Creator must have been distracted that day. A round ball of a man whose height wouldn't have been much over five feet.

With apparent contempt for his tour guide role, Flume continued his drone.

"With most of that 3% found underground or from glaciers, means less than 1% comes from lakes, rivers, and dams like this one. So, a precious commodity, in very short supply. Amazing to think the world survives on just one per cent of its natural supply of water. In time, if not already, water will be considered more valuable than gold."

"Do we take drinking water too much for granted?" asked Mack. "With our growing population and rainfall now at its lowest in 50 years, won't future storage and supply become a serious problem?"

"No pictures here," said Flume, after Mack had scored a batch of quick-fire shots, just as they arrived in the central control room.

"Why's that?" said Mack, lowering his camera.

"This is a restricted area. I'll have to ask you to remove those images."

Mack did what he'd done many times before, faking a manoeuvre that suggested deletion, then declaring. "Ok they're gone."

His fingers were well crossed, hoping he wouldn't be asked to prove they'd been wiped from his cam's memory. Because they hadn't.

Immediately, covertly, he buttoned-on for video. With his camera hanging innocently from his shoulder, he casually panned keyboards, dials, screens, and operatives. Not sure what he was looking for but ensuring broad coverage of Metro Water's 'mission control', for scrutiny later.

"To answer your question about future supply. It will come down to public education. Adapting to tougher and tougher restrictions," said Flume with his ever-ready supply of stats and data. "Australians are the world's greatest per capita users of water with an average household consuming 340 litres per day. They've got to learn to get by on a lot less. That's the equivalent of 1450 cups of coffee a day."

"Really? Fascinating!" said Mack with a touch of sarcasm. "So apart from demanding the homes of Australia use less of the precious drop, I imagine, preserving, securing, what's left, is vital?"

"Apart from rainfall, we can control every other aspect. Warning systems for flood alerts, even alarms flagging imminent algae or toxic blooms. Surveillance cameras monitor all of Lake Jacaranda's boundaries. The perimeter is fenced off from the public, barring all vehicles, horse riders, campers, and bush walkers. Anyone caught can be fined up to $40,000."

Flume gave off an air of superiority, like a judge passing sentence.

With permission, Mack had been taping the interview and was now ready to ask a leading question. He couched it carefully, delivering it casually.

"What did you make of that call to a Sydney radio station recently from a man claiming the city's water supply could be under threat?"

"He was a total crackpot. Our security systems are impenetrable. It would be almost impossible to break through our defences."

"Almost? Magnus that suggests there's a slim chance some bright spark, could pierce your protective shield."

"No way, I'm 100% confident the city's water is rock solid safe. Anyway, I don't want this tour to spin doubt in people's minds that their drinking water could somehow be at risk, 'cause it's not. Now, I'll take you down to our pumping station, Jacaranda's engine room."

Mack knew he'd ruffled Flume's feathers. While he wanted to press the man further on security issues, he believed his point had been well made. He was in no doubt, now, that management at Lake Jacaranda Dam was blissfully unaware how pregnable their defences were. It was obvious they hadn't received any direct threats. Yet. And, they'd have no idea Vic Denton's report was in the hands of, who knows what kind of criminals. At this very moment extremist left-wing groups, terrorist organisations, or deranged individuals with ransom demands on their minds, could be planning to poison the city's 'well'.

Lake Jacaranda supplies three quarters of Sydney's drinking water. Right now, 5.5 million people, in 2.5 million homes, have no idea that the next time they turn on the taps, everything could change in a flash. With a threat to lives and livelihoods.

52

Investigation into the death of Wes Markowitz was moving at a snail's pace. Due to torrential rain on the night of his murder there were no witnesses to the hit-and-run horror. No one saw him mowed down. Twice. Detective Inspector Deacon of the Homicide Squad was frustrated at the lack of progress. Surveillance cameras in the vicinity proved to be useless, either providing vision of the appalling weather conditions, or not working at all. The blue/grey paint samples and glass fragments from a car headlight found at the crash scene were traced to the Ford range of passenger vehicles but did not identify one model in particular. That left a needle-in-a-haystack situation with potentially tens of thousands of cars under consideration. Dozens of panel beaters had been visited. Not one had repaired or seen a Ford with the kind of frontal damage expected following collisions with a brick wall.

Interviews were conducted again with newsroom staff at the TransNational Times. Most of the journalists and editorial staff who worked with Wes Markowitz admitted he was a cantankerous pain-in-the-arse who made everyone's life a misery. But when asked if there was anyone who clashed with him on a regular basis or was in constant disagreement, one name kept on emerging.

The security guard who witnessed the punch-up, in which Markowitz was clearly the aggressor, was quick to point out that the passive victim had sprayed vitriolic hyperbole in threatening to get even. As he broke it up the guard was convinced this fight was far from over. He believed there was an outstanding score to be settled. It wasn't looking good for the man who had received a blooded nose.

Management weighed in too. Both Richard Ogilvy and Mason Green acknowledged there was a well-known stand-off between the two men but stopped short of suggesting murder as an outcome to their hatred for each other.

That left one interview. The head of the entire media group of companies was to give his thoughts on the brilliant, award-winning photographer who had visited him to take pictures for the thirty-year anniversary edition of his flagship, the TransNational Times. During that photo shoot the angry photographer had made it clear his Chief of Staff at the newspaper was a "liability" and he would do anything "to see him on his way".

After a lengthy interview with the influential media magnate, Detective Inspector Deacon, delicately posed his last questions.

"Sir Phillip, do you think Mack Grayson is capable of murder?

"Sadly, yes I do."

Do you think Mack Grayson could have murdered Wes Markowitz?

"Certainly, I do."

53

With Quentin Street's tragic demise, the permanent position of host for TNT was now up for consideration. An immediate replacement was required and after his recent debut performance there was one obvious candidate. Too obvious perhaps. Head of TV, Richard Ogilvy would have the final say. The programme's Executive Producer, Clyde Jameson, was in favour of cashing in on Mack Grayson's impressive rise in recent weeks. Ogilvy wasn't so sure.

"There are a number of qualified presenters, with more experience, more runs on the board, who logically should be considered before a decision is made," pressed Ogilvy.

"Richard, with the ratings hike every time Mack has a story on TNT, it's money in the bank for the Network. Since his original fire story more advertisers have been buying spots in the programme. It speaks for itself. The ratings the night Mack hosted were the highest in months. To blood a host, who is not as familiar to our viewers, could have a negative effect."

"If we put Mack 'in the chair' then it must be understood this is a temporary move while we consider our options following Quentin's untimely exit. After a few months we review and if all goes as well, as you believe it will, we'll sign him up permanently," said Ogilvy. "And one more thing."

"Yes?" said Clyde, doubtfully. What condition was Ogilvy about to apply now?

"Mack will still be in the field for key stories. That water contamination story remains a priority."

"Deal," said Clyde, jumping up. "Just one problem."

"What's that?"

"We haven't mentioned any of this to Mack, yet."

54

It seemed like any other morning. Five million city folk waking up to another day in the harbour city. A sunny prediction, with a promised high of 25 degrees, windless, not a sign of rain. Perfect.

That was until attempts were made to fill kettles, take a shower, or water the garden. As taps across the city were being turned on, there was no water, no flow. Nothing.

Through some extraordinary engineering backflip Metro Water's central pumping system had been thrown into reverse, draining all the water from homes and businesses, across the city. Every tank was now empty. In an instant there was no running water, not one available drop, right across the metropolitan area.

Metro was immediately inundated with calls. As were police, local councils, members of parliament, hospitals, radio and television stations.

A stunned city was in panic mode.

There was no water, anywhere.

Mack was in the same predicament as everyone else, missing his morning shave and shower, normally followed by a cup of coffee. Two cups, to be precise. He had a feeling in his bones this shutdown of the city's water was the beginning of something, about to become far bigger.

In his car, on the way to work, Mack thought of someone who would be plugged in to the emerging catastrophe. He switched on Radio A2Z. Dino Lombardi was in full talk-back mode, fielding calls from distressed listeners. Mothers with babies, confused school kids, teachers, hairdressers, priests and a fire chief, praying no one would be in need of his brigade's services. No one was able to start their day as normal.

A sudden realisation, as to how much one took for granted the availability of water, every time one turned a tap.

Dino was totally in the dark. His team's repeated calls to

Metro Water for an explanation or action plan had drawn a blank. No one was answering phones, texts, or emails. The usual fount of information was struggling to cope with the deluge of irate, frightened citizens, flooding his switchboard. A screaming Tower of Babel. Dozens of voices. So many questions. Not one answer.

Why was there not one drop of water across the entire city?

Aerial photos of Jacaranda Dam on TV had shown an inactive spillway, no water cascading down its concrete causeway. It was as if every free-flowing water source had been suddenly, permanently, shut down.

Mack rang the mobile number he had been given to organise his recent tour of Lake Jacaranda's catchment. Surprisingly, his guide that day, Magnus Flume, Metro's new Operations Manager, took the call. If he'd known it was Mack, he probably wouldn't have answered.

"Magnus, its Mack Grayson. You ok? What the hell's going on?"

"It's chaos, we've completely lost control. Some outside force has shut down all our systems."

"You said they, who's they?"

"We don't know yet, we were told an announcement will be made shortly. Mack, they've taken over the whole plant and reversed the pumping systems, draining the city of every last drop. There's no running water, anywhere."

"I thought you had a state-of-the-art, failsafe system to combat any cyber-attack."

"That's what I was told by my Board."

"That's what you told me on my recent visit. I think you called it '100% rock solid safe'. Couldn't be further from the truth," pressed Mack.

Flume's voice was trembling. "Whoever this is knew our weak spots, knew how vulnerable we were. How they got hold of the minute details of our security operations stumps me. Once they breached our supposed secure firewall, they were able to penetrate deep into the network and literally take it over."

Mack knew exactly where the information came from. Whoever stole the briefcase from his car now had the all-important guidelines to controlling the city's water. A road map authored by former Operations Manager at Metro, Victor Denton. He'd revealed several specific areas where the organisation was vulnerable to attack. Problem was, he had been quite specific in detailing exact methodologies and passwords to breaching the security blanket. He'd highlighted examples needing immediate closure and renewed protection. Now those instructions, routes to a systems takeover, were in criminal hands. But who were these savvy villains?

"You say there's to be an announcement. When, how, where?"

"At midday we'll be informed of their demands. It'll be broadcast through the 'coms' network in Jacaranda's control room."

"So, they've taken over internal communications as well?"

"A deep, authoritative voice advised they had taken control and we should await further instructions at midday."

Mack saw the escalating problem only too well. There was also a silver lining. He had a plan. He just needed Magnus Flume and Metro's board to give it the green light.

"Right now, the city is paralysed. Not a drop of water is available to any household, business, hospital, no-one. It's a State of Emergency. We need to calm the city as best we can, as soon as possible. Everyone needs to be told exactly what's happening. Let me bring in a news camera crew to record the midday announcement. Metro's Board must then make a statement to pacify a confused and terrified community. You'll need a spokesperson and fully detailed media release information at the ready. We'll then monitor your action plan, your response to the city."

"But we don't have any procedures to respond to such an emergency," said Flume, his voice breaking.

"What! You must have measures to at least explain what's happened, what you're doing to rectify the situation, how you'll provide regular updates."

"We never anticipated such a disaster, it was never considered a possibility, not in a thousand years."

"I don't believe it. While you hope for the best you must always prepare for the worst. For any eventuality. For starters you'll need to answer questions on alternative water resources from neighbouring catchments, not affected by the shutdown. Presumably their water tankers can truck in vital supplies. Most importantly you must declare the trust, the confidence, in your IT experts that they can break through this cyber stranglehold and restore supply. Bottom line, you need to have the city's water flowing again ASAP."

It was obvious Flume was losing his grip.

"The IT boys are working on it, flat strap, but I fear the sophistication of this attack may be beyond them." Flume cleared his throat, trying to sound as though he was still in charge.

"Anyway, Mack why should you, why should TransNational TV get the exclusive on this crisis? Shouldn't all media organisations be involved?"

In the little time left, before the midday showdown, Mack stressed how there was only one option if total pandemonium was to be avoided.

"For a start, you don't want hundreds of media storming your headquarters creating hysteria, predicting the end of the world. Metro Water would be seen struggling to calm the baying mob. Faced with such delicate circumstances one camera crew recording proceedings would make sense. The information you release to us, we'll then share with the national media. In addition, we can distribute it to anyone you nominate."

Mack piled on the enormity of Metro's responsibilities in such an unprecedented moment of crisis, while opening the door for TransNational TV to play the lead role.

"Of course, depending on how this announcement goes you'll need to alert and brief the police, emergency services, defence forces, mayors of all local councils, and most importantly Federal and State Governments. If you need help with that, we can certainly assist with the communication process."

Mack knew he was flying a kite trying to hijack a media scoop, like no other. Offering to contribute to Metro's overall media strategy would give him and TransNational TV access to the key organisations involved and their plans when, and if, push came to shove.

With only an hour to the 'midday announcement', a desperate Metro board had little choice but to agree to all of Mack's recommendations. Unanimously. He immediately phoned Richard Ogilvy, giving him a lightning brief on the chaos at Metro and the exclusive opportunity for the Network to dominate news dissemination. An excited Ogilvy agreed to despatch a full crew and outside broadcasting unit to cover the 12 o'clock event and for any subsequent interviews or visual opportunities that might ultimately arise.

It was decided not to televise proceedings 'live' as the midday message could panic the city, if demands or threats were aimed at destabilising the community. It would be better to control, perhaps sanitise, the content by releasing edited information later. That would reassure millions of people expecting explanations, demanding answers.

Ogilvy had made it clear in the few short hours since the wholesale shutdown of the city's water supply many normally calm individuals appeared on the edge of hysteria. They hadn't been able to shower, wash hair, clean teeth, operate washing machines or dishwashers, boil an egg, water the plants. No coffee, no tea. Not today. And most important of all, no one could have a drink of water.

Metro Water's board members met for crisis talks to discuss its emergency strategy. After discussing who should be the company's spokesperson, Magnus Flume was appointed their public relations trouble-shooter. Mack was convinced they'd made the wrong choice.

This entire conversation with Flume had been over the car phone. As he approached Lake Jacaranda the first thing Mack saw was its dry spillway. With recent doses of heavy rain there should have been significant run-off. Today, not a drop. The shutdown was complete.

Mack parked his car, making his way to Metro's main gate. A media scrum of press, radio and TV crowded the space, some shouting into the intercom demanding a statement, an explanation, answers, anything. Stark proof Metro's silence had already exacerbated the situation.

There was no way Mack was going to gain access through this entrance, without the building being stormed. He backed away and rang Flume. There was a secure emergency exit point on the far side of the dam, he would be guided from there. He rang Ogilvy giving similar directions for TransNational's news crew, already on its way.

Just thirty minutes to go before everyone would find out what was going on, who was holding the city hostage, what were their demands. If the city's 'tap' was to remain turned off for days, maybe weeks, the consequences would be dire. Millions of people without running water presented numerous social, economic, and public health challenges.

A community grappling with its short-term prospects may have to face longer term instability.

Desalination plants inactive for years would have to be recommissioned converting sea water into drinking water. That could take weeks, even months to become fully operational.

Short term solutions would need to be quickly introduced. Improvisation would be the ultimate key.

The TV cavalry from TransNational finally arrived with minutes to spare. They rushed to set up. Since no one knew what was about to happen, it was difficult to know how best to position three cameras, a lighting rig and sound-catching gear, to record the unfolding drama. The midday deadline came and went without any announcement. It gave Mack and his crew precious extra minutes to stage manage Metro's control room space for a potential 'live cross' to the Network's newsroom or perhaps a direct link, to an anxious television audience.

From lounge rooms to offices. From retailers and council offices to schools, universities, and hospitals. Everyone on tenterhooks, wanting to know when the water might flow again. At Dylan and Jake's schools hundreds of pupils struggled with toilets that failed to flush while at Amy's it quickly became a public health hazard with students being sent home.

Observe and record everything, was the instruction but it was agreed nothing would be released to the public until more was known about the nature of the threat. Richard Ogilvy instructed the news director at TransNational News to issue low key bulletins, calmly advising viewers, information would shortly be released by the station. An advisory to standby for the latest on the water crisis. An audio version of the announcement was released to radio stations alerting citizens to tune to TNN for a major announcement. Despite Mack agreeing to inform other TV networks of the broadcast details, Ogilvy decided they be kept out of the loop, for now. This was to be TransNational's exclusive, at least initially. Once TNN was established as the main information source it would then be the guaranteed box seat for all ongoing communication, throughout the crisis. In theory.

Suddenly, a booming voice echoed across Metro's operational area. Breaths held, everyone feeling the gravity, the intensity of the moment.

Cameras rolled, sound needles twitched.

Good afternoon.

Listen very carefully. I will only say this once.

We have taken control of Metro Water's entire network.

For the next 24 hours the city will have no water.

Plenty of time for you to consider your predicament.

Millions of lives are now in your hands.

If our demands are not met, be warned, we will contaminate the entire catchment.

We can also initiate widespread flooding of the Lower Jacaranda Valley.

You can prevent all this from happening.

You must deposit $100 million dollars into nominated overseas bank accounts.

Upon receipt, we'll release your precious resource back to the community.

Failure to comply and we will implement Strike Two.

That will create your living nightmare.

"Who are you, why are you doing this?" Magnus Flume's croaking voice asked the question on everyone's lips.

"There will be no questions."

Flume persisted. "There's no way the city will be held to

ransom like this."

"No questions."

"And what exactly is Strike Two?"

"You have 24 hours."

With a feedback crackle, the bass male voice disappeared. Its distorted delivery, totally unidentifiable. If its 'otherworldly' sound and threatening content were designed to terrify, it had succeeded. For a moment, nobody spoke, nobody moved. Mack broke the silence, with a whistle.

"100 million to get the water back on. Got that kind of money Magnus?"

"Who's got that kind of money. Pay up and who's to say they wouldn't be back for more, next week," Magnus shrugged.

Mack knew the next move had to rest squarely on the shoulders of Metro's cyber security geeks, to shore up defences and plug the gaps asap.

"Meanwhile what do we tell city folk, the police, State Government, hell the Federal Government? We've only got bad news to share. We have to convince the city that Metro has negotiations under control and are fully confident of an early outcome. Meanwhile, urging the community to remain calm etc. "Magnus, the key communication is going to be Metro's contingency plan, what happens in the interim. How do you supply water to five million people over the next couple of days?"

"And what do I say in a 'live cross' to everyone in this city, in ten minutes time!?"

Mack, suddenly, was acutely aware he was well out of his depth. A short while ago, he was a photojournalist, working within the comfort zone of decades of experience. Now, he found himself catapulted into the front line, the sole journalist, responsible for the most delicate of communications amid, potentially, the most calamitous of emergencies.

As Magnus entered crisis talks with his management, Mack phoned Richard Ogilvy, advising him of the ransom demand and the risks of non-compliance. They hurriedly discussed what, with Metro's vital input, should be released to the general public. The imperative being, to avoid widespread panic.

There was no time to prepare a script. There would be no autocue as back-up. Mack hurriedly wrote some head points, as guide notes, while his crew readied itself for a 'live-cross' to the nation. It was decided that while the incident was Sydney centric, it would be important to alert the rest of the country. Neighbouring states and cities would be pressed to offer assistance, mobilising their support. Importantly, to ensure their own water resources were fully secure, well protected. The nation should be placed on full alert.

At the last minute, Magnus rushed in from his meeting with Metro's Board and briefed Mack on the company's game plan. It had suggested Magnus should be part of this TV communique and explain his company's position. To prove he was not up to the task, Flume had raced over to the corner of the control room and vomited into a wastepaper basket. Metro's spokesperson was clearly not available for comment.

The senior camera operator, acting as studio director, gave a ten second countdown, as all of the Network's on-air programmes, were about to be interrupted. An on-screen graphic **Breaking News** appeared with a low key subhead of **Sydney Water. Latest.**

Then, it was live to the control room at Metro Water where Mack was standing in front of a bank of monitors. Monitors that were frozen, currently blank and inoperable.

"Good afternoon, Australia. Especially concerned folk of Sydney.

My name is Mack Grayson from TNT, TransNational Tonight, coming to you live, from the control room of Metro Water's headquarters, at Lake Jacaranda.

Metro's management has asked me to explain exactly what has happened to Sydney's water supply. The Network's computer system has been hacked following a cyber-attack. The city's water has been cut off. All water tanks have been drained.

Metro's crack team of IT specialists are now tackling the problem, confident of regaining control.

The hackers are yet to identify themselves or declare their objectives. Negotiations have commenced and we're planning on an early resolution.

For the next 24 hours, Sydney will be without water. After that, while we anticipate the return of supply, there are no guarantees.

We urge neighbouring communities with reservoir and catchment capacities to remain on standby. They may be required to assist in transporting urgent supplies, especially for hospitals and emergency services.

Drinking water is clearly our key priority. If you have bottled reserves it goes without saying, please use sparingly.

Meanwhile Metro's website will keep you up to date with developments. TransNational News will deliver regular bulletins, as information comes to hand.

Please take care. Look after each other. This is Mack Grayson.

Mack thought the content of his delivery bland and insubstantial, providing no explanation or grand plan to satisfy millions of deeply concerned citizens. He was quickly corrected with a call from Richard Ogilvy.

"Cool and calm, delivered in a storm. You couldn't have said it better without frightening the community, any more than it already is. Obviously, you couldn't say anything about the ransom demand. Not yet anyway. TransNational now has a major responsibility to keep the public informed. It's a heck of challenge, at the same time an extraordinary opportunity for this Network.

"Mack, I think you've just become our resident mouthpiece for communicating the fragile predicament the city now finds itself in.

"No water for five million people, who could have imagined?"

55

For a few weeks TransNational Tonight (TNT) had trialled several Network presenters in the current affairs chair, once occupied by the recently deceased Quentin Street. Following Clyde Jameson's chat with Richard Ogilvy it was decided, before making a permanent announcement, experienced candidates would be auditioned to avoid any favouritism outcry, over the 'blue eyed, new boy'. Three different talking heads were given the opportunity to shine. Despite best intentions the seasoned talent failed to hit the mark, and viewers knew it, many ringing in or posting online comments, wondering why the obvious choice had not been installed.

The choice of TNT's new presenter was finally made, but was this the day to advise Mack he'd scored the gig?

Driving away from Metro, Mack's head was spinning. He had just spoken to the nation. He'd spun a yarn, suggesting all would be resolved within a day or two. It was kilometres away from the truth. If Metro couldn't regain control of its plant systems and restore the water supply within the next 48 hours, the city would be plunged into chaos. That's unless someone wrote a cheque for $100 million dollars. If both scenarios failed the ugly spectre of Phase 2 would raise its head. Whatever that was, it didn't look good.

His mind was in overdrive, full of confusion, a jumble of thoughts, no order, no priority.

The first thought was to return home and check out how his family was coping.

His second thought was to go to the office and plan a news update strategy, once Metro provided a progress report.

Mack's third thought was to head for a supermarket and stock up on bottled water.

A fourth thought was to have a quiet drink, with the one person who he knew wouldn't give him a hard time. He reached for the phone. Before he could dial Sacha's number, it rang…

"Detective Inspector Brian Deacon, Mr Grayson, we need to talk."

56

Mack arrived at Inspector Deacon's office, after a longer than usual road trip to the CBD. Just two hours ago he'd spoken to the nation. He thought his tone had been calm and re-assuring, without hinting at panic. It looked as if he'd failed. Vehicle congestion had brought main arteries to a standstill. The resulting traffic jam resembled a car park. Thousands of cars were heading for shopping centres and supermarkets, no doubt, in a race to join the queue, for bottled water. The whiff of pandemonium hovered in the air. Mack knew there were several other places he either wanted or needed to be. It was hard to turn down a request from the man leading a murder enquiry.

"I appreciate it's hardly the time to be having this conversation Mr Grayson. "I know you're tied up in this water problem, right now, but it's important we have this little chat. There have been some disturbing developments in the deaths of Wesley Markowitz and Quentin Street."

"Happy to help," he lied, "what would you like to know?"

"Mack how would you describe your relationship with Wesley Markowitz?"

"It's no secret, we intensely disliked each other."

"It's important you know we've spoken to a number of people who witnessed you threatening Mr Markowitz. To that point it was believed you could physically harm him, given the opportunity."

"There has only been one occasion where our disagreement became physical and that was in the Times newsroom. It was witnessed by numerous people, including security personnel. Some of them, no doubt, you have spoken to. I received multiple blows but chose not to retaliate."

"I have been told you made a number of verbal threats, suggesting you intended to get even, at a later date."

"It was the heat of the moment. I had a swollen, bleeding nose, following Markowitz's attack on me. I was angry, it doesn't mean I wanted to kill him, if that is what you're implying?"

"That is exactly what I am suggesting Mr Grayson. Where were you on the night of July 16?"

"I have no idea, I'd have to check my diary. My wife would probably know."

"It appears, she has a better memory than you."

"What do you mean?"

"She distinctly remembers you were late home that night. She told us she had no idea, where you'd been. It seems your whereabouts were unknown around the time of Wesley Markowitz's murder."

"This is absolute bullshit. I'd been working all hours on numerous stories for the Network. I could have been anywhere. I'll check my diary and let you know where I was, who I was with."

"Mack, do you by any chance own a blue, Ford, motor vehicle?"

"No, No I don't. But my son did."

"Your son did, where is it now?"

"It was stolen a few weeks ago."

"Was it reported to police?"

"I don't believe so, it was an old wreck of a Falcon. Only worth a couple of hundred bucks. No insurance on it. My 17-year-old son Dylan had been learning to drive. He's on his P Plates."

"I'll need to talk to him." Deacon was sensing the glimmer of a breakthrough.

"Now, perhaps you could help me with this one?" said Deacon rotating his laptop to face Mack. He pressed 'enter', rolling the black and white footage.

A surveillance camera revealed a man walking away from a front door. The image was quite clear. The person's identity, without any doubt.

"What were you doing at this address, Mr Grayson?"

"When Quentin Street didn't turn up at work and wasn't answering his phone, I was asked to host the show, for one night. After the programme had been to air, I dropped by his place, on my way home, to see if he was alright. Also, to assure him that I was not about to steal his job.

When I rang the bell and knocked on the door, there was no reply, so I left."

"There are no images of you arriving or door knocking, just you leaving. Did you enter the house that evening?"

"Certainly not. This is ridiculous. When he didn't answer the door, I rapped on the side window, loud enough for anyone inside to hear. I finally came to the conclusion, no one was home."

"Interesting, early the next morning he was found dead, hanging from a beam in the lounge room. Do you know anything about that?"

"This is mad, why don't you check the CCTV footage of me arriving, knocking on the door and the window.

"There are no pictures of you arriving, just leaving."

"Are you suggesting from these pictures, I'd just left the house and closed the door behind me, after taking someone's life?"

"Your words Mr Grayson, your words."

57

He should have been at home, being the responsible family man. Calming a wife and three children. He should also be at the office, liaising with Metro Water, working with the team at TNT, planning the next water crisis bulletin.

His gruelling interview with DI Deacon had totally thrown him.

Allegations of murderous intent, against not one but two individuals, had truly rattled him. How was it that there were so many witnesses convinced he was quite capable of ending Wesley Markowitz's life? Nobody appeared to be speaking up for him.

And how strange, there was only half the CCTV footage of him at Quentin Street's home. The missing portion would have proven his version of events. There was no doubt. He was beginning to feel he was being set up.

Before he tackled any of the now urgent demands of the day, he needed a brief moment to escape the unfolding drama. Some 'time-out', a chat with a non-judgmental, non-demanding ally, who might make him smile, laugh even.

A drink in the middle of the afternoon was not normally his shtick but after ringing her and finding her free, they met in the Back Page, the back bar at the Times watering hole, The Page and Inkwell.

"Every time I see you, your life is off-the-scale complicated, while your career heads for the moon. But this has got to top it all," Sacha embraced Mack, planting a meaningful kiss on his lips.

"Stop the world, I want to get off," sighed Mack. "Too much happening, too fast. I just had to have a moment, with a friendly face. Yours."

"At the surgery, I had a patient cancel on me, so I was able to make a quick dash, I've got twenty minutes."

"I haven't even got that. Right now, I should be in so many other places."

"I saw your address to the nation, didn't everybody? Jeez what a mess we're in. What do you think's going to happen?"

Mack realised Sacha was the first person to ask what the emerging water catastrophe might mean to the city. He knew so much more than had been revealed in his TV address. Especially about the ransom demand.

There was no way, he could share the true position. If people were worried now, he couldn't imagine the fallout tomorrow, if Phase 2 was brought to bear. Whatever that was.

Mack ordered two vodka and tonics. They came in cardboard coffee cups. The bar's dishwasher full of dirty glasses, had no water to wash them. Reality was already hitting home.

"It's not looking great. We must have faith in Metro's computer boffins, fixing the security breach, in time. Meanwhile, we all must somehow, get by, without water. Cheers," said Mack, raising his cardboard cup.

"So, what's the latest with the Wes Markowitz enquiry? I gather it's now a murder investigation."

"Yes, it appears, I'm the main suspect."

"What! You are kidding?"

"Jacki has already put me in the frame, by saying on the night Wes was killed, I wasn't home."

"Why on earth would she do that?"

"She clearly doesn't like me very much."

"But dob you in, for murder?"

"It didn't help when I couldn't remember where I was that night, when interviewed by police."

"What was the date?"

"July 16"

"Sacha reached for her bag, retrieving her diary."

"Oh no, you won't believe it?"

"What's up?"

"That was our boozy evening in the cocktail bar at the

Majestic, when we dissected our marriages, our careers, our lives."

"Of course, and it proves I couldn't have murdered Wes Markowitz."

"Yes, but I would have to come forward and say I was with you?"

"Your husband and my wife will want to know about our little get-together. They'll want to know why the secret meeting, what did we discuss?"

"We could be in a heap of trouble."

"Hopefully, better than being a murder suspect!"

As they made their way to the pub's carpark, they suddenly found themselves holding hands. The vodka and tonic spike had loosened inhibitions. Within seconds long held, unspoken desires fast tracked into an embrace, neither wanted to unlock. When lips finally parted and lungs came up for air, a breathless exchange.

"Is this a good idea?"

"Totally not. Your car or mine?"

58

Mack pulled up outside his house and sat in the car for a few minutes. He needed to go in but knew the reception he'd receive. All he would get would be long, unfriendly faces, amid a barrage of unanswerable questions, about the water emergency.

His phone rang. It was Clyde Jameson, wanting to know where he was. Mack explained he needed a moment to connect with his family, after the day's dramas.

"I'd rather be telling you this, to your face, not over the phone," said Clyde.

"Sounds ominous?"

"Well, its good news actually, for you. So much we need to talk about."

"Still sounds ominous?"

"As you know we've been trialling various hosts for TNT. Richard Ogilvy and I have come to the conclusion that you should be Quentin's permanent replacement."

"When I get this monkey of a water crisis, off my back. Taking 'the chair', that would be great."

"No time for that. Following your broadcast today, TransNational must stitch up the overall communication, on this growing emergency, as soon as possible.

Tonight's half hour of TNT along with most TV programmes across the city is being taken over, appropriated, by the government with public service announcements. Telephone hotlines, emergency centre locations, information updates and bulletins are about to crowd the airwaves.

After that, from tomorrow it will be over to us with our regular nightly half hour. And if the ransom isn't paid this could be going on for a while. Who knows how long? Every day communicating progress and promoting calm will become even more challenging. Your hosting of TNT needs to be inextricably linked as the ongoing 'go to' source for the general public."

"You already have a couple of hosts for the immediate needs. How soon do you want to involve me?"

"That's why I wanted to see you, face to face"

"How soon?"

"I want you to start tonight assisting the government announcements. And from tomorrow hosting the programme nationally every night.

Be here in an hour, for tonight's run through."

59

For someone, who many would consider a high achiever, a rising star, with a growing fan club and a man who had just been appointed host of the nation's top rating current affairs show, you would think he'd be appreciated, congratulated, even loved, when walking through his own front door.

Not in this household.

Admittedly communication with the inmates recently had been rare and brief. There had been an unusually demanding job to wrangle. In fact, many jobs and it was only going to get more frantic.

Guilty he was. Popular he was not.

He received a cursory hug from Amy and a chorus of grunts from Dylan and Jake. As usual Jacki was absent. The children fending for themselves, yet again. Leftovers of a 'takeaway' meal were scattered around the kitchen, dirty plates piled high, in the sink. With no water, the kids knew they were off the hook with washing-up duties.

"How's everyone coping with the water situation?" Mack asked casually.

"The boys smell, they haven't had a shower," said Amy holding her nose.

"And the toilet stinks, there's no water to flush you know what," whined Jake.

"Doo-doos," explained Amy, as if clarification was required.

"Yes, thank you Amy, I think we know the problem." Mack attempted another cuddle. It was shrugged off.

"What are you going to do about it, Dad?" said Dylan, with a genuine look of concern. And an expectation he'd get a satisfactory reply.

"It's all in the hands of the management over at Metro. They reckon they'll have it sorted, hopefully tomorrow or the day after," Mack lied. "We'll just have to see."

"Can't YOU do something, Dad?" persisted Dylan.

"Well, I am. I'm hoping to keep people informed with developments. Pass on updates, progress reports, any tips or advice to help people through this difficult time."

In millions of homes Mack assumed the same questions were being asked, with no real answers to satisfy questioners.

All this was happening in just the first 24 hours since the water was cut off.

What would it be like if this went on for days, for weeks?

60

Mack hadn't told his kids from tonight he was going to be TNT's new permanent front man. While it may have been a major fillip in his life, to the children, it was just another wedge, in the ever-widening gap between them.

In the car, on his way to the studio, he turned on the radio. Whichever station he tuned to, growing concerns were being expressed. Metro had issued media releases saying they were still working on the problem. It didn't sound convincing or re-assuring.

Public health issues were becoming increasingly evident. With no running water and no flushing toilets in hospitals, aged care facilities, schools, hotels, and businesses, as well as homes, temperaments were frayed. The mercury was rising.

Bottled water had already run out in most supermarkets, gas stations and corner stores. According to one radio reporter, ugly scenes had been witnessed across the city.

Mack turned up the volume.

"Panic buying of water has seen large crowds storming retail outlets creating violent scenes. Fights breaking out in supermarket aisles, shopping plazas and car parks. A man loading his van with cartons of water was attacked by an angry mob, who split-up the proceeds, each making off with a number of 'six packs'.

There have also been reports of a shooting and two stabbings, following arguments over bottled water.

Mack turned off the radio, as he pulled up in front of TransNational's HQ. TNT would be on-air in two hours' time. This would be his first night officially, as the programme's host. A part of him wished he was on the other side of the world, anonymous, on a photo shoot in Afghanistan. Anywhere but here would be good. Instead, he was facing his city's biggest crisis ever. And his life's greatest challenge. What's more, he was expected to be the voice of reason, the sane influence, installed to calm a public on the edge of hysteria.

"Big day today, Mack, an even bigger night tonight," an under-pressure Clyde Jameson declaring the bleeding obvious, as he directed Mack into the sofa opposite his.

"We've had promotional ads running all afternoon flagging this evening's programme as the 'must see' latest, on the water crisis. Blanket commercial spots too on radio stations across the city, urging people to tune in. We've swamped the airwaves with advertising, hopefully the competition is still struggling to get its act together.

Not to stress you out Mack but tonight's audience will be the largest in the ten-year history of the programme."

"Thanks, I really needed to hear that. Don't stuff it up Mack. I hear you."

"No, I'm sorry, Mack but it's important you appreciate, how vital this opportunity is, how crucial your role of anchor will become in the overall mix of our communication. "We are making sure the entire TransNational network, of newspapers, television, and radio, puts its combined shoulder to the wheel. As a result, many of the Group's staff from other TV programmes have been re-assigned to assist us in producing and shooting up-to-the-minute advisories and alerts for TNT. "Keeping the population informed, keeping them as calm as possible, that's what it's all about. "This looks like it's not going away, anytime soon. Reference to the threats of water contamination or ransom demands are totally off limits. Naturally we'll be keeping that information from the public for as long as possible. Mack, you've given us a head-start with your earlier address from Metro. People clearly trust you. This will be a continuation, with your ongoing calming influence establishing us as the ongoing source for the latest information."

"Are you sure you want me to make my debut on the flying coat-tails of this public emergency? There must be other presenters who have had years more experience in live television." "You've proved yourself Mack, more than once. Your ability to read a situation and spontaneously react, is a natural attribute. Your calm presentation resonates with viewers. We're going to need that, starting right now.

Now, let me take you through the proposed rundown for tonight."

61

The luxury apartment on the 45th floor had been a regular setting for their secret meetings. Trysts would be too strong a word. She hadn't let it get that far, to be a tryst. He clearly enjoyed himself. She just pretended. Ever since she had given him early access to groping opportunities, she had rationed him, with promises of more, all in good time.

His impatience with being granted such small rewards and insistence that he deserved so much more, was sounding like a well-worn gramophone record, on repeat.

"Tell me what you'd like? Let me just this once. What have I got to do?"

She knew the game she wanted to play. She'd invented the rules. He was happy to wield his executive power, his reputational influence, in exchange for her delivering a favour or two from time to time. Anyway, he genuinely thought she was falling for him, with the possibility of dipping their collective toes, into his favourite hobby of wedded bliss. Just one more time. She kept the flame flickering in his mind, that it was not out of the question.

Could he make marriage number six work? First, there would be the question of disengaging with the incumbent, wife number five. His hired private detective had already compiled an extensive dossier on the antics and misbehaviour of the about-to-be-ex, that would guarantee him his most economic divorce settlement to date.

Although there were no wedding bells on Jacki's radar, she was planning to be free of her husband, before fielding any fresh offers. Already, there was marked progress. Her octogenarian squeeze had come to the party. He'd given a statement to police that it was very likely Mack Grayson had murdered Wesley

Markowitz. A decision he believed he reached all on his own and not because of her deftly applied manual skills.

His appetite so strong, his unquenched desires so in need of release, she knew he was capable of so much more. If needs be.

His testicles were firmly in her hand. Figuratively and physically.

62

"I saw it in the local paper. 1972 Ford Falcon, station wagon, 450 bucks. I beat him down to $400," grinned Dylan.

"When was this?" Inspector 'Deeks' Deacon, was taking notes.

"Sometime middle of May."

Deacon took down registration details and grazed the scant paperwork on offer. A handy bonus was a photograph Dylan had taken just after he bought the car. The Inspector studied the image, wondering if this could be the Falcon that mowed down Wesley Markowitz. Twice.

"How would you describe the colour?"

"Probably sky blue originally but years parked in all sorts of weather, it had faded to a sort of blueish-grey."

"So, obviously, you hadn't owned it very long?"

"Only a couple of months before it was stolen."

"When exactly was that?"

"July 16."

"How do you know it was the 16th?"

"I was supposed to be driving a couple of mates to a soccer match we were playing in. When I went outside to put my gear in the car, it was gone. We ended up going by bus."

"What time would this have been?"

"Around 5 o'clock?"

"You hadn't noticed it missing before then?"

"No, I hadn't used it since the previous evening, so it could have gone any time."

"Why didn't you report it missing?"

"To be honest, the main reason was the 'rego' had run out. It was illegally on the road. Also, I didn't think the police would be interested in a 400-buck wreck, that was uninsured."

"Whoever stole your car would have had to break in somehow. Pick the door lock or smash a window?"

"They wouldn't have to."

"Why?"

"It wasn't locked."

"What, you might as well have handed them the keys."

"Well, I did, sort of."

"What do you mean?"

"The keys were in the ignition."

63

The following morning, Dino Lombardi had been on-air for five hours, the most demanding five hours of his life. Radio A2Z had been the go-to station for the petrified and overwhelmed. Callers bleating their fears, many openly weeping, as they described individual predicaments, urgent needs. With little positive news to share he couldn't offer much in the way of comfort or re-assurance. The shock-jock's show normally ran for three hours but management had decided, with his rising public profile, it would be wise to extend the programme by two hours to keep listeners tuned to one major information source. Dino wasn't sure. He was beginning to think the longer it went on the more uncertainty he was projecting. For that reason, he was glad to be broadcasting from the studio in his home and not from station HQ. Just in case irate listeners turned up at the office, to spray bile or vent spleens. He felt safer on his home patch.

Things went from bad to worse when Metro Water's spokesperson attempted to allay fears and gain the public's confidence in his organisation's handling of the crisis. In his 'live' interview with Dino, he told listeners everything was under control, when it clearly wasn't. He explained Metro's IT team was hoping for a breakthrough, later in the day. He didn't sound convincing. Dino prodded him to elicit a more positive vibe, but his interviewee failed to take the bait, unsure how far he could stretch a lie. His explanation on how the hackers had penetrated Metro's supposed impenetrable security shield was weak. His status quo on negotiations with them, to reach a successful conclusion, even weaker. Shoring up public faith with his assurances was fading fast.

During Dino's interview with Magnus Flume, the airwaves were blitzed by anxious audience talk-backs. Folk ringing in with serious and genuine concerns. As each caller's panic bubbled to the surface, Flume was unable to pacify them with positive indications of when supply would be restored.

Calls from organisations that rely on water showed just how many operations and businesses were unable to function without nature's heavenly drop.

First it was the city's metropolitan fire chief.

"We have a serious emergency. My phone's ringing off the hook. Brigades across the city are asking what they should do if there's a fire. Sounds strange doesn't it, fire stations unable to fight fires. Without water there's no way we can protect citizens and their properties. We are physically incapable of rendering any assistance."

A theatre nurse from one of the major hospitals phoned in, sharing bad news.

"We have cancelled all surgeries, until further notice. Water is a vital component in preparing sterilised equipment, prior to surgery. Staff can't scrub-in without running water. Surgeons and theatre staff have been stood down, leaving dozens of critical patients waiting for crucial operations."

An irate man, running a chain of car washes, was seething mad.

"I'll go out of business. With no water my entire operation has ground

to a halt, forced to close down. Are you going to compensate me for loss of business?"

Flume: *"I suggest you contact your insurance company."*

"I don't think I'm covered for a public utility's monumental stuff-up. Maybe I'll have a go at your insurer!"

The talkback onslaught continued unabated. Whether it was plumbers lamenting the obvious, icemakers, landscape gardeners or the owner of a mobile grooming unit for dogs, it was the same.

"We can't operate until you sort out this disaster and get the water back on."

Frantic plights from the general population showed just how the crisis was striking deep into hearth and home. And how Flume's attempts to put minds at rest were failing miserably.

A desperate diabetic with polydipsia, explained how his condition, an uncontrollable urge to drink water all day, had sent the frequency of his anxiety attacks through the roof. What should he do?

Flume's intelligent response?

"I suggest you talk to your GP or buy some bottled water." "That ran out ages ago." "Well then, you may have to wait, till we can get the water back on." "When will that be?" "Hopefully, later today." "I don't believe you."

Nobody did. And so, it went on.

"My 85-year-old mother needs to take her tablets. She can't swallow them without water."

Flume: *"Why don't you try milk?"*

"She's lactose intolerant, what useless advice."

With no drinking water it especially meant there was no coffee, no tea, to calm, already, jangled nerves. And not a drop for cooking, washing, or showering. Every organisation, every business was suffering. From hospitals, schools, day care centres and doctors' surgeries to market gardens, pubs, hotels, and restaurants. Not a soul left untouched, everyone affected in some way. Commercially, domestically, or both. Every business, every home had dried up.

And there was another major issue looming, that most people had been ignoring. The fact that millions of backed-up un-flushable toilets were about to deliver everyone's worst nightmare.

If there was no water in coming days, the city could be facing an unprecedented, out-of-control, public health crisis.

64

As Mack listened to Dino's show he became increasingly mindful of the heat in public sentiment. To sow more doubt, more vague promises had to be avoided at all costs. Tonight would be his big test. He knew he had to ramp up the rhetoric, to sound genuinely positive, impress upon the audience solutions were in hand. With the hackers due to declare their hand tomorrow, tonight's TNT show was primarily a 'steady as she goes' stabiliser, involving key city council, government, and emergency service bigwigs, as interview subjects.

Clyde as TNT's boss made it quite clear the programme should be seen as the key information source, with municipal office bearers convincing the population, putting minds at rest. Everything possible was being done.

"All you have to do Mack is anchor the discussion."

"Oh, is that all!"

"It's important that we share the opinion of each of these individuals, within their level of responsibility, their contribution to sharing the workload. These are the people who will provide the answers, the guidelines and action plans. Through them, we're the conduit toward advising the community of what's up ahead."

"Why are we not including Metro Water in the interview line-up?"

"I am not convinced they're capable of calming a city, nervously perched on the edge of its seat. I have discussed this with the State Premier and the Lord Mayor. They have seconded key staff to Metro in an attempt to solve their cyber seizure crisis. Also, to guide them on how to communicate progress, especially after the hackers' next announcement.

"So, who's in charge of negotiations, Metro or the politicians? There's still the burning question of a $100 million dollar ransom."

"Metro will be seen as the recipient of the demand and the day-to-day contact but there will be a team of experts, behind the scenes, providing them with substantial back-up."

"Is the ransom going to be paid?"

"No way. There's no guarantee that if the money was paid, the threat wouldn't be repeated the next day, for even more money. No, now's the time for negotiation. Let's hope it works, the alternatives don't look great."

Mack had already been to the wardrobe department and kitted out with his on-air attire. No suit this time but a collared shirt and jacket, to replace his T-shirt and shorts. In the end, he kept on the shorts. He argued, no one would see them below the desk. And a bonus. He managed to convince Clyde a tie would not be part of his rig.

A fleeting visit to the make-up department, to 'powder his nose', and he was onto the studio set, into the presenter's chair, introducing himself to the night's special guests. Two minutes later, after a ten second countdown, from the studio's floor manager, his first night officially as host of TNT was under way.

After Mack's brief welcome and introduction, a taped scene-setter rolled to air. A five-minute pre-recorded package on the city's reaction to its water shutdown. The day's grim pictures of supermarket queues, fights in the aisles and arrest of protesters, trying to break into Metro's city office. Vision of numerous taps being turned on, with not a drop of water to be seen. Followed by vox pops of concerned citizens, sharing their worst fears. All typical images and comments, highlighting the city's early struggles as they faced the frightening possibility. Life without water.

This backdrop to the emerging crisis set the agenda for the round-table discussion. Then the rotating auto-cue assisted a nervous Mack to deliver his opening comments.

"Tonight, a nation outraged, as our harbour city is held hostage.

Water, cut off, in an attempt to bring Sydney to its knees.

Australia's fighting spirit, the nation's fundamental belief system, must not allow this to happen.

To have our precious natural resource compromised by a cyber-attack is totally unacceptable, un-thinkable.

We must however confront the harsh realities of this challenge as we contemplate our place at the negotiating table with those who threaten our precious natural resource.

We must return our lives, your lives, to normal, as soon as possible. Understandably, everyone is asking, what happens next?

So many questions.

Tonight, some of the answers, as we fight back.

With me in the studio, three people determined to guide us through these challenging times.

It was a lively Q and A with the New South Wales State Premier, Sydney's Lord Mayor, and the State's Chief of Emergency Services. Mack asking the questions, his calm interrogation eliciting answers that weren't always what viewers wanted to hear. To be offering false hopes at this stage, would have been foolish.

The panel's selected answers, loaded with optimism, spoke the honest truth:

"From what we know, so far, the city's water catchment is being held hostage by what's known as Ransomware, a sophisticated cybercrime technique. In simple terms, encrypted data has taken over Metro's entire operation. Our aim with the assistance of some of the nation's top IT cyber-hack-

ing specialists is to intervene and regain control. The main objective is to re-activate decryption codes to restore the utility's information systems and return water supplies to the people of Sydney. If we are forced to confront a stubborn adversary, we are confident we can negotiate our way toward an agreeable settlement."

"We will adopt a 'contain and negotiate' role, guiding Metro toward the best possible outcome, in response to the Hacker's demands. Once we know what we're dealing with, our skilled negotiators will work towards a satisfactory conclusion. The bottom line is everything is negotiable. The ultimate goal being a 'win-win' result."

"When we learn the full extent of the challenges confronting us, we'll have a better understanding of the problems facing the wider community, together with an idea of delivering requisite needs and services. We can then respond with a well-orchestrated plan, with resources secured locally and, if necessary, from interstate. Hundreds of professionally trained personnel remain on standby."

"It's important to remember we have emergency procedures and powers that can be immediately brought to bear, setting aside existing legislation, if necessary. Suffice to say, for occasions like this, the nation's defence forces can be mobilised, at short notice. Details of these arrangements remain confidential, for security reasons, until the course of events dictates otherwise."

Mack wondered whether these chipper *'we've got it under control' 'we can cope with anything'* statements exhibited too much optimism. As far as he knew there was no clear response plan. This impression of preparedness could backfire when the true picture revealed itself. Conversely, he had to admit to himself, to imply the opposite, to hint that administrative chaos reigned supreme, would be disastrous.

Fortunately, his journalistic smarts were on full alert. He was learning fast. Tell them as little as possible, drip-feed them *'need to know'* information and avoid a panic, at all costs.

Few people were aware of the real scenario. Just a handful knew the finite detail or the size of the ransom's monetary threat. Mack was one of them. If folk knew they were part of a major stand-off with *'pay up or suffer'* consequences, there would be riots in the streets.

They would soon find out the true picture. Unless someone came up with the $100 million dollar ransom money, the spectre of the hackers' threatened, *Phase 2,* loomed large.

Phase 2 whatever it was, would obviously be more onerous than *Phase 1,* which had already crippled the city. What could be worse than no water? Could dire predictions be ramped up further?

The city was about to find out.

Until then Mack and his studio guests needed to maintain civic calm. Having set the scene, by bedding down the realities of the situation, his questions then began to explore solutions, support mechanisms and the various authorities, that could now assist the cause. This time their answers were more cautious, designed to engender confidence in the availability of vital resources.

With the accent on hoping for the best, while preparing for the worst, it was a risky ploy, that could easily unsettle already disturbed citizens. A grand plan, nonetheless, accentuating help was on its way. Government, municipal and volunteer forces, were standing by, ready to swing into action. It was definitely the intention, but Mack was sure at this early stage, it may not be much more, than a wishful thought.

So many elements to organise, so little time.

The three TNT guests did their best to re-assure the TV audience with the status quo and action plan:

"First and foremost, some relief for city hospitals who, without water, have been forced to close surgical units and cancel crucial operations. Hospitals outside the affected area have offered their operating theatre facilities. Critical patients in need of urgent procedures can be transported with their surgical teams for immediate treatment. It's a far from perfect situation but for cases facing 'life and death' scenarios this is the best, the only solution."

"The main concern for the city's five million inhabitants is obviously the supply of fresh water. This evening hundreds of trucks from local and interstate storage facilities are bringing bottled water to our city. Bottler plants, supermarket warehouses, discount chains are also assisting the emergency. We will be setting up hubs, distribution points for the hand-outs. Locations and details regarding per capita allowances are being determined as we speak."

"Bottled water is only one of our urgent requirements. Large volumes will also be required for major institutions, hospitals, schools, aged care facilities and most importantly, homes and businesses across the city. Water tankers from state and interstate facilities are hurriedly being pressed into service. They will be filled from their own reservoirs and driven to Sydney. Distribution will be according to acute needs and priorities. We stress the need for calm and patience as details regarding release of water to the community will be decided, fairly, in order of priority."

"Right now, we are unsure if the city's main water catchment at Lake

Jacaranda is a viable source of clean, unadulterated, water. Since the reservoir was seized and all pumping ceased, its purity is now questionable. Until we have clarification as to safe usage, no independent withdrawal or extraction can be undertaken. With no filtration process currently in operation, this precaution must remain in place until further notice."

Phones rang hot at the conclusion of TNT's effort to educate, inform, and pacify. Initial reaction was it had failed miserably. Viewers were dissatisfied, many seething with anger. The main gripe? They didn't want to know what interim measures were in place. They demanded to know when water would be restored to the people. With the temperature rising, one could smell an uprising. Street protests?

Clyde Jameson and Richard Ogilvy relayed supportive comments to Mack, but it was clear they'd been hoping for a more positive reaction from viewers. Mack attempted to counter their disappointment with the fact the audience response should not have been unexpected. With no water to drink, wash or cook and no indication when it might flow again, their immediate future, to them, naturally looked bleak. And with no water for homes or businesses, at what point would their lives, as they know it, grind to a halt? A frightening prospect.

Distressed callers to TNT had glimpsed a world without water and were obviously terrified.

Tomorrow might bring answers. Not necessarily the one they were praying for.

65

Over at Lake Jacaranda's Metro headquarters, its cyber-security team had been burning midnight oil. The past 24 hours had seen its exhausted IT department joined by an army of hired experts, the best computer brains with specialist knowledge of cyber-crime. Their objective, to break through the hacker's cast iron grip which was holding the city to ransom. Progress had been slow. Despite applying the latest sophisticated intel and technology, they were still locked out. It appeared the ransomware's penetration began with a camouflaged phishing attack, a social engineering tool designed to steal user data undetected. This initial assault on the water utility's computer system was triggered when every employee's email account was bombarded (phished) with fake messages. On the surface, these communications appeared genuine. Individual's names, familiar departmental details and accurate references had given each email total legitimacy. Staff had been instantly deceived. Invited links and advisories recommending routine maintenance had been innocently opened and processed. Each missive was a trap, leaving the heart of the organisation's computer network at the mercy of the hackers. Unwittingly, dozens of employees had been party to the attack, allowing unfettered access to Metro's nerve centre. In so doing, it gave permission for the attackers to wreak havoc. Total control of entire systems, encrypting files, rendering them inaccessible. It had paralysed Metro and given hackers the autonomy to do as they wished.

Recovery in the short term appeared impossible. It would mean rebuilding the entire IT system and database from the ground up. For that reason alone, the chance of regaining control within the limited time available, was not only fast diminishing, it was also unrealistic. In fact, impossible.

The only communication from the anonymous hostage-takers had been direct. The 24 hours in which to raise the ransom money were fast diminishing. If it wasn't delivered Phase 2 of their threat hovered like the proverbial Damocles. The not knowing and the speculation of possibilities ranging from further cessation of supply to water contamination and poisoning, shredded already frayed nerves.

66

"There's this 1972 ageing Ford Falcon sitting at the kerb, outside Mack Grayson's house, unlocked, keys in the ignition. His son reckons it was stolen sometime on the 15th, 16th of July."

'Deeks' Deacon stubbed out yet another cigarette before pinning a blown-up print of the photograph Dylan had given him, onto the Incident Room whiteboard. Squad members leaned forward gaining a closer look at the grey-blue wreck. Sarcasm on the loose.

"What a peach, that'll pull the girls!"

"Crappy rust bucket, surprised it went at all."

Deacon continued. "All right, all right. Now someone sees it's an easy 'get', jumps in, drives off, and on the evening of the 16th with the rain pissing down, commits auto murder. They then dump the car. Open and shut case, you might say. Mack Grayson had the motive and access to the means. He borrowed his son's car with the intention of killing Wes Markowitz. The murder weapon was parked at the bottom of his driveway, for fuck's sake. Remember also, flakes of blue paint were found at the scene and more than likely came from the Falcon. We know he and Markowitz hated each other. Witnesses have told us of constant shouting matches and flare-ups at work. And there was a fight that got real ugly, with Grayson threatening to settle the score at a later date.

And how about this? His wife says he wasn't even home that evening. He's yet to provide an alibi for his whereabouts."

Nods and grunts around the room suggested general agreement. They wouldn't have to look much further for their murderer.

"Everything points to him, but I'm not convinced yet. He flatly denies any involvement. There are no eyewitnesses to the hit and run. We don't have the Falcon to lift any prints, test for DNA or check for samples of the blue paint.   I also don't think he'd be that stupid to use his son's car to kill his nemesis."

A lone voice in the squad room: "Maybe he's covering for his son who lost control of the Falcon in that filthy weather."

"What, his son murdered Markowitz? Why would he

do that?"

"To get even with his dad's persecutor?"

"Give me a break, I think not!" barked Deacon, continuing.

"Bear with me, So, if it wasn't Mack Grayson, who else could it be? Someone with a grudge? "You could argue that anyone could have been driving that Falcon. It's no secret Markowitz had a stack of enemies, many submitting written complaints against him or resigning from the Times because of constant harassment and bullying. There would be many who were no doubt delighted when they heard he'd been 'offed.'

"Or could it have been a stoned driver forced to destroy the evidence after crashing their car in torrential rain. A drunk driver covering up a fatal accident?

"I still think Grayson has a lot of questions to answer. We can't rule him out.

"And here's something. There's already one person who clearly wants to bury him. His employer, the Chairman of TransNational, Sir Phillip Daniels, seems more convinced than anyone that Mack Grayson murdered Wesley Markowitz."

67

"You're probably the only person who can unscramble this disaster and get the water flowing again."

"True, but Metro would never admit they were wrong and

that I had the answers to fix their problem."

Running out of ideas, Mack had called Vic Denton sounding him out before the hacker's next broadcast. Desperate for ideas, anything at this eleventh hour that might offer a solution to the escalating public emergency.

Vic had written the damning report. In the wrong hands, it now provided the road map, the complete guide to creating a disaster, of epic proportions. But the only man who could possibly save the city from the looming crisis had his hands tied. Metro had publicly bad-mouthed him and widely questioned his credentials. Backing down now would be an admission that the utility's management had been wrong all along. Allegations of negligence in its duty to serve the public would almost certainly bring weighty legal implications leading to multi-million-dollar payouts.

Before his resignation he'd designed a programme aimed at recovering lost data creating ghost systems to circumnavigate the hack. He never got to finish the project. Offering up his untried theory in an attempt to regain control could have severe repercussions and jeopardise negotiations. Especially if it was wrong.

With hackers maintaining their stranglehold on the city's water supply Metro may, in the end, have no choice but to involve Vic Denton. Once their own cyber rescue efforts had failed. It would be their last resort.

68

"*This is Dino Lombardi on Radio A2Z, 'trying to shape you a better world'.*

I'm not sure how to react to this latest news but so often in a crisis folk will take matters into their own hands. Today is no different.

A group calling themselves the 'Water Warriors' has broken through a security fence at the city's main reservoir on the western shores of Lake Jacaranda. Eyewitnesses report, that earlier in the day, a water tanker was stolen from the Council compound in the CBD. It's now being used to pump directly from the catchment and once filled, is redistributing to hundreds of waiting vehicles. Lines of angry, frustrated folk are waiting with jerry-cans, bottles and buckets, any portable receptacle that will hold liquid. Fights are breaking out as desperate individuals jostle and compete for the front of the queue. Cars are banked up for kilometres, blocking the highway as more and more people realise they can't live without nature's magic drop. Outraged by this vigilante takeover, Metro Water says these individuals are not only stealing, but they're also trespassing, violating government property, more importantly, risking life and limb. A genuine health risk exists, as the quality of water being siphoned off could be highly questionable. The shutdown of the city's supply has meant there's no active filtration in operation. And with Metro no longer controlling the output, there's the danger hackers could contaminate the reservoir, at any time, without warning.

While the midday update from those holding the city to ransom, is just minutes away, I appreciate five million of you remain on tenterhooks.

237

We're in this together. As we wait for the latest information, remember I'm with you every step of the way. As soon as I know the latest, you'll know the latest.

Until then this is Dino Lombardi, signing off for Radio A2Z, 'hoping to shape you a better world. Eventually."

69

The breakthrough by supposed computer boffins, charged with restoring Metro's systems and wrestling back control of the city's water supply, turned out to be wishful thinking. Pie in the sky. All that had been achieved in the past 24 hours was the tearing of hair amid blasphemous outbursts. Occasional forays down hopeful rabbit holes came to nought. Between them the nation's leading cyber security experts had produced absolutely nothing resembling progress. Vic Denton's predictions were now frighteningly real. Metro was a sitting target with easy access to its systems, leaving the organisation wide open to piracy and pillaging. They were the chickens he had warned would come home to roost. No one had believed him. **Strike One** had been an unmitigated disaster with all its failed attempts to regain control. Now, in just a few minutes, everyone would learn of their fate thanks to **Strike Two**, whatever that was, from whoever was holding the city hostage.

Assuming no one was prepared to stump up $100 million

dollars of ransom money. Clearly no volunteers there. There had been much discussion, consternation, over what might happen when push came to shove. At whose feet would the responsibility lie when forced to negotiate a payout of serious dollars? Would it be Metro Water, the City Council, State or Federal governments or a combination thereof? So far, no takers, amid widespread ducking for cover.

With Mack's growing status as the TV front man for communicating the latest developments in the escalating drama, he'd set up camp with a camera crew at Metro's Lake Jacaranda HQ. Whatever was about to happen he wanted not only to witness and record the exchange but also have the opportunity to contribute, where practical, to any response.

Unfortunately, Metro's Operations Manager, the go-to-man throughout the crisis, so far remained its spokesperson and chosen negotiator. He had been appointed media contact for all enquiries. His statements, rubbery faltering communications, had done little to calm an already disturbed public. While he'd be supported by far more qualified professional negotiators from police, military, and security backgrounds, for some reason he was to remain the chief mediator. On his shoulders, an outcome that could expose him as an increasing liability or anoint him as a saviour. As Metro's key representative emerged from his fifth visit to the bathroom in the past hour, Mack realised that determination may have already been reached. Here was Magnus Flume, the utility's frontline answer to solving the unfolding crisis. No time to reflect on why he'd not been replaced by someone more competent, because promptly, on the dot of midday, a familiar voice boomed itself into Metro's control room. Wireless headsets and microphones were switched on, portals to one another, in different locations, especially the board room. It immediately facilitated confidential communication in the control room, away from 'hacking' ears.

"Good afternoon gentlemen… What a disappointment you are. You had a simple task to perform.

Instead, you chose to challenge us. Not a wise decision.

A real 'dog's breakfast', if ever I saw.

Your best brains couldn't get within a mile. A total failure.

I think our point is made." The bass male voice gave a sarcastic chuckle.

"Exactly what is your point?

Sweating, Magnus Flume, tried to sound and look officious. A difficult ask, as his diminutive five feet of height with a triple chin disappearing into the top of his open neck shirt, reflected the opposite.

"And what can we do to bring this nightmare to an end?"

The commanding voice continued to dominate the Control Room.

"You can end your nightmare, as you call it, whenever you like. You're the reason it's gone on this long. Meet our demands and your problems are over. It's that simple."

"The lives of hundreds of thousands, millions are suffering as a result of your actions," whined Flume.

"Well, you know what to do to end their suffering, don't you? And if you don't act soon, they'll be suffering even more, and it'll be all your fault."

"We're quite prepared to negotiate but your terms are unacceptable."

Static in Magnus Flume's earpiece signalled a board room directive, to negotiate downwards from the $100 million dollar ransom figure.

"We can't raise that kind of money."

"Rubbish. Of course, you can."

"We might be able to agree on one or two million perhaps?" Acting on orders, Flume attempted a lowball starting point.

"You must be joking. Where did you get the idea we're willing to negotiate? $100 million is what we want. 100 million is what we're going to get. $100 million deposited into nominated offshore bank accounts."

"That's not going to happen."

*"Well then, **Strike Two** it is."*

"**Strike Two**, exactly what **is** that?"

"It's easily explained since you have failed to comply with our request."

"Your demand," Flume interjected, almost assertive.

"Request" corrected the voice "It's good news, bad news. I'm afraid."

"The good news?"

"The good news is the water will be turned back on at 7.15 this evening. Just 15 minutes after Mr Grayson's programme goes to air. He can share the good news with the city…as well as the bad."

"The bad?" said Mack.

"While the water may be turned on, at some stage in the following 24 hours it will become unsafe to drink or bathe in."

Flume spluttered "What in God's name are you thinking, you can't…when…?"

"That's for you to find out. Any time you want to avoid a major disaster, you know what you have to do."

"How do we contact you?"

You don't. When you're ready to meet our demands, we'll know."

How?

The question remained in the air, unanswered.

"And Mr Grayson?"

"Yes" Mack, surprised he was being singled out.

"Be careful when you camouflage the truth to your viewers, to the city at large. If you continue to sugar-coat the real situation, we may have to intervene. When everyone knows what's really at stake, they'll see there is a simple solution.

See you in 24."

"Who are you, why are you doing this?" Mack's attempt to quiz his inquirer was cut short.

With a static crackle, the doom-laden voice made its exit.

70

When Clyde Jameson received Mack's account of the hacker's ongoing demands, he knew TNT had to again play a crucial role in preparing five million people for the next phase of the crisis. This evening's programme needed to trumpet the welcome return of the city's water supply, albeit short lived. At the same time, it needed to warn of unspecified dangers lurking ahead.

With potential civil unrest reaching boiling point, the focus would have to be on maintaining calm while the supposed experts negotiated a settlement or compromise. There were just 24 short hours in which to secure that breakthrough.

As head of TV, Richard Ogilvy, now had a dual responsibility. First, to ensure the Network was across the latest detail with regular 'breaking news' updates. At the same time, providing suitable entertaining alternatives. Programmes to divert worried minds. He had a left-field inclusion for tonight's TNT and dropped by Clyde's office to discuss.

"Tonight, Mack must make it crystal clear to viewers. While the city's taps will be flowing again every household, every business must be prepared for what's to come."

"Problem is, we don't know what **is** to come," said Clyde, raising his eyebrows.

"Look, when we get wind of what it is, we interrupt all programming to alert, to advise, to back off, whatever. It may save lives."

"Until then, it's the lull before the storm. We need something positive for tonight's TNT, to distract people from the obvious."

"Which is why I'm here. We've been offered a major world exclusive. Django Marx wants to break his silence."

"What! You **are** kidding. Australia's, one of the world's, greatest rock stars ever. Where's he been hiding?"

"He's not spoken for years. He's re-invented himself, prepared to talk frankly for the first time, about anything, the drugs, his marriages, the group's lengthy hiatus, everything. His band, FarQ, has re-formed with a new album to spruik, on the eve of a twenty-country global tour. Live and exclusive on TNT, the band has agreed to play some of its biggest hits from the past, along with selected highlights from this new release. We'll heavily promote it across all media and run the interview and performances over three nights."

"That's magic, true gold. Whoever pulled that off deserves a medal."

"You're looking at him," said Ogilvy with the broadest of grins. "The band is recording in Studio One right now and Django's available after that, for Mack to interview."

"And to grill," laughed Clyde. "That's one hell of a life, to reflect on."

"With just three hours before you're 'on-air', limited time to pull all this together. This evening's piece should just be edited highlights of the interview and a 'live from TNT' music clip. It's really a flag waver, the teaser for longer packages, over the next two nights. Should be a ratings blockbuster." An excited Ogilvy banged his fists on Clyde's desk.

Clyde chipped in. "We'll need a scene-setting historical flashback as an intro to tonight's piece. A backgrounder that tells the international success story, the album sales, the awards, the millions of fans, the drugs."

"The jail time?" added Ogilvy.

"Everything. I'll get a researcher to chase up archival footage of the band performing, plus interview sound grabs from their heyday in the 1980's. A journo with a quick script and an editor with fast hands can whip it into shape."

"Better brief Mack quickly too. Remember all this comes

after his 'City Water Latest' with imminent warnings of 'God knows what'. He's going to be a busy boy," said Ogilvy, stroking his ponytail.

71

Dino realised he'd been forced to share the limelight, unwittingly. While he commanded radio's airwaves as the city's leading talk-back host, Mack had, in lightning quick time, leap-frogged him gaining pole position in the popularity stakes. Mack's intimate involvement with water crisis communiques, alongside his growing TV popularity, had already amassed a legion of fans. At the same time Dino's listener ratings had dipped. He had to somehow regain the spotlight, be first with developments, impress upon his audience he was the 'go-to' man for the latest information.

Within minutes of the hackers broadcast Dino began broadcasting confidential details of the ransom demand 'live' on his afternoon show, placing him in the box seat, hours ahead of Mack's planned evening delivery.

"Folks, at last, I can bring you good news regarding our water crisis. The first person from any media organisation with the latest developments direct from the Control Room at Metro Water. Relief is within sight. Listen carefully, as we still face a number of significant challenges.

For those of you who can't wait to turn on your taps, drink a glass of water, boil the kettle, take a shower or flush that 'can', Dino can tell you from 7.15 tonight, you'll be able to do all of those things.

But you'll have to be quick about it. Sometime in the following 24 hours, those holding your city hostage are threatening to contaminate the water. We're told, it will then be impossible to drink or bathe. You are warned. Your health, your family and friends' wellbeing, is about to be challenged.

To make matters worse, the hackers won't tell us exactly when they plan this attack or what toxic surprise they have in store. So, prepare yourself tonight by filling up every available water container or bottle because you may only have a small window of opportunity to stockpile drinkable water. Most importantly. Don't rely on household water tanks being a viable ongoing source. Remember, those holding us hostage can reverse pump and suck your tank dry, as they did before.

Right now, the city, the state, Metro Water, in fact everyone in this city, all of us, are being held captive until a ransom sum is paid. Let me be the first to inform you that the cost of restoring the city's water supply to the community has been set at $100 million dollars. Unbelievable. Right now, we face an astounding $100 million dollar ransom demand, before our water is returned to us.

The powers that be, civic, government and utility, are attempting to negotiate a settlement to bring an end to this crisis. Progress so far, has been slow. Having failed to reach an agreement there appears to be no sign of an early breakthrough.

But with my contacts, close to the action I'll bring you details as soon as there's a breakthrough. Till then prepare yourselves. From 7.15 this evening start filling up and storing water. But remember, after that, I repeat, your water could be contaminated, possibly poisoned.

When I know more, you'll know more. This is Dino Lombardi, 'trying to shape you a safer world'."

72

Following Metro's 'control room' exchange with the hackers, it was agreed Mack would frame that evening's TNT programme to prepare the city's five million inhabitants for the good, the bad and the ugly. Three key positions. The availability of fresh water, the doubt associated with how long it would be available and the potential life-threatening dangers, up ahead. Injecting some calm into this adversity would have to be the main objective. Any reference to a stalemate over ransom negotiations would naturally be avoided. And no mention of the $100 million dollars. That figure could seem insurmountable to stressed citizens, already in a state of panic.

Driving back to the Studio to link up with Clyde's team and prepare script content for that night's show, Mack tuned in to Radio A2Z. He wanted to see how Dino might be struggling to keep the news-flame flickering, without much in the way of heartening news to report.

Catching the last couple of minutes of Dino's explosive rant and self-congratulatory breast-beating, Mack nearly drove off the road. He couldn't believe his ears. How could Dino be so irresponsible? Everything Mack heard contradicted what he planned to say that night on TNT. Now, he would have to respond to an agenda set by Dino. Either that, or deny it, altogether. Looking at his watch, he knew the reckless radio jock would have just come off-air. Immediately, he dialled his mobile.

Dino had been waiting for the call. Before Mack could even speak, he launched his attack. "You can't own the drama Mack; this emergency is not a one network exclusive."

"You fuckwit, you have just put the entire city unnecessarily on edge."

"They needed to be warned Mack. And if you're not going to tell them, then I had to, they deserve to know."

"You didn't need to reveal the ransom amount and the breakdown in negotiations. Where did you get that information? Those exchanges were confidential, behind closed doors."

"I have a source."

"Clearly. Who?"

"Let's just say someone close to the action who believes your role, your value, is grossly exaggerated. They were happy to give me the inside drum."

"Well, the two of you have just thrown the panic lever toward chaos. Be it on your head if this leads to more people taking to the streets. Well done, Dino."

Amid a tirade of expletives Mack ended the call, immediately punching in Clyde Jameson's number.

"Been trying your number for a while," said Clyde "Presume you've caught up with your mate Lombardi, shouting his mouth off?"

"Can't believe he'd be that stupid. Now, we have no choice but to follow suit, making a 'silk purse out of a mad sow's ear'. Lives are at stake, and he chooses to turn this into a TV versus radio ratings contest. A stunt to advance his own cause, to hell with the fall-out."

"Mack calm down, what is done, is done. We'll deal with him later. For tonight we need to concentrate on the facts, with the emphasis, on the positive."

"Is there a positive?"

"Hear me out. If they're true to their word, we know water will start to flow again during the programme. The programme you host. We've got to milk that connection, because it links you as the city's main source for answers. The hackers have chosen TNT as the outlet to announce its moves, channel its intentions. At 7.15 tonight, fifteen minutes after the programme starts, we will signal the good news. Taps can be turned on again.

I've booked advertising spots on all TransNational TV and radio programmes. We'll be urging folk to tune-in for breaking news. Not everyone will have heard Lombardi's outburst. 'Mr Trustworthy' Mack Grayson will bring you the very latest. Mack, we can make this work, in our favour."

"But the water could be poisoned at any moment, and we'll be encouraging people to drink, to store, contaminated water."

"I have an idea we're discussing with Metro right now that might solve that problem."

"What's that?"

"You don't need to worry about it, right now, there are more important fish to fry."

"What could be more important?"

"At the end of this evening's show we'll be televising highlights of an interview to be shown in its entirety over the following two nights. It's real left-field stuff to divert the city's attention, from all this madness."

"What interview?"

"The one you're about to conduct."

73

Sacha decided she had nothing to lose, visiting Inspector Deacon to provide Mack with an alibi. He could not have murdered Wes Markowitz on the night of July 16. She could prove he was nowhere near the scene of the hit and run. They'd met for drinks in the cocktail bar at the Majestic. Sacha would confirm they were there all evening.

She advised Deacon if he wanted further proof, he could interview the barman who'd served them some especially stiff Margaritas. He would confirm they were the last to leave the cocktail lounge at around 1am, closing time. The young hotel employee would, no doubt, remember their lively conversation too, on the likelihood of being called up to serve the nation, as part of the conscription programme announced by the Australian Government. Sacha's two boys, Mack's son, Dylan, and the barman had all been in the government's sights, age-wise, as potential recruits for the armed forces.

As she signed her statement Sacha got the distinct impression the homicide detective was visibly put out, seriously disappointed she had come forward voluntarily, putting Mack convincingly in the clear. He'd now have to find something else to keep his only suspect in the frame.

The more difficult task for Sacha now was providing a credible explanation for Jacki. Why was she out drinking with her friend's husband? Why hadn't she or Mack mentioned it? Whatever they decided, Sacha wasn't about to quiz her supposed best friend about whether she was having an affair with her husband, the real reason for meeting with Mack. With his marital relationship at rock bottom, he'd agreed with Sacha she should initially break the ice with Jacki. But first they had to come up with a plausible excuse for their secretive drink.

74

TNT Studio One: Pre-Recorded Interview Mack Grayson with Django Marx, legendary front man with rock band, FarQ

"After a self-imposed exile of 20 years, you now emerge from hibernation, declaring your retirement from the music world, a little premature. What happened?"

"Quite simply, unfinished business. I have to confess I missed it all, I

missed making music. A couple of months back, the band got together for the first time in forever. We re-lived the magic, it felt so good, jamming the whole day."

"Not, the whole night?"

"Those days are over man, I've finally grown up, I enjoy my sleep too much!"

"That doesn't sound like the Django Marx we all knew and loved. The controversial, hard-drinking, night owl rocker, consumer of interesting substances."

"Yeah yeah, I know, I think back and go, oh my lord, did I really do all that? I'm a changed man. You heard it here first. Regrets, I have a few. Actually, a lot!"

"What might they be?"

"Where do I start?"

"How about when you stabbed that journalist? After getting out of jail you refused to speak about it."

"Man, do we have to?"

"How about this, you answer some of the questions people have been wanting to know for years and we'll give your new album generous air over the next two nights."

"I'll think about it."

Mack swivelled his chair, delivering straight to camera.

"For the next two nights join us for a TNT exclusive, as we take a trip down rock's memory lane with FarQ. The only Australian band to sell more than 300 million albums worldwide. Here in the TNT Studio, they'll perform some of their biggest hits from the past as well as tracks from their new album, Diddling with the Devil. And from the legendary front man, answers to some of those questions you

all have been waiting to hear."

Mack swivelled his chair back to the ageing rocker.

"Is that a deal, Django?"

"We'll see."

The muso with the signature eye patch delivered a wry smile, revealing that famous gold tooth.

The on-screen image then dissolved from the interview two-shot to the newly recorded studio version of the band's biggest hit, Love Muscle. Intercut with this brand new, present-day rendition, edited archival footage from three decades ago. That was when Django had hair halfway down his back. Quite different to today's look. A definite time warp manifestation, with the wild rock n' roller of yester-year, now sporting a 'number-one' buzzcut.

When the performance clip ended the screen was filled with reminders of the water crisis, repeated information from Mack's earlier alert and warnings.

The programme's credits rolled. Another TNT came to a close.

Clyde Jameson was unusually euphoric. "Nice one Mack, that should be a ratings bolter, pull a sizeable crowd over the next couple of nights, too. Great, that Django's playing along with our obvious tease. We'll use some of those comments in our overnight promo."

Mack knew he had a distinct advantage. During the band's early days of sex, drugs and musical mayhem he had joined them on a tour of the United States taking pictures for Rolling Stone magazine. He'd got to know Django well, very well. During the four week assignment he and the front man had become close sharing all the joys of life on the road. Mack had been between marriages and felt almost obliged to help out with Django's constant workload, satisfying the ever present troupe of groupies. Post concert parties they yarned, smoked and popped pills and in that short time became sworn brothers promising to keep in contact. So when Django was approached by TNT and informed Mack would be the interviewer for a tell-all sit-down he instantly agreed. His known hatred of the media had been legendary. He had not spoken to anyone from the press in over two decades.

"Talk about mellowed. He's clearly experienced a metamorphosis, so out of character. That alone, will intrigue viewers. They'll want to watch, just to see if he lifts the lid on all the gossip and scandal from the 80's and 90's. It's going to be up to me to extract those gems."

Before the 'Django exclusive' filled the closing minutes of the programme TNT's water crisis special had worked a dream. For a start, widespread pre-promotion, spruiking Django's appearance, giving his first interview in 20 years, sent TV sets across the city into meltdown. His 'second-coming', doubled up with the latest from Metro Water, meant the already top rating show was likely to achieve stratospheric audience numbers that night, possibly its best ever.

The hackers had knowingly selected 7.15pm for the temporary return of running water. They knew TNT would be on air from 7pm affording them a highly visible platform to advise the city's population on the status quo.

Their three critical proclamations. The brief availability of fresh water, the imminent threat of contamination and thirdly, how meeting their ransom demands could solve everyone's problems. After Dino Lombardi's negative spray Mack needed to lace his communication in positive thoughts with hopeful outcomes.

Dino's irrational, irresponsible outburst had been designed to set the cat amongst the pigeons, aimed at drawing listeners away from TNT, towards his radio station, but it had failed.

Inadvertently, Dino had diverted traffic away from his radio station, in particular his own prime-time show.

75

Two hours before the show Mack had returned to the Studio following the hackers' latest revelations and been briefed on multiple fronts about that night's programme rundown. Clyde had brought him up to date with the grand plan for communicating the latest on the water crisis. He also outlined the bright idea he'd alluded to over the phone, following negotiations with Metro Water. Mack was then rushed into 'make-up'. While receiving a powder base to hide a shiny visage and a hair-brushing to straighten loose locks and eyebrows, a segment producer briefed him on the interview. Fortunately, the backgrounding he received with a list of suggested questions was fulsome and impressive. This ten-minute familiarisation was all he was going to receive before going face to face, one on one, with probably one of the world's most successful rock gods, ever. But there was a bonus. The added knowledge gleaned from a certain US tour by the band

76

It has oft been said if you can remember the 1960's, you really weren't there. A decade when the most innovative music known to mankind flourished as part of a pop/hippie culture, with a nod toward psychedelia and mind-altering substances. Bands like the Who, Cream, Rolling Stones, Pink Floyd and the Doors exploded on to the scene garnering fandom devotion, hitherto unseen.

There are those who wrongly believed the 1970's were then welcomed as a recovery from those heady 60's but it was just another decade with its own set of musical extremes and tempting stimulants.

Which brought us to the 1980's.

With a two-decade head-start the foundations were locked and loaded. The music scene was well established with the spectacular rise and fall of brilliant, talented, often flawed individuals, well documented. Many eminent musos entering and re-entering rehab clinics, attempting to quit life threatening habits. One such survivor was the front man of the most successful Australian band of all time, singer/songwriter/heroin addict, Shane Williams, better known by his alter ego Django Marx.

His explanation for such a colourful handle? An obsession with Django, the title character from a 1960's spaghetti western and Groucho Marx from the Marx Brothers, an American comedy act, popular early last century.

Django had been in various forgettable bands in the late 1970's, honing his unusual raspy vocals, writing, and performing songs, for which he was fast becoming noticed. Critiqued in several music industry broadsheets, hailed as the man to watch.

While providing backing vocals at a recording session for a dog food TV commercial, he met guitarists Sandy Lane and Chance Likely. There was instant synergy. Three weeks later, after recruiting drummer, Dave 'Chip' Fryer, they would form a four-piece outfit that would go on to set the music world on fire. On one occasion, quite literally.

They called the band, FarQ.

It was clear from the start that Django was a lyric genius. He wrote all the songs on their first album, 'WeFarQ', debuting in the Top 10, after heavy radio airplay. The second week it was at Number 1, just as they were departing on a national tour. Selling out to packed houses with hysterical fans wherever they went, a new rock phenomenon was born. Each song's lyrics spoke volumes to its young audience. At last, a band that represented their thoughts, their fears, their aspirations.

Their second album, 'FarQ2', launched them internationally

and for the next five years, they were permanently on the road. Stories of excessive behaviour followed them wherever they went. Alcohol and drug binges, trashed hotels, groupie sex scandals, even rape allegations. But nothing would deter from rave reviews, multi-million sales and live performances, considered unparalleled in stage presence and virtuosity. In that time Django managed to get himself married and divorced twice, spent three months in jail for attacking a journalist and faced numerous drug charges. He also managed to collect a swag of awards including the most 'influential songwriter of the decade'. In just ten years the band had sold over 300 million albums, believed to be an all-time record, internationally.

Dogged by controversy, generally involving drug and alcohol fuelled public episodes, they managed to generate negative press wherever they went. Nowhere, more than France. The final night of a concert series in a Paris theatre had put an abrupt end to their frantic touring schedule. A large part of the group's stage presentation was a mesmerising lighting rig working in tandem with stunning pyrotechnics. A flare used to start the fireworks had accidentally ignited wall panels of flammable acoustic foam. Within minutes the fire spread as toxic black smoke engulfed the auditorium. Hundreds stampeded toward the exit. Tragically, fifteen died. Scores were injured, treated for burns, smoke inhalation, or were crushed, trying to escape. The group's management was found to be culpable and the tour manager, overseer of the firework installation was charged, receiving a six-month jail sentence.

Shamed by the international media the band retreated

toward hibernation. Over the next sixteen years they released nine albums in absentia from fans and public appearances. Choosing to make music in private, releasing highly acclaimed material, with minimal fanfare.

While their music remained in the hearts and minds of music lovers across the globe, a constant when it came to radio airplay, the four musicians to all intents and purposes disappeared from sight. Touring was over for good.

Never say never. Every itch, in the end, must be scratched.

Django Marx explains.

"I never thought I'd say this but the best drug of all is adrenaline. Standing on stage in front of a hundred thousand fans at an open-air concert. They're belting out the words to a song you wrote. It just has to be the greatest feeling, validation to a songwriter, that you've reached out and touched so many. They got your message. I've missed all that."

The first words from rock music's most celebrated exile in almost 20 years. Waist length hair had gone, replaced by a stubbled bronzed dome. The eye patch remained. His signature adornment following the loss of his right eye when glassed, by a now ex-wife, on finding him in bed with one of his backing singers.

Frank and direct as always. Django was back, full of remorse.

"Paris hurt us real bad. We all felt appalling guilt. While none of us was directly responsible for the fire, all those people in the theatre that night had come to see us. Fifteen people died because they loved our music. That's hard to live with."

Contrite, with a softer side, never seen before. Age may have wearied him, but he showed a genuine awareness of the influential sway a rock band can have on adoring audiences. Good and bad.

"I'll be 65 next year, there's a good chance I might finally be coming of age! Me, all grown up. Surely not! Anyway, it prompted me to call the boys. Was it time to emerge from hermit status? They were as enthusiastic as I was. Big question was, did we still have the goods? We got together for a massive jam. It was as if we'd never been apart."

"And that led to you releasing your first album in eight years, 'Diddling with the Devil'. The title suggests some kind of relationship with Satan. Is this a flashback to your chequered past or the fact you can now reason with those dark forces?"

Django Marx had agreed to an exclusive interview, a no-holds barred chat with Mack Grayson. No question was off limits.

"Ahh the tough questions first?" chuckled Django.

Mack: *"In a couple of tracks, I detected self-doubt in the lyrics. Quite profound, unusually honest. Was there a bit of soul searching, trawling past events, confronting regrettable moments, perhaps?"*

Django gave a broad smile, flashing his gold tooth. *"There was a lot of dirty washing to launder, seriously cathartic stuff. "In the sober light of day without the constant fog of drugs and alcohol, I surprised myself how much I remembered. It's been good therapy putting those memories to music. Mack, not all those memories were bad!"*

Mack: *"One track 'Sky High' was about that altercation at 30,000 feet with two flight attendants, a journalist and a plane load of passengers heading for New York, forced to make an emergency landing in Dublin.*

Django: *"We'd just finished a 50-gig tour of the UK, had been partying all night and piled onto the 747, a little worse for wear. A journalist had* booked a seat near mine and proceeded to harass me over being a drug addict, a poor excuse for a human being, a bad example to young people etc etc. He then laid into me about my voice. So, I stabbed him!"

Mack: *"You stabbed him with a sharp pen, in the arm, in the face and neck. You punched two members of the cabin crew, knocking one unconscious. You had to be restrained, tied to your seat."*

Django: *"I got three months in prison to think about all that. We had to cancel the remainder of the world tour. Received a lot of bad press. After that I spent a long stretch in rehab, again. Looking back now I realise what an idiot I was, living the rock star bullshit. Would you believe, it turned out the journalist's daughter had left home after family fights, over her obsession with FarQ? He obviously saw the opportunity to give me a free character assessment. He wrote a scathing article about our sky-high meeting. I deserved every word."*

Mack: *"Despite the controversies FarQ has been Australia's most successful band of all time. True survivors, about to release your twelfth album and starting a global tour. Looking back on your contribution to music, your achievements, the record sales, the concerts, the awards, how would you sum it all up?"*

Django: *"Now that I'm clean, drug free, I can honestly answer that question. No self-centred, smug, pat on the back, how great we were, stuff. Honestly, it all comes down to the fans.*

"Without them we were nothing. With them we are everything. The fans truly understood the lyrics in our songs, our rage against the system.

"How would you like to be remembered?"

"As spokesmen for a generation. We spoke their politics, felt their frustrations, massaged their dreams. The band's name gave them permission to stamp their feet. And respond with their personal battle cry. FarQ"

Note to Readers: Selected moments from a two-hour interview with FarQ's helmsman, Django Marx. Seen over two nights on TransNational Tonight (TNT), intercut with past hits and highlights from their new album, **Diddling with the Devil.** A TNT entertainment exclusive during the city's public health emergency.

77

That night's TNT opened with a Django teaser. A compile of edited highlights from his interview with Mack, that hinted at so much more. Added to that, a tantalising morsel, a 20 second clip from FarQ's new album.

Mack opened the show on the dot of 7pm.

"Good evening and welcome to this special edition of TNT, I'm Mack Grayson.

Tonight, the very latest developments on the city's water emergency. And stand by for the return of water to your homes. Get ready to turn on the taps. That's live here on TNT.

A little later a special treat to lift our spirits Django Marx, stripped bare. FarQ's controversial front man talks for the first time about his wild past. The highs, the lows, the fame, the women and yes, those drugs. Back from the edge, reformed, reinvented, with a new album. He says, he's ready to spill the beans on his extraordinary life.

"All that and a lot more, a little later.

"But first, the latest on the city's water crisis. Rumours and misinformation have been circling all day. Many of you will be worried and confused by these mixed messages. Tonight, I share the truth and deliver the facts, with latest instructions, direct from the control room at Metro Water.

"Let's start with the best news. If the people holding Metro's Jacaranda Reservoir hostage are true to their word, your taps will start flowing within the next few minutes. I'm standing here in TNT's staff kitchen waiting, along with all of you, for that moment when our precious drop makes a welcome return.

Mack places his hand on kitchen tap in readiness.

"At 7.15 we've been advised fresh water will once again be flowing across the city. You should plan to bottle and store as much as you can, as quickly as possible. Speed is of the essence as this opportunity will only be with us for a limited time.

"Please listen very carefully. The people threatening our water supply plan to then turn our taps against us.

"Not long after giving us back our water, they intend to contaminate it, making it impossible for us to drink or wash ourselves.

"To put it bluntly, they're threatening to poison our 'well'.

"I share your outrage, your obvious fears at this news.

"We don't know exactly when this will happen. We're told it will be some time in the next 24 hours. If we are to believe those holding us to ransom the next three hours will be uninterrupted. So, it could be in 4 hours' time, or 10 hours from now. We can only guess.

"I hear your cries of 'When will we know it's safe to drink or take a shower'?

Bear with me, we have a solution.

Since the hackers' 'cyber malware' staged its takeover, it meant they can now dictate through-flow of either fresh or contaminated water, whenever they choose. Since we don't know exactly when this horrific event might occur, we have to remain alert, vigilant and smart. So, we have established a counter-manoeuvre. To avoid the constant threat of water pollution, frequent sampling is the only way to alert and forewarn ourselves, if supply is being compromised.

TNT has consulted with Metro Water's scientists who have developed a monitoring system to warn us when our water supply has been compromised, potentially dangerous, if consumed.

"Since all of Metro's computer and lab technology is in adversarial hands, independent testing can only now be conducted manually. Every quarter of an hour Metro now plans to test the water to confirm suitability for human consumption. Staff will be working around the clock to produce these results for immediate release to all TransNational TV programmes. The moment there's any suggestion that drinking a glass of water, or taking a shower might cause harm, broadcast programmes will be instantly interrupted to deliver that crucial information.

"So, to confirm, TransNational TV will be providing a 24/7 news-cover advising the city on all 'breaking' items with a special focus on water quality, every fifteen minutes.

Live Action on TNT... Mack turns on the tap, water begins to flow.

"Isn't that a welcome sight? Fresh water returned to millions of us, across the city. Friends, while that may seem great, let's not get carried away with this apparent gift. It could become a poisoned chalice. While life returns

to normal, it could quickly change. Since we don't know how long before it's taken away from us again, we need to act now and we need to act fast.

"A couple of important reminders.

"Don't forget. As your water tanks begin to re-fill, it will bring you short lived joy. Remember, our 'cyber hackers' have the ability to reverse pump and suck them dry, as they did before. Don't assume you'll have a back-up storage supply. Because you don't.

"For the latest information keep an eye out for regular TV bulletins. TransNational programmes including TNT will tell you if the water's safe or when it should be avoided. If in doubt, wait for the next test result for confirmation.

"Finally, the good people at Metro, along with State and Federal cyber specialists are doing everything possible to bring this ransom stand-off to a satisfactory conclusion. You've probably heard all sorts of outrageous amounts being demanded. Don't worry about those figures. Let's leave negotiations to the professionals. We'll get there, we're going to bring this emergency to an end.

"Act fast, heed the warnings, best of luck to you all.

"As you start bottling water and taking that shower, a quick change of pace, a sneak preview of tomorrow night's programme. Django Marx, music's grandfather of rock, speaks for the first time about the mad world he inhabited for twenty years.

Good night, stay safe. I'm Mack Grayson."

(Roll Django interview highlights and music clip)

78

It's just three people.

Choking the city to a standstill.

Between them they've managed to bring a population of 5 million to its knees. They've paralysed Sydney, hung it out to dry, held it out to ransom. Shock and awe, their plan appears to be working like clockwork. And if we are to believe their threats, they've only just got started.

The most computer and IT savvy of this sinister trio, a systems genius known to his crew as Hal. So named, following Stanley Kubrick's 1968 movie masterpiece 2001: A Space Odyssey. In the film, Hal is a sadistic, super-intelligent computer that seizes control of a spaceship. Kubrick had created the computer's three-letter name from the easily decrypted acronym of IBM.

Hal, the computer mastermind, had successfully devoured Vic Denton's damning report, the one stolen from Mack Grayson's car. In his report, he had revealed secret codes and passwords which, in the wrong hands, would provide an easy hack into the company's computer nerve centre. Ultimately it would breach all defences, taking control of the entire network.

Which is exactly what happened.

This computer whiz also had a pilot's licence and owned a 500cc motorcycle. The same motorcycle, that assisted its pillion passenger, in lifting Denton's classified Metro manual from the back seat of Mack's car. The pillion pirate, the second member of this elite cyber-hacking triumvirate is the booming voice of gloom delivering daily ultimatums to Metro's control room.

The third partner in this band of fortune hunters is the brains behind the ransom heist. An especially smart individual, with a military-styled approach to the entire operation. This tactical and strategic hot shot had meticulously planned every aspect of the operation, to the most minute detail. And so far, everything had gone exactly as planned.

Right now, this alliance of three were gathering in their command centre foxhole to prepare for the moment when they would 'programme' the return of water to the city. Albeit, for a short while. They wanted to witness how Mack Grayson communicated this newsworthy moment on TNT. How he might explain the next challenging ordeal, previously referred to as **Phase 2**.

As they observed the live telecast they noted how Grayson's delivery was slick, confident, well-measured. At the same time, they were convinced his super-calm demeanour would have masked a genuine concern for the dark cloud looming on the city's horizon. Not wanting to panic his audience, he must have been acutely aware of the fast-approaching storm. But failed to show it.

While surprised at the knee-jerk initiation of Metro's testing regimen, every fifteen minutes, they saw it as nothing more than a small hiccup in their overall vision for total dominance. It could even provide city folk with a false sense of security. They'd believe there was no need to worry. After all, wouldn't they be informed the moment Mother Nature's liquid pearls were threatened? Surely, all they had to do then was just turn off the taps. Simple? Perhaps not. Our trio of evil-thinkers already had an idea to override complacency. Anyone choosing to gamble risk over common sense would do so at their peril. The old adage, 'you can't legislate against stupidity,' a stark reminder. First up, the temporary restoration of the city's water supply. At 7.15pm, with the computerised, pre-programmed input from the cyber group's bunker, Metro's pumps at the Lake Jacaranda reservoir were primed and activated. Fresh water was available to hundreds of millions of taps. It had only been a little more than a day, but the cyber-inflicted drought had created wholesale havoc, leaving the city's administrators and the people they served, in no doubt as to how vulnerable they were.

Held to ransom by an invisible enemy.

One could almost hear the joyous cheers, collective sighs of relief, as the city's millions were re-united with the most natural of resources. Drinking, cooking, showering, and flushing once again became the routine of life. It was as if a long-lost friend had miraculously returned, after an unbearable separation. Just 30 hours apart from that special someone, always taken for granted.

If there was a lesson to be learned, perhaps it was to value such a vital relationship in future.

A friend who could so easily become an enemy.

A deadly enemy, laced with poison.

79

They had been best friends since high school. Bridesmaids at each other's weddings, godparents to each other's children. Forever an integral part of each other's lives. Inseparable. Until now.

Since Mack's 50th birthday party, relations had soured. Communication had withered to a standstill. There had been no argument or disagreement. Not yet. Just a void. At Mack's birthday celebrations, Sacha had confided in Jacki her suspicion that Dino was having an affair. Was it possible that Sacha's best friend, had stolen her husband?

Since then, an agonising silence, until today. Both their marriages severely challenged. Mack's relationship with Jacki was fast becoming terminal. She had signed a police statement failing to vouch for his whereabouts on the night of the Markowitz hit and run. Just another reason for the ever-widening gap between Sacha and Jacki. For your now former best friend to have snitched on her husband placing him in the frame for murder was unforgiveable. Sacha had volunteered to put the fire out. She had visited Inspector Deacon at the Homicide Squad to confirm she'd spent the entire evening of July 16 with Mack, in the cocktail lounge, at the Majestic Hotel. That was the easy part. Mack and Sacha now had to explain to Dino and Jacki why they had met for a marathon five-hour drink, what they discussed and why neither of them had mentioned it. With Mack's persona-non-grata, at home, at an all-time low, it was decided Sacha should go first.

She'd just finished late surgery at her medical practice and was driving over to Jacki's. She had rung in advance to make sure she'd be home. Miraculously, Jacki had picked up. Previous attempts to drop by had failed, as her mobile phone always went straight to message bank. And it didn't help that she never returned calls. Each time Sacha rang the home landline, one of Jacki's children answered, declaring they didn't know where their mother was, or when she might be home. That alone rang alarm bells. Just another unanswered question. Were her godchildren being neglected?

Amy answered the door, giving Sacha a familiar lengthy hug followed by a long face and "Haven't seen you for ages Aunty Sash, it's been sooo long."

"I know, it's not good enough, is it? I've missed you. How's everything going here. The water's back on, isn't that great?"

"I know and my stinky brothers still haven't had a shower, they pong!"

"Well, they better be quick, we don't know how long fresh water will be available. Where's Mum?"

"She's upstairs on the phone, talking to a man."

"How do you know it's a man?"

"Just before you arrived, I heard her say, *You're the man, you make the decision.*"

"Is that right? It could have been your Dad?"

"No, he never rings on the house phone. Anyway, she

wouldn't take it upstairs if he called. She'll be down in a minute."

"Ok. I might just borrow your bathroom a moment, while you still have water."

Closing the door behind her Sacha quickly rang Dino's number, hardly surprised to find her husband's phone engaged. Immediate irrational thoughts. Of course, he wasn't available to take her call, he was talking to Jacki. Who else would he be talking to?

Was this the end of a very long road? The inevitable had flashed its intentions for quite some time. Being truly honest to herself, marriage to Dino had been rocky, for eternity. Their careers had taken off in opposite directions. Both had been successful in their different spheres, but neither had an overlapping interest in the other's progress or achievements. Now, with their teenage sons almost independent of their parents the family hub had disintegrated into bland indifference. Neither Sacha nor Dino had done much to rescue it. It was clear no one was happy in this family.

Theirs had been a long, drawn-out courtship since meeting on the strangest of occasions, a Christmas party at a greyhound racing track. The attraction was instant. Total opposites, but they had rung each other's bells. She was at university, studying medicine. He was hosting a midnight-to-dawn, graveyard shift in a nondescript country radio station, 200 kilometres out of town.

Years later, on one of their infrequent weekends together she accepted his umpteenth proposal. Dino had worn her down in her fifth and final year of medical school. The long-haired disc jockey from a colourful Italian family had finally scored his bride.

Sacha knew it wasn't a perfect match but to spite her disapproving parents launched herself, headlong into the marriage. The wedding was held in the sheds of Dino's family business, a market garden, specialising in organic vegetables. The alcohol-charged feast, sprinkled with well-lubricated speeches, ensured the early departure of Sacha's tee-total family. From that moment on, the marriage was under the hammer.

With their careers diametrically opposed and separated by serious kilometres, the bride and groom were struggling from day one. Sacha was working as an intern in the maternity unit of a large public hospital in the city, devoting evenings to her specialty subject, reproductive issues confronting women, in particular, infertility.

Dino on the other hand was still cruising radio's country circuit and while his profile was on the rise, he was yet to attract the attention of the metropolitan majors. Sacha occasionally travelled to the bush for passionate motel weekends but the cavernous gap between them was forever widening. Their careers, their interests, their friends, dwelled on different planets. When Sacha became pregnant, Dino landed a gig in Sydney and for a brief moment, domestic bliss broke out, in the city. Within two years, Sacha, pregnant with her second son, had become a full-time general practitioner. Dino was working the afternoon shift on a top rating station in the city. Once again, the Lombardi family unit lurched toward momentary survival.

Despite marital ups and downs their careers soared. Dino as

a top radio talk-back host and Sacha, a leading fertility specialist with her own medical practice.

Their private lives were something else.

"Important phone call, just had to sort a few things." Jacki descending the stairs, threw a well-aimed glare at Sacha.

"Why don't we leave the kids to the TV and go into the garden. Drink?"

"Love one."

Without asking what drink was preferred Jacki took a bottle of white wine from the fridge, grabbed two glasses from a cabinet and walked through the open door to the patio. You could cut the tension, even with an unusually blunt knife.

Jacki wasted no time, with an opening, vicious spray. "We were best friends, shared everything. What happened? I feel so let down, badly, Sash." Feigning hurt, she reached for a tissue and blew her nose.

"YOU feel let down? You're never home, you don't return calls, you're permanently off the air, where have you been Jacki?"

"Where have **I** been?"

"Yes!"

"More a question of where have **you** been? No doubt fucking my husband at the Majestic?"

"That's not fair."

"Too right, it's not fair, when your once-upon-a-time best friend sneaks off for the night with your husband."

"It's so not like that."

"I've always thought you two had an eye for each other."

"That's utter bullshit."

"So, what lame excuse have you dreamt up for me?"

"I'm having a tough time at home, Dino ignores me, he's permanently unavailable. Even the kids have noticed there's something wrong. I still think he's having an affair."

Sacha threw it out there, looking into Jacki's eyes to see if there were any tell-tale signs, indicating she just might be the 'other woman'. Not a flicker.

"I gather things haven't been too great with you and Mack either."

"What makes you think that?"

"For starters, you telling Inspector Deacon, Mack wasn't home the night Wes Markowitz was run down.

"Well, he wasn't."

"He's your husband, father of your children. Jacki, you put Mack in the frame for murder. You never gave him a chance to explain where he was."

"Where was he?"

"With me at the Majestic. Both of us miserable with our marriages. You hadn't returned my calls. Dino was in another world. Mack under stress, with no one to talk to. We needed a drink, a number of drinks."

"Where in the Majestic, one of the rooms, I suppose?"

"In the bar, all evening and there's a witness. Inspector Deacon has already interviewed him."

Jacki burst into tears.

"My life is such a mess, you wouldn't believe it, I've..."

Sacha got up to leave before there was any chance, she might feel sorry for Jacki. Their relationship, their friendship was over.

Mission accomplished, she'd soothed the way for some kind of truce between Jacki and Mack. She'd now spin a similar story to Dino. He wouldn't care anyway. For the marriage or his diminishing friendship with Mack.

As she waved the three TV-glued children goodbye, she wasn't sure when next she'd see them.

Even more convinced now, their welfare was a growing concern.

As Sacha closed the front door, Jacki tilted the final drops from the wine bottle into her glass and smiled at the evening sky.

80

People weren't exactly dancing in the streets, but the return of free-flowing water had been greeted with renewed appreciation for nature's drop. Nerves remained on edge as residents hurriedly showered, laundered, and bottled. No one knew how long they had, before the whole system, might crash and turn against them. Again.

While the main concern was the threat of contamination, advance warnings were in place. When the hackers struck, the public was assured a fail-safe testing procedure, would detect any problem. Metro's scientists would be checking water samples every 15 minutes for signs of toxic interference. In the event of a noxious reading, a warning would immediately be released to key television outlets. In other words, stay tuned to TransNational TV stations for the latest, in particular TNT, the programme hosted by Mack. The city faced its greatest challenge in living memory. It wasn't just each person, each home for themselves. This emergency had rallied and bonded the entire community. Beyond the city precincts extraordinary gestures of support from numerous sources. Water tankers trucking supplies from outside the Jacaranda catchment area had commandeered a car park at a major sports ground. Defence force personnel were handling distribution. Bottling companies had donated pallet loads of water, as charities manned sites, giving away thousands of cases, cartons, and six-packs.

Then there were the Samaritans, who called themselves The TapDancers.

In a little more than a day, twenty thousand people outside the city area had signed up to The TapDancers' website. Its aim was simple. Individual homes, outside the city limits, pledging their taps, to the common cause. Everyone wanting to 'fill up' was welcome. Just arrive with containers, jerry cans, bottles, any type of water carrier. Anyone wanting a shower, bring a towel. Some even offered baby bathing facilities. All of them providing tea or coffee with the vital ingredient, so lacking in the city.

This charitable gesture temporarily eased the situation, saving the water shutdown from becoming a total catastrophe. A heart-warming example of how in a crisis communities can bond and rally, volunteering to help people they've never met.

Hoping if the situation was reversed, others would come to their rescue.

Within hours Rotary Clubs had taken up the cause alerting regional branches to assist in spreading the message, urging participation from homes and businesses. Suburbs, even streets, became instantly labelled TapDancer supporters, radio stations broadcast sites with multiple tap access points. But as the queues lengthened nerves became frayed, the fear factor ever present, the future a complete unknown.

More than two hours passed without incident.

The wait was on as five million people anticipated the possibility of **Strike Two.**

Whatever that was.

81

Dino realised he'd missed the bus. By a mile. His earlier on-air rant boasted claims of a 'deep throat' within Metro Water, feeding him the inside drum on ransom negotiations. Problem was the leaked information failed to attract an audience to his radio programme when it really mattered.

Instead, the city had tuned in to the heavily promoted TNT, hosted by Mack. It wasn't just the latest on the 'water crisis' that pulled massive TV ratings but the celebrity drawcard. The exclusive appearance of rock legend, Django Marx.

Dino's bitter feelings toward Mack, growing by the day, soared to new heights. Last night's confession from Sacha that she'd spent an evening with TV's rising star, without mentioning it, had been the last straw, plumbing new depths to his crumbling marriage. Whatever friendship may have previously existed with Mack was now cactus.

With a disintegrating private life and a radio programme losing its grip on the water emergency, it had crushed his usual rock-solid self-belief. He was desperate to reverse the slide, vowing to drive a sizeable nail into the Mack Grayson juggernaut currently dominating the airwaves. He was not used to being in the back seat. All his life he had been a battler taking on anything, anyone, that got in his way. At high school he was teased and bullied for his long hair, skinny frame and clipped Italian accent but he railed against the schoolyard bullies eventually earning their respect, His ability to talk non-stop on almost any subject and lace it with humour began to impress his detractors. From these soapbox rants it was clear what kind of career would suit him best. His meteoric rise in talk-back radio was well documented and now with hardly a foot out of place, the thought of failure terrified him. What could he do? TransNational had highjacked the disaster turning it into a ratings blockbuster for Mack to helm, leaving the rest of the media in its wake.

Dino thought having a spy in the boardroom at Metro would guarantee regular scoops from the frontline of this unfolding drama. Now, without that advantage, he needed to address the declining radio audience as well as his damaged ego.

The management at Radio A2Z made it quite clear they were far from happy with Dino's performance. Why wasn't he closer to those negotiating with the cyber hostage-takers, the key players like Metro Water, the State Government, City Council, police and security forces?

Dino knew exactly what they were implying.

Mack Grayson was in bed with key elements of the decision-making establishment, why wasn't Dino?

Mack Grayson has got a march on the rest of the media, why hasn't Dino?

Mack Grayson has seized control of Metro's day-to-day communications, what's Dino going to do about it?

It was a classic case of how each and every news hound within a major event's media scrum, strives to be head and shoulders above the competition.

Newspapers, magazines, radio, television, news wires, websites, social media. All battling for supremacy in a cut-throat media world.

Dino's radio programme, part of the 24/7 news cycle, was just one of the talk-back platforms jostling for attention in a crowded marketplace. He knew the routine, what was expected, how it thrived and survived on input, feedback, opinion, and debate from a demanding audience. Especially with a blockbuster event like this one. Listeners, callers, contributors came in all shapes and sizes, ready to spar. The well-informed, the self-opinionated, the smart, the unhinged, the alcoholically over-refreshed, the bloody-minded, the argumentative, those who like the sound of their own voices, they're all there. The lifeblood of chat radio. The host is the ringmaster who duels with callers, wrangles the issues and decides who gets to expand on their thoughts and theories, who gets cut short, who gets cut off. Engaging with the audience for an average three-hour 'live' programme every day is physically and mentally challenging for the presenter. Factor in their hours before and after the show, keeping up with the issues, planning for tomorrow, putting out fires, lighting new ones.

It's an ascent and descent of a different mountain every day utilising techniques few get to master. Even fewer get to summit.

Dino was almost at the peak and to stumble now would be an agony. He needed to bust a gut to avoid failure. He wasn't sure whether it was his injured pride, or a desire to get even with Mack, that was driving him. By combining both motivations he was pumped, rearing to go. Juggling his options, acutely aware the 'water crisis', was already the city's biggest public emergency ever. A story that would be remembered, re-visited for years to come. He wanted to play a critical role, be close to the action, communicating progress to the masses. Deep down he wanted to be seen as one of the main media players. **The** main media player.

He wanted to snatch the profile someone else had already secured.

Management from Radio A2Z wanted him to cover the very instant water was returned to the city. It had to be **the** radio moment. The evening's highlight. While Mack Grayson's TNT was only on-air for half an hour, Dino should prepare himself for a long night. He would be 'live' throughout the evening. A distinct advantage.

With his production team he considered all the obvious tools from the talk-back armoury. The tried, tested and proven methods were always the best. They settled on 'live' interviews from the field, engaging with those most affected. Families, the aged, the disabled, children, the business community. Add to that Metro Water, State and Local Governments, the waterfront would be covered. Everyone involved in wrestling the crisis. Also involve umbrella organisations, emergency services, hospitals, charities, defence force units, the army of volunteers. In addition to this wall of communication and intelligence, regular updates and advisories. Keeping the city fully informed.

The objective? Reach out. Care. Inform. Show heart. Exhibit warmth. Could it be 'Dino, the voice of the people!? Broadcasting from key suburbs, canvassing reactions from the true sufferers, easing their pain. All with the sole purpose of becoming radio's lead commentator. The 'go-to jock' for the latest information.

Live radio from the 'burbs', in homes, in hospitals, retirement villages. The public's joy at being able to turn on their taps was palpable. Dino had interviewed everything that moved and every 15 minutes gave the latest result from Metro's scientists. So far, the water was safe and drinkable.

During the evening a regular stream of callers with observations, concerns, and questions. Lively conversations. The evening had gone well, Dino felt more confident. He'd struck a chord. He had made a difference. It was solid progress, but he knew he was going to need more. Much more.

He took the next call, offering his usual greeting.

"This is Dino, what's on your mind?"

"Dino, I told you it would happen, didn't I?"

"Who's this?"

"Long before the shutdown, threats to poison the water, I said it would happen. I warned you."

The voice sounded familiar to Dino, slightly distorted, like before.

"I remember you. You made all sorts of wild claims but never identified yourself."

"Well, now you know, I wasn't making it up."

"Who are you?"

"Someone who knows what's going on."

"Are you with the people holding the city to ransom?"

"No, No, but I know what they're up to, what they're planning next."

"What are they planning next?"

"Strike Two."

"What's **Strike Two?***"*

"If the money is not paid, the City's water is in for a nasty shock".

"What kind of shock?"

"You'll see."

"How do you know all this?"

"Let's just say I know. Listen up. I have a message for the entire city. The water may be flowing into your homes right now but sometime in the next 24 hours, if the ransom isn't paid, **Strike Two** *will be launched. All I can tell you is the consequences of not meeting their demands could be fatal. I shouldn't be telling you this. Up until six o' clock tomorrow morning you're safe. After that, any minute of any hour, could prove catastrophic.*

"They don't know I'm doing this."

"Who are you?"

"I've said too much already. Remember, after 6am everything changes."

The line went dead.

Instantly, the radio station programme was flooded with calls from listeners who had heard the phone-in. Should they believe what they had heard about **Strike Two**, the threats, the 6am reprieve tomorrow morning?

Dino immediately replayed the interview on-air as the radio station's management issued directives and press releases to the ransom negotiating team and the wider media, about possible breaking news on the water crisis. Was it news, was it fact, could it be acted upon? Dino argued it was the second time this caller had provided accurate information, suggesting it was someone close to the action. A credible source? Water quality would still need to be tested every fifteen minutes until 6am tomorrow. At which time they'd know whether the information Dino received was reliable. It was anyone's guess what would happen on or after 6am.

Strike Two apparently?

The evening had started with Dino under immense pressure. Beginning to wonder whether his best days in radio had been and gone. Tonight, broadcasting 'live' from the suburbs changed everything. Connecting with people that mattered, those worst affected by the cyber-inflicted drought. He'd enjoyed the buzz, reaching out to his audience, offering comfort, delivering advice, face-to-face, rather than from a sterile studio closet. He had spent too much time in air-conditioned comfort.

He and his producer agreed to be more actively involved with outside broadcasts in future.

Now, all of a sudden, 'mana from heaven'. Dino's programme, the only programme in the city to be chosen by this whistle-blower informant. He prayed his mystery caller's knowledge was genuine. If it was, his programme would be credited for communicating another nine safe hours to gather and store water. Nine hours also for the city to decide whether to pay a $100 million ransom. As the city taps flowed, Metro's scientists continued water sampling every quarter of an hour. Dino waited patiently, whiling away the time, with the knowledge he may have just scored a direct hit.

On Mack Grayson.

82

The night was uneventful. Water to all households remained freely available, without a glitch. Each quarter-hour test, from the Metro laboratory, relayed via TV bulletins, declaring it safe to use.

The clock rolled toward 6am. The moment after which **Strike Two** might apply. No change. Taps continued to flow, unaffected.

Dino's prediction, thanks to his informant, had proved accurate. 7, 8 and 9am came and went, without incident.

Then, at 9.10am all hell broke loose. Metro's lab team confirmed an unidentified foreign presence in the water.

An alert notice was prepped for immediate release. Advising consumers to shut down all water sources and outlets.

Urgent: Act Now

A suspicious, potentially dangerous chemical agent has been detected in Metro's main reservoir. Significant water contamination is expected to reach all consumers before 10am.

Do Not Drink the Water. Do Not Cook with the Water. Do not Wash or Bathe

IMPORTANT: Only Use Stored Water Supplies

Before the urgent directive could be televised via a TV news-flash, it was masterfully disabled.

Knocked out by an instant power failure, across the city.

Widespread outage meant Metro and its testing lab crashed, suddenly shutting down. With no electricity, TV channels primed to disseminate the crucial warning message, were paralysed, unable to broadcast vital instructions and survival tactics.

This communications inertia presented an alarming predicament. A double-edged sword. If no warnings could be issued by any authority, no warnings would be received by any consumer.

Millions of innocent folk were just minutes away from possibly the most terrifying moment of their lives. Totally unaware some evil threat was now gushing through Lake Jacaranda's pipes, surging toward homes and businesses.

83

Seizing control of a water utility's command centre is an extraordinary feat requiring exceptional IT expertise. No argument. Metro Water's bible of operational procedures, Professor Vic Denton's stolen manual, had provided the cyber highway to the facility's inner workings. All the guidelines, access codes and passwords clearly identified. Ready for use, or abuse.

But shutting down the city's electricity network was a whole new ball game. Hijacking vast areas of the metropolitan grid system would surely be impossible. A bridge too far, requiring exceptional knack and know-how. A magician with an extraordinary skill set. Hal, computer genius and systems mastermind, one of the three conspirators behind Metro's takeover, was certified an ethical hacker. He hacked for a living. Just the man for the job. Over the past three decades, he'd worked for numerous government departments and corporations on systems security and protection. As both a cyber forensics analyst and a cyber security engineer, he was widely recognised as one of the nation's leading professionals in the hacking trade. No longer wishing to work for other people he'd decided it was time for a change. Time to use his obvious talents on one major, financially lucrative project, for personal gain. And early retirement.

Within half an hour, Hal had infiltrated and overpowered

the electricity grid's key systems. Wizardry at work. Firewalls designed to allow or block specific traffic had been easily penetrated or circumnavigated. Since most power plants and sub stations had switched from manual to remote access, it had made them vulnerable to attack. By disabling the systems infrastructure Hal could unplug sub stations one by one, remotely. Accurately planting erroneous signals had cleverly disabled all protective systems. Both the transmission and distribution frameworks were now totally under his control. Exposed and in jeopardy, the city had been rendered powerless.

Hal couldn't help thinking how another potential ransom prospect, another river of gold, was staring him in the face. Common sense prevailed. Save it for another day. There's work to be done, here. First.

With the power down and contaminated water coursing its way toward city taps, Metro Water's lab team was frantically testing samples to identify the suspect chemical, its strength and toxicity.

When the latest results came in, frenzied pandemonium broke out.

84

It's dangerous, it's corrosive, it can maim, it can kill you. In the wrong hands sodium hydroxide can wreak unmitigated havoc. And right now, it **was** in the wrong hands.

Commonly referred to as caustic soda or lye, it's mostly used in detergents, paint strippers and soap manufacturing. It's also the main ingredient in oven and drain cleaners. Large quantities can immediately bring a solution to the boil, its acidic potency capable of decomposing roadkill. And it boasts even darker efficiencies. Murderers have utilised a heated version to dissolve human bodies, destroying all evidence, within three hours.

Understandably, its acidity is lethal. Just handling sodium hydroxide has horrendous consequences. Contact with the skin can lead to severe chemical burns, scarring, even blindness. Swallowing as little as 10 grams can be fatal. Children mistaking it for a soft drink have died.

Then, as if with a Jekyll and Hyde split personality, it can also undergo an unbelievable transformation, a metamorphosis with redeeming qualities. Sodium hydroxide's most extraordinary property is that when heavily diluted it forms a crucial part, of the overall balance in a city's drinking water. It raises ph. levels, minimises corrosion and acidity, while removing heavy metals, to produce the perfect drop.

The problem arises when cyber extortionists seize control of each element of a water utility's ebb and flow.

Metro Water's holding tank, containing sodium hydroxide, should be releasing no more than 120 parts per million. The actual reading was catastrophically off the scale. The recorded amount of caustic soda was now one hundred times greater than the safe level. An astronomic 12,000 parts per million. A toxic overload designed to induce panic, perhaps loosen purse strings on ransom demands.

And with a sudden electrical blackout, no one could be warned about the acid concentrate surging towards them.

The cyber terrorists had ensured Metro was unaffected by the power cut, as its turbine and back-up generators had been isolated, continuing to pump the poison closer and closer to city taps.

In less than an hour the reality, the full nightmare would be known.

85

The deafening siren in Metro's control room announced the presence of a chemical overload in the system. Flashing lights accompanied a verbal drone, on constant repeat.

"Danger Level Output….Danger Level Output….
Danger Level Output"

It was just after 9am. It had been quiet all night with fourteen hours of uninterrupted flow. Nothing of concern to report. 'All Clear' safety bulletins had been released every fifteen minutes.

Mack had been conducting interviews with Metro scientists, administering the test sampling, when the alarm sounded. The latest reading declared sodium hydroxide levels to be 100 times greater than the strict national standard.

Caustic soda, a certified killer, was on the loose. The liquid's lethal capabilities, racing toward millions of innocent men, women, and children.

An **Urgent, Act Now** alert was prepped for immediate release to TransNational TV and radio stations, warning citizens of the imminent threat. Then, another crippling blow.

Suddenly, with no warning, a total power blackout across the entire city.

Immediately, the planned 'news flash' communication ground to a halt. No danger warning could be released.

Remote-controlled, cyber sabotage was at work once again.

Obviously, no coincidence, the only place with full power was Metro Water, its pumping stations continuing to operate at full capacity. Precious minutes ticked by. The outcome seemingly inevitable.

Mack instinctively dialled a number. Someone he thought would know how to apply the emergency brake to this runaway train.

"Mack, electricity's just gone off, you too?" shouted a clearly nervous Vic Denton

"I'm at Metro, only place with power. Our cyber friends upped the dosage of sodium hydroxide a hundred-fold. It's on its way to the city, we can't warn anyone, we can't stop it."

"Mother of God, that stuff can kill."

"What can we do?"

"Nothing Mack, it's remote controlled, they're running the show."

"What can **I** do, to override the system, take an axe to a computer, something, anything?"

"Let me think."

"No time for that, just 20 minutes before it reaches the city."

"How about blowing up the turbine, powering the pump system!" quipped Vic.

"How do I do that?"

"You can't be serious?"

"Never more so."

"Without explosives, set fire to the entire engineering hub. Pour fuel on hot engine parts and supply lines. Together with the flammable vapour you should have instant ignition."

"Over my dead body!" yelled a spluttering Magnus Flume, racing into the lab with a security guard in tow.

"Don't tempt me!" glared Mack. "Magnus, thousands of lives are at risk. Horrendous chemical burns. Imagine what drinking that acid will do."

"You can't blow up the plant."

"We just need to disable it, while we negotiate our way out of this disaster."

"What about the city's water supply?"

"It's about to be poisoned. We must act now."

Mack ran to the stairwell leading down to the power plant, the utility's engine room. The security guard moved to block his path. Quick punches to the head and gut and the guard doubled over, collapsing on the floor.

It was now a race against the clock. Locking the door behind him, Mack descended into the bowels of the engineering plant.

He couldn't help thinking how a photo-journalistic commission to a war-torn, dangerous, hot spot anywhere in the world would be especially preferable right now. In contrast, he had landed himself the most extraordinary life or death assignment.

If he was truly honest, he'd rather being sharing Margaritas with Sacha.

Instead, he was about to blow up a water treatment plant.

"Now Vic, where am I going, what am I doing?"

86

Drifting toward oblivion.
A life well lived.
And fortune favoured.

Lingering images.
Looking down on adoring faces.
Gig after gig, night after night, hotel after hotel.
Life on the road, on a bus, on a plane, on a stage.

Theatres, arenas, stadiums, open-air concerts.
Constant applause, encores, standing ovations.

Night clubs, good friends, willing women.
Searing highs, depressing lows.
With and without chemical joy.
In a studio, in an interview, in a daze, inner turmoil.

Aching hearts in Paris.
No satisfaction from platinum sales.
Always somewhere else, being something else, for someone else.
Lost.
At home.
Just me and her, going nowhere.
Misery, a close friend.
Pass the bottle, chop up the powder, prepare the fix.

Here's a song.
Just need some words
About how I gave an interview yesterday.

Didn't realise it was my last.

87

Launch day for the new album. The world's music media gathering en masse. Physically and online. Anticipation for a private 'live' concert spruiking new material whilst proving earlier brilliance was no fluke. Baited breaths. Did they still have it?

Back stage, three of the band's four members twitched.

Sandy Lane, Chance Lively and Chip Fryer were feeling the pressure. Their first public performance in twenty years.

About to emerge from the wilderness,
where the tragic spectre of Paris had hovered.
A fire that claimed fifteen beautiful people.
Dimmed but not forgotten.

Rehearsals rocked, everyone relieved they still had it.

Their peer hierarchy about to witness, about to judge. Scribes, eager promoters, booking agents, venue managers had packed the 500 seat Trocadero Theatre. Everyone hoping to snare a piece of the action following the 'second coming' of one of the greatest rock acts of all time.

The scheduled start time had been and gone by thirty minutes. No one on the audience side of the curtain seemed concerned. Such delays were common.

On the other side, a different story. Three band members primed to deliver. Desperately in need of a fourth.

At the front of the stage an unmanned, lone microphone, awaited vocal accompaniment.

The singer nowhere to be seen hadn't answered his phone.

88

The plant room fire had taken hold within minutes. Mack had been guided by Vic Denton on the best and quickest way to disable the gas-powered turbine. Lube oil released from a resource tank onto hot metal surfaces did the trick. A spark completed the ignition, triggering an inferno. He had beaten a hasty retreat as the resulting explosion demolished the space, shutting down the power source, silencing the pump network. With the necessary damage complete and the outflow of sodium hydroxide halted, Mack immediately switched on deluging fire sprinklers to drench the area. Mission accomplished. So he thought.

While the community had been saved from a potential disaster it was now without water, one more time. And the authorities needed someone to blame. As Mack emerged into Metro's control room, instead of congratulations and applause, he was handcuffed and led away. No consideration to his life-saving efforts, he'd destroyed public property, beaten up a security guard and left the city, critically, without its water supply.

Sir Phillip Daniels immediately demanded Mack be removed from his position as host of TNT. While Clyde Jameson supported his anchor-man he had no choice but to support the chairman's directive. Facing civil charges, Mack would need to be stood down until the police investigation concluded.

Over at Radio A2Z, Dino went joyfully overboard, pouring verbal bile on Mack's temporary demise. Citing unforgiveable criminal behaviour resulting in millions of dollars' worth of damage. His assault on the security guard had left the man hospitalised, following a head injury received when falling unconscious to the floor.

Ever since the shock jock's whistle-blower had predicted safe water usage up to the moment **Strike Two** began, his audience figures had begun to climb. He wanted to capitalise on it even further, now Mack was off-the-air, gagged.

Vic Denton had caught Dino's anti-Mack rave, calling the radio station to castigate the talk-back host.

"Through his actions Mack Grayson saved this city from a major disaster. If he'd not acted hundreds, if not thousands of people would have died or been severely injured."

Dino: *"He destroyed Lake Jacaranda's power plant and has now robbed the city of its water."*

Vic: *"Repair measures are in place and with provisions like The Tap Dancers, there are numerous contingency procedures already in place."*

Dino: *"You seem to know a lot about the specifics of Metro's modus operandi."*

"I used to work there."

"Did you now. What was your role?"

Vic knew he must tread carefully. Obviously not revealing his former position and intimate knowledge of Metro's weaknesses. Definitely no reference to authoring a certain manual, now in the hands of cyber terrorists.

"Just a middle manager in IT, nothing important."

"Shame, I was hoping you could give me the inside drum, what's going on to solve this ransom crisis."

"Sorry, no I was just ringing in to support Mack Grayson's heroic efforts."

"Because I get the impression from my whistle blower...Do you listen to this programme?"

"Not often."

"You're forgiven. I've got this whistle-blower who appears close to the people demanding a ransom. I've talked to him off-air. He tells me they've got hold of a document, a roadmap to seizing control at Metro. It was stolen. Someone snatched it, taking off on a motorcycle.

"You're kidding?"

"No, just thought you might know something about that document?"

"Sorry, can't help, above my pay grade. Anyway, give Grayson a break."

"Thanks for calling. This is Dino, what's on your mind?"

As he cradled the phone, Vic Denton's intestines performed a somersault. Troubled by something he'd just heard. Something very few people knew.

And he was sure Dino Lombardi was not one of them.

89

With Mack stood down from his TNT hosting duties and his role as Metro's media go-between suspended, he wasn't present for the cyber attackers' next bulletin in the utility's control room. Since their acid attack had been thwarted and the turbines silenced it was expected to be a particularly hostile broadcast.

Replacing Mack, a TNT crew had been installed in the utility's control room to record proceedings. With a direct link back to the TV programme's offices where Clyde Jameson and his 'disgraced' host watched on a monitor.

"I've definitely up-ended their grand plan. But what's next, what horror awaits us now?" said Mack.

"At least with no water flowing, they can't poison us with chemicals."

"Don't worry, whatever it is, we can guarantee it won't be pleasant."

With a static crackle the familiar booming voice from cyber space joined the room.

"How disappointing. You were warned. If you didn't pay the ransom, you would suffer. When are you going to realise there is only one solution to your city's dilemma? Rather than pay the money, you decide to risk the lives of millions. You then blow up the plant. Where did that get you? Back, where you started. What a 'dogs' breakfast.'

"You were about to poison the city, we had little choice," argued a whining Magnus Flume.

"I'm tired of reminding you. You had. You still have. A definite choice. Pay up and be free of all threats. Just a hundred million dollars, all your problems go away."

"I'm authorised to offer you 10 million, that's our limit. That's it."

"You haven't been listening. I've said it before, I'll say it again, 100 million, no negotiation."

"10 million is our offer."

"You leave us no choice. Key suburbs will now be targeted with something far worse than our little chemical experiment. Since you have rendered the pump turbines inoperable, we are forced to take more drastic measures. We suggest you alert all levels of Government; this is no longer just a Metro problem. Prepare yourselves for **Strike Three.***"*

"And what exactly is that?"

"Bacillus anthracis. It's a deadly bacterium."

"What!"

"Better known as, Anthrax.

You have 24 hours.

Come up with the money, or the city faces a biological attack."

Mack and Clyde Jameson looked at each other, wide-eyed.

"Mack, what on earth's happening?"

"I've no idea. But from the little I know about Anthrax, we're in serious trouble.

90

Django Marx was celebrated in death more than he was in life. The rock star's demise shocked the music world and shattered his legion of fans. FarQ's comeback album *Diddling with the Devil*, recorded just before his fatal heroin overdose, was already storming the charts internationally. Posthumous awards awaited its creator.

The outpouring of love across the globe had been phenomenal. Candlelit vigils, tearful singalongs, sit-ins at his record label, a mountain of floral tributes at his grave site. The grief was palpable. Shrines were created at venues commemorating key moments in the group's historical rock calendar. You could pay your respects at the Django Marx altar built to salute FarQ for drawing a massive crowd of 264,000 in May 1996 at Predio Rural, La Colmena, in Buenos Aires, Argentina. A world record, to this day.

There were also daily street gatherings at a New York needle exchange that Django had attended (regularly) and later sponsored. The most extraordinary, the most moving, was at the Paris theatre, the venue where the tragic fire had halted the band's stratospheric rise. It became an instant religious sanctum, thousands making a pilgrimage to the site of FarQ's last 'live' concert. The group had been devastated by the inferno that brought an abrupt end to their live performances and hectic touring schedule. They withdrew into hibernation, setting up a trust fund for the families of the fifteen fans who perished. To this day they still donate 30 per cent of their earnings to French charities dedicated to youthful pursuits. As they continued to release albums from relative obscurity, their commitment, their ongoing support toward the teenage victims never waned. This generosity of spirit coupled with their musical genii ensured the fans remained loyal to the very end.

Immediately before his death the world hadn't heard a word from Django. He hadn't given an interview in over a decade. He hated the media. Various scribes had given him such bad press, he'd rejected all subsequent approaches. It didn't take long for news to surface that a 'one-on-one exclusive' had been recorded just days before he died. A nightly current affairs television show in Sydney, Australia had recorded a lengthy, no holds barred, nothing off-limits, exchange. With a magic bonus. FarQ had performed 'live' on the programme, showcasing past hits together with tracks from their about-to-be-released new album.

It was as if every TV station on the planet wanted to get

their hands on this interview and performance material to satisfy gagging audiences. Highlights were immediately edited into a two-hour 'special' and packaged for sale internationally. Django's illuminating commentary on the peaks and troughs of rock stardom were intercut with impressive studio performances, proving the band was still a class act.

But it was his frank delivery on the Paris theatre disaster, the perilous relationship with drugs and a genuine regret over his run-ins with the law that revealed raw, honest, humility. At the close of the interview, he'd been asked how he and FarQ would like to be remembered. At the time he would have had no idea how prophetic, how tragic, how soon his words would be shared with the world.

"How would you like to be remembered?"

"As spokesmen for a generation.

We spoke their politics, felt their frustrations, massaged their dreams. The band's name gave them permission to stamp their feet.

And respond.

FarQ!"

Django's parting gift. A battle cry, for the youth of the world.

Through all the hype and hoopla associated with the worldwide distribution of the Django Marx 'special', the profile of one man was to soar, gaining him global notoriety. Mack Grayson, host of Australian current affairs programme, TransNational Tonight was the interviewer who had unwittingly drawn the final breath from the fabled front man. Magazines and radio stations queued up to interview him. TV variety shows across the English-speaking world set up 'live-crosses' to chat by satellite.

He became an instant international celebrity.

At home it was a completely different story.

91

Inspector 'Deeks' Deacon had become a constant in Mack Grayson's life.

First it was over the 'hit and run' murder of Wes Markowitz. The toxic relationship between Mack and the now late Chief of Staff of the Times had given Deacon his prime suspect. Quite possibly, his only suspect. But the night Markowitz was mowed down, Mack had the perfect alibi. A five-hour drink-fest in the cocktail bar of the Majestic Hotel, confirmed in a written statement by Sacha Lombardi. Deacon was still convinced Mack had something to do with the grisly murder.

Then, there was the suspicious death of TNT's host presenter, Quentin Street. Found hanging in his apartment alongside a typed (not handwritten) unsigned suicide note. Deacon believed it could have been prepared, by anyone, not just the victim. While a collapsed relationship suggested a broken heart prompted him to end his life. Deacon had other theories. Security camera vision showed Mack leaving the premises after he'd checked on Street, who had failed to turn up for work. He denied being inside the residence, protesting that video evidence had been doctored. Then, there was the question of the chair that was climbed upon and kicked away by Street. Or was it? At the crime scene, the final resting place of the chair was further than any suicidal person could have propelled it. According to Deacon. Another reason why he refused to rule out foul play was because one person would be the principal beneficiary from Street's demise. The one man who would step into his shoes and take over as the TNT anchor.

So it perhaps came as no surprise to Mack that Deacon summoned him to police headquarters after Django Marx' fatal heroin overdose. Especially since it resulted in the most watched TV special of the year, with celebrity status for the interviewer.

"He told me he was clean, hadn't touched the stuff in years. An absolute tragedy, I was blown away when I found out."

"Were you now? Interesting. You certainly benefitted from his death."

"What do you mean by that?"

"Your interview with him has made you a media superstar around the world."

"Maybe, but I didn't kill him. He died by his own hand."

"How do you know?"

"The coroner reported he'd overdosed on impure heroin, laced with a potent, synthetic opioid. It didn't help that he'd exhausted all needle sites on his body and ended up injecting into his eye."

"You could have accessed the heroin knowing it could kill him."

"Are you suggesting I then stabbed him in the eye to advance my career? Give me a break."

"Three people die and so much good fortune comes your way. Don't you see why you're a person of interest, three times over? It's quite ironic. All your gains have come to nothing since you're now suspended from every one of your television roles."

"When the true story, the real story comes out, how my actions were totally justified, how thousands of lives were saved, I'll be cleared."

"I think you'll find blowing up a public utility and beating up a security guard is likely to earn you a lengthy jail sentence."

92

Ever since he'd called up the radio programme and spoken to the city's leading talk-back jock, he knew something was seriously adrift.

Very few people knew about 'the manual'. Even fewer knew it had been stolen, let alone snatched by motorcycle thieves.

Across the road from the station's head office, he watched the main entrance. The show had just ended, and he was hoping to catch up with its presenter.

It was the second day he'd staged his stakeout, on the off chance of tackling the man who appeared to know far more than he should.

Two hours had passed and just as he was about to abandon his park bench and interrogation plan, the building's revolving door delivered two men in animated discussion. A heated exchange. An argument, that lasted all the way down the steps to the pavement. Pedestrians steering a wide berth to avoid flailing arms. Finger pointing continued with raised voices. Traffic noise drowning out angry words. One man was receiving a dressing down, possibly a threat from a superior, obviously unhappy about something.

Turning on their heels, they headed in opposite directions.

This was the opportunity he'd been looking for. Having just received a verbal hammering, his target might hopefully be caught off guard. Another confrontation, so soon after the first, a moot moment to pounce.

"Mr Lombardi?"

"Yes."

"A quick word if I may, about the cyber terrorism threats you've been covering on your programme."

"What! Sorry! I'm late for an appointment."

"Do you reckon your whistle-blower knows more than he's letting on?"

"Excuse me! Who are you?"

"An interested listener. Someone who'd like to see the end to this water crisis. On air, you mentioned a 'manual'. Have you seen it; do you know who's got their hands on it?"

Brushing his interrogator aside, a flustered Dino walked on.

"Look, I'm in a hurry. What's this got to do with you, anyway?"

"That manual has all the answers to the shutdown at Lake Jacaranda. In the wrong hands it's dynamite and you seem to know something about it."

"What makes you think that?"

"You mentioned on-air it was stolen by someone on a motorcycle. I am one of very few people who knows that."

"What's so special about you?"

"I wrote that manual, I feel responsible for its disappearance. I've been helping with the police investigation," lied Vic Denton.

Lombardi appeared taken aback.

"I don't know any more than what my whistle-blower has told me. I've shared everything with my radio audience. And the station's management has passed all details to those investigating the Metro incident."

"If it's publicly available information, where can I get hold of a copy?" "Give me your card and I'll get one of my producers to deliver the file." "How do I know you'll provide all the information, all the paperwork?"

"I want this off my back as much as you do. My management want me to ride a white charger through this whole ransom debacle. I've just been roasted, trust me I'll deliver. When you've reviewed the material, come back and we'll discuss it on air. It may bring the whistle-blower out of his bunker and give us something valuable to work with."

Denton handed over his card, then watched the radio man walk away and turn the corner. Vic knew he'd never receive that file. He felt a sudden urge to follow.

Easier to observe from across the street rather than

shadowing directly behind, he kept a safe distance. Watching Lombardi make several quick phone calls. During one, he had whipped out a business card from his pocket and began to recite its details, before barking some inaudible order. He appeared agitated, constantly looking around as if he expected someone to be tailing him. Could his recent conversation with the author of the Metro manual have rattled him for some reason? Occasionally he glanced across the road forcing Denton to try on a sun hat outside a pharmacy or take cover behind a magazine lifted from a newsagency's rack.

Eventually Lombardi reached his destination, greeting two people outside the city's top dining address, the award-winning Italian restaurant Scaramouche. Denton had heard it was owned by some media baron, a man who somehow had managed to juggle 5 wives, over a 40-year period.

Lombardi's two dining companions looked like a father and daughter. A well-dressed man in his 80's escorting a beautiful blonde woman, at least forty years younger. She greeted Lombardi with a hug and a kiss on both cheeks, suggesting she knew him well. A firm handshake between the two men showed a respectful formality.

They entered the restaurant, Lombardi first, followed by the woman. The elderly gent was last, reaching out to the advancing backside, giving it a more than friendly squeeze. Denton noted this was no father and daughter duo, before ringing Mack to give an account of the street meeting and surveillance. With no reply and not wanting to leave a message, he decided he'd try again later.

93

She pulled up in the restaurant's vestibule, turned and hissed.

"Don't you ever do that again."

"Couldn't resist it. Sorry."

"No, you're not."

"No, I'm not." he chuckled.

The staff offered multiple welcomes. Bowing and scraping before leading the party of three to a private room. The manager was all eyes and teeth with clasped hands, eager to ensure everything was perfect. The restaurant's owner was hosting an important lunch.

As before, the suite showcased her favourite blooms, dahlias, orchids and birds of paradise. She was getting used to this showering of affection. As he, similarly, was getting used to her increasingly blasé ripostes. The familiar tease, laced with a hint of hope. Both persevered, with diametrically opposed aims. Quite oblivious.

The third member of the dining party was employed by his host. They were known to each other, meeting on several occasions but could never be described as friends. When an invitation from the chairman of the nation's leading media corporation was extended, it was received with immense intrigue, accepted with gratitude. Assuming there would be a gaggle of media types for some TransNational function, he was surprised to find himself as just one participant of a very small lunch party. With the city in an enforced drought, thanks to cyber terrorists, he thought his talk back programme's city-wide influence and its recent spike in audience ratings might have something to do with it. Unusual though, that the founder of a media empire would want to engage personally with a talk-back jock, rather than through the radio station's management. Not here at a lavish lunch for three. And certainly not with his ex-best friend's wife, making up the numbers. He was shocked at her presence. They had recently seen each other, and she'd made no reference to the upcoming luncheon or the fact she was especially friendly with his boss.

He suddenly wasn't very hungry, which was good because there was to be a limited menu thanks to the water crisis.

An award-winning Californian pinot grigio was poured by the right-handed sommelier, with professional aplomb. Left hand, firmly planted in the small of his back. Attention to detail at Scaramouche was top drawer, truly five-star. A waiter with an over exaggerated Italian/Anglo accent, waxed in minutiae, before taking orders. Then a lengthy silence before the door to the suite closed, with an unusually loud click. As if some ominous announcement was imminent.

Raising his glass, Sir Phillip Daniels was quick to propose a toast.

"Here's to an enjoyable lunch, an interesting discussion and an outcome more than satisfactory for everyone."

Dino Lombardi raised and sipped the pinot, not quite sure where his afternoon was heading.

"Now, today's conversation will remain inside these four walls. If ever challenged, I'll deny any reference to it. For both your sakes, I insist you also remain tight-lipped. Permanently.

"As you know Lombardi, Mack Grayson is currently suspended from hosting duties at TNT, while police investigate the incident at Metro Water. In addition, he's currently under suspicion for the murder of Wesley Markowitz, the former chief-of-staff at the Times. Police also consider him a person of interest in the hanging death of former TNT host, Quentin Street and the fatal drug overdose of Django Marx."

Dino was quick to correct his host. "None of those allegations have been made by police, publicly. As I understand it there's no evidence to prove he had anything to do with any of those deaths."

"That's where you come in, Lombardi. You're going to make it widely known that the police are vigorously pursuing Grayson in relation to these crimes, with charges expected soon."

"But that's not true."

"You will make the announcement just after I have terminated Grayson's contract with TransNational, following the negative publicity over the Metro bombing. Not to mention the other incidents police are already investigating."

Dino was about to arc up when the door opened. A waiter wheeled in a stainless-steel trolley groaning with starter options and an ice bucket with another bottle of the prized pinot. Putting his manners aside, Dino reached for the wine, topping himself up, downing a full glass, in one gulp. Discretely, the waiter settled plates, refilled glasses, bowed and departed. A second quiet fell over the room, as cutlery grazed bone china and assorted selections of antipasto were dished onto individual platters.

As he gripped roasted eggplant and frittered sardines with a pair of silver tongs, Dino maintained a stunned silence. Why had he been singled out to create wild defamatory accusations against his former close friend? Admittedly he detested the man. Their recent altercations over on-air disagreements had them indefinitely at arm's length. But to dob him in for murder was totally out of order. He wouldn't do it.

"There will be no discussion, this is my directive to you, it will be carried out," Sir Phillip, glared his insistence.

"Jacki, you don't believe Mack's involved in any way with these deaths, surely?" Dino's eyes pressing the question.

"I really don't know anymore, he's been so erratic, rarely at home, no idea where he is, what he's been doing, who he's with. Several times the police have brought him in for questioning. He had no alibi to confirm his whereabouts on numerous occasions. They remain suspicious. Obviously not satisfied with his unsubstantiated explanations."

"I'll have to talk to homicide detectives, get an update on their investigation."

"That won't be necessary, I've spoken to Inspector Deacon, Chief of the Homicide Squad. I've told him what we're planning, what you will be announcing. If asked, he'll confirm Mack Grayson as a person of interest, facing serious criminal charges. I've made it worth his while, he won't be letting us down."

"Why are you doing this? You'll be crucifying the man,

destroying his reputation, ending his career, he may never recover. What about his marriage, his kids?"

Looking to Jacki, Sir Phillip placed his hand on top of hers. "Grayson has completely abandoned his marriage, Jacki and the children. Under the circumstances, with her husband a murder suspect, I think she's holding up remarkably well."

"Phillip has been amazing; he's seen me through this unbelievable nightmare."

"I can see!"

Dino's mind was in overdrive. Mack was being stitched up for murder. Sir Phillip had senior police in his pocket and Jacki appeared to have Sir Phillip in hers. As waiters cleared away remnants of the entrée, the table's diners exchanged glances that spoke volumes without words. When the main course was wheeled in Dino decided he'd like the staff to witness his next statement.

"I'm not going to accuse a man of murder, when he hasn't been charged with anything."

"Save your thoughts a moment Lombardi," Sir Phillip, in a loud voice with a raised hand.

"I will not be party to false allegations; you can't force me."

"Lombardi!" Bellowed Sir Phillip. Dismissing staff and confirming, from now on, they would serve themselves, pour their own wines. Knowing nods between the restaurant's owner and its manager ensured they would not be disturbed. Sir Phillip used the next 30 seconds to collect himself before launching into his ultimatum.

"Lombardi I am confident you will do as you are told."

"Why would I be that stupid, that reckless? My career would

be in ruins."

"Because I have your balls in a vice. Sorry my dear."
Jacki nodded, as if the comment, was quite acceptable to her.

"This morning Lombardi, I declared my marriage well and
truly over. My wife, correction, my ex-wife, has been a very
naughty girl."

"What's that got to do with me?"

"Everything Lombardi, everything."

Slipping a hand inside his coat pocket the media titan
produced a batch of photos, tossing them on the table, laying
them out in front of Dino.

"In my own home Lombardi, in my own bed, you violated me."

Sir Phillip had always suspected his wife, Florence, kept a
secret lover. A hidden camera in the Daniels' master bedroom
now confirmed the man's identity. The photos of the easily
identifiable naked couple were impossible to deny. Dino tried,
anyway.

"It was just a one off, we both decided it wouldn't happen
again."

"Bullshit." Sir Phillip, the hand in his other pocket, withdrew
a small tape recorder, placing it on the table, turning it on.

Recorded voices: "You look as though you could do with a
serious workout? (Dino) "Can't wait. Tuesday and Friday next
week as usual? (Florence)

"Just the once, was it? That was recorded by a waitress I
engaged, wired for sound, at TransNational's 30th anniversary
celebrations, at my beach house."

Jacki remembered the evening well. When the flirtatious

knight attempted to charm her on a tour of his private art collection, triggering an interesting relationship, with vastly different agendas.

"Lombardi, perhaps you now see, why you have little choice. That's if you want to hold on to your job, your radio audience, your reputation, your marriage, your children, your family and friends. Have I left anyone out? And the scandal, the shame. Imagine being exposed as the man who stole Sir Phillip Daniels' wife. The gossip columnists will have a field day. Some of the more tasteful, partly clothed photos, would also look good, gracing front pages."

Dino stood to leave "And all this, so you can bury Mack Grayson, and steal his wife?"

He made his way to the door, turned, pointing at the two remaining diners.

"Perhaps I should tell your story instead. And how you stitched up an innocent man?"

"Very unwise Lombardi, very unwise."

The door slammed shut. Dino's voice clearly heard from the other side. "Just watch me."

94

While Mack was officially under investigation by police, temporarily stood down from TNT hosting duties, he still felt an underlying obligation, a genuine commitment to Sydney, especially his TV audience. During the water crisis he was confident he'd served the community as best he could, considering he was a novice at playing TV presenter. The feedback suggested he had connected well, with the local population. Informing, guiding, warning with his now familiar reassuring tone.

With the imminent threat of an Anthrax attack, he'd been rendered helpless. Impotent. He wanted to contribute in some way and wasn't convinced the city elders, emergency powers at their fingertips, could wrestle the looming catastrophe effectively. The $100m ransom payout was beginning to look like the best option in avoiding a disaster of cataclysmic proportion. And yet no one was making a move toward writing a cheque.

The more he delved into the impact and likelihood of an Anthrax strike on innocent city folk, the more he was convinced everything should be done to prevent it from happening. Somehow, it had to be stopped before it started.

Mack's research had unearthed disturbing facts, confirming Anthrax as a deadly bacterial horror no sane person would visit upon anyone. The potential havoc wrought by this biological killer would be horrendous. And yet someone was about to unleash it, with all its unforgiving capabilities.

A contagious disease carried by infected cattle and sheep, Anthrax easily spreads to humans via exposed cuts or abrasions. The threat of a weaponised version that could easily be introduced to an unsuspecting community was frighteningly real. Microscopic spores of Anthrax are invisible, have no taste or smell and can survive for decades. In a laboratory it can be converted into powders or sprays and released with dramatic health consequences for anyone who comes into direct contact.

Afflictions come in the ugliest of forms. The biggest worry is you have no idea it's eating away at you, both inside and out, until it's too late. From enormous suppurating skin ulcers to agonising abdominal pains leading to the vomiting of blood. Terrifying for the victims and fatal in 75% of cases.

A New York study carried out in 2003 terrified everyone who read it. It claimed the airborne release of just one kilo of Anthrax via aerosol-ised distribution could result in one and half million infections and up to half a million fatalities.

Alarm bells rang loud. Anthrax is widely available on the world market through a global network of germ banks. More than 40 of these organisations offer Anthrax free of charge or are prepared to negotiate exchange deals involving other deadly organisms. Worse news still. Mack discovered the existence of a bio-engineered Anthrax, resistant to all known antibiotics and vaccines, had been developed in a Russian laboratory. It was now available for sale internationally.

The more information he gleaned, the more concerned he became. If the cyber terrorists had got their hands on one of the more virulent Anthrax variants, the outlook was nothing short of an unmitigated disaster, threatening the lives of countless innocent souls.

But there was one saving grace. A mini silver lining. With Metro currently unable to distribute any water, thanks to Mack's fire-bombing of its pump turbines, it could mean Lake Jacaranda might be spared an Anthrax attack. While the water supply might escape the deadly poison, it meant the city would, more than likely, face an anthrax attack in a completely different guise. Away from the reservoir, perhaps. Descending on a vulnerable population of five million, through some other means.

More questions than answers.

95

He'd been trespassing there, monthly, for decades. Not once had he been challenged. Signs warning him of heavy fines, blatantly ignored. There were miles of foreshore to choose from, but the familiarity of his personal campsite gave him, in his book, quasi-ownership. A private beach space, hidden from the road, where he could fish, swim, read and sleep, uninterrupted. The perfect hideaway.

Noting the moon was almost full, he lifted the barbed wire and crouching, ducked through the gap in the fence. Navigating the space, without snagging his jacket on the barbs. As he made his way to the favoured spot, his body cast a squat moonlit shadow, in the way a fairground mirror distorts the human image.

Under menacing dark clouds, a chilly wind was rustling the tall grass, still wet from the afternoon's drizzle. His cold ears were telling him he should have brought a woollen beanie.

Hardly a perfect night for angling but he needed to get out of the house, away from a nagging wife and an insufferable mother-in-law. An unwelcome guest who came for a weekend and had now been under his roof, almost a month.

Setting down his tackle, a folding chair and backpack, complete with a thermos of hot tea, he prepped rod, reel, and line. Attaching a plastic worm as his lure, he began to trawl the lakebed edges and drop-offs, where trout and perch were known to hide from predators. Innocent fish, blissfully unaware the most dangerous predator lurked on the shoreline, not in the depths of the reservoir.

He had fished all his life with both his father and grandfather as tutors. They had taught him about patience and the appreciation of peace and quiet. How the wait may not always be rewarded but the desire to return with a 'better luck next time' attitude must remain a certainty. A fixture. And so, just being there, wrapped in his cloak of peace and quiet he was at one with the world. Complete. Content. Satisfied. Catching something, anything, would be a bonus. Last year he took a couple of hours to finally land a 5 kilogram trout that had fought valiantly for freedom and failed. The monster had fed his family for a couple of days.

With the wind picking up and the now persistent rain unyielding, he had slipped on a poncho and anchored his beach umbrella deep into the soil. A distant thunderclap announced more foul weather ahead. The temperature was dropping noticeably. He decided on one final cast, then would call it a day. Returning to the cackling hens in his lounge room was not a joyful prospect but preferable to pneumonia.

He knew the lull before a storm was prime time for hooking fish. As the rain aerates and cools the water's surface, it attracts insects from nearby embankments. Drawn toward this tasty snack the trout leave their usual hideouts in pursuit. Placement of the bait amidst this airborne activity increases the chances of a 'catch'.

Or so the theory goes.

Nothing, not even a single bite, was letting him know there was any interest from beneath the lake's surface. And with the rain now relentless, bordering on downpour, his misery level peaked. He began to reel in the untouched lure. Almost back to the shore's edge where his rock ledge overhung the deep drop-off, the line became snagged. He walked first left, then right, attempting to free the hook. Bending, releasing the rod at various angles and heights without any luck.

Just as he was about to give up, cut the line, pack up and head home, it freed itself. He started to reel in, immediately noticing there was something still attached. It wasn't a fish, there was no resistance. He had caught something. Whatever it was, it was now heading to the surface.

As it emerged into the now pounding rain it glinted as a lightning flash revealed it to be circular and shiny. Halo-like. Deciding not to remain a moment longer, he tossed the object into his backpack, broke camp, heading for home and a hot shower.

Later that evening, in the shed at the bottom of his garden, he took a close look at the result of his fishing endeavours. The night's catch was perfectly round, chromed with fragments of glass, jutting from its frame. And it bore something else, forcing his heart to skip a beat. Without doubt, quite distinctive, embedded in the rim, were three teeth. Three human teeth.

He knew they were human. One of the teeth had a mercury filling.

96

Their street exchange had obviously rattled the radio man. Vic Denton was convinced Dino Lombardi knew far more than he was letting on. And from the panicked phone calls that followed, he was obviously sharing his concerns. Dino appeared especially disturbed by Vic's admission that he was assisting police with its terrorist investigations.

"We need to talk, something's not right, I think your radio mate might be involved." Vic had rung Mack.

"What's happened?"

"Can't discuss over the phone. Where can we meet?"

"How about the Page and Inkwell, the pub over the road, from the Times?"

"See you there in an hour?"

"I'll be there."

Intrigued as to why Vic was acting with such caution, Mack had been experiencing his own unsettled thoughts.

He'd been pursuing theories as to the likely next move by the cyber terrorists, how an Anthrax threat might be used against the city. Since repairs to Metro's pump turbines were far from complete, water distribution and therefore the poisoning of supply was no longer possible. Out of the question. So, how else could the city be threatened?If not from the land, what might the possibilities be from the air?

As soon as he investigated the implications of an airborne attack, he was horrified by what his research revealed. A U.S. government analysis as far back as 1993 determined that 100 kilograms of Anthrax spores dropped from an aeroplane, upwind of Washington D.C., would kill up to three million people. The area blanketed by the anthrax cloud would have to be quarantined for up to 30 years while it was cleansed of its toxicity. Surely no one would be mad enough to inflict such devastation upon any community. Or would they?

Masquerading as a detective from the local police station, Mack had contacted the two local aerodromes enquiring if any light planes had been hired in recent times. Just the previous day, one of them, Winston Aero, had received confirmation for the booking of a Cessna 188 AGwagon. It was unusual but they would be paying by cash and providing their own pilot.

When Mack asked what the main use would be for such an aircraft, his heart missed a beat.

"Primarily it's employed as a low flying crop duster."

The booking was for the next day.

97

Human teeth embedded in what looked like a motor vehicle's headlight rim.

He was convinced his 'find' was quite extraordinary. No doubt of significance to someone. The fisherman had pondered over his 'catch of the day' for a while, unsure whether to hand it in to police. Admitting he regularly trespassed on government property, to go fishing, was something he really wanted to avoid. In the end, conscience got the better of him.

He dropped it off at his local station, telling the desk sergeant he had found it near the reservoir. He hoped he wouldn't hear another thing.

Later the same day he received a call.

"Where exactly did you locate this item?" demanded Inspector Brian Deacon.

The angler spent the next three hours in the back of a police car and on the shoreline of Lake Jacaranda. Initially, he claimed the location of his discovery was situated just outside the perimeter fence. The homicide inspector didn't believe him, issuing a firm warning. Withholding evidence in a murder enquiry could have serious consequences.

He had no idea his little fishing expedition could possibly have made such an impact. Given little choice, he led the policeman to the exact spot, where he'd reeled in the auto part with three human teeth attached.

Deacon was immediately on the phone. "I want the dive team down at Lake Jacaranda, pronto. With a crane on standby. And let me know ASAP if there's a link between the new headlight evidence and the deceased's dental records."

98

Vic Denton left his city apartment, deciding to walk the two kilometres to the Page and Inkwell. He was convinced Dino Lombardi was somehow involved in the city's ransom heist. Or for some inexplicable reason, he was withholding vital information.

Ever since Vic handed over his business card to the radio shock-jock hoping to receive the file on Lombardi's whistle blower, he'd heard nothing. What's more, he'd got the impression his phone was being tapped. Strange clicking sounds could be heard during many of his calls.

He knew Mack had been friends with Lombardi for years but their relationship recently had soured. By sharing their doubts about the loudmouth Italian, he hoped it might shed some light on his erratic behaviour.

It was a warm afternoon as he made his way across town. All pedestrian lights turned green just as he reached each crossing, suggesting he'd arrive at the pub earlier than arranged.

Soaking up time, he slowed his pace, grazing a few shop windows on Sydney's George Street. Store sales were on. 50% discounts on leisure wear beckoned. A spruiker standing in an open doorway urged passers-by to enter.

But it wasn't the bargains that caught Vic's eye. A mirrored reflection in the glass projected an image, that suddenly increased in size. Advancing closer and closer. Faster and faster As he turned to face the accelerating object, it headed straight for him.

Several motorised cyclists had been tearing up the footpath, weaving in and out of the human traffic. Most hell bent on reaching destinations in record time to deliver takeaway meals, while still hot. Believing they had a God-given right to treat sidewalks as racetracks. Avoid the city's road systems and terrorise pedestrians. Almost a sport.

It happened so quickly. Which one was it?

Pram pushers shouted at them, old folk waved walking sticks, normally placid shoppers baled them up, issuing finger-wagging character assessments. But like flies, the more you swatted, the more they bore down, pedalling even faster. Anonymous, speeding cyclists, behind helmets, goggles and camouflaged clothing with no visible registration plates. If you wanted to lodge a formal complaint it would be impossible to identify one rider from another.

The guilty biker had already disappeared into the ambling throng, blending with the rest of the two-wheeled pavement pests. Virtually invisible. Printed on the back of his thermal bag 'Winged Waiter', a cartoon image of a tuxedoed maître d' in-flight, holding an outstretched tray. No food deliveries on this stolen bike. Instead, it was dishing out a deadly message to Vic Denton.

To date, this mobile madman had successfully evaded all the authorities investigating the Metro ransom crisis. To date, his contribution to the drama and chaos had been the most daring. First, as the motorcycle wizard and thief, who stole Professor Denton's explosive security report. Then as the cyber attacking computer genius who took control of Lake Jacaranda.

There was still more to come. As an experienced pilot, he was planning to fly a light plane on the most daring of missions.

Whether on the ground or in the air, 'mayhem' was his middle name.

Everyone nearby couldn't fail to hear it. A skull hitting the kerb with a resounding crack.

Blood poured from his nose and ears. His body still, lifeless.

99

The submerged wreck broke the surface of the reservoir, water cascading from its crumpled bonnet. Earlier police divers confirmed a motor vehicle had been located at the bottom of the lake, near the spot where an angler had been fishing for trout. Underwater, churned-up mud had made it impossible to identify the make or model. A crane manoeuvred into place, hooked and raised the auto's remains for all to see.

Blowing out a cloud of cigarette smoke, Inspector Deacon offered a rare smile. Despite extensive frontal damage it was, without doubt, an aged Ford Falcon. And with fading blue-grey paintwork exactly as described by its owner. Matched by a photo now pinned to the squad room's 'incident' whiteboard.

As the Falcon was loaded onto the back of a truck, one thing instantly struck the homicide detective. One of the headlight rims was missing.

100

Mack sat in a corner booth at the Page and Inkwell nursing a glass of red wine for over an hour. Why did Vic Denton want a private chat, away from eyes and ears? What was it that couldn't be discussed over the phone? Another quarter hour passed, no answer following calls to mobile and message bank. Mack increasingly uneasy. Events of recent times hinted grim possibilities. There had to be good reason for Vic's 'no-show'.

Pulling the pin, he decided to head home.

He was still suspended from TNT on-air duties, having gone from the busiest man in television to a thumb-twiddling inertia. The stand-in host for the programme, a cocky thirty-year-old, with obvious intentions of making his position permanent, was far better than Mack had hoped. He prayed his loyal audience would welcome him back once he was cleared of charges over the destruction of Metro's pump turbine. Repairs were well underway, but the resumption of full flow capacity was still days away.

There was hope an ancillary system might provide a temporary 'stop gap' with a previously retired turbine pressed back into service. Vic Denton had confided to Mack this secondary plan, conceived whilst he was still employed by Metro. It would require previously untested computer programming to successfully override all existing programmes. If it worked, it would regain control of the utility's information systems. If it failed the cyber-hackers might retaliate, inflicting further pain on the city. The existence of this 'ace up the sleeve', the possibility of water back on-line sooner than anyone could imagine, had to be kept under wraps at all costs. Until then, the wider community's support and cooperation would be key to survival. Trucked supplies from neighbouring water catchments together with the now expanding network of TapDancers, were the only lifelines for five million people living on the edge, without water.

As he pulled up outside his house, the phone rang. It was Clyde Jameson with distressing news.

"Mack, Denton's been in a serious accident. He's undergone emergency surgery, looks like he may have to be placed in an induced coma. According to witnesses, interviewed by police, a motorised cyclist mowed him down, the unidentified rider bolting from the scene."

Mack was glimpsing a change of fortune, the ransom

holders displaying a hint of panic. "First, they cut off the water, then attempt to poison it with sodium hydroxide. Now, with the threat of an Anthrax attack and what appears to be an attempt on Denton's life, their grand plan is beginning to show cracks."

Praying he would survive the night and be conscious in the morning, Mack planned on visiting the hospital, hoping Vic would be able to explain what happened. More importantly perhaps, what was it he urgently wanted to discuss.

After slipping his key in the front door, he was immediately pounced on by an enthusiastic Amy, quick to announce that Dylan, was planning to join the army. The federal government's conscription programme was now in full swing and had prompted the lad to consider his post-school options.

"I'm going to a lecture thing tomorrow," said Dylan enthusiastically.

"That's great," Mack high fived his son.

"Just a 'look-see' at this stage as I'm pretty sure my exam results won't qualify me for much in the way of job opportunities."

"Wise move, well done. Check out IT options you may be able to specialise in. That's your obvious strength."

"At least Dylan's career prospects are not in tatters." Jacki emerged from the kitchen, displaying her usual hostility. "Suspended from TV hosting duties, facing multiple charges, potentially a prison sentence. Isn't your life a 'dogs' breakfast'? What sort of example is that to the kids?"

"Jacki, one of your rare visits to the homestead, how nice to see you." Mack returned the sarcasm.

"Thanks to your act of vandalism there is no running water

across the entire city."

"Mum, Dad, stop it please." Amy appealing to her parents. Her brothers remaining silent, glued, as usual, to the TV screen.

"People seem to forget my actions prevented a deadly toxic chemical from entering everyone's homes. It could have killed thousands."

"For good measure, add to that, you're a suspect in a murder investigation."

101

The teeth extracted from the Ford Falcon's headlight rim were a perfect match, confirmed by dental records of the deceased. Not that he doubted it for a moment, but Inspector Deacon was now convinced he had the auto weapon used in the brutal slaying of Wes Markowitz.

All he had to do now was find the person who was driving the vehicle and charge them with murder.

Already, he had his suspicions, but he now had an additional incentive. If he could successfully charge Mack Grayson with the 'hit and run', his weighty house mortgage might just disappear. A twenty-eight-year unblemished law enforcement career was about to be severely challenged. His unquestioned honesty, integrity and 'life by the book' had been legendary. But the long hours, poor pay, a painful divorce had all taken their toll. Now, with a new wife, a Brady Bunch combine of five children and a home purchase that was killing his pocket, the remedy appeared very attractive. And imminently available.

Sir Phillip Daniels had convinced him that there was only one suspect in the murder of Wes Markowitz. That guilty party should be locked up, the key thrown away. Simple. Make it happen and Deacon's home loan would be confined to the trash can. History. The Ford Falcon instantly went under the microscope. The stripped vehicle bombarded with DNA swabs, targeting seats, dashboard, steering wheel, doors, handles, everything lab techs believed might have received human contact. Anyone leaving their 'autograph' at a crime scene could be identified as the offender thanks to the indelible fluorescing DNA substance. A car that was 20 years old would obviously have had multiple owners, multiple DNA identities. Eliminating previous drivers and passengers would not be easy but Deacon knew exactly where he wanted to start.

With nothing to fear, Mack and Dylan Grayson agreed to be tested. Since Mack had never driven the car, he was confident he'd be cleared. Whereas Dylan expected to be pinged as the owner-driver but be absolved from culpability.

When the results came back both Graysons were confirmed as having a DNA presence within the vehicle. One was immediately ignored. For the other, Deacon visited Mack at home and in front of his children, launched into familiar police talk.

"Macdonald Grayson you are under arrest for the murder of Wesley Markowitz. You do not have to say anything. But it may harm your defence if you do not mention when questioned something which you later rely on in court. Anything you do say may be given in evidence."

"I've never driven that car, not once. As you know, I have an alibi for that night."

In total disbelief, a stunned Mack was handcuffed and taken down to the police station for questioning. The look on his children's faces rocked him to the core. Jacki's facial reaction bordered on bewildered amusement. Any concern totally absent. Something Mack would never forget. Or forgive.

102

Questioned for four hours before being charged with Markowitz's murder, Mack was finally bailed, after putting up his home as collateral.

Deacon had presented new forensic evidence suggesting the time of death was now confirmed to be in the early hours of the morning of July 17. Long after Mack and Sacha said they left the Majestic's cocktail bar. That would give Mack plenty of time to take Dylan's car and mow down Markowitz. And all the easier when it was known the vehicle's keys were already in the ignition.

That information, coupled with the concocted DNA result from the Ford Falcon and Mack knew he was being stitched up for a crime he clearly did not commit.

It hadn't helped that while he said he'd never driven Dylan's car he was forced to make an admission. He remembered being a passenger, the day his son bought the $400 wreck. It was just a quick five-minute spin around the block. That would have been the only time his DNA could have attached itself to the vehicle.

With a court date yet to be set, Mack was hoping to prove his innocence long before legal processes were brought to bear. Long before influences of those hell bent on destroying him and his reputation, could attempt to saddle him with a guilty verdict.

He'd spent the night in a police cell and upon release decided he wasn't going home. Formally charged with murder, it would be hard to explain to the children, especially with Jacki pouring fuel on an out-of-control fire. After stopping at a supermarket to buy a change of clothes and basic toiletries he checked into a budget motel, in a dingy backstreet, away from prying eyes. After a quick shower, he was back in the car heading for the hospital, hoping Vic Denton had survived the night.

"He wakes occasionally, keeps mentioning the name Dino. Does that mean anything to you?" asked the attending nurse on Vic's ward.

"No, it doesn't," lied Mack. Not wanting to share any detail of the mad world he currently inhabited.

"He lapses in and out of consciousness, always in a state of delirium. It'll be a few days before we know how well he's recovered from the surgery."

With a multitude of tubes feeding lifesaving drugs into Vic's comatose body, Mack decided to sit with him a while, in the hope of catching a lucid moment.

An hour passed as he wondered whether Vic would ever fully regain his faculties. His pale face beneath a heavily bandaged skull signalled recovery was, more than likely, a long way off. After grazing well-fingered magazines from the ward library, fully informing himself of celebrity gossip from bygone years, he got up to go. Turning at the door, telling himself he'd drop by later to check on any progress, Vic's eyes momentarily opened. Recognising Mack, he gave a weak smile, before closing them again.

Moving to the bedside he picked up Vic's hand. "Good to have you back. How are you feeling?"

Eyes opened again, this time with a firm glare. He gripped Mack's hand, "I see you!"

"I see you too Vic. What can you tell me about Dino and what happened to you yesterday?"

"No, I see you."

"I know you see me. What did you want to tell me before your accident, that you couldn't tell me over the phone?"

"Go back to where it started. Wise up, I see you, before you see me, easy as."

103

Gaining nothing from his bedside vigil with Vic, Mack jumped in the car and dialled the one number where he knew a friendly voice would answer. She picked up, sounding delighted to hear from him. They arranged to meet.

While waiting for her to arrive he reflected on the hurtful things Jacki had said, especially in front of the children. One comment in particular had disturbed him and he couldn't quite put his finger on what it was.

"The Majestic Hotel cocktail bar, where else?" said Sacha spreading her arms in greeting, inviting a meaningful hug. The scene of numerous Margaritas and an alibi for a 'hit and run'.

"Apparently not," said Mack with a long face.

"Oh no what's happened now?"

"Not good news I'm afraid."

"Me too."

"What's up?"

"Dino wants a divorce."

104

Dino's life had somersaulted through an avalanche of horror and confusion. Could he now wrestle this chaos toward an opportunity?

So far, he had failed to pronounce guilt upon Mack.

Sir Phillip's death knell announcement on Mack's career had been bugled to the media at large. The star TNT presenter, now charged with murder, had been immediately sacked from the

TransNational Media Group.

This should have triggered action from the radio shock-jock. Under threat, the directive from the media baron had been blunt. As soon as the dismissal was made public, Dino was to crucify Mack on his radio programme. An on-air savaging, that would destroy the man. Dino's former close friend must also be painted as a person of interest in the deaths of former TNT host, Quentin Street and rock music legend, Django Marx.

Dino faced the toughest of decisions.

If he caved-in to coercion, his career would be over. Eventually he would be exposed as a liar, a trapped blackmail victim, knowingly peddling false information, meddling with the legal system. His sideboard of trophies and awards for exposing rorts, scandals and ne'er-do-wells, would be brought under the microscope and questioned.

If he refused to comply with these orders, he faced public ridicule and humiliation. Bedroom photographs and audio grabs, proving his steamy, ongoing affair, with Sir Phillip's now ex-wife, would be splashed liberally across the media to shame him. At the same time providing bucket loads of sympathy for his boss. This time it wouldn't be Mack's reputation at stake. It would be his. All the obvious ramifications with family, friends, his marriage, his loyal listener audience, not to mention Radio A2Z's management. Apart from releasing saucy snapshots and audio clips, Sir Phillip would demand his head. An unceremonious axing would terminate all future career aspirations.

While he was still to decide whether he would comply with

the demands, one of those ramifications had already been delicately addressed.

When Sir Phillip blatantly brought it to Dino's attention that 'the game was up' he had convinced himself it was decision-making time for his unhappy marriage. The need for a dramatic change, a confrontation, bringing a fresh start. Some order from the chaos. In so doing, wipe the slate clean to pursue a future with his new love, Florence.

Perhaps a knee-jerk reaction but a hastily arranged frank and sad exchange with Sacha suddenly seemed paramount. Bringing to a head something deeply troublesome for years. They had drifted so far apart, pursuing radically different lives and careers. Never wanting to tip over the marital apple cart and face the honest truth. They should now admit their marriage had been a disaster. As a result, their children had grown up in a dysfunctional household. So now, confront reality, embrace cold hard facts, and pull the plug.

At their hurriedly convened meeting Dino spilled details of the imminent media storm about his exposed affair and imploding career prospects. Sacha was outwardly shellshocked by the revelation while her inner self quietly registered a hint of relief. The news was devastating, the impact on their two sons immeasurable. But the future suddenly glimpsed a silver lining.

Without argument and with little discussion, they reached consensus. Divorce being the obvious solution, they agreed to walk towards an amicable settlement. Details to be thrashed out. Deep down both knowing that 'amicable' may not be the word they would use to describe it when it was all over.

Sacha had then asked the obvious question. "So, who is it you've just destroyed our marriage for?" bracing herself for the obvious reply.

"It's Flo Daniels."

Bursting into tears, first at the revelation of her husband's affair. The hurt sizeable. The deep-down betrayal visceral.

The shock had then morphed into instant relief. The other woman wasn't Jacki. She had suspected her former best friend for quite some time. Recent strange and distant behaviour had delivered mixed messages. That overheard phone call in the garden when Dino had said he was talking to a male work colleague.

Sacha had clearly heard Jacki's voice. What was that all about?

Numerous indicators suggesting she might well have had designs on her husband. All leading up to that unforgettable evening at her house. A showdown over those secret drinks with Mack at the Majestic. That's when their relationship, their friendship, hit the wall. Ironically, that was also when Jacki accused Sacha of having an affair with Mack.

"Florence Daniels, how disappointing Dino, that brassy tart, how could you? I thought it might have been someone else, someone with a bit of class."

"Like who?"

"Doesn't matter. But it does explain why you've been so distant. Both your sons have missed your intimacy in their lives. I knew you were unhappy, guessed you must have found a new playmate but Florence Daniels! Dino!"

"She's an amazing woman, a lot more to her than you see on the surface."

"I'm sure. Quite a surface too!"

"Don't start. We plan on living together."

"Do you love her?"

"I do."

"Dear God! Give me strength! Don't suppose she's going to get a farewell present from Sir Phillip. Going to cost you. Two separate overheads to support."

"Don't worry I've got that covered."

"Can't imagine how. Anyway, I'm going to move out for a few days while you get your sex life in order. I suggest you clear out asap. Explain to the boys, your decision, your future plans. When I get back, I expect there to be no evidence, you were ever here."

105

Florence 'Flo' Jones no longer titled 'Lady' or bearing the Daniels 'handle' had been shown the door by her now ex-shining knight. Forced to resume her original surname. Sir Phillip had waved a not inconsiderable cheque before Miss Jones's greedy eyes. Upon acceptance, it declared the end of their marriage. No comebacks, no further demands. Her signature on divorce documentation, confirming its finality was duly inked.

While she'd enjoyed her time in the sun as Lady Daniels, she realised the clock had been ticking dangerously close to midnight. Her affair with Dino Lombardi was either going to be discovered or the lovestruck couple would have to publicly extricate themselves from unhappy marriages to set up shop together. Such was their unplanned plan.

At his Scaramouche luncheon, Sir Phillip had made the decision for them. Confronting Dino with damning photographic and 'sound bite' evidence that his wife had been in a long-term sexual relationship with the Italian lothario.

That same morning, before the grand reveal at their tense lunch, the media magnate had given his fifth wife her marching orders. Florence and Dino had been forced into hastening their next move. Dino calling Sacha for urgent talks. Florence seeking out rental accommodation until something more permanent could be considered.

Most importantly, what was Dino going to do about Sir Phillip's threat?

"Bury Mack Grayson on your radio programme or suffer the consequences."

Could all this underhand skulduggery really be about giving Sir Phillip instant bidding rights for the hand of Mack's wife, Jacki? No doubt, much more than a hand.

The media magnate had never failed at anything before. Billionaire status suggesting his Midas touch always struck gold when it came to matters of business. But four, now five, failed marriages and his weakness for beautiful younger women yet again displaying an ageing Achilles heel. Could it just be blind lust? An old man proving he still had the pulling power. Not just in the boardroom, but also the bedroom. Was he not aware, if his grand plan came off the rails, he could be wading into a conflagration of unprecedented repercussion? And a media field day, like no other. Not to mention monumental legal consequences.

Had the veteran corporate warrior finally lost his grip?

106

The City had submitted ransom offers of 20 then 30 million dollars which were immediately rejected by the cyber-hackers. They insisted it was 100 million or suffer the consequences. As the last gasp 'talks' evaporated, the familiar voice boomed into Metro's control room, advising everyone their time had run out and the threatened biological attack was now the only course of action.

Mack had been in Clyde Jameson's office, hearing the announcement, piped through to his office from Metro HQ.

Its doom-laden messaging had continued.

"It didn't have to come to this but since you have chosen to ignore multiple warnings and opportunities, making a total 'dog's breakfast' of negotiations, you give us no choice but to now launch our assault. Within the hour a part of your city will be under siege and under a cloud. Which part, I hear you ask? You'll just have to wait and see."

The usual static crackle signalled end of communication, followed by deathly silence.

Mack stood up and made for the door, a quick glance back at Clyde. "I think I know what they mean by 'under a cloud."

Dashing to his car he dialled the one number that might confirm his suspicions. His squealing tyres exiting TransNational's carpark, as he headed out of town.

"Good afternoon, Winston Aero,"

"I rang you a couple of days ago, from the city police about a Cessna crop duster you were chartering for aerial distribution this week." Mack successfully repeating his performance earlier in the week, impersonating a detective from the local precinct.

"Strange you should ring at this moment."

"Why's that?"

"It's being prepped right now; he's loading up as we speak, should be airborne shortly."

"Who's he?"

"The pilot who made the booking."

"What's his name?"

"Let me see. On today's flight plan, the name he gave was Mack Grayson.

"What's he doing now!?" Mack was shouting, as he turned on to the highway, nosing north, with a half hour drive to Winston Aerodrome.

Lifting his binoculars, Chas Winston, owner of the charter aviation business, completely mystified by what he saw. "He's wearing a full protective suit, a Hazmat. Can't imagine why he needs such precautions for a fertiliser drop. He's tipping bags of white powder through a loading hatch, into the storage hopper, forward of the cockpit."

"You must stop him!"

"What! Why"?

"Stop him from taking off. He plans to drop a deadly poison on the city."

"That's absolute madness. Why would anyone want to do that?"

A frustrated Winston waved his coms phone in the air before slamming it down on the chart table. "I can't raise him on the digital two way, until he's on board, plugged in, ready to leave the ground."

"Can't you refuse permission to take off?"

"I'm in the control tower, he's on the other side of the airfield. He could take to the air, any time, with or without my permission."

"You've got to stop him. I'm on my way, but he'll be airborne, before I can get there."

"I'll drive over, try and hold him up, till you get here."

"Good man. Consider him dangerous."

"I'll be right, I'm a black belt in Karate."

"You're going to need it!"

107

The city had tried to bargain its way to a lower figure and failed. Non-negotiable. $100 million it always was. $100 million it would always be. **Strike Three** bells were now ringing.

This time the terrorist group had dramatically raised the stakes. They were about to launch their most daring attack yet. Their end game. Biological warfare.

Hal had arrived at the airfield with two bulky shoulder bags. One packed with sealed pouches of Anthrax spores. The other with full protective gear, an impermeable whole-body Hazmat suit and hood, for the safe handling of hazardous material. The deadly toxic powder was to be loaded into the Cessna crop duster. Once airborne the plane would fly over a selected target before dumping its lethal load. While the pilot would emerge unscathed, thousands of unsuspecting innocents below would be guaranteed inexplicable misery.

Once Anthrax was released into the air and breathed in, blameless victims would experience extreme flu-like symptoms, leading to grave illnesses. For many it would mean a painful, inescapable death.

Having donned the Hazmat suit Hal began the dangerous, precarious task of filling the plane's forward bin with the noxious white powder. Ensuring there was no spillage.

Hoping he wouldn't be disturbed during this delicate

procedure, he was to be out of luck. It started off as just a speck, in the distance. As it loomed larger, it was clearly heading his way. Through his Perspex visor he could see Winston Aero's fuel tanker was now speeding across vacant runways from the far side of the airfield. Hal cursed the clock. Five minutes from now and he would have been airborne. Hurriedly he split open the remaining anthrax pouches, tipping them into the storage chamber. The last bag was still in his hand when Chas Winston leapt from the tanker's cab and raced toward the Cessna.

"What's with the Hazmat suit for a fertiliser drop, Mr Grayson?"

"Just precautionary, it's a rich concentrate, don't want to breathe it in. It's seriously toxic, I'd keep your distance."

"If that's so, won't it affect people once it reaches the ground?"

"No, it breaks down, dilutes in the atmosphere, as it descends."

"I've been doing this work for years, that's utter bullshit." Winston stepped forward. "I'd like to see the label on that packaging."

"No problem, here, take a look."

As Hal handed over the remaining open Anthrax pouch, he gave it a sizeable fist bump underneath, showering the contents over Winston. A direct hit on his face, his hair and over his clothes.

"You've just been served a death sentence."

"You bastard, what is this?" spluttered Winston spitting out a glob of white powder.

"Anthrax. Breathe it in my friend, say goodbye."

Winston launched himself at the crazed pilot. With limited mobility in the cumbersome suit, Hal, lost balance, falling back against the plane's wing, next to his open toolbox. Before he could reach in and grab a spanner Winston had moved in, wrestling him away. As a black belt, he knew his well-practised karate kicks to the throat, jaw or head would be futile, because of Hal's hood protection. Instead, he readied himself, attack style, for a 'spinning roundhouse kick' designed to knock Hal off his feet. Known as the 'sledgehammer technique', it nearly worked. Hal managing to deflect the blow with a neat side-step and deft hand manoeuvres, suggesting he was more than familiar with advanced level martial arts.

As Winston mounted a second attempt, Hal was more than ready with his response. The kick's thrust swiftly neutralised by lightning-fast reflexes and instant blocking moves. Shocked by this highly effective defensive manoeuvre Winston overbalanced. Staggering headlong toward Hal, who stepped sideways, swiftly slamming the plane's wing flap down on Winston's head, rendering him unconscious.

Hal lost no time in preparing for immediate departure. After closing the Anthrax hopper, he removed his Hazmat suit. Flying the plane whilst wearing it, would be impossible. He hoped exposure to any of the white spores would have been minimal. Climbing into the cockpit he opened the throttle, before turning on the master switch and fuel pump. Once fully primed, he triggered the ignition, readying himself for take-off.

As he taxied toward the main runway, he could see a car

making its way from Winston Aero's admin building, at speed. Glad to see its destination appeared to be the spot where the fuel tanker was parked. Hal was straightening up on the flight strip, quickly gathering speed. Eager for an early exodus before anyone else tried to interrupt his battle plan.

Seeing the crop duster preparing for take-off the car immediately changed course. Mack, driving at breakneck speed across the airfield knew he had to intercept the Cessna, prevent it from leaving the ground.

He'd noticed the abandoned fuel tanker and with Chas Winston nowhere to be seen, he had assumed the worst. The plane loaded with Anthrax was about to wreak havoc. An aerial blitz upon innocent city folk. It had to be stopped.

Hell bent on overtaking the plane and cutting it off, Mack decided he would first come alongside to see if visual communication was worth a try. As he drew level, he could see the pilot laughing like a mad man, pointing and clapping hands like some demented clown. Any chance for rational exchange out of the question. With very little runway remaining, the pilot at full throttle was reaching take-off speed. Mack swerved the car in a threatening manner, hoping to force the plane off course, at least slow it down. Without success. With less than 50 metres of runway before a looming bank of trees spelled trouble, it was time for drastic action. Without a second thought, Mack pulled the steering wheel hard right, colliding with the plane's midsection in a shuddering crunch, releasing his car's airbags. The crop duster veered violently off course as part of its landing gear and one wheel broke away. Somehow, the pilot managed to wrestle back control whilst maintaining enough speed for a take-off attempt. Minus one wheel and leaning heavily to one side the Cessna revved to screaming pitch, gradually lifting into the air. The pine trees at the end of the runway had their top one metre shredded, as the plane's propellor tore through the greenery. Amazingly the crop duster remained airborne. As he gained altitude the victorious pilot could be seen offering a visible fist pump, followed by a single finger salute. Mack was out of the car, shouting at the Cessna's disappearing tail. The plane with its deadly cargo was on its way, a biological horror with frightening potential.

Where was the plane heading?

Who, what, was the target?

Everyone seemingly powerless in preventing this from becoming a full-scale human tragedy.

108

Over at the parked fuel tanker Mack groaned on seeing a body covered in white powder. It had to be Chas Winston. They'd only met over the phone, when Mack had passed himself off as a detective from the local police station. Winston had volunteered to intervene with no idea of the danger, he was likely to face. Mack felt instant pangs of guilt. Risking everything he knew about the dangers of close contact with Anthrax, he read Winston's pulse, confirming he was still alive. He then tore off his shirt and bandaged the man's bleeding head wound. Ringing '000' he advised the call centre operative it was an emergency. The patient had been exposed to a highly toxic substance. Protocols for full hazard protection would need to be strictly observed.

His next call was to Clyde Jameson, right now, the only person he truly trusted. Mack ostensibly was off duty, persona non grata and to many people, strictly 'on the nose'. His movements over the past couple of hours could only be described as being of a freelance nature. There was no way he could raise the alarm by calling Metro or anyone in authority, forewarning of an impending disaster. Clyde had backed him all the way from his TNT arrival and meteoric rise, through the firebombing at Metro, the murder allegations, up to his suspension, as host of the programme. Someone who wouldn't question him and had the ability to execute the almost impossible. Millions of lives hung in the balance.

"Clyde, its Mack, listen very carefully. We have a major emergency. I'm at Winston Aerodrome. Just failed to stop a crop duster loaded with Anthrax from heading towards the city. We face a mega disaster unless it can be stopped. The authorities must pay the $100m ransom for the terrorists to abort this mission."

"I'm dialling Metro now. You ok?" Clyde sounded relaxed, undaunted by the task.

"Apart from being covered in Anthrax, I'm fine".

"What?"

"Tell you later. The city's in your hands. God speed."

As he ended the call, he could see an ambulance with a fire engine escort, racing toward him. A groggy Chas Winston was making the effort to sit up, rubbing a swollen head, looking quite disorientated. Mack had just introduced himself. It was the second Mack Grayson, Winston had met in one day. This one wasn't the pilot but was the police detective he'd spoken to earlier. A police detective who apparently wasn't really a police detective! Maybe the head injury had led to his brain playing mind games. He was just glad someone had turned up to rescue him.

Mack fully briefed the medical and rescue personnel before excusing himself. He needed to warn his family. Their suburb could be among the crop duster's targets.

He rang the home phone and Jacki's mobile. No reply. Not wanting to leave alarmist messages, he headed back into town. Not a joyful thought. His last visit to the house resulted in checking into a motel to escape Jacki's acid tongue.

Ringing Sacha to warn her of the possibilities of an aerial bombardment he discovered she was home alone. Her two sons were with their father who was trying to explain how his extra-marital affair had led to their parents splitting up. Mack explained he was also without family and staying in a motel.

Hardly surprised by each other's news, they agreed to meet that evening.

109

"Good news, bad news, Mack. The city has agreed to pay the ransom. Now, the pilot won't respond. We can't stop him. Our cyber-hacking friends seem to have lost radio contact with the plane. Looks like their man's gone rogue."

Clyde had pulled off the impossible, convincing Metro to stump up the $100 million, only to find the threat of an Anthrax strike even greater. Minutes from now in some innocent suburban quarter thousands of individuals were oblivious to the looming aerial attack.

And there was nothing anyone could do to stop it.

"Chas Winston might have a solution. It's his plane, he's got a digital two-way link. He might be able to make contact. At this moment, he's in an ambulance, enroute to hospital."

Mack dialled up Winston. It was answered by a paramedic with muffled voice. Everyone on board the ambo was wearing full Hazmat protection suits with hoods. The patient was only just compus but once briefed on the dilemma, seemingly wide awake, full of ideas.

Attempts to contact the plane and abort the mission were repeatedly blocked by the pilot but Winston managed to establish the Cessna's exact location through a GPS portal he'd created for emergencies. It confirmed the crop duster was approaching the city's western suburbs but had not confirmed a final destination.

All he could see was a 'WWW' reference signifying the common host name for the World Wide Web. The well-known prefix, the link to any one of a billion websites. Unfortunately, not one site in particular that might reveal the plane's actual target.

Winston relayed his findings to Mack and Clyde as precious seconds ticked by. Useful information but without a geographic endpoint, nerves were fully jangled.

"What's with 'WWW' and no web details or site reference. Why enter 'WWW' with no additional info?" queried Mack.

"Could it be something that's familiar to the pilot. He could be using 'WWW' as an abbreviation?" offered Winston.

"'WWW' could be a stand-alone?" suggested Clyde.

"What do you mean?"

"A site that has three 'W's in its title?"

"You mean like Western Waste Watch?"

"Yes!"

"That makes sense."

"What's out in the western suburbs that has three 'W's in its name, that could be a sitting duck in the event of an aerial attack?"

"Let's see."

"Oh hell!"

"What?"

"I know exactly where its heading."

"Give it!"

"Wizard's Wonder World."

"No! Of course."

"Wizard's Wonder World is the city's biggest amusement

park. With school holidays now, there'll be thousands of kids with their families. All blissfully unaware of the deadly white storm approaching."

"It gets worse," added Winston.

"It can get worse?"

"The plane is quickly losing altitude. Must be heading toward the drop zone for a low-level fly-by. Ready to dump its load."

"Those poor people."

"They haven't got a chance."

110

With Mack's family miles from the Wizard fun park's location, there was no need to warn them of a possible Anthrax attack. Others would be suffering instead. Poor souls. Almost back in town when he received a phone call from the most unlikely of people. Dino.

Clearly not a happy man. Talking gibberish, offering apologies, not his usual cocky-confident self, at all.

"Hold up Dino, start from the beginning."

"Mack, my life is falling apart. I don't know where to start. I must destroy you, or I'll be destroyed. You're being stitched up for murder, I'm being forced to crucify you 'live' on my radio programme. Bury you, your reputation, your career. If I don't, my life, my job, will be wiped out. All because I'm in love with the wrong person."

That last comment sent a shiver up Mack's spine. Was Dino about to come clean about his affair with Jacki?

"I love her Mack and it's got me in all sorts of trouble. And I'm divorcing Sacha."

If he could have reached down the phone and punched Dino, he would. Instead, he gave him a free character assessment.

"You've been a complete arsehole, Dino. Totally irresponsible over the water crisis. Broadcasting misinformation, frightening an already confused population. Now your weird, irrational, behaviour following your lunch with Sir Phillip Daniels."

"How do you know about that lunch?"

"Vic Denton caught up with you outside your radio station. He then followed you to Scaramouche, the restaurant where you dined."

"That's where it all fell apart."

"Certainly did, especially for Vic Denton. In a coma following a cracked skull. You might know something about that?"

"It wasn't meant to be that way."

"So, you did have something to do with it?"

"Look, I'm just letting you know the police, that Inspector character."

"Deacon."

"Yeah, Deacon intends to spit-roast you alive. He's being paid off to ensure you swing for the Wes Markovitz hit and run murder. Also, he'll use trumped-up evidence to put you in the frame for Quentin Street's hanging."

"Who's providing the cash?"

"Sir Phillip Daniels."

"What! He's trying to put me away. Why?"

"He wants you out of the picture so he can pursue bride number six."

"Who's that?"

"I thought you knew. Why, Jacki of course."

"You gotta be kidding. So, who's the woman you're in love with?"

"Flo Jones. You used to know her as Lady Florence Daniels."

111

With a spare half hour before he was due to catch up with Sacha, Mack dropped by the hospital to check on Vic Denton.

Sadly, nothing had changed. He was still in a critical state, disoriented, talking in riddles. While the neurologist was pleased with his progress, he wasn't prepared to predict long-term recovery prospects.

When they were alone, Denton beckoned Mack closer, keen to whisper in his ear. Paranoid, as if someone might overhear.

"I see you, Mack."

"I see you Vic."

"I see you, Mack."

"I really do see you too Vic."

Here we go again thought Mack. How sad this brilliant

scientist had been reduced to such childish banter,

"Wise up Dino, remember I see you before you see me, easy as."

"It's Mack here Vic, not Dino. Is there something you want to tell me about Dino?" A confused look followed by an open mouth. Denton obviously struggling to answer, but no words came out. At that moment a ward orderly arrived, carrying a tray with Vic's dinner. Mack decided it offered the perfect moment to leave.

He wanted to be on time for his date. Well, it felt like a date.

Wildly pointing his knife and fork at Mack, Vic offered some parting advice.

"Go back to where it started, wise up, I see you, easy as."

112

A knock on the door immediately triggered an increase in his heart rate. A joyful surge that announced an about-to-be moment he never thought possible. Not in a month of Sundays. Or any day of the week. Who would have thought both their marriages would implode at the same time? He'd been rocked by Dino's shock revelation that Jacki was now in the arms of Sir Phillip Daniels. More surprised than upset. And a decision she'd failed to bring to Mack's attention. He couldn't wait for that showdown. At the same time, acutely aware of the impact their separation would have on his three children. Then, Dino asking Sacha for a divorce, having swept the 84-year-old knight's ex-wife off her feet. Equally shocking but in many ways perfect. Delicious timing.

Tonight, neither had to justify sharing this moment to anyone. She had rented an apartment while husband Dino packed up his life and removed himself from the family home. And he, escaping Jacki's poisonous tongue, had arranged temporary lodgings in this basic, very basic, motel. It had all started with their drink fest at the Majestic Hotel's cocktail bar, sowing the seed of something neither was brave enough to articulate at the time. It was there, that night, when they both realised their marriages were doomed. Unsaid feelings, the exchange of meaningful glances, had then suddenly taken on a life of their own, in the Page and Inkwell. At their meeting in the Back Page bar, she'd offered to provide him a genuine alibi for the night he was accused of murdering Wes Markowitz. That shared relief spilled over into the back seat of his car where they relieved each other of several buttons and a couple of zips. Frantic passionate minutes that stopped short of carnal ecstasy. Only just. An agreement was reached. There'd be another more romantic occasion, where true feelings might be properly expressed. Preferably, at the soonest. "Welcome to my palatial home."

Closing the door behind her, Mack swung his arms 360 degrees, helicopter-style, showing off his humble motel accommodation. Displaying obvious embarrassment. The room bathed in burnt orange exhibited shades of the 1970's. Above the bed a framed print of Vincent Van Gogh's Sunflowers, attempting to blend in with a faded gold candlewick eiderdown. Overall, a cringe-worthy artistic statement. He apologised for the drab surroundings, explaining it was an interim solution, somewhere to lay his head, until life turned a few decisive corners. Hopefully for the better. Because for a murder suspect, someone accused of blowing-up the city's water utility, who's also charged with assaulting a security officer, one's future could look especially bleak. They wrapped their arms around each other, sharing the embrace in exquisite silence. Breaking away, then holding at arm's length, locking eyes before leaning in with impatient mouths. A deep, sensual kiss each had long awaited, dreamed of, yet never believed possible. Not one grabbed like teenagers fooling around in the car, as in their previous encounter. This kiss, delivered with such passion, instantly led to each undressing the other.

The next minutes intensified feelings, hinting new futures, as shared pressures drifted away. Liberating all tension their mutually climactic romp reached a crescendo neither had experienced in almost forever. Prompting an exhausted rollover and a shared gaze at the ceiling. A brief hush broken by uncontrollable laughter.

After a while, words. Not the obvious ones. Not about the water crisis, the murder charges, the family breakdowns or two looming divorces. Sacha was first.

"More than anything else, whatever happens from hereon, our children must be the priority."

"I totally agree. My three and your two are about to have

their lives turned inside out. We both have school leavers this year too and the possibility of 'call ups' to the armed forces. But first I must unshackle myself from the mounting list of trumped-up charges against me."

Sacha turned to Mack, leaning on one elbow. "How are you supposed to wrestle a corrupt system designed to bring you down, whatever it costs?"

"I have a crazy plan. Wing and a prayer, it might just work."

"What is it?"

"More important things first," said Mack leaping out of bed.

Opening a cupboard, he withdrew three bottles, setting them down alongside coffee mugs. From the fridge, a lemon. From the freezer, ice cubes.

"What are you doing?" an intrigued Sacha, swung her legs out of bed.

Mack poured slugs of tequila, orange liqueur and lime juice before adding lemon wedges and ice, whisking the concoction with a fork.

"Not quite how they should be, but this moment has to be celebrated."

Handing a mug to Sacha, they clinked two roughly conceived margaritas and toasted themselves.

"To us."

"To justice

"A better tomorrow."

113

Mack Grayson was the last person he expected to see. Dropping by the police station, without appointment or courtesy call.

Deacon hid surprise, as he delivered his opening quip. "Thanks for the warning. Come to finally confess, make an official statement. Wise man."

Closing the homicide inspector's door behind him, Mack sat down and leant forward.

"You're the one who needs to confess. Bribery and corruption between a senior member of the police force and a knight of the realm. That's a hanging offence!"

Turning a noticeable shade of red, the Detective stood up for his terse response.

"What bull are you talking Grayson? Evidence against you confirms, as charged, you murdered Wes Markowitz."

"Charged yes, because of cooked evidence thanks to a greased palm. Yours!"

Mack blasted Deacon, going into detail about how he and Sir Phillip Daniels were in partnership to destroy him. And that it wasn't just the Markowitz death but also fabricated allegations for his involvement in the departures of Quentin Street and Django Marx.

Apart from what Dino told him about Deacon being on Sir Phillip's payroll he was spinning his wheels. He didn't know the detail or how much money was involved but by the look on the Inspector's face, Mack knew he'd just reeled in a bent copper.

"Utter bullshit. You're off your head. I flatly deny it."

"I've a witness who'll corroborate all of this. You're a dead man walking, Deacon."

Mack was giving the impression he knew far more that he did. Hoping he wouldn't be asked to expose Dino as his source or details of the Scaramouche luncheon where beans were spilled.

The shocked look on the policeman's dial was priceless.

Deacon had received rock solid assurance his agreement with Sir Phillip Daniels was strictly confidential, exclusively between the two men. How had Grayson found out his murder charge had been hastened thanks to the promise of a generous cash incentive? A sizeable bribe designed to line the detective's pocket once trumped-up evidence concluded with a guilty verdict.

Sticking to his guns, appearing to be in full possession of the facts, Mack then threatened to release the damning evidence to all relevant authorities.

"I'm sure the Police Integrity Commission will have a field day. And my growing list of media contacts will splash you from newspaper headline to TV news bulletin."

Deacon didn't need to be Einstein. He knew if this information was made public, his career was over. Criminal charges would be laid. A public shaming guaranteed.

The implications of Sir Phillip's involvement in this corrupt behaviour were something else altogether.

Mack had then offered the 'get out of jail card'.

"I don't know why I'm being so generous. You don't deserve it but there's a way out of this, where you get to escape unscathed."

"What's the plan before I agree?"

"You really don't have a choice."

For the Detective to have the slate wiped clean there was a solution to his dilemma. Perhaps a few opportunities to absolve him of crooked conduct.

First up, the Wesley Markowitz murder charge.

Mack pointed out there was a major flaw in the pathology of the police investigation into the Markowitz 'hit and run'. Deacon had overlooked a key factor, in fact missed it altogether.

When Mack smashed into the Cessna crop-duster on the airfield at Winston Aerodrome it had immediately released his car's inflatable airbags. It later dawned on him that DNA airbag analysis from the wrecked Ford Falcon, raised from the depths of Lake Jacaranda, would be able to reveal the true identity of the driver, Markowitz's killer.

Of all the DNA samples the police crime lab took from the vehicle, deployed airbags were not among them.

Mack was aware DUI cases and motor vehicle accidents provided irrefutable DNA evidence from engaged airbags that would confirm a driver's identification. Undeniable proof, who was behind the wheel.

The crashed Falcon's airbags would have only been engaged once in their life. Just once on the night of the deadly incident. Mack explained to Deacon how only one person could have come into direct contact with them. One person who would, on impact, have shed their skin cell's singular DNA autograph.

Without doubt, that person would be exposed as the driver. The murderer.

Sweating profusely with a shattered look, like trapped wildlife caught in a headlight beam, Deacon caved in with an exhausted sigh.

"This stays strictly between us?"

"Of course. That's if you do what you're told."

"Which is exactly what?

For his first assignment Deacon had to fast track the airbag laboratory tests. To prove his confidence in the outcome, Mack agreed his murder rap should stand until DNA results revealed a new suspect, formally identified, and charged.

Once that was established with Mack no longer facing trial for murder, his link as 'a person of interest' in the deaths of Quentin Street and Django Marx had to be immediately dismissed. Both cases were obviously part of the 'stitch up' between Deacon and Sir Phillip casting doubt on Mack's involvement in the two other 'suspicious' deaths. In particular, the selected use of closed circuit TV footage giving the impression Mack had been in Street's house and party to his hanging. Edited tape sequences that showed Mack arriving and leaving without entering the property should be restored to the official record and filed, without fail.

Deacon would also be required to provide a report for the coroner concluding Street and Marx's departures were by their own hand. Confirming without doubt, from a police standpoint, both were suicides.

It was payback time and this was just the starting point.

The levelling of scores would be gradual. And why the hell not? Mack's life had been catapulted into misery. As an innocent man facing serious jail time, he'd been publicly humiliated, stood down from his dream job, pilloried before a growing television audience and shamed in front of his family. Inspector Deacon had been the one wielding the axe, creating fake evidence and charges just to feather his own nest. Panic and greed had got the better of him.

"I'm behind in my mortgage repayments. Could lose the house altogether. Police salaries are not overly generous. With a new wife, five kids between us, we are struggling to keep our heads above water."

"Enter the shining knight, Sir Phillip Daniels, with an offer you couldn't refuse."

"He wants to pay off my entire mortgage with one cheque."

"That would have been a few years of a Detective Inspector's salary."

"Too right. $850,000 to be exact. All my home loan. You should know, I haven't received one cent yet."

"I feel so much better!" Mack's sarcasm, bitter.

"It was all contingent on you being found guilty and sentenced. Right now, I wish I'd never agreed to it."

"Bet you do. Bit late for that. You've ruined my life, you bastard."

"Never been tempted before. A reputation for always playing it straight. My career's been full of citations, awards, promotions."

"Congratulations. Now, you've thrown it all away. You should be the one going to jail. You were prepared to see an innocent man convicted and jailed for a murder he didn't commit."

There was one further charge Mack was also keen to address. After saving the city from the cyber terrorists' attack with sodium hydroxide he was accused of blowing up Metro's water turbines and assaulting a security guard. While Deacon wasn't directly involved with that case Mack insisted he wield his influence on the relevant investigating officers to plead special consideration. Thousands of lives were rescued from what could have been a major disaster. There would have to be mitigating circumstances galore. Unless of course, Sir Phillip Daniels has been waving his cheque book around there, as well?

"I can't guarantee wiping those charges."

"With such a great incentive, I can't see you failing. Don't let me down. Just in case you change your mind about everything we've discussed."

Mack held up his mobile phone.

"I've recorded every word of our little chat. Your admission of fabricated murder charges. Your bribery confession. Everything. It's all here.

Oh, not a word to anyone, especially Sir Phillip.

I'll be in touch."

114

"This is Dino Lombardi on Radio A2Z. Friends, I have devastating news to share. Having always strived to endorse fair play and root out evil, I now find myself utterly ashamed. I have let down my city, my country, most importantly you, my loyal listeners. My dictum, my credo, had always been clear. To help 'shape you a better world' I have failed my own philosophy and committed a cardinal sin. I have betrayed you.

At any stage during this confession my employer is likely to shut down my microphone, call in security staff and alert police. This will probably be my last broadcast. Ever.

You have all suffered a crisis of monumental proportion. With the severance of your city's water, the attempt to poison its supply and now the latest threat of an Anthrax attack on our community. You deserve an explanation.

I shamefully admit to being the architect of the cyber assault on Metro Water. There were three of us. Each involved for totally different reasons. Together we thought we could pull off a daring ransom heist, with expectations Metro would cave-in early, submitting to our demands. $100 million didn't seem an unreasonable figure. It had to be substantial to be taken seriously. It was the equivalent of $20 per head for the City's population of five million. What was planned to be a simple 24-hour turnaround, led to days of failed negotiations, chemical threats and a bombing of the reservoir's pump turbines. It was never meant to have such a catastrophic outcome. With the city still negotiating its way toward a satisfactory conclusion, it has been a total failure.

Despite massive regrets, any apology now will seem meaningless.

So, why did we create so much misery and confusion? What was the prime objective for hijacking Metro Water?

I can only speak for myself.

My reasons were threefold. And not as obvious as you might think.

Number One. *It may seem trite, even outrageous, but I genuinely believed there were to be benefits from creating such widespread chaos. For me, it was the most important reason of all but never intended to cartwheel out of control, so disastrously. Never intended to create widespread suffering. It was designed to show Australia and the world the vulnerability of our natural resources. How easily they can be hi-jacked, held to ransom by cyber terrorists. How supply can be so easily threatened. How distribution can be shut down with little resistance.*

And we proved it.

How weak was the protective shield, in just one public utility, Metro Water. We've shown the world how easily an organisation's systems management can be penetrated, taken down by a smart cyber genius, one of my so-called partners in this experiment. And how, it all comes at a staggering cost, to a city, to a nation, not to mention the human toll. As a result, the Metro communications takeover immediately became a highly visible case study. It has been seized upon, scrutinised and debated, all around the globe. It had sounded a harsh warning. Overseas news outlets devoured the story, promoting discussion on the universal implications of cyber-attack inertia, suggesting so much more has to be done. The message was clear. Act now or ignore at your peril. And it goes so much further than the Metro example. A universal siren was blaring wider international implications, where the true impact would be felt. Consider governments, corporate entities, institutions, grinding to a halt, threatened by cyber-sophisticated individuals, collectives, even other nations. Each with their own criminal intention to either gain control, make demands, or hold to ransom. Imagine the impact of permanently crippling a federal parliament, grounding an airline, silencing a telco or neutering a national television network. All eminently possible with an ever-growing list of potential targets. Without controls national economies could be crushed, paralysing thousands of organisations, businesses, government departments. Until the world is shocked into a confrontation with its IT insecurities and its weakness in combatting communications terrorism, it will always run the risk of being cyber-raped. The Metro experience is a worldwide wake-up call. To urgently review and re-write systems defence policies. Preferably with guaranteed impenetrable firewalls. If there could ever be such a notion?

Be warned. There will always be a fresh posse of hacking genii ready to launch the next wave of computerised magic, utilising new-fangled data tricks. And if the risks aren't heeded and cast-iron protections locked solid, we can't say we weren't warned. Before the next frightening cyber-crime intimidation strikes at mankind's heart, expect insurance companies to re-think policy liabilities and risk with laser-like focus. Future claims and payouts could run into billions of dollars, with one extreme outcome. Premiums will rocket themselves to the moon with fees quite literally, out of this world, astronomic. Leave it too late and desperate prayers after the event will be pointless, never to be answered.

None of this may make sense. The pain and inconvenience to you, your family and friends, is understandably immeasurable and cannot be justified by our actions. All I can do is explain my reasons why

Number Two. *While still committed to exposing the world's cyber vulnerabilities this reason was my personal 'call to arms'. Wedded to all the warnings mentioned in Number One and the total lack of action* *internationally, my intentions locally were two-pronged. And selfish.*

The objective was to create and host a covert natural resource ransom drama. At the same time be the one to negotiate the solution.

My radio programme would become the conduit for information. The source for updates, resolutions, calming advice. Problems asked and answered.

My intention was to be the covert villain, create the emergency, then gain the reputation as the gung-ho saviour.

One of my cyber team of three, the IT boffin, also doubled as whistle blower. On the inside, in the know, he fed us problems on-air we already knew, because we had instigated them. Then we set about solving them. Smoke and mirrors.

The idea was to make me the city's talk-back focal point and information guru, as my radio station basked in ratings glory.

It got out of hand for which I'm genuinely sorry. No longer the possibility of hero status for me. In fact, the opposite. I no doubt face numerous criminal charges.

And yes, the drama is far from over. The city is still without water.

Number Three. *Now, this one may seem obvious. Had the $100 million ransom been paid, the money would have been split three ways.*

Before you vent spleens over us potentially profiteering from such destructive, irresponsible, behaviour, most of my share would have been used judiciously to promote a renewed focus on cyber 'insecurity'.

You may not believe this but as described in reason Number One I am an advocate for change, passionate about education, broadening awareness, plugging yawning gaps. In my opinion, the future stability of the planet depends on it.

However, I must confess, some of that money would be useful right now, helping to mount what could be my expensive legal defence!

So, those were my three reasons, dear friends. And, if you're still listening, I have a few more things I have to share. They could provide vital insights, perhaps even offer some enlightening mitigation.

The latest tactic for non-payment of the ransom was to aerially bombard the fun park, Wizard's Wonder World, with deadly Anthrax spores. This would result in the killing or infecting of thousands of people, whilst poisoning the local environment for decades.

I refuse to support such an outrageous proposition.

The pilot of the plane also happens to be the computer expert who initially brought Metro Water's systems to its knees. A short while ago he took off on the flight from hell, promising to rain chaos on a fun-loving public. On board he believed was the most toxic of cargos. What he didn't know was I had switched the Anthrax for pouches of harmless powder.

By now he will have dumped his consignment, satisfied he'd just delivered death and destruction on a terrifying scale. This man is a dangerous, psychologically deranged individual, totally out of control. He should never have been allowed to go this far. Finally, perhaps, some redemption. My decision to swap the Anthrax for an inert substitute has saved a multitude of innocent folk from life threatening illnesses. Even death.

The pilot, who I only know as Hal, clearly has no concern for the human suffering he thinks he's just created. I want nothing more to do with him and urge police and security forces to intercept him at Winston Aerodrome, where he's shortly expected to land. He should also be questioned about the mowing down of Professor Vic Denton by motorised bicycle. And the motorcycle 'snatch and run' of Denton's report on Metro's security deficiencies.

One final proclamation. I was recently threatened with losing my job, by the owner of this radio station, media baron, Sir Phillip Daniels. He ordered me to broadcast details that an innocent man was guilty of murder. He advised me police hierarchy had been incentivised to participate in this outrageous claim and that I must follow suit or sacrifice my career. I refuse to be part of his insane demands and now, with nothing more to lose, share this information, so others can investigate and prosecute these allegations.

Looking through the glass divider from my studio into the radio station's production office I see several people have now gathered, including some in uniform. No doubt, waiting to escort me elsewhere. Also, I see the woman I love. She knows nothing of what I have just shared with you. Flo, I'm sorry, I'm in deep trouble. Our future maybe a little delayed.

Friends, thank you for listening to my confessional. I don't seek forgiveness; I just hope a little clarity may have brought some order from all this chaos.

In closing, I was only trying to 'shape you a better world.'

"Signing off for the last time, this is Dino Lombardi for Radio A2Z."

Mack had turned on the radio just as Dino began his mea culpa. He heard his exposition, the stripped bare honesty, the frank admissions of guilt. The flaws in his grand plan had finally dawned on him. While magnanimous in theory, holding 5 million people to ransom to prove his point was obviously excessive, clearly criminal. But Mack was grateful the shock-jock had decided against falsely accusing him of murder, live on-air. Dino's morals and media ethics had finally won through.

What especially struck Mack was the public revelation that Sir Phillip had maliciously set him up for the Markowitz murder, with obliging assistance from the senior officer leading the investigation. Charges against the media titan could very soon be setting a multitude of cats among nervous pigeons. Exorbitantly priced lawyers would already be licking their lips, sharpening their knives.

Overall, it was hard to believe Dino had managed to create so much bedlam without being suspected. He had brought the city to crisis point, destroying his life in the process. Adding to the woes, his new relationship was about to be interrupted with a stretch at His Majesty's pleasure.

Mack called Sacha to inform her of Dino's shock announcement. She had missed his cathartic radio outburst and was blown away by the frank admissions. Her immediate concern was how her two sons would take the news that their father was the architect of the city's water drama. Mack outlined his next move, with Sacha immediately offering full support.

In more ways than one Mack realised his former close friend was in serious trouble.

115

Blunt reality, the city was still without water.

Emergency supplies trucked in from outside Lake Jacaranda's catchment, supplemented by the TapDancers' network had only been a temporary fix. Residents were increasingly desperate, anxious for a return to normality.

Mack believed a breakthrough should now be a realistic prospect. Dino's confession had brought his part in the cyber to an end. And police would now be heading to Winston Aerodrome to apprehend Hal, the mentally unstable pilot, returning from what he believed was his 'deadly' mission.

That just left the third member of this destructive trio to be tracked down and silenced.

While this progress signalled an improvement in the situation the stark reality remained. The entire communications system at Metro Water was still in 'shut down', in criminal hands. It was one thing to round up the cyber conspirators but to reconnect the city to its water supply would be a greater challenge. One had to assume their cooperation would be out of the question, especially since no ransom money had been paid.

Vic Denton was the only person with a possible solution, having worked on the rejected escape formula before his resignation. Vic was still recovering in hospital. Mack decided it was time for another visit, hoping he'd receive more than the garbled ramblings offered on the last occasion. He was to be out of luck. As soon as Vic saw him, he began his unintelligible gobbledegook, spinning a similar message to before.

"Now Mack, wise up. Remember it's all about the day before, I see you, before you see me, easy as."

His recovery from the brain injury had been painfully slow. The doctors still cautious about long-term prospects, repeating the previous prognosis, that it was too early to tell.

Over at TNT Clyde Jameson had been monitoring the latest demands from the depleted cyber-attack team. Just one person remaining. The 100 million dollar ransom had not been paid since Hal had refused to abort the Anthrax aerial attack. Communication with his remaining partner in their operations centre had completely broken down. Right now, neither were aware the deadly poison had been swapped for a harmless powder, both assuming the fun park's crowd had been bombarded with the toxic horror.

"To restore water to the city, we make one final offer. Five million dollars and all your problems are over."

"The pump turbines have not been fully repaired; you can't restore supply."

Operations Manager Magnus Flume had at last found his voice, wielding it with authority. A first for him.

"After all the chaos you've created, you don't deserve a cent."

"Nice try. We know about the reserve turbine. Overhauled and primed for action. We could be pumping water right now. I'll check back in an hour. Five million dollars. Don't disappoint."

The usual static crackle ended the message.

Clyde rang Mack relaying the latest demand.

"With Dino and Hal out of the picture it just leaves one final member of the team who obviously wants to make a quick deal and a hasty exit. If only we knew where he was operating from. It must be a sophisticated set-up to have mounted such a complex cyber-attack in the first place, then to take-over the entire power grid."

"I've got an idea where it might be," said Mack heading for the door.

116

Mack had wondered if the distorted voice, booming its demands into Metro Water's control room, might have been Dino's. He knew now, that was impossible. While the shock-jock was in the studio confessing to his radio audience the remaining member of the cyber squad was clearly somewhere else, making their final pitch for a ransom payout. Dino couldn't have been in two places at once.

So, who was the last man standing in this triumvirate, and where was he?

"With Dino Lombardi under arrest and Hal, the mad computer freak, in custody we should be able to wrap this up. Hopefully we can now catch the third partner in the act of badgering Metro into approving a five-million-dollar settlement."

"Where exactly are we going?"

"To make you the hometown hero. With a bit of luck, you get to arrest the last member of the cyber syndicate."

Mack had contacted Inspector Deacon telling him to drop everything. Following their last meeting he knew the corrupt cop would do exactly as he was told. He was needed to oversee a raid on what was possibly the cyber attackers' HQ and to mobilise 'back-up', with an armed squad, just in case muscled security offered any resistance.

"If I'm right, the operating base for our cyber gang has been this well-hidden location. I'm presuming it doubled as the IT systems command centre as well as the broadcast hub that communicated with Metro and the media. A sophisticated mission control. Because it's situated in a private residential area it didn't draw attention to itself. If it had been in a commercial or industrial environment, it would have been more easily detected and exposed. We'll be there shortly."

"How do you know it's this particular home?"

"A wild hunch. Pray and hope, my motto."

"Something else you can pray and hope over."

"What's that?"

"I've received the DNA results from the Ford Falcon's airbags."

"And?"

"Looks like you're not off the hook."

"What do you mean?"

"It shows you and your son Dylan are still suspects."

"What. Bullshit!"

"Look, a child shares 50% of its DNA with a parent, which is confusing, presenting a possible mix-up and a real dilemma. That's unless one of you really was driving the car the night Wes Markowitz was murdered."

"Why would I force you to test the airbags to identify the killer, if Dylan or I were guilty?"

"The reliability of DNA evidence submerged in water at Lake Jacaranda is no guarantee of accuracy. We're going to have to run the tests again."

Mack slammed the steering wheel with a closed first. "There's got to be an explanation."

"We'll need to take fresh swabs from everyone in your family, finally eliminate or confirm whose DNA is on those airbags."

"Including my younger children. You're kidding?"

"Everyone."

"But they don't even drive, Jake's 12, Amy is 8."

"Until we check and eliminate everyone, we can't move on. Who knows, it could end up being someone outside the family, someone who shares a partial DNA."

Mack pulled up half a street away from the target's premises, his head chock full of quandary. Suddenly, he was back in the frame for murder. With the Tactical Response Unit leaping from the van pulling up behind, it was no time to dwell on Markowitz's death. The raid was in progress.

As Mack approached the house, he reached into his pocket for the key.

The armed squad was first into the open hallway, Mack and Deacon next. At some lower level the booming voice was delivering its familiar tone as ground and upper floors were swept for any sign of residents or security personnel. Nothing. Mack slowly descended the spiral staircase leading to the basement. He had been here many times but never below stairs.

"It's a simple decision, pay the money and water will be returned to the city today."

Quietly opening the door marked 'Do Not Enter' Mack held his breath. Would he set off an alarm announcing his presence, might there be a security detail, some human resistance, perhaps an armed response? No challenge. Instead, he absorbed an extraordinary spectacle. Confronting him, a mesmerising array of electronic equipment. An audio-visual extravaganza.

A full bank of monitors, scanners, microphones, printers, keyboards, cameras, and speakers. All this apparatus and gadgetry installed among several raised stacks of computer hardware. The combined sight resembled a veritable Aladdin's cave, illuminated control panels flashed their lights. Sound needles twitched, as they registered vocal highs and lows. And in the middle, oblivious to Mack's presence, wearing noise-cancelling headphones, over a baseball cap, was the remaining member of the cyber syndicate. Making a final bid to land a multi-million-dollar payout.

A batch of monitors displayed the 'live' action from inside Metro's control room, relayed by magic-eye cameras no doubt previously planted by the hackers. A familiar face filled one of the screens.

"Mr Flume wouldn't you like to see an end to this agony, once and for all?"

"Why should we pay you one cent? You've done nothing but create total chaos. Your Anthrax attack has devastated the city, proving you have no regard for human life."

"Bit late to do anything about that. Only question now is, do you want water returned to the city?" the male voice, sounded increasingly impatient.

With Deacon at his side and two armed police in the doorway Mack tapped the shoulder before him. The body let out a shocked yell, immediately swivelling in its chair. For a moment, total silence. Just a noticeable whirr from one of the many machines crammed into the bunker studio.

The stunned look was short lived as if this moment had been expected. With two out of the three cyber-criminal perpetrators now in custody, it was just a question of time before the last domino fell and the remaining member reeled in.

Mack leaned forward and removed the headphones. As he lifted the baseball cap, blonde hair cascaded across narrow shoulders. Despite the litany of crimes and charges about to be levelled and the deep resentment at the betrayal he'd been subjected to, the beauty was still hard to ignore. He had willingly fallen under a spell and shared what he believed to be a truly mutual love. That was a long time ago. And from this moment, officially over.

"Jacki, what **have** you done? What's happened to you?"

First silence, then "You wouldn't understand."

"Try me. You were once a happy housewife with three kids. Now you're likely to be charged as a terrorist, extortionist, blackmailer, placing thousands of lives at risk. My God, an Anthrax attack, what were you thinking?"

"That wasn't my idea."

"You went along with it."

"Dino and Hal were the mission drivers I was just the gopher accomplice, operating from here, Dino's home studio. Every communication with Metro was scheduled during the day, it was perfect. No one was home. Sacha was at her medical practice; their children were at school."

Jacki lent forward swinging the boom microphone toward her.

With the press of a button, a voice-changer device immediately distorted her dulcet tones into the business-like male.

"You all thought you were dealing with Mr Big, the tough guy, it was just little old me," said Jacki in her electronically induced bass voice.

Mack looked at Deacon who was gathering himself from the shock that Mack's wife was the third member of the city's cyber heist.

"So, what's all this got to do with Sir Phillip Daniels?"

"He's got nothing to do with it, he has no idea I'm involved. He's just helping me cope with my disastrous marriage." Said Jacki.

"Does that include him telling police he thinks I murdered Wes Markowitz? I wonder who encouraged him to make that statement."

Jacki ignored the question. "How did you know I was involved?"

"First time, when I was robbed of Metro's security manual, while picking up pizzas. I was jumped by a motor cyclist with a hooded pillion rider. Only you and the kids knew where I was. Coincidence? I doubted it. In my tussle with the disguised, masked pillion pirate, I noticed they had silver nail polish with pink glitter just like you had painted on the previous night, with Amy, at home. When I got home that night, you had wiped off the polish. So I wasn't 100% sure it was you.

"My suspicions were piqued when Metro failed to comply with broadcast demands. Each time the voice referred to the utility's poor response effort as a "real dog's breakfast". An unusually rare comment. Then at home, on the very same day, you used the term a "real dog's breakfast" again. With your strange behaviour and constant absences, it all began to add up."

Jacki leapt to her feet, eyes daggered. "I hate you. You had it all, the fame, the recognition, the accolades, I just wanted something for me. It was all about you. I **so** hate you."

"I hope you think it's all been worth it. Plenty of time to reflect, while you're separated from three amazing children. Sir Phillip can't help you now. Deacon she's all yours."

The inspector charged and handcuffed Jacki, before leading her up the spiral staircase, toward an inevitable jail cell.

117

With the ransomware heist brought to its knees and key players now behind bars, it begged a question, for which there was no immediate answer. How do you restore nature's magic drop to five million people when data control systems channelling its distribution remain in the grip of jailed cyber hackers? In taking over Metro's computer network they had effectively shut down all its communication capabilities, rendering it powerless. They were the only ones who could turn the city's taps back on and had flatly refused to assist. Their attempts to negotiate reduced jail sentences if they cooperated by resuming supply, had instantly failed. There had to be another way. Anything to avoid kowtowing to those who had orchestrated such a public disaster. While ad hoc emergency procedures, like TapDancers, had saved the day and were still operating, they were only meant to be a temporary fix. A 'back to normality' demand from an increasingly impatient general public, was now posing a serious problem. With key offenders in custody the city's population immediately expected to be on the receiving end of free, uninterrupted, no longer compromised, water.

That was impossible. Damage to Metro's IT infrastructure had been terminal. Mack knew it would require a total overhaul and re-programming of trashed systems before operations could re-commence. That could take months, there had to be an alternative. A magic formula, some counter measure, anything to return tap water to the people.

He remembered when Vic Denton was Metro's Operations Manager, he claimed to have devised a revolutionary plan to kick-start crippled IT systems. Something to do with tracing a cyber-attack back to the very second before it struck. He never had the chance to test his theories, resigning in disgust when his report on the utility's security weaknesses had been comprehensively rejected. With Denton's reputation at Metro in tatters and his current brain injury restricting meaningful conversation, Mack felt he had no choice but to take a gamble. Desperate times invite desperate measures. He'd begun to wonder if Vic's garbled raves from his hospital bed may have been suggesting key details, solutions to releasing Metro from its lockdown paralysis. Could his gibberish have been communicating vital instructions?

"Go back to where it started... Wise up... I see you... before you see me... easy as."

Knowing Denton was persona-non-grata at Metro and Mack, still with a murder charge, labelling him a serious liability, his next move had to be handled with extreme care. Running the gauntlet and testing Denton's wild theories would require access to Metro's computer nerve centre and cooperation from its top systems analysts. Mack would need to enlist the full cooperation of a key individual, on the inside, to open doors and circumnavigate red tape. Perhaps someone who needed to bolster his public image. Someone who had been forced to operate outside his comfort zone, about whom Mack had never exposed his inadequacies. One obvious candidate.

Magnus Flume had been Vic Denton's replacement. There appeared to be no love lost between the two of them. Misunderstandings, rumours and general scuttlebutt had given each a distorted view of the other. But when it was pointed out that, through a suggested leadership role, Magnus could be seen as the hero who returned water to the people, he instantly guaranteed unqualified support. In a flash, he bypassed strict company guidelines, calling the organisation's IT chief to convene a crisis meeting.

Hours of theorising at IT HQ then led to several failed attempts to re-gain control of Metro's core computer operations. It was abundantly clear the department's combined brains trust was incapable of offering workable solutions to reverse the meltdown. This heartened Mack, believing his hunch was now worthy of a trial run. He launched his theory.

"Is there any way of knowing the actual data base readings, the precise programming across the entire network, at the exact moment the cyber-attack took place?"

"What! why? We want to move on, move forward, not drag up ancient history," offered one of the 'so-called' communications gurus.

"That ancient history, as you call it, was the moment your entire operation crashed, thanks to a daring hack by a single operator. Your inadequate computer protection allowed the network to be comprehensively hi-jacked. What I'm trying to do, with information I've received, is to go back to where it all fell apart. The point where you allowed your supposed impenetrable information epicentre to fall into enemy hands." Complete silence as red faces and tight lips absorbed the criticism, hoping perhaps the ground might swallow them up. Mack knew he now had the room's full attention, and its complete cooperation as he swung his rescue plan into operation. A theoretical plan held together with crossed fingers. He needed to rely on his memory of Denton's obscure rants repeated ad infinitum during every hospital visit. Deciphering the baffling spiel and converting it into useable data, might just provide the key to unlocking the entire Metro network.

"Go back to the beginning... Wise up... I see you... before you see me... easy as."

"We need to return Metro's information hub back to its optimum efficiency. Take all programming, all systems back to the second before the cyber-attack, the last point at which everything was fully functional."

"You're mad! Why dwell on the moment the firewall failed?" yet again the chief dissenter expressed severe doubt.

"That's exactly where we should be! The precise moment Metro's communications hub caved in. It will allow you to analyse what went wrong, to rebuild, ensure it never happens again. Your flawed cyber-defence system is obviously corrupted. That's where you must start. Rectify now or face further attacks."

Mack couldn't believe how his lack of knowledge, his common-sense reasoning, had the IT experts finally agreeing with his logic. The systems failure that collapsed an entire city's water supply had been laid firmly at their door. They were well aware they needed this opportunity to redeem themselves. After surviving the challenges of recent days Magnus Flume was exhibiting unusually heightened confidence. Firmly grasping the nettle, he spoke with conviction, making it quite clear they should now proceed with Mack's rescue plan. And so, the metaphoric computer clock was dialled back to midnight on the 23rd of July. The date and time when Metro's entire information system collapsed, plunging the city into its worst ever drought. Data systems were re-programmed, re-calibrated to the exact moment the city was robbed of its precious drop. It had been Mack's interpretation of Vic Denton's bedside drawl of "Go back to where it started." "Go back to where it all began" A feasible guess with no guarantee of success. One needed 'part two' of Vic's secret formula to match up with 'part one' if there was to be any chance of success.

Mack wasn't quite sure where to start.

118

Sir Phillip Daniels' world had tilted on its axis.

He had been delighted to hear the city's water crisis had come to a sensational close, with three individuals apprehended and charged. That was until he heard the names of those responsible. The first bombshell, when one of his TransNational employees, Sydney's number one talk-back radio star Dino Lombardi, was named as the ringleader. While that news shattered the media baron the next name came as an even greater shock. Jacki Grayson was declared a key member of the syndicate that sought to relieve the city of 100 million ransomed dollars.

Dreams of making Jacki his wife number six, and retiring to his beachside penthouse, suddenly evaporated. He felt duped, devastated, desperate. He had no idea Jacki had been living a double life and how she had used him to convince police her husband Mack, was Wes Markowitz's killer.

Sir Phillip's troubles were only just beginning.

Allegations made by Dino Lombardi that the media magnate had blackmailed him into declaring, on his radio show, that Mack Grayson was a murderer had been investigated. Whilst Dino's honesty and integrity was questionable, it helped that the policeman reviewing his claims had a similar threatening experience from Sir Phillip. Inspector Deacon had then turned the tables on the once shining knight, declaring he'd attempted to bribe him into charging Mack with murder. Despite vehement protestations and legal representation, Sir Phillip was accused of bribery and corruption, scheduled to face court the following month.

There was another reason why Deacon was now totally convinced Grayson had nothing to do with the 'hit and run' killing. Results from fresh DNA swabs on the airbags of the Ford Falcon wagon had just been received.

At last, conclusive, indisputable proof of who murdered Wesley Markowitz.

119

"Back to the start... Wise up... I see you... before you see me... easy as"

Metro personnel in the IT control centre had re-programmed the entire network, painstakingly backdating all data entries to the very second before the cyber meltdown. The last point at which the system had worked perfectly. Smug operatives stood back with folded arms, advising Mack from that moment, he was on his own. Informing him, for the hardware and software systems to now magically merge and resume full operational capacity, it would require a lengthy password. A password no one at Metro knew, except former employee, Vic Denton. All that was known about this secret password was it contained a total of nineteen characters, numerals, or symbols.

"I reckon you have a few trillion permutations to consider. Best of luck."

An unhelpful voice from the analyst throng smarting from Mack's earlier barbs. How their ineptitude had caused Metro's IT debacle in the first place. Their support from this moment would be limited. He knew he faced an uphill struggle but refused to be rattled by negative taunts. Without referencing Vic as the source of his coded information he started outlining key thoughts, writing them up, on a large whiteboard.

"Information I've received suggests the starting point must include the line '**I SEE YOU BEFORE YOU SEE ME**' as the central driver to the password."

"That's 21 letters, you've already surpassed the required nineteen characters."

"Yes, but if you break them down into single letters '**I SEE YOU BEFORE YOU SEE ME**' can become **ICUB4UCME** which is only nine characters."

The cynics tossed glances at each other as if to acknowledge there might just be something in Mack's plan. Pressing on he spelled out another Vic Denton bedside rave on to the whiteboard.

"Now ahead of those nine characters we have **WISE UP** and by following the same principle if I pluralise the letter **Y**, to make two **Y's** then add a **U** and a **P, WISE UP** becomes **YYUP**. Altogether we would then have **YYUPICUB4UCME**. That's 13 characters, still six to go."

The atmosphere in the room was shifting to the positive. No one cared where Mack's coded pearls came from if they led to a breakthrough. The prospect of a systems resumption that could end the city's water crisis, lifted the mood considerably.

"When it comes to the password's closing clue, **EASY AS,** I'm flying a kite here. I'm guessing it could simply convert to **ECAS.** If we've got everything right the combination so far reads **YYUPICUB4UCMEECAS**, Only problem is that totals 17, leaving us short by two characters."

Magnus Flume broke the silence.

"You've only got capital letters and one numeral. Nothing 'lower case', no 'symbols', Characters that provide extra security, that's what's missing? Taking our example. If you place a lower case **'s'** alongside two identical capital letters, it will indicate a plural. In other words, **YYUP** (WISE UP) with a lower case **'s'** could become **YYsUP.** And since **WISE UP** is an exclamation, one might reasonably expect it to be followed by the symbol **!** I'm suggesting the two missing characters are a lower case **'s'** and an exclamation mark. **YYUP** therefore becomes **YYsUP!**"

As Magnus's suggestion created a spate of high fives Mack was quick to offer words of caution.

"Hold up, bit early for celebrations. If we're wrong, it's back to the drawing board.

WISE UP I SEE YOU BEFORE YOU SEE ME EASY AS may have morphed into **YYsUP!ICUB4UCMEECAS** but was it the password to restart Metro Water's control systems? Mack initiated a trial run with the utility's IT geeks backdating the programme to midnight on the 23rd of July. The last second before the network crashed.

Whirring computers began to digest the password as the crucial question hung in the air.

Was Vic Denton's bizarre outburst from his hospital bed about to solve the water crisis, or had it just confirmed the confused ramblings of someone recovering from brain surgery?

They didn't have to wait long for the answer. A chorus of groans reverberating around the IT control room as the screen lit up with 'Invalid Password'. Criticism was immediately levelled at Mack, his far-fetched acronym theory had clearly failed. Knee-jerk alternatives were then wildly bandied around. It was obvious no one had a clue. Temperature in the room was rising.

Mack held up his hand calling for silence as voices attempted to shut him down.

"Listen up. Listen up. I'm convinced we are on the right track." he lied.

"You have no idea, just a shot in the dark." Yelled one of the earlier naysayers, all of a sudden feeling vindicated.

"We knew this trial may require some finessing and that's what we must now do."

"Waste of time."

"Anyone got a better idea?"

Silence.

"I'm confident we have everything right. We just need to make two simple changes. Remove the exclamation mark after **YYsUP!** that's wrong. Instead for the absent symbol we place an apostrophe for the **YY'sUP**

For the second time the computer network was primed to receive the password. Mack held his breath as the revised offering of **YY'sUPICUB4UCMEECAS** was typed and entered.

120

Dylan, Jake and Amy were mortified to hear their mother had been charged as one of the cyber terrorists who'd brought the city to its knees.

Worse was to come, after Inspector Deacon announced Mack was no longer a suspect in the hit and run murder of Wes Markowitz. Fresh DNA evidence from the Ford Falcon's airbags had now identified the guilty party.

June 16 was a stormy night with torrential rain. That evening, it would be alleged, Jacki Grayson had lured Markowitz to his death after impersonating nurse, Janet Strange, from St Margaret's Hospital. Over the phone, in a disguised voice, she had lied, telling him his son had died following a skateboard accident. She had remembered an article Wes had written about his horrific upbringing in a Romanian orphanage and how by drenching himself in downpours had helped douse memories of appalling conditions and savage beatings. Believing news of his son's death would send him out into that night's deluge, Jacki had pursued, mowed down and murdered Wes Markowitz.

The latest and final DNA test proved conclusively Jacki had

been at the wheel of the Ford Falcon.

The combination of charges from terrorism to murder meant she would now spend the rest of her life behind bars, wondering whether the vendetta against her husband had been worthwhile. Jealous of his life, dissatisfied with hers, failing to give him an alibi on the night of the murder, sleeping with an influential media baron to fulfill her objectives, had all failed. And not one dollar from the attempted 100-million-dollar ransom heist.

Mack had his suspicions Jacki may have been involved in the Metro Water cyber-attack and was hardly surprised when it was confirmed. But this was different. When your wife of 18 years is accused of murder, a murder for which she intended you to be found guilty, the shock, the hurt, the anger, was indescribable.

Sacha and her two sons were living their own nightmare. Coming to terms with Dino's role as kingpin of the city's water crisis. His attempt to alert the world to global weaknesses in the protection of key utilities had backfired big time. While attention to vulnerable resources had been well drawn the impact on millions of people, their lives and livelihoods had proven catastrophic. Add to that exiting his marriage to join forces with Sir Phillip's ex, Florence Jones. His shame was now complete leaving his two boys shattered and a wife battling to provide them solace. Secretly, she harboured a personal relief.

Two families had now been drawn together. A combined five children, an unattached mother and father, all rocked by a scandal of immense proportion. A storm nevertheless, with potential to be weathered.

Not long after fresh, unadulterated water, had been restored to the city and Mack released from all charges related to the destruction of Metro's turbine he was reinstated as host of TransNational Tonight. He managed to successfully distance himself from his wife's role in the cyber-attack, declaring no knowledge of her involvement. This was aided by revealing in minute detail each stage of the crisis, and how his actions saved the city from imminent disaster. Viewer ratings soared. TNT had become the information platform for the return of order, with Mack the popular 'go-to' host. The Grayson home had been placed on the market. Mack's mountain of newspapers and magazines, previously stacked from floor to ceiling, had found a new address. This time, uncontested. Along with Dylan, Jake and Amy, he'd moved into the Lombardi's former marital home. With Sacha and her two sons. Five children, two adults. A combination of seven. Soon to become six. One of the siblings had recently passed an interview and IQ test and was shortly to appear in uniform. After its recent recruitment drive Dylan had been accepted by the Australian Army for its forthcoming induction programme. His special interest in IT duly noted. Another member of the Grayson clan was also exhibiting the family's familiar pluck and personality.

"Hello, this is Amy Grayson, can I help you?"

Each time the house phone rang there was a race to answer, Amy always the first to pick up.

"Dad there's a man on the phone for you."

"Who is it?"

"He says he's been trying to track you down."

"What does he want?"

"Apparently, it turned up at the same shop."

"What did? Let me speak to him."

Mack immediately recognised the voice.

"You're the cab driver who pawned it after that night at the city fire?"

"I always felt bad about that, I can now get it back."

"I really appreciate your call but I never want to see it again, I no longer have any use for it but thanks for letting me know, thank you."

Mack ended the call. Everyone looking at him for an explanation.

"Something I don't need anymore, I'm planning on buying a new one, anyway."

From the other side of the room an open hand, raised to the mouth, was followed by a sizeable blown kiss.

END

CHARACTERS IN TAP DANCERS

Mack Grayson	Photo-journalist, TV Host, Hero
Jacki Grayson	Wife to Mack
Dylan/Jake Grayson	17 year old/12 year old sons
Amy Grayson	8 year old daughter
Dino Lombardi	Radio A2Z, Shock Jock
Sacha Lombardi	Wife to Dino, GP, Medical Practice Founder
Wesley Markowitz	Chief of Staff, The TransNational Times
Mason Green	Publisher, The TransNational Times
Sir Phillip Daniels	82 yr old Founder TransNational Media Gp
Lady Florence 'Flo' Daniels	Sir Phillip's 34 year old Wife.
Phil 'Lockie' Lok	Veteran Cam/man, TransNational TV News
Richard Ogilvy	CEO TransNational TV
Clyde Jameson	Exec. Prod, TransNational Tonight (TNT)
Quentin Street	Presenter, TransNational Tonight (TNT)
Supt. Rick Charles	Fire Chief
Jack Rankin	Council Safety Inspector
Duc Tran	Hero Fireman
Olga/Nina	Russian Mother/Daughter, Fire Survivors
Brian 'Deeks' Deacon	Detective Inspector, Homicide Squad
Professor Victor Denton	W-blower, Former Ops Mgr Metro Water
Django Marx	Legendary Front Man, Rock Band, FarQ
Magnus Flume	Current Operations Manager, Metro Water
Hal	Cyber Criminal, Computer Genius
Chas Winston	Owner/Manager, Winston Aero